POLONAISE

Doris Leslie

SAPERE
BOOKS

POLONAISE

Published by Sapere Books.

24 Trafalgar Road, Ilkley, LS29 8HH

saperebooks.com

ISBN: 978-0-85495-539-8

For Ann Driver

PART ONE: WARSAW 1828-1830

ONE

The diligence, packed to capacity, stank of perspiration, of patchouli, and the unpleasant reminder, with every snore that he emitted, of the garlic sausage upon which Professor Jarocki had that morning breakfasted. The day had been hot, the evening bid fair to be hotter, with the promise of storm in a saffron sky and clouds like dark somnolent dragons hiding the dregs of the sun.

Between the professor and an ample blonde, Frédéric sat wedged. The blonde with her *ya*s and *na*s and baggages, and a hideous bandy-legged dog of no breed or shape ever seen in Poland — or in any Christian country, come to that — had boarded the coach at Frankfort-on-the-Oder. Thence, throughout the journey, she had engaged in lively conversation with her hitherto silent fellow passengers, and in particular with the portly advocate from Posen in the opposite seat; he, very obviously, had an eye for her. The English consul, returning from Berlin to Cracow, who, notwithstanding the heat, was wrapped like a mummy.in a tartan shawl, vied with the advocate for the lady's attention till the talk turned beyond her range — and Frédéric's — to politics, when the professor shook himself awake to say, to everyone's alarm, 'The megalosaurus is an important type,' and went to sleep again.

Frédéric envied Pan Jarocki the ease with which he could adapt himself to the miseries of Prussian travel and the indigestibility of Prussian food. In short, this longed-for visit to Berlin had proved for Frédéric a disappointment. For that, however, in all fairness he could not entirely blame Berlin or the Berliners, even though he did with all his heart detest these Germans with their pudding faces, their flat heads and disgusting table manners.

He had been more favourably impressed with the capital than its inhabitants. To the city he conceded a pleasing cleanliness and order, spacious well-built streets, good beer and better opera. Given a happier choice of travelling companion than a professor of zoology on this, his first sortie from the homeland, Frédéric judged he might have profited in cheer if not in learning — if, for instance, he had visited Berlin with Jasia, or Julius or Titus. But God forbid he should complain. His papa had sent him forth with the best intentions and a well-filled purse, and he had made good use of his time and money. He had seen something of the world: not much, to be sure, and not nearly enough, but a glimpse to set him aching to see more. He had bought an old edition of Mozart's sonatas and a new edition of Bach's fugues. He had bought two pairs of lavender gloves, a bottle of Cologne water, and a cravat that he regretted. The Berliners had no taste. He had also in his valise some trifles for his sisters, a fan for his mama, and cigars for Papa Nicolas. And if Titus and Julius should ask him of the women — of whom this fleshly charmer here beside him with her elbow at his ribs and her scent and her dog and her giggles was a fair sample — he could honestly aver, 'The dowdiest, most monstrous frumps ever in nightmare conceived, and how any man, Pole, German, or whatever, could bring himself to — ' well, and there it is!

But aside from all this, reflected Frédéric, repressing with a writhe the charmer's insinuating elbow, aside from all this best forgotten he had seen much to be remembered. For while Pan Jarocki and his professorial colleagues had mumbo-jumboed at the zoological museum, Frédéric had been free to explore. The musical library at Schlesinger's... There he had browsed in sheer delight upon the original scores of the masters, and had dared to hope that one day he too might come to Schlesinger's. Maybe. Or maybe not.

To none — not Jasia, nor Julius, nor Titus, but to his heart alone had he confessed it. In Berlin at the head and front of music he would sit, acknowledged, not as the boy prodigy of Warsaw, who had played before the Czar of Russia when he had visited the capital and been graciously presented with a ring; no, not as pianist would he arrive, but as composer. Alas! How far removed from too-eager anticipation of that journey to Berlin was the reality. He had called on every music shop in town unrecognised. None in that city nor any other save his own had ever heard of him or of his Rondo (Opus 1) published in Warsaw when he was fifteen and dedicated to Madame de Linde, the Rector's wife, with whom he played duets.

That was three years ago. He now aimed higher, had aimed perhaps too high. What of rings and things from emperors for the trick of playing? Your fingers must die with your body. The music you make lives on. Quite so. But one must learn to know one's limitations, nor be discouraged by the first rebuff, even though it knocked you flat ... to rise again.

What then had he hoped, had prayed for when he started, on this two weeks' jaunt to Germany? That Schlesinger would salaam to his Mazurka in G Major for its originality, its charm, its — yes, admit it now — its sugar candy? Graceful, Schlesinger had called it in his non-committal letter. *Your harmonic sequences are most persuasive* ... but not sufficiently persuasive to persuade. Well! He deserved it. And in the darkness of the diligence he burned. That he should dare on a moment's impulse to force an entrance to that sanctuary with his scrawled offering, and demand reception, to be received by Schlesinger himself.

Schlesinger, with oriental caution and politeness, had professed to know the name. He was lying through his nose — *an even bigger one than mine,* thought Frédéric, recalling once again that shaming interview, that oily eye upon the score, unblinking, supercilious. And he had stammered painfully, 'I would, *mein Herr*, have copied it more clearly had I thought — had known — you might — would — have permitted me to call without appointment.'

'My dear young sir,' the smiling Schlesinger corrected, 'the pleasure is altogether mine. No appointment with me is ever necessary — or requested. I am only a music seller.' His eye reverted to the lamentable script, erased and blotted: shocking. 'However, I will read it.'

Read it? Schlesinger would never read it. None but Frédéric *could* read it, who in execrable German and an agony had bleated, 'If, *mein Herr*, you would allow that I play it for you here, I could the better show —'

He was not allowed to show: he was shown out.

He had left with Schlesinger the address of his hotel. The script was returned with a brief platitudinous letter, which Frédéric held in the flame of a candle till the words blackened and were lost to him — and to posterity, happily for Schlesinger.

The incident, though shattering, had no profound effect. His spirit's eloquence was yet to be unfolded. That much within himself he knew, and for the rest — he had his life before him, and all of Bach and Mozart for his soul.

He went to no more music shops. Instead he attended Congress meetings with the bald-heads of the Zoological Society, and sat, on one occasion which was followed by a concert, in the same row as the Crown Prince, Spontini, and yes — Mendelssohn!

All eyes for him, Frédéric heard nothing of the lecture, nor would he much have understood it if he had. Mendelssohn! Within an arm's length distance, if it had not been for those two monstrous *Frauen* in between; though to be sure, after the Schlesinger fiasco, even had he found himself in the next seat to Mendelssohn, he would have had no courage to approach him. Enough that he might gaze, and make a surreptitious drawing of the man's beautiful profile to show Titus.

What else could he tell his friends? Of the ghastly dinner given by the naturalists as finale to the Congress, where he sat like Saul among the prophets, caricaturing all the savants on his cuff, ate too much of that most frightful sausage, mixed his drinks, and lay all night sick and sorry? How Jasia would laugh, and Julius and Titus, when he told them of that disconcerting contretemps with none other than the Chamberlain himself, Baron von Humboldt. ('Oh, yes, my dears, these scientific stick-in-the-muds are very much *bon ton*, I do assure you!') His Excellency, dressed in what appeared to be a kind of livery, was mistaken by Frédéric for a lackey and bidden, 'Fetch my hat.' Too rich! But blame the beer and Rhine wine. And nothing more convivial than that had he to tell, save just one stroke of luck.

The *Herr Direktor* of the Zoological Society, Professor Lichtenstein, *confrère* of Pan Jarocki, and a member of the Singakademie, had given Frédéric a permit for the opera. That was something, and worth the penalty of Congress meetings. He had heard Spontini's *Ferdinand Cortez*, Cimarosa's *Il Matrimonia Segreto* — not bad, and well conducted — and, at the Singakademie, Handel's *Ode for St. Cecilia's Day*, which almost approached the sublime.

And at this point in meditation, Frédéric fell into a doze and dreamed of a choir of angels…

The diligence bumped and clattered over cobblestones, and halted with a jolt that flung Frédéric out of heaven into a hell of fuss. The blonde shrieked: '*Gott im Himmel!* Robbers!' Her dog began to bark, the advocate to swear, the Englishman peering through the breath-fogged window said, 'I think we have stopped at an inn,' and the professor, waking, uttered, 'God be thanked! I have an appetite.'

The guard appearing at the door of the diligence announced, '*Gnädige Frau, meine Herren*, we have arrived at Züllichau. There will be here a change of horses and a two-hours wait.'

Followed more commotion. None except Pan Jarocki desired a two-hour wait, Frédéric least of any, in this benighted place. He had hoped to be at Posen before dawn where at least he would find the comfort of a bed to take the ache out of his bones. He was stiff from head to foot.

Plucking the professor's sleeve, he entreated, 'Sir, could we not proceed from here by post-chaise?'

'Eh? By post-chaise? Is your father then a millionaire, or am I?' demanded the professor. 'Are you crazy? It would cost three hundred zlotys to proceed from here to Posen in a post-chaise. Be thankful for the chance to stretch your legs.'

'They'll need some stretching,' grumbled Frédéric as he hopped out of the diligence in the wake of Pan Jarocki. But he was glad to be rid of the charmer. Much more of her scent and he'd vomit.

The landlord, in a fluster at this unexpected visitation, bestirred himself to offer of his best. While the professor gave his order for the meal, and the blonde and her advocate paired off together to the exclusion of the Englishman, whose sole desire seemed to be for a can of hot water and a shave, Frédéric wandered into the inn parlour. It in no way differed from a dozen such where on his journey to and from Berlin Frédéric had rested; scrupulously clean, smelling of pitch-pine, and sparsely furnished — save in one respect which all other hostelries had lacked — a grand piano.

A piano in the parlour of an inn — incredible! He sat and rattled off a few arpeggios. *Sancta Cecilia* — and in tune! After sixteen hours jolting in a diligence, to find an instrument good enough to play on must, he thought, be a presentation from the gods.

He began to improvise and those who heard his music one by one were drawn as to a magnet. The blonde, in an ecstasy of sentiment and tears, sobbed on the advocate's shoulder. The Englishman, who had come from his shaving to investigate the source of sound so unaccountable in such a one-eyed hole, stood dabbing a cut on his chin where he had let his razor slip in his wonder. The landlord, torn between the will to produce a meal fit for an Orpheus and the wish to hear him out, padded back and forth between parlour and kitchen with his wife in a scold at his heels.

'Sheep's head! You have forgot the drink. Must I do all the work while you stand gaping? Have I four pair of hands to fetch and carry?'

'Never,' declared the innkeeper, 'has such a one since Mozart played like this. A wizard!'

'I'll wizard you!' cried Madame. 'Go! Draw the beer and bring a bottle for the Englishman. He asks for *Liebfrauenmilch*. Will you lose good custom with your folly?'

Frédéric, oblivious, played on, and in the doorway, cloaked and hooded for departure, a young girl listened, tranced.

Only Pan Jarocki stayed unmoved while impatience lent an edge to appetite. These digital gymnastics were no novelty to him, who strongly disapproved such choice of a profession. Often enough he had warned his good friend Nicolas not to pander to this nonsense. Music. The arts. Those were all very well for the wealthy *dilettanti* of this world, but not for the son of a father who, for all he earned sufficiency of income as head of the most select Young Gentlemen's Academy in Poland, was no Croesus, and could not hope to furnish Frédéric with more than an inadequate allowance. The boy had extravagant tastes.

He had also, Pan Jarocki considered, a brain — if he chose to use it. True, he had only just managed to scrape through his finals at the Lyceum, but that was because he had devoted more of his time in the last three years to his piano playing than to his studies. A mistake, the professor reflected, a very grave mistake on the part of Monsieur Nicolas to have encouraged the boy to appear on the concert platform. Adulation, admiration — all that gushing fiddle-faddle from the ladies might turn his head, but would never fill it. And what, ruminated Pan Jarocki, of this trip to Berlin wrested at last and with much hum-humming and ha-hahing from friend Nicolas, as experiment to see if contact with the greatest scientists in Europe could induce the boy to abandon his minstrel's gallery for worthier heights?

The venture had not proved a success. Far from weaning Frédéric from music, the meetings of the Congress had occasioned quite an opposite effect. It was with the utmost difficulty that the professor had persuaded his young charge to attend the lectures, or to evince the slightest interest in scholarly debates. On the contrary, the boy had brought an unbecoming levity to those learned gatherings that the professor had greatly deplored. On visits to museums he had pointedly evaded the antiquarian section, but had rhapsodised at length upon a score of Mozart. He had pined for a piano and suggested, with some impudence, that Pan Jarocki should demand one from the Congress. He had filled a notebook, not with notes, but with disgraceful caricatures of the assembly, among which Pan Jarocki had been forced, regrettably, to recognise himself. Small gratitude indeed for sponsorship, and small wonder the professor was aggrieved.

He had watched this youngster from the cradle, had hoped to see him with a tail of letters as long as his own tacked to his name. But what letters worthy of any name could be tacked to Frédéric's — in music? Yes, if the lad were to prove himself a Beethoven that might be something, truly. Frédéric, however, was no Beethoven. His compositions, to the mind of Pan Jarocki, were distressingly flippant. Dance music. No more, no less. Only listen to him now! Tinkling on the innkeeper's piano! A waltz measure which even Pan Jarocki, who did not profess to be a master of the arts — or music — knew to lack breadth and grandeur. Such elaboration, such embroidery, such melodious shakes and trills, not unlike the song of the *Daulius luscinia* or common nightingale, mused Pan Jarocki, who, though entirely unimaginative and virtually tone deaf, could not but admit the boy was gifted. But the professor's heart misgave him as to where such gift might lead. A piano player was held by Pan Jarocki in not much more esteem than a play-actor. There had even been some talk at one time, he remembered, that Frédéric might choose the stage as a career, since he had shown himself so excellent a mimic. That lunacy, however, had been crushed. Of the two evils piano-playing was decidedly the lesser.

The professor shook his head. Strange indeed that his friend Nicolas, himself a man of parts and understanding, would not see eye to eye with him in this all-important question of Frédéric's career. Perhaps — confess it — Nicolas was just a thought inflated with the high society that Frédéric from the concert platform had attracted. Princes, counts and countesses visited the house of Monsieur Nicolas, whom Pan Jarocki knew to be enamoured of a title. The son, he feared, had inherited that weakness along with his love of dress. French blood will out. Certainly Frédéric had gained an entrée to a world that would never have received him had he taken a professional degree. But Warsaw was not London, Paris or Berlin, and Frédéric, almost entirely self-taught, was hardly likely to attain a European reputation.

In short, Pan Jarocki concluded, while his sinking stomach reminded him that he had waited half an hour for his dinner and was content to wait no more — in short, he would concern himself no further with what, after all, was none of his affair. If Nicolas was content to see his son a second-rate pianist and could afford to keep him should he starve — and 'God above! Am I to starve?' shouted Pan Jarocki. 'Hi! Landlord!'

The innkeeper came hurrying. 'Yes, yes, *mein Herr*. I go to fetch the wine.'

'Never mind the wine,' bellowed the professor, 'feed me. Where is that Wiener schnitzel?'

'Directly, sir. It is all but now prepared. I wait only for the sauerkraut. A genius!' the landlord added with emotion. 'Your son, *mein Herr*, he is a genius.'

'He's not a genius and he's not my son,' growled the professor. 'I have a fancy also for a *Leberwurst*. Tell the boy to come to table — and make haste!'

The landlord bolted, shocked. Profanation! These Poles! Savages indeed. Though, to be sure, the *Junge* who played like a divinity was no savage. None other, the landlord was convinced, than Michael the archangel, come to bring a blessing on the house.

With the candle glow upon him as he sat, rapt, one could almost have believed it. The chestnut hair, gold-pointed where it caught gleams of light, seemed to form a halo to that serene young brow. The eyes, coloured like old brandy, held a clear startling brilliance that might, however, have been caused as much by fever as by fervour. The flush on either cheek where the transparent skin stretched tight across high cheek bones may have testified to some organic frailty. The mouth, both whimsical and womanish, was retrieved by a jutting fortress of a nose curved like a scimitar, the only male feature in his face... As if God, thought she who from the doorway watched him, had begun to make a girl, and decided just too late to make a man.

The music ceased; the boy rose from the piano, his face a little pale, his eyes wide and full on hers that held him, wondering.

He advanced a step towards her, unconscious of the furore his playing had aroused, unaware that the blonde in a rapture embraced him, that the Englishman, shaken from reserve, had wrung his hand, that the advocate was shouting to the ceiling his *bravo*s, *bravissimo*s, and that the landlord, hugging two bottles of wine, had hysterically blurted, 'Young master — I too play the piano, I too have music in my soul. But I have missed my vocation... I thank you, master, I thank you from the bottom of my heart, as Mozart, could he have heard you, would have thanked —'

And suddenly where she had stood was empty. She had vanished. Was she a ghost, a spirit conjured by his vision? Was he mad?

Breaking free from his encircling admirers, Frédéric rushed to the door. A post-chaise laden with luggage was drawn up under the arch of the courtyard. The night was black as ink, starless, moonless, but the light from the open doorway shone full on her face as she stepped into the chaise followed by a grim attendant, who closed the door of their conveyance with a slam.

In a frenzy Frédéric darted forward and swung himself on to the step. If he lost her now he must lose her for ever, unless he learned her name and destination. He saw her eyes dipped in shadow, her red mouth tremulous with smiles.

'So — you *are* real!' he gasped in French. 'I thought perhaps I'd dreamed you. Where are you going? Tell me and I'll follow you. Must you go now — this minute? Can't you stay?'

He heard the ripple of her laughter; she shook her head and her hood fell back revealing a glossy tangle of dark curls, the whiteness of her throat.

'How beautiful!' breathed Frédéric. 'Who are you? Tell me,' he whispered, 'your name.'

He saw her lips move in answer, but the tumult of his heart drowned her reply.

'Mademoiselle! For shame! To give your name to a stranger.' A very ogress of a woman, with a face as full of teeth as a shark's, now intervened between the panting Frédéric and the lady, with an order to the post-boys to drive on.

'No!' cried Frédéric, madly. 'Not yet. Wait!' And as the horses sprang forward he jumped down, dashed round to the far side of the carriage and was up again on the other step

pleading through the window, 'Pardon, Mademoiselle, but —
pray repeat the name. You said?'

'Constantia Gladowska.'

'The saints be praised! That is a Polish name!' And now he
spoke in his own tongue. 'Do you go to Warsaw? If so I swear
I'll follow —'

'Mademoiselle,' the ogress hissed, 'this is insufferable!'

'*Tais-toi, Élise.*' And as a goddess might have smiled, so did
she. 'Yes, monsieur, I go to Warsaw. We shall meet again …
perhaps.'

'No, not perhaps. For certain!'

The post-boys lashed their whips, the chaise lumbered out of
the yard with Frédéric on the step clinging with both hands to
the window frame, his face not six inches from her own. 'I
have been waiting for this moment,' he panted, 'all my life.'

'Oh, sir, surely not!' A more uncomfortable moment could
scarcely be conceived. *Jesu Maria!* Was ever anything more
crazy? 'Sir, I command you to get down.'

The grinning post-boys stayed their horses. The chaise
halted, and Frédéric, crestfallen, feared he had dared too far;
but her eyes, starry in the darkness, dared him farther.

'I shall be behind you,' babbled Frédéric. Then his foot
slipped from the step and he tumbled in the gutter.
Undaunted, still talking, he picked himself up. 'I too,' he told
her, 'go to Warsaw. I live there.'

'I know.' Her voice came floating on a whispered laugh, 'I
know you live in Warsaw. I have heard you play in Warsaw …
Monsieur Chopin.'

TWO

Thirty-six hours later he was at home again. His delayed arrival, due to the heavy rains, had thrown the household in a ferment of anxiety. His mother, half demented by visionary alarms of bolting horses, highwaymen, and the coach overturned in a ditch, was ready to believe her son arisen from the dead when he appeared.

The journey, for all his horrific account of its discomfort, had not laid a damper on his spirits. Enthroned in the place of honour, his father's chair, with a sister chattering and questioning on either arm of it, he sat, and told them all there was to tell — with reservations; not, however, omitting a side-splitting account of the final Congress dinner, while his mama in silence and her heart at rest, rejoiced.

His papa, hands beneath his coat-tails, his back to the stove which had been lit to warm the prodigal's return, made vain attempt to raise his voice above the din.

'Louise! Isabella — pray let me speak. I have no doubt, my son, that your sense of humour has been amplified at your hosts' expense, but in what other respect have you profited by this experience? What, may one ask, have you learned?'

'Enough,' said Frédéric, sobered by that hawk's-eye glance upon him, 'to know that I shall never be a scholar. I have sat through endless lectures and debates that might have been in Hebrew — so much I understood of them. These scientific ghouls who feed on the bones of dead animals, know less of life than any clod of a peasant who works with the beasts of the field. No, Papa,' Frédéric spoke with clear finality, 'this visit to Berlin has served its purpose as far as I and my future are concerned. I alone am the best judge of my capabilities — and limitations. I am more than ever now determined to make music my life's work with — or without — your permission.'

His sisters gasped at his audacity. His mother gave him a small private smile. She knew, as she had always known, his destiny, from the moment when, at the age of four, she had found him sobbing under the staircase during a musical *soirée*. A trio of gifted amateurs had been playing Mozart. The music had wakened him where he lay in his cot in the room above, and he had come barefoot in his nightgown to hear more.

'But, my darling, it was beautiful. Why do you cry?'

'Because it was *too* beautiful. It hurts.'

She had feared for him then, and she had gone on fearing. How would life deal with one so sensitive? How could she guard this delicate rare bud from the frosts of a boisterous world? It must be placed in a hothouse under glass and sheltered, watched…

His frail health was her first charge. None of her children was robust, and their mother went in terror of that dread disease that had taken, in her fourteenth year, her youngest girl, Emilia. Frédéric was always catching cold, and though the doctors could find no evidence of pulmonary trouble, they had warned her that he might not go unscathed.

Yet for all his mother's cosseting he remained unspoiled. The comradeship of the boys of his own age with whom at his father's school he was educated, or that streak of common sense, the heritage of his French blood, may have acted as a buffer to maternal adoration. True, he had his moods. He swung to extremes; he alternated between heights of hysterical exuberance and depths of a morbid despair, that drove him to describe himself as the E string of a violin on a contra-bass.

His talent for caricature, a saving grace, enabled him to see not only the absurdities of others, but his own. If God — and his mother — had started out to make a girl of him, at eighteen he was more than half a man. And so his father's eye had noted.

'It is evident, my son, that what you have lacked in learning, you have gained in — observation,' Nicolas commented drily.

The boy reddened. His papa had a disconcerting trick of dragging out a secret from its cache. Did he already guess, then, that the miracle for which he had been waiting had come to him, and that his heart was now ensnared and given — to a girl whose face he had glimpsed in the dark? Was it possible that his papa's all-seeing eye had followed him from the inn at Züllichau to Warsaw, had watched the arrival of the diligence in the market place where he had left his luggage with the postmaster, and Pan Jarocki with unfeasible excuses, and had made a bee-line for the town hall, to enquire breathless of a clerk for a directory or register of names of recent visitors — for any sign or clue to guide him in his search for her — his star?

But though he did not over-estimate his father's perspicacity, Frédéric had overlooked his father's blood. He, who, wholly French, had been initiated into the mysteries of manhood with the cracking of his voice, gave a less innocent interpretation to the flush in his son's cheek and his newly acquired assurance. Nicolas smiled. *Tant mieux!* Though for his part he would not have sought the alcoves of Berlin for a first adventure.

'So,' said Nicolas, 'you have decided as I knew you would when I sent you on this mission to the scientists. All has solved itself as I foresaw. You have given me the final proof, if proof were needed, that my good friend Jarocki was wrong — and I was right.'

Frédéric stared, then took a breath. *'Ma foi! Mais ça c'est trop fort!'* he exploded. 'Do you mean to tell me that I have been made to suffer at those meetings — and how I suffered! — in order that you might prove to Pan Jarocki that I'm a dolt, an imbecile, a failure? You know as well as I that I'm no scholar — but at least I have taken my degree —'

'By a hair's breadth,' put in his father.

'Certainly! But still I've taken it. And I could take a doctorate in music blindfold if I wished, but I don't wish. Music can't be taught and learned like algebra.' Then at his father's twinkle, Frédéric's indignation fled. 'Still, Papa, I'll forgive you — for the comfort you give me. This means, doesn't it, that I need no longer call myself an amateur? From now on I shall take my music seriously and earn a living by it — if I can. No more gratuitous performances. I shall charge high fees for my engagements,' cried Frédéric, excited by the vision of all Europe at his feet — and all his laurels won at Hers. 'And you will allow me to go on studying counterpoint with Elsner, won't you? I swear I'll work as I have never worked before. Improvisation comes too easily to me, but now I promise you I'll learn all there is to know of theory — if you'll let me still continue with Pan Elsner.'

'We'll see what we will see,' was all the answer that he got; with which ambiguous reply he had to be content. He knew his present cause was won. His future rested with himself and with the gods.

The house of Nicolas Chopin, situated in one of the best residential districts of Warsaw, was spacious enough to be divided into private apartments for the family, with accommodation in the school quarters for some two dozen boys. A corridor led from the boarders' dormitories to the residence of Monsieur Chopin, and was guarded by a baize-covered door.

It was past midnight when Frédéric, who had sat late talking to his father, mounted the stairs on his way to bed. A stifled giggle, a sibilant 'S-st —' halted him, and his candle held high to investigate, he saw the door of the corridor cautiously opened, while a grinning face with a finger to its lips appeared in the aperture. The body to whom the head belonged, next revealed itself, clad only in a nightshirt.

'*Casimir! C'est toi!*' exclaimed Frédéric, and still clutching his candle, he flung his arms round this apparition, and kissed it heartily on both cheeks. '*Qu'est-ce que tu fais donc? Comment ça va?*'

It was the rule at Monsieur Chopin's academy that the young gentlemen should speak nothing but French, and indeed, most of them, like Frédéric, were bilingual.

'Careful! Careful! Don't make such a row,' Casimir warned him. 'Barcinski sleeps with one ear open. Look, you're dropping grease all over me! I heard you arrive and thought you would never have done jabbering. My room has been moved to the one above your salon since I was made a monitor. Did you know I've been promoted to monitor while you've been away? I have a bedroom to myself at last.'

'Come to mine,' said Frédéric, 'we can't talk here.'

'Yes, but what if your father finds me there?'

'He won't. I'll lock the door.'

Casimir Wodzinski, although a head and shoulders taller than Frédéric, was his junior by two years. His brothers, Felix and Anton, had recently left the school for the University. Frédéric, who had known all three of them since childhood, was accustomed to spend part of his holidays at Słuzewo, the country seat of their father, Count Wodzinski.

'I must hear all about your doings,' said Casimir, when the door of Frédéric's bedroom had been shut and bolted. 'Why did you not write to me? You wrote to Titus.'

'How do you know? Is Titus in Warsaw now?'

'No, not now. He was here for three days last week and Monsieur gave me permission to go out with him. We sat in the Botanical Gardens and he read me bits from your letter. I was so jealous I could have killed him. So now you must tell me verbatim all you have seen and done.'

'I will tell you all tomorrow — or at least all,' said Frédéric loftily, 'that is fit for you to hear.'

'Listen to this braggart!' cried Casimir, turning up his eyes. 'He's grown mighty superior, the little Fryck, since he's lived among those pigs of Germans. Would you have me believe that you have sampled all the delights of Sodom and Gomorrah in a fortnight? I'll wager you've lived as pure as any young miss in a convent.'

'Not from lack of opportunity — *nor* invitation, I assure you,' retorted Frédéric. 'I swear I'd as lief couch with a hippopotamus as with a German *Frau*.'

'*Tiens!* Then you visited no brothels?' persisted Casimir, surprised. 'Have you had no experiences — no adventures? I've heard that Berlin is second only to Paris in its variety of entertainment.'

'Truly!' exclaimed Frédéric. 'The cub of *homo sapiens* is a filthy inquisitive beast with a voracious appetite for garbage.'

'Huh! Garbage be damned! A man must learn, and we must all begin.'

'Yes,' Frédéric smiled to himself, 'and we can all choose our beginnings.'

'Then what have you been doing?' Casimir demanded. 'Do you mean to say you sat in the pockets of these greybeards all the time with your nose glued to a case of specimens? For my part I would not call *that* any peep-show!'

'You disgust me,' said Frédéric coldly.

Casimir grinned. 'Very well, then. I disgust you. Why? Because I'm an animal, a cub — with a cub's desires and appetites — and curiosity? Yes, I'm human — sub-human, if you like — and you, my Fryck, are superhuman, above mundane affairs or fleshly interests. Although I cannot help but feel that there is more in this marked ascension to ethereal planes than meets the eye. So I disgust you? *Alors, parlons d'autres choses.* These hippopotami, then. Did you play to them?'

'Play? The only piano I laid hands on was at an inn between Posen and Züllichau.' For the slice of a second Frédéric's eyes were closed; he opened them to ask, with a carelessness that was a trifle overdone, 'And that reminds me. I suppose you have not heard by any chance the name Gladowska?'

'Gladowska? No. And why should a piano at an inn remind you of — whoever she is?'

Frédéric gave a shrug. 'Merely a sequence of thought. A chance encounter *en route…*' He rounded sharply upon Casimir, who sat on the floor with his chin to his knees and in his eye a dangerous impish sparkle. 'Hadn't you better be off to bed? You will catch cold sitting there in your shift.'

'Thank you. I don't feel in the least cold. The weather indeed is oppressively warm for the time of year. A chance encounter *en route*? Come! That sounds as though it might have possibilities. Gladowska. Is she the latest rival to Maria? Who, by the way, sends you all sorts of loving greeting in her last letter to me — and a row of kisses at the end for her own Fryck. It seems you've made a conquest there, *mon vieux*, but if I find that you have trifled with the affections of my innocent young sister, it will be my painful duty to call you to account.'

Cursing himself for not holding his tongue — for now Casimir had pounced upon that name, it was certain he would never let it go, Frédéric sought, unconvincingly, to temporise. 'Maria! The dear child. Next time I pay a visit to Służewo, I hope your parents will allow me to give her music lessons. I have observed that she is developing a talent.'

'Yes,' Casimir agreed, 'and for more than the piano. Don't forget how last holidays I caught you with her in the arbour in the moonlight and that you bribed me with the promise of a penknife not to —'

'And don't *you* forget,' Frédéric interrupted with some haste, 'that I've been travelling five days and nights. I'm sick for want of sleep. I wish to go to bed.'

'I am not preventing you. Gladowska,' Casimir complacently repeated. 'I'll remember that name.'

'I advise you not to,' said Frédéric, glaring. 'I only mentioned it *en passant*, and you are quite wrong in your suspicions — whatever they may be. I've only seen her for two minutes in the dark.'

'Darkness lends enchantment. And is it necessary to *see* — when love is blind?'

'Will you go?' urged Frédéric, scarlet. 'Or must I call Barcinski to come and throw you out?'

'Talking of Barcinski,' Casimir continued, undisturbed, 'reminds me that I saw him behaving in a most singular fashion while he strolled in the garden last evening. I must tell you —'

'I would much rather you didn't.'

'I must tell you,' Casimir irrepressibly proceeded, 'that I watched him from my window, unobserved. His perambulations up and down commanded my attention. Suddenly he stood stock still, unbuttoned his jacket and took from his breast pocket something which my straining eyes discovered was a glove. A pink, lace-edged kid glove. And with his face upturned in such an ecstasy you'd have thought that he'd seen God, he raised that glove to his lips and — kissed it!'

'What if he did, you gossiping fool? I suppose even a schoolmaster is not entirely devoid of sentiment.'

'On the contrary, he is so full of sentiment that he has set us all transposing Sapphic odes instead of Aristotle.'

'You bore me,' said Frédéric, freezingly. 'Now will you go?'

'Certainly, my angel — I am going,' Casimir, rising, edged towards the door. 'I only thought you might be interested to know the owner of that glove.'

'*Sapristi!* Are you insinuating it was mine?'

'You flatter yourself. No, my dear, it was your sister's. Isabella's.' And in a hurry Casimir departed, leaving Frédéric aghast.

Was this to be believed? Barcinski, the resident master, and Isabella? No! Impossible. He was twice her age. Even that, though, didn't make him very old. And Frédéric recalled how for the past six months Isabella had evinced a penchant for the classics, and had been taking Latin lessons with Barcinski. This, then — unless that jackass Casimir had drawn too vividly upon imagination — was the result. What, Frédéric wondered, would his father have to say, if Barcinski's passion for Isabella were returned?

He was not left long in doubt.

Isabella came to him next morning in tears and with a tale. Since Frédéric had been away (but this must be kept the greatest secret), Barcinski had declared himself — indeed, he was most desperately in love. Isabella, too, confessed that she was not indifferent, but Papa — she was half distracted! Pan Barcinski had insisted that he should approach Papa with a formal offer for her hand in marriage. There must be no subterfuge, and so Anton...

'And who,' enquired Frédéric, 'is Anton?'

Isabella blushed. 'That is his name. I implored him not to be precipitate...'

But it appeared he had not heeded her entreaties. He had taken himself and his proposal to Papa, to be emphatically rejected — and threatened with dismissal. Moreover, all communication between the lovers was forbidden, the Latin lessons had stopped, and Isabella was in two minds whether to kill herself or elope with Pan Barcinski.

'That,' said Frédéric, 'would be the happier solution unless Papa relents.'

'He won't relent. He has other plans for me and Louise. He has lost his head completely since, thanks to your concert-playing, we moved in high society. I don't *want* to move in high society!' sobbed Isabella. She was a year older than Frédéric, but in her high-waisted muslin gown, with her flaxen curls in the prettiest disorder, she looked the merest child.

'You could marry a prince,' said Frédéric.

'Who? What prince? Not that pig-faced son of Radziwill? I'd sooner die. I *shall* die,' Isabella hysterically stated, 'if I lose Barcinski. You alone in all the world can help me, Fryck.'

'I?' quoth Frédéric, startled. 'Don't you bring me into it, no fear! I'll have nothing to do with —'

'Yes, you will,' cried Isabella. 'And you *must*! I will tell you how. Mama can refuse you nothing, and Papa can refuse nothing to Mama. Listen, my little cabbage — I entreat you — if you would only ask Mama to intervene —'

So she coaxed and wheedled. For her love's sake, Fryck *must* exert his influence. If he had ever loved he would not be so hard. Unsympathetic! How could he who played to melt a stone be so unkind? Had he no heart? Was all the tender music that he carried in his fingers mere trickery, then? *Not* born of his soul?... He *had* no soul! He was a popinjay, a conceited, smirking parrot, with an acrobatic trick to charm the ladies. His was not *true* music, as anybody but those cackling countesses would know. 'Oh,' Isabella wrung her hands, 'was there ever anybody so unfeeling? How you grin!' Her nails itched to tear that grin from off his face.

'But,' Frédéric dispassionately argued, 'you can't throw yourself away on a schoolmaster. You're young. You have your life before you.'

'My life is finished,' declared Isabella, 'if I am not to marry him whom I adore.'

'I can't think how you *can*,' persisted Frédéric. 'He's old, he's grey, he stutters —'

'He does *not* stutter. He has the slightest hesitation in his speech, which I find most intriguing. Nor is he grey. True, he has a *mèche blanche* which everyone considers very chic. And so do I. And as for old — he is not turned thirty-eight.'

'And you are just half that. I think it very wrong in Pan Barcinski,' Frédéric pontifically pursued, 'to take advantage of the opportunity afforded to him during Latin lessons to make love to you.'

'He did *not* make love to me during Latin lessons, though I've no doubt he would have done so if Mama had not been always present with her knitting. I was not allowed to be alone with him a minute — in *her* sight. And now I'll never be alone with him again.'

'Serve you right,' rejoined her brother, callously. 'Behaving like a kitchen-maid and sneaking out to meet him on the sly.'

'Well, I'm sure I wish I were dead!' wailed Isabella. 'I would never have believed *you'd* turn upon me in this fashion. And since when have you become so virtuous, pray? Everybody knows how you behaved at Służewo with Maria and she only fourteen. You should be ashamed!'

This *tu quoque* retort might well have ruined Isabella's hope of an ally in her brother, who wisely refrained from over-protestation, waxed cold as she waxed hot. 'Give me credit, idiot, for better taste. Who am I to play with schoolgirls?' Who indeed, whose heart enshrined a goddess? 'And if you think that *I'll* encourage you in this absurd intrigue, you are mistaken.'

With shattering dignity he wheeled to leave the room, his sister abject at his coat-tails. 'Oh, please — please, Fryck darling, no! Pray don't take offence at a mere *blague*. Oh, God! What did I say? Nothing. Only some teasing nonsense of Casimir's — you know how he never can stop teasing. Forget it. Only help me now. None but you can help me. If you would only plead for me with Mama — she would marry me to the chimney sweep if *you* approved the match. If you would sing his praises to Mama — tell her how scholarly he is — he will be offered a professorial chair at the Lyceum — that is *certain*. In all Poland there is no greater master of the classics. He reads Greek as easily as I read French. Ah, Fryck! I'd do the same for you and more if you should ever need it...' And so on.

Then in a moment's flash it came to Frédéric that he might turn his sister's cause to his account. She, who had no more to do than pass her time in paying calls and chattering over tea-cups — surely she might glean some useful information concerning the *demoiselles* of Warsaw? Through Isabella he might trace the whereabouts, the comings and the goings of his lady. She might be visiting with friends. Warsaw perhaps was not her native city: if it were, he felt convinced he would discover her. No city in the world could contain her long, without his knowledge. That was sure.

And so it came about that confidence for confidence was presently exchanged, and promises extracted. Frédéric would intercede on behalf of Isabella, if Isabella in return would devote her energies to the search for his Gladowska. He gave her ruthlessly the margin of a week. If at the end of that time her investigations had proved unsuccessful then Isabella's love was doomed. He told her flatly, that far from aiding her, he would encourage opposition.

'A week? Merciful heaven!' Isabella's entreaties and tears began anew. 'How terrible, how *more* than heartless! And why the devil,' she turned upon him in a pretty fury, 'can't you look for her yourself?'

'I too shall be untiring in my efforts,' Frédéric assured her, 'but you can venture where I should fear to tread. I can't sit round a tea-table purring with grimalkins as you can, my little kitten, and lapping all the gossip of the town. Nor can I go bandying her name in my enquiries without attracting unwelcome attention to myself — and her.'

'But suppose I never find her?'

Frédéric smiled. 'You *will* find her. Warsaw is not the universe. And think of the incentive.'

'I never heard anything so shameful! This is bribery. Corruption. A week! God *knows* I'll never find her in a week!'

'You may find her in a day if you put your mind to it,' said Frédéric.

'Little toad!' screamed Isabella. 'This is *too* cruel — and monstrously unfair!'

'There is, I think, an English proverb,' Frédéric told her, 'which says, "all is fair in love."' Laughing, he took her face between his hands. Come, dry your eyes, *ma poupée*. There's no need for tears. I have a presentiment you'll find her.'

'You and your presentiments!' scoffed Isabella. 'I hope indeed, for my sake, you are right.'

But he was wrong.

It may be that the week's limit was extended and Isabella given a reprieve, while the search went on and Monsieur Nicolas remained immovable. Certain it is that not only Isabella but Louise, the elder sister, was admitted to the secret, and heaven knows who else besides, for we find him writing to his friend Titus Woyciechowski that *Six months have now elapsed and I have not set eyes on or exchanged a word with her of whom I nightly dream, and who has inspired me with the adagio of my Concerto in F Minor, also this little trifle of a waltz I send to you...*

Six months is a long time to dream; too long for Isabella, whom desperation had emboldened to dispense with Frédéric's doubtful intervention, dare defiance of her father, and vow she'd marry Pan Barcinski out of hand. So much for that, and far too much for Frédéric. He, when parental consent to the betrothal had been at last obtained, found the ecstasy of lovers gall to his taste — and to his condition, which may have accounted for his desire, not without reluctance granted, for another holiday abroad: this time to Vienna, and not with Pan Jarocki.

Accompanied by a couple of young friends, music students from the Conservatoire at Warsaw, Frédéric set out on his excursion; but although we find him armed with introductions from Pan Elsner and Zwyny, who, since his childhood had been his one and only teacher of the pianoforte, it seems that Frédéric had no immediate intention of appearing on the concert platform in Vienna.

Since his return from Berlin, he had been studying with a feverish determination to perfect his technique. He kept a piano in his bedroom and at all hours of the night — to wake the servants overhead, who had it firmly fixed that the young master was mad — he would jump from his bed to set his fingers singing some elusive harmony snatched from a dream: to make articulate the voiceless passion, the melancholy yearning of the artist heard above youth's flame and clamour, and youth's exaggerated crude perplexities. In such moments, when in the tragic brevity of revelation he beheld a lifted new horizon and learned the secret things that belonged to him and to his God, then and then only did he know his aim and purpose, as surely as he knew his time was short.

But though his instinct yearned towards creation, the light of his extraordinary gift as an executive could not be subdued. That visit to Vienna marked the first milestone along the way of his career; it revealed him, outside the limited acceptance of his own small world, as an artist of the rarest quality, a new exponent of a new school, whose spontaneous improvisations defied all orthodoxy.

The astounded critics, forced to revise their academic code, were redundant in their acclamation of:

This young pianist from Poland who comes before us as a master of the first rank. The exquisite delicacy of his touch, his indescribable dexterity, his finished shading and portamento reflect the deepest feeling; and his compositions which bear the stamp of genius, present a virtuoso who, without previous blast of trumpets, appears as a brilliant meteor in our midst.

Thus the *Allgemeine Musikalische Zeitung*, which for all its fulsome praise does not seem to have inflated him. In those letters that have been preserved, and which give us his own recording of the causes and effects of his first appearance in Vienna, it is the boy and not the artist who is speaking, unaware of latent powers — or afraid of them.

To his parents, August 3th, 1829:

My Dear Ones,

Here I am, very well — and happy. I don't know why but I appear to astonish the natives and I am astonished that they find anything to be astonished at! Thanks to Elsner's letter of recommendation Haslinger gave me an exceedingly friendly reception. He made his son play for me, showed me everything of musical interest that he has, and apologized for not introducing me to his wife. (He said she was not at home!)(But in spite of his overwhelming politeness, he has not yet printed those things I sent him and I did not dare ask him about them. However, while he was showing me all his most enviable editions, he informed me that my Variations will probably appear in the Odeon *series next week. I didn't expect that!*

He strongly advises me to give a concert here. In fact, everybody I meet seems to think the same. Herr Hussarzewski who invited me to dinner last night was quite enthusiastic about my playing, and Herr Blahetka, a journalist, whom I met at Haslinger's also urged me to give a concert. So does Count Gallenberg, the Director of the Opera House, where I heard some shocking bad concerts. He endorses Haslinger's opinion that the Viennese should hear me play my own compositions. Everyone tells me that now is the most favourable time for me to appear because Vienna is starving for new music. All this fuss about me and I can't make up my mind!

I seem to have met almost everyone of note in the musical world and Haslinger promises to introduce me to Czerny. As to Vienna — I am utterly infatuated with this beautiful gay city. They want me to stay here for the winter. Shall I?

P.S. Well! I have decided. I am to give a concert. Blahetka says I am certain to cause a furore. *Everyone is very amiable. Count Gallenberg in particular, as I am to play at his theatre and* nota bene — *without pay!*

The members of the orchestra positively cringe to me when I walk in arm in arm with the Director of Italian Opera. Just imagine! Both Graff and Stein have offered me pianos. I have chosen a Graff which I prefer. It is to be hoped Stein won't take offence!

And so — God help me… (Don't worry.)

And three days later this:

My Dearest Parents,

You know from my last letter that I have been persuaded to give a concert. Well, yesterday (Tuesday) at 7 o'clock in the evening at the Imperial Opera House I made my first bow to a Viennese public! When I see you I shall be able to tell you more than I can write. At any rate I wasn't hissed!

As he was to pay me nothing for it, Count Gallenberg hurried on the preliminary arrangements. Here is the programme.

Beethoven's Overture (Prometheus).

My Variations.

Songs (Fräulein Veltheim).

My Cracovienne.

My Rondo.

But the orchestra accompanied so abominably at rehearsal that I was obliged to substitute a Free Fantasia for the Rondo.

I must confess I was not at all satisfied with the Fantasia, but the public must have liked it if one can judge by the tremendous applause I received…

My friends were scattered about in all parts of the house so that they might hear remarks. Celinski will tell you he heard nothing unfavourable either from the critics or the public. Hube reports the only severe criticism

— and that from a lady! 'It is a pity the youth has so little presence!' Still — if that's the worst that can be said of me I don't care.

I improvised from 'La Dame Blanche' and also — because I felt I must have a Polish theme — I chose 'Chmiel'. The public to whom our national airs are entirely unknown seemed quite electrified, and my spies in the pit said the people began a regular dance on the benches!

There does, however, seem to be an almost unanimous opinion that I play too softly or rather too delicately for the public here. They are more accustomed to drum-beating. I am afraid the newspapers will say the same thing, especially as the pianiste daughter of Blahetka — the musical critic whom I met at Haslinger's — drums dreadfully.

Never mind, if the newspapers cut me up so much that I shall never dare appear before the world again I have resolved to become a house painter! That would be as easy as anything and at any rate I should still be an artist!

In a letter to his friend Titus Woyciechowski after a second performance, when his first success had been repeated, he speaks with more assurance.

Just imagine my playing twice here in the Royal-and-Imperial-Theatre and in so short a time! This is how it came about. Haslinger (who is going to publish my Variations) told me it would be to my advantage to present my own compositions, as my name is yet unknown in Vienna and my music difficult to play and understand.

The members of the orchestra evidently thought so the way they cursed my badly written score at the rehearsal.

I began with the Variations (dedicated to you!) — which were to come after the Rondo Cracovienne. They managed to get through the Variations but the Rondo was so entirely beyond them, owing to my frightful scrawl, that twice we had to stop and begin all over again. I ought to have put pauses below instead of above.

Anyhow, the gentlemen were so full of grumbles and grimaces, that I felt much inclined to announce myself sick — or dead — in the evening.

At last Baron Denmar (the stage Director), seeing the mauvais humeur *of the orchestra and my unhappy plight, took pity on me and suggested that instead of playing the Rondo I should improvise. Whereupon the orchestra began to pull more faces, so that in the end and in desperation I consented. And who knows whether my success was not due to the calmness of despair, for in spite of this discouraging beginning, I was not in the least frightened when I sat down, pale, to a magnificent instrument — a Graff — the best in all Vienna.*

A very painted young man turned over for me, and whispered boastfully that he had done the same for Moscheles, Hummel, Herz, etc., when they *played in Vienna. You can imagine how I felt then!*

However, all went well. I was enthusiastically received and recalled four time after my Variations. The Improvisations went even better — they were followed by storms of applause and even the orchestra clapped!

By universal request I was induced to play again the following week. And this time I did *play the Rondo, having copied it for the orchestra to read and they were so delighted with it that they (the orchestra) actually recalled me twice! I was also obliged to repeat the Variations — at the request of the ladies, and especially Fräulein Blahetka who is herself a* pianiste *of considerable réclame in Vienna.*

She is seventeen. Very pretty. She has given me an autographed copy of her own compositions as a keepsake. I think she likes me!

Do forgive me writing so much about myself…

It was excusable. His letters to his family and friends, poured forth in the first fever of excitement, express his naive exuberance and wonder at the enthusiasm with which he had been greeted by the musical élite of Vienna. But, though half-drunk with those first sweets of success, his appetite for such was soon appeased, and before he left Vienna we find him writing home:

If ever I longed to be with you it is now. I have received a great deal too much kindness, but under no circumstances will I give a third concert. I only gave a second because they forced me into it — and because I thought people might say I was no good because I'd not been asked to play again!

What do you think? Blahetka said he was surprised that I could learn so much in Warsaw. I told him that even the greatest donkey must learn something from Zwyny and Elsner!...

At any rate I need no longer be regarded as a student.

Once back again in Warsaw, however, these triumphs were forgotten; and it is as student still that, untiringly, he applied himself to his finger exercises at the piano in the attic room his parents had prepared for him as a surprise for his return.

The entrance opening directly upon a short flight of stairs, concealed by another door, secured privacy in this retreat, and there at a shabby old writing desk retrieved from the lumber room he composed... *Nothing*, he writes to Titus, *worthy of God or man.*

So much for his own opinion of his Rondeau à la Krakowiak (Op. 14) and the Trio (Op. 8) just completed.

He was in that state of emotional upheaval when his senses craved for some magnetic centre, when his youth and all his youth's impulse, invested with unstable flickering impressions, sought fulfilment. His music could no longer exclusively possess him; he hungered for a more acute awareness of his being. He had fed on dreams and from dreams and visions only had created.

Yet in this bewildered maze of adolescence he had imaged a reality, tremulous, importunate, constantly dissolving and recurring, though none the less persistent. But that shadowy passion for her whom he named his 'Ideal', held perhaps less of love than love's reflection…

He went haunted. He saw her everywhere: on his lonely walks, when, sick of his music and his scales, he would leave his piano, and wander with his thoughts of her through the network of narrow streets that lead from the Stare Miasto to the oldest part of the city. There in the market place he loved to stand and watch that vivid fantasy of colour and movement with its background of tall gable-roofed houses, their façades covered with a dazzle of intricate designs in paint and sculpture, untouched and undisfigured by the passing of five hundred years. The peasants, who came from near villages to buy and sell, were an endless joy to him. He delighted in the primitive flashes of sheer red, orange, green or blue of their national dress: the swathe of sash or shawl, the embroidered tunic of some wealthy farmer, and here and there, in sinister contrast to that gay-patterned motley, the traditional black of a Jew's gaberdine, the shuffling uneasy walk of one who had no right of way outside his ghetto.

And sometimes, in the villages beyond the city's walls, he would watch enraptured the dances of the country folk at the end of a market day, when, steeped in Slavic rhythm he would stroll homeward in the dusk, his mind busy with exotic cadence and sweet melancholy, to capture from that heavy-hoofed peasant dance with its wild insistent throb and beat, the very soul and essence of mazurka: or perhaps, in some such mood as this, a figure, young and hooded, would detach itself from those unseen who passed him on his way, and by some trick of light, or magic, would transport him and set his own heart dancing a mazurka, that he must follow where she led and overtake her, with her name in a rush on his lips — to be greeted by the blank stare of a stranger, twice her age and as handsome as a turnip! Alas, not her whom he for ever sought and never found.

All hope at last expired, he came to think that she had never been, save in his own obsession that had called her to him in his dreams, to torment him with this mockery of love. And when, resolutely, he decided to erase her from his thoughts, when the vision of her faded and grew dim; when on a day that he had arranged to meet his friend Titus Woyciechowski at a café in the town; when for the first time in more than half a year he had ceased to think of her, or at least to think of her without a pang, she came to him.

Nor, unbelievably, did he know her to be there, not three yards distant from his elbow, as he stood in a moment's pause outside the Conservatoire examining a poster that announced the arrival of Paganini in Warsaw… No pricking of his thumbs and no 'presentiment' warned him that Constantia Gladowska had returned.

THREE

At a table outside the Café Fukier on the Stare Miasto, Titus waited — and waited.

It was, however, not unusual for Fryck to be an hour late for an appointment, and Titus had time not only to spare, but to waste. His father, a wealthy landowner, who had died while Titus, his only son, was still in petticoats, had left him a fortune and a castle at Poturzyn. Having recently attained with his majority full possession of his heritage, Titus found himself a gentleman at large with the choice of a career as arbiter of fashion or patron of the arts. He combined both with some success.

Between this young elegant and Frédéric had existed, since their early schooldays, a friendship of the closest intimacy. But, reflected Titus, as he sipped his vodka, the patience of even the most devoted and tolerant of friends is by no means inexhaustible. Or was it possible that he had mistaken the day or the location of this rendezvous? And taking from his pocket a crumpled scrawl he read:

My dearest Soul! I must — I positively must see you. You cannot imagine how dreary Warsaw has become. (*That, my friend,* interpolated Titus, glancing with disfavour at the stolid bourgeois occupants of neighbouring tables — *that goes without saying. To exist among such* canaille *is surely worse than death.*) *If it were not for my family I could not endure to go on living here. How dreadful it is to have no one with whom to share one's thoughts, to be unable to express one's innermost secrets to any living soul...* (*With exception,* suggested Titus, *of Julius and Jan, the Radziwills, myself, and both his sisters. He is so charmingly ingenuous, the little Fryck). How often I tell my piano all I should like to tell you. You know what I mean. (Do I? observed Titus. I wonder.) Listen, my friend. I cannot stay here in Warsaw. I am suffocated. I want to return to Vienna — with you! What joy if we could go together. We will discuss this further when we meet. You say you will be in Warsaw on Tuesday. Come to Fukier's at four o'clock. I shall be there, waiting.*

Decidedly, thought Titus, *it is not I who am at fault: and it is I, not he, who am still — waiting. Today is Tuesday. This is Fukier's. Our Fryck appears to be in desperate mood, or was, when he wrote that letter. As for me I do not dance attendance on a caprice.*

'Waiter! Another vodka!'

But Frédéric arrived before the drink: breathless with haste, pink with excitement, hot, and stammering.

'I've seen her! I have talked with her! She's here!'

'Who? Where?' asked Titus, in some bewilderment. 'Sit down, my dear fellow, and explain yourself. Waiter! *Two* vodkas.'

'Oh, God! A miracle!' ejaculated Frédéric, and sat, his face bowed on his hands, his shoulders shaking. 'A miracle has happened — is happening. The blessed Saint Anton has heard my prayers — I have seen her — have spoken to her. At last! For the better part of a year I have waited — and despaired. Now she is here again — in Warsaw. In a fur-lined tippet and a cherry-coloured hood. She has hands like flowers and her eyes are blue. I had thought them black, but I had only seen them in the shadow. In the light — blue as gentians — or the eyes of those strange oriental cats. Do you remember how enraptured you were with the sapphire eyes of Princess Radziwill's Mongolian kitten — or was it Siamese?'

Titus began to be alarmed. Could it be that Fryck had lost his wits? 'Drink this,' he said soothingly. 'It will calm you.'

'Thanks, thanks.' With a sweep of his arm Frédéric upset the glass of vodka. 'A thousand pardons! What a clumsy oaf! But, happily, *not* over your exquisite new trousers. I wish,' said Frédéric covetously, 'I could afford your tailor. Is lavender the latest shade?'

Titus, relieved at this return to norm, admitted that it was. 'I am told from a friend who writes from London, that d'Orsay has made it all the rage among the *ton* — but it was Brummell, I think, who first introduced the strap under the boot to render the trouser creaseless. We are always ten years behind the *mode* in Warsaw. I do agree, though, that my tailor has quite surpassed himself. I, of course, gave him my instructions. I am told also that King George has grown so enormously fat that he dare not follow the fashion. Not even an English tailor, than which there is no better in the world — can fit *his* calves with skin-tight *pantalons*. He drives out now, they say, in a closed carriage with the curtains drawn for shame that his people should see him. General opinion seems to be that he is dying. I have it on the best authority that —'

'Dead or alive,' Frédéric interrupted, 'I am not interested in England's preposterous king, although *she* tells me that her great-grandmother was English. So I ought to adore the English for her sake. She has, now I come to think of it, the English figure. Slight and *svelte*. Englishwomen on the whole are not remarkable for beauty. They have such dreadful teeth. Her teeth are unbelievable. Each one a pearl. But her figure — not the *embonpoint* of a *prima donna* who from deep breathing exercises is so abnormally developed that she carries a mountain on her bosom — which I find quite disgusting and which always spoils the *sight* of any opera for me, that I have to shut my eyes to hear it. No. She, although a singer, is a sylph. Slender. Young — older perhaps than I or even you — but still, she's young. Somewhere in the early twenties. Is this mine?'

And taking the glass of vodka that had been placed in front of Titus, Frédéric raised it to his lips. 'Believe me, this is a great event. I drink to her — and to all the magic she has brought me. If I loved the shadow of a dream, how much greater is my love for the reality!' He drained the glass, then dashed it to the ground and set his heel upon it, declaring, 'No other lips shall touch where I have breathed her name!'

'What name? Will you tell me who,' demanded Titus, 'is responsible for this hysteria?'

'You may call it hysteria. You may call it imbecility, you may call me a besotted ass. I am in love.'

'Yes?' murmured Titus, taking snuff.

'I cannot expect you to understand,' hissed Frédéric. 'You have not seen her. You have not dreamed —'

'According to the doctors, all dreams are due to indigestion,' said Titus, glancing at his watch. 'My carriage is waiting at the town hall to drive me home. From your letter I imagined you to be in direst straits. I am delighted to find you now in seventh heaven. But such celestial heights are not for the earth-bound.' He rose. 'Goodbye — till you regain your reason.'

'Don't go!' Frédéric made a grab at his friend's arm. 'No doubt you think me crazy. Perhaps I am. I am! And so would you be too if — but let me tell you! Pray, my dear, sit down again, and let me tell you...'

And he told.

It seemed Constantia Gladowska lived in Cracow, but on that unforgettable occasion when he had met her at Züllichau she had been on her way to Warsaw, where she stayed for one week only at the house of an aunt, which accounted for the fact that he had not seen her since. She often came for a few days to Warsaw. She had been present at one of his concerts — that was how she had recognised him, and known his name. She had been studying singing in Vienna, and had now returned to Warsaw to study at the Conservatoire. 'She said that she was to make her début here in April.'

'When you,' suggested Titus, 'will be making your return visit to Vienna.'

'I?' screamed Frédéric. 'Vienna? Do you imagine for one moment that I would leave Warsaw now — for Vienna?'

'I see,' said Titus, and he smiled.

'You do not see!' shouted Frédéric, to raise a titter from the occupants of other tables already much diverted by the behaviour of these dandiacal young men. 'And for that I pity you — for you have never loved.'

'Nor have you,' retorted Titus, flicking invisible snuff from his sleeve. 'You are a Narcissus, in love with no one but yourself. How can you be in love with some smirking flipperty-gibbet whom you meet for five minutes in a droshky?'

'I did *not* meet her in a droshky,' denied Frédéric, loudly. 'I met her in —'

'Hell's torment!' It was now Titus's turn to shout. 'Do I care *where* you met her — whoever she may be? And if she is that creature of whom you have been writing me seventeen-page nauseating rhapsodies, the majority of which I put to some more useful purpose than to read them, I assure you — then let me now repeat — I'm sick to death of her! I came here to meet you, to talk sense. I return home in ten minutes.'

Frédéric's jaw dropped. 'Then you are not staying here the night?'

'Have I not already told you I am returning to Poturzyn *now*?'

47

'I am sorry.'

'No, *mon ami*,' said Titus, beckoning the waiter, 'you are not sorry. But I am. Sorry indeed to see you in such case. I had hoped to discuss something of more interest than these mawkish vapourings. I had hoped to hear of your latest works — your future plans. Only yesterday I received a letter from my mother who is in Leipzig. Your fame, it seems, has carried there.'

Frédéric sat up. 'Really? Leipzig? Who can have heard of me in Leipzig?'

'Oh, nobody — nobody at all,' Titus laconically announced, digging in his pocket for a coin to give the fawning waiter. 'You may or may not have heard of Schumann.'

'Schumann?' repeated Frédéric, open-mouthed. 'Not Robert Schumann?'

'Is the name Robert?' asked Titus coldly. 'That I did not know — but I *do* know that he is considered a young man of some musical significance.'

'Significance!' breathed Frédéric. 'He is a master. The greatest of all moderns —'

'Perhaps not quite the greatest,' murmured Titus. 'He seems to think there is a greater yet. He may be over-generous, but it appears —' and Titus stood to lay his hand for an instant on Frédéric's shoulder — 'it appears that when he first heard your Variations played before an enthusiastic audience of students, he greeted the finale with the remark, 'Hats off, gentlemen! A genius!'

Frédéric paled. 'Is this true?'

'Is my mother a liar?'

'But —' the colour rushed back to the boy's face — 'this is too fantastic. Schumann — to say that of me — of *me*? My Variations? *Your* Variations, Titus.' He seized his friend's hand

and crushed it to his lips. 'You inspired me to write them. God! I can't believe that Schumann said — No! Impossible!'

'All things are possible.' Titus withdrew his hand to fasten with a jewelled clasp the velvet collar of his cloak. 'I don't tell you this to flatter you, my Fryck, but to spur you to greater effort. Don't waste your opportunities and the gifts that God has given you on feminine rubbish.'

Fists closed, scarlet, Frédéric sprang to his feet. 'Do you dare to call her —'

'I dare,' Titus interrupted smoothly, 'to speak my mind to a friend.'

'Even friendship can be strained,' Frédéric flung back, 'to demand apology — or account for such outspokenness.'

Tiens!' Titus cocked an eyebrow and reached for his cane. 'Will you fight me for it? Here is my weapon — ready.' He whipped a sword from its malacca case. 'And I'm the better duellist, I fancy.'

'Name me coward,' panted Frédéric, 'and I'll knock the teeth out of your head. My choice is pistols — not a dandy's sword-stick.'

'What?' Titus laughed, and replaced the sword in its innocent sheath. 'Between *us* — words? Do you think I'd fight you — for a woman? For her, who since time's beginning has been the root of all man's evil? The greatest mistake the Creator ever made was that act of manipulative jugglery He performed on Adam's fifth rib. Until then man had been sufficient unto himself, with all the best of *him* and the worst of *her*, combined. Then God thought fit to divide man into halves — ever since when, the two halves have been trying to be whole again. For my part, I would say — leave well alone. I have no desire — yet — to seek my *lesser* half; and I pray,' eyes up, devoutly Titus crossed himself, ' that I remain for ever self-contained.' And ramming his beaver at an angle on his head, he strolled away across the market square.

But for once Frédéric did not follow at his heels. He stayed where Titus left him, bemused with love and vodka, in Elysium.

He had sought and found, was anchored: not to a mirage, diaphanous, elusive, visioned through the mists of unreality, but to reality itself.

The 'mawkish vapourings' deplored by Titus found voice in stronger essence than the calfish adoration of a boy who had no words to speak his love; but while he stood dumb before her, his spirit spoke in its own boundless language.

Within a month of that second meeting with Gladowska, he told Titus in a letter, *I have written a few études. They will need some playing.*

Thus unheralded save for that one laconic statement were the first of those astonishing impressions launched on the piano-playing world, though not till five years later to be recognised.

There in the quiet of his attic room he sat at his piano, pouring through his fingers the changes of his mood, as flame and joy and darkness took their turn in his articulation. But she, the source of it, went unconscious of her part in immortality. She, preoccupied with her affairs, her pending début, and no lack of other suitors in every way more eligible than he, had not much time for a girlish youngster in his teens, who stood stammering and pop-eyed when they met, which seemed to be six days out of every seven in the week.

Then, when his unfailing appearance on the steps of the Conservatoire proved more than mere coincidence, she ceased to smile upon him, and refused his escort home.

Agonised, Frédéric watched her go. The tilt of her chin, her veiled glance, the very swing of her skirts as she walked told him he had displeased her. But till now she had been gracious; had talked to him of this and that: of how hard she had been studying; of the students' concert in which she had taken part: what the critics said of her — and of Paganini, who had come and gone. How her eyes had sparkled when she spoke of him!

Yes, admittedly — a player.

'But more than a player! A supreme artist.' She repeated it. 'Supreme!'

'A great executive,' he mumbled, 'certainly.'

'But more — much more than that! He has no rival.'

'Surely Slawik,' he had dared to argue, 'is almost, if not quite, his equal, considering his years. He is young and Paganini —'

'Is he old,' she flashed at him, 'I was completely overwhelmed. He moved me to tears.'

This was unendurable.

'Slawik,' he offered, desperately, 'is to my mind the greater violinist. He is marvellous. Ninety-six staccato notes in one bow! I would not have believed it if I had not heard him. Have you heard him?'

This was a direct challenge, and she not disposed to take it from one who had no status, no right to contradict. A stripling, who had played in public only twice — and that for charity, unpaid. An amateur.

She knew nothing of his recent triumph in Vienna, and cared less. There were pianists at the Conservatoire of greater worth than he. True, she conceded him a certain quality of emotional appeal. That evening at the inn when he had played, unconscious of an audience, she had been quite enchanted, but fundamentally, to her mind, he lacked depth. She did not much believe in him. She believed, however, greatly in herself. Soon she would prove, not only to this little fatuous calf, but to Warsaw, Paris, London and Berlin, that her voice was unsurpassable. Had not Ernemann declared that no singer of her years could be compared to her? And was she not invited to appear before the court at a *soirée musicale* in company with all the stars in Warsaw?

But not Chopin. He had not been asked to play at court, even though he had been presented by the Czar of Russia with a ring. But that was as a prodigy. And now, like all such *Wunderkinder*, he had passed his zenith. He was and would remain a mediocrity. This she gave him quietly to understand in her glance, faintly mocking, in her tone, cruelly careless.

'So! You do not play with us at the *soirée*? I had hoped to hear you. There is always a great attendance during the Diet sittings. Perhaps later...?'

'Yes, Mademoiselle, perhaps later. I do not compete with ... angels.'

He could have bitten out his clumsy tongue for that. She passed it over, and returned with claws, to scratch. 'I am astonished that you are not invited.'

'I,' he said, 'am not at all astonished. Why should I, a mere beginner, be invited?'

She was drawing on her gloves. Her vulture of a maid, holding her portfolio and muff, stood grimly at her side. He heard whispers.

'Mademoiselle! Will he keep you here all day? Pray come along. It is unseemly!'

'Yes, I'm going. My muff, Élise. Brr!' She shivered, divine in her fur bonnet. 'I am frozen. There is skating on the river. Do you skate, Monsieur Chopin?'

'I —' he began eagerly, ' would adore to skate with —'

'Come, Élise.' She took the words from his mouth and trod on them. *'Au 'voir,'* her laughter tinkled, *'Chopinetto'.*

Chopinetto? Was it insult or endearment? Who could tell?

'May I escort you —'

'No. And, if you please, I insist you do not follow me, nor plant yourself so often on these steps to watch my coming in and going out. I do not care for such attention, I assure you.'

Damnation. Death.

Shattered, dismissed, humiliated to the snow beneath him, there he stood. Tears sprang smarting to his eyes. Was he a girl — to weep? In what way had he offended? In every way — by word and deed. Yes, evidently. He must not come here again to throw himself, his love, his longing, at her feet — to be spurned. To hell with her, and with all women! How right was Titus to shun them like the plague. And how dared she to put him down and take him up and play the cat's game to his mouse? Was he not man enough to speak and assert himself?

In two strides he overtook her. 'Mademoiselle!'

She frowned. 'Still here? You are persistent.'

'Yes. Forgive me. I have waited. I swore to find you … you remember?'

'I remember that on one occasion you amused me. You do not amuse me now.'

He turned from red to white. 'I apologise for my intrusion. I shall not intrude again.'

He bowed and went. Her laughter followed him. Seething with rage and misery, he dashed home to plunge into the solace of his music, the dark melancholy, perhaps, of the *étude* in E Flat Minor, with its youthful exaggeration of despair.

There are some who say he was incapable of love: that he was the lover of himself more than of any woman. It may be so: even that long association which shadowed all the last years of his life may not have penetrated deeper than the frail shell that enclosed the man and not the soul of the musician.

But that Constantia Gladowska did profoundly stir him, and that through her he suffered as only the very young can suffer — to forget — is certain. That he was unaware of his own potentialities is certain, too. He believed that he was small; she made him feel smaller. He knew nothing of his greatness, except in those rare moments of illumination when all vital force and purest energy unite to grasp at knowledge, to see, to touch, before the curtain falls...

It was about this time that Nicolas Chopin, spurred by Elsner, decided his son must give a concert and repeat in Warsaw his Viennese success. To the practical mind of Nicolas, the boy could turn his music to more lucrative account than scribbling sheets of manuscripts that might never find a publisher. There was no money, Nicolas maintained, in composition. Not one in thousands made a name or income for himself writing music. More could be earned in two hours on the platform than two years at a desk with a pen. Even Beethoven died poor.

Thus Chopin's first appearance as a paid performer took place on March 17th, 1830. But although the hall was packed to capacity, he did not receive from his compatriots in Warsaw the wholehearted acclamation accorded to him in Vienna. Nor did his Concerto in F Minor produce the effect that he had hoped for. *The first allegro,* he said in a letter to Titus, *is obviously unintelligible to the masses. There were a few 'Bravos' at the end of it, but I think only from those who wanted to show that they understood serious music! The Adagio and Rondo seemed to go better, the applause sounded genuine as far as one could judge, but my Pot-pourri on national airs was a complete failure and the faint — the very faint — clapping was evidently intended to let me know the audience was bored!'*

Nevertheless, this setback did not deter him from giving another concert the following week. Gladowska may have had her share in his determination to regain lost ground. He had been greatly cheered that she was not present to witness his discomfiture: this he learned when he waylaid her once again.

'So! You have come back?'

Her laugh had lost its sting: her eyes were a deeper, warmer blue behind the dark fringe of her lashes. The day was warmer, too, the biting frosts of the last few weeks had melted. Spring was on its way; in her fur cap snowdrops clustered. She was more beautiful than he had dreamed.

'I —' his voice stuck in his throat — 'I have not been away.'

'I thought perhaps you had left Warsaw.'

'Then you did not know — you have not heard? I gave a concert.'

He half suspected her surprise was feigned. 'A concert? You have given a concert? No. I heard nothing of it.'

'Why should you? The papers scarcely spoke of it.'

'If I had known that you were playing, Monsieur Chopin, I should have been there to applaud you.'

'You might not have heard me, Mademoiselle. I am told I play too softly.'

'Your playing is exquisite — in a room.'

That thrust went home. He knew then that she had read the criticisms of his performance, in which one and all complained that he was scarcely audible in the back rows.

'If you will honour me by your presence I will play again — next week.' He said it on an impulse, smarting from her cut, more than ever determined to show her and those swinish critics that he followed no school but his own. His music and his playing were unique. One day she and the world would accept it: but the whole world's praise, he told himself, would be well lost for hers. Let the world rot, if by his music he could win her, and make her eat her words. What words? She had said nothing that could be taken as offence. No, not in words so much as in faint mockery and implication. She made him conscious of his youth, his inexperience. Plainer than words she had told him he was raw.

And now, committed, he must at all costs reappear.

He went in panic lest it might not be possible to arrange another concert. His papa would have to be consulted. Would he be willing to finance a second loss? The first concert had not cleared its expenses.

He need not have feared his father's disapproval. Nicolas was in complete accordance. 'You cannot be judged by a first concert. In this case, *mon fils, c'est le deuxième pas qui coûte.*'

Much more than his father guessed depended on this second step, which judging by results must have been a giant's stride. The interim before the day arrived was passed in a state of nervous excitement, which subsided in one of his violent colds.

Deaf to his mother's entreaties and his father's orders, Frédéric refused to stay in bed, but sat all day and half the night at his piano. He must, he insisted, practise every hour before the concert; he dared not slacken off, nor — as his mother urged him — could he possibly postpone it. If he did, everyone would say he was afraid to appear again. And if he did not appear again, he would be marked down as a failure. Did his mama then wish him to be a failure? Did she want everyone in Warsaw from the gutter to the court to jeer and point and say 'There goes little Chopin — yes, that one with the formidable nose! He once thought he was a pianist or even a composer. Ha! Ha! Ha! How inexpressibly droll. He is now a commercial traveller in ladies' corsets...'

Of course, if his mama wanted him to sacrifice his life's ambition he would do so for her sake. If at this critical moment in his career she would make of him an imbecile with her ceaseless fussing and her camomile tea, then he would sell ladies' corsets — or retire to a madhouse. But in the meantime he implored her to leave him here in peace and let him practise. Sacred Name! Why must he be tortured?... And so on, till he was in a fever and his mother in a fright.

The doctor, sent for, came long-faced, with medicine to purge him and plasters for his chest. Frédéric, who would have none of him or of his physic, called — one may believe he screamed — for his friend Jan.

'Jasia! I want Jasia — only Jasia can soothe me. Do you not understand? I am an *artist*! I cannot suffer these upsets. You strangle inspiration at its birth. I had conceived and now I'm empty — *une fausse couche*. I will *not have* these interruptions! Pardon, Mama, but if you give me tisane I shall vomit. Send for Jasia if you love me. Yes, my cough is better. No, I have not spat blood, but I shall — to burst my lungs — if I may not be left alone with my piano. God send me patience. Send me Jasia!'

His father, who, fortunately for Frédéric was lecturing his students at the university that morning, knew nothing of these tantrums. Madame Justina, poor woman, left to deal with them, despatched Louise to Matuszyński's lodgings with a note.

Jan, a young medical student, second only to Titus in Frédéric's adoration, arrived in answer to that urgent summons prepared to find the invalid at point of death. He found him at a Graff piano in a shawl.

'Jasia! My soul! How good — how good of you to come!'
Frédéric rushed to embrace him. 'Now you shall hear my
Adagio to the F Minor concerto. I have improved it.'

'Why two pianos?' queried Jan.

Frédéric explained, 'I hired this. It is to be taken to the
concert hall. I myself prefer a Pleyel, but a Graff has a louder
tone. They shall not say again that I —' A fit of coughing
shook him, choking the words in his throat.

'Get back to bed,' Jan commanded, 'or, you'll not be fit to
play on this or any other instrument.'

He was a lean, dark-browed, elderly young man with a keener
sense of duty than of humour. Bound to his own work he
disapproved of and discouraged any relaxation in his friend.
Frédéric's interest in personal adornment, his passion for
perfumes, his love of flowers — a bowl of violets, his
favourites, was always to be found in season, in his room — all
such lighter shades of life were held by Matuszyński in almost
Lutheran abhorrence. 'My black shadow,' Chopin called him,
and turned to Titus for the sun.

'This confounded cold has gone to my lungs,' said Frédéric.
'Do you think I shall be well enough to appear on the platform
in thirty-six hours from now? Feel me.' He took Jan's hand and
held it to his forehead. 'How I burn! Feel me here —' he
banged his chest. 'It's hollow. Have you brought that
newfangled what-is-it? — that stethoscope, to listen to my
breathing?'

'I need no stethoscope.' Jan unbuttoned the front of
Frédéric's shirt, laid his ear to the boy's narrow chest and
tapped sensitive long fingers here and there. 'You crackle like
old parchment,' he said, when he had done. 'I would like to
take you with me to the mountains. I would like,' he added
thoughtfully, 'to specialise in pulmonary disease.'

'Good God! I hope you don't think I show any signs of it!' cried Frédéric, alarmed. 'Why do you pull such a face at me — you solemn black old crow? Bluebeard!' He touched Jan's lantern jaw, grimacing. 'Ugh! Don't you ever shave? You've a three days' growth at least. Me, I can't grow a beard. It would be as easy to grow potatoes on *my* chin. But I'm thinking of cultivating one whisker on the right side of my face — the side that I show to the audience.' He burst out laughing, then finding no response from Jan, he frowned. 'My faith! You look as glum as Hamlet. What do you mean, I crackle? Is it serious to crackle?'

'It means,' said Jan, surlily, 'that you must go back to bed and not dance about half-naked.'

'How can I go back to bed when I must practise my concerto? Do talk sense. You — who are always hammering at me to work — you who growl and snarl at Titus when he comes to town to take me on the razzle — now you say "Go back to bed," and with my concert facing me three days from now! Do you realise *that*? You don't, of course. And why have you not returned to me my Polonaise? I have asked you for it fifty times. Tell me — did you like it? Don't you think it breathes the very spirit of our Poland? Ah, my friend! You little thought your puny sweet caramel Fryck could produce the cannon from a bed of roses — did you? I wrote it in a thunderstorm last summer. I didn't much care about it then, but looking it over the other day I saw its possibilities — and more. Actually, as I saw it when —' he paused and clutched the air — 'when I *seized* it in its passing — for that is how music comes to me, in one flash, to be captured before the light goes out — like — like — O God! Why have I no words? How I envy writers who express themselves in the scratching of a pen. Here I have to drag *my* soul from my entrails. No!

That's clumsy. Hideous. My soul floats from my fingers. One day I shall do a series of these Polonaises. In this, my first, I see how I can bring to the piano the living symbol of my native land, a pageant of life and death and love and war: the turmoil and tribulation we Poles have suffered and endured, and the mortal cry of our endurance. I shall paint in music the martial splendour of our history, and in undertones of green and grey the vastness of our plains and the joyous colour of our peasant dances — like glorious bright butterflies darting through the mists of Poland's tears. Yes! We Poles have suffered — but we shall live to rise again, and it is our *resurrection* that I —' He choked. 'Hell's fire! *Curse* this cough!'

Then Jan took him bodily and put him back to bed and stayed with him all that day and night. Jan could always succeed in asserting his authority where Justina and Nicolas had failed.

In the morning the fever had abated, although the cough remained. But Jan was satisfied no major complications would ensue.

For twenty-four hours Frédéric worked almost unceasingly at his piano. On the day of the concert and unheedful of his mother's scoldings he went out, muffled to the chin, to the Church of the Holy Cross. There, before the altar he knelt to pray for his success, and light a candle at the feet of Madonna.

He rose from his devotions, comforted, to see a kneeling figure that drove the blood from his heart to his head. Constantia! It seemed fitting he should find her there in that sanctuary, her eyes uplifted, and, in the tinted window light, gentle as the Virgin's, while her fingers strayed from bead to bead and lingered on the gold cross of her rosary.

Unobserved, Frédéric stood gazing, until a glance from her rendered him more than ever dizzy... She had seen him, she had smiled! And rising, beckoned him with a gesture to her side. 'Wait for me at the door,' she whispered, while he, weak-kneed and palpitating, wondered what new cruelty lay beneath this startling kindness. 'I am alone,' she said.

Alone! Was this an invitation? Alone and unattended by her ogress of a maid. For the first time in all their meetings he could talk with her, unwatched and undisturbed. O Most Merciful Beloved Virgin! A *thousand* candles could not suffice to render thanks for such beneficence.

How he got himself outside the church he never knew; nor how long he stood there in the biting wind, chilled to the bone, and coughing to kill himself. Much he cared for that. 'Wait,' she had commanded. 'Wait for me.' He'd wait for all eternity with that promise in his ears, unconscious of the figure he cut wrapped in his cloak — shivering, blue-nosed, and sucking a belladonna pastille for his cough.

'Poor Chopinetto!' In the moment's agitation he had not realised that she had come, and, from the step above was laughing down at him, framed in the stony façade where in carved nooks and crevices starlings chattered and grey pigeons preened and pecked. 'You look,' she told him, while bareheaded, trembling, he bowed over her careless hand, 'so exactly like a little pinched owl with that enormous beak jutting out over your muffler.'

Red with shame he tore the muffler from his throat. 'I have had a cold on my chest, but I am better...'

It must have been the divine reflected glory of the Virgin's glance that in the church had softened hers, for now her eyes were cold as the sky, or the grey stones behind her. How could he have thought her eyes were blue? They changed their colour as she changed her mood — to torture.

'So you play again tonight,' smiled Constantia, addressing not him, but a point above his head, to shame him further, for his lack of height. If only God had given him six inches more! 'Now *that* I call really brave,' she said, and stepped down till she stood at his level, but taller than he, still.

'I do not think,' he was stung to retort, 'that it needs much courage to face a Warsaw audience. If this were Vienna, for example —'

'Pooh! Vienna!' She dismissed Vienna with a shrug, and looked him over, her smile curling up the corners of her mouth. Something mischievous and faun-like in that smile seized him with an unconscionable desire to take and shake her: strangle her and leave her lying bruised and ravaged — his! And with that frenzy on him, he swayed a little where he stood and let her words drift by him. 'I have studied in Vienna! The Viennese are all for show and tinkle-tinkle waltzes. I hear that you write waltzes, Monsieur Chopin.'

Now how had she heard that? None knew but Titus that he had written one to her. Had Titus gossiped, in his jealousy, to link her name with his and make him a laughing-stock — a byword for his folly? God! This woman — how he loathed her — and how unutterably he loved her! If he could kill her where she stood and stamp upon her corpse!

Her next words were still more agitating.

'I have taken tickets for your concert in the, front row, so that I shall be certain to miss nothing. Is it true that you have borrowed a Graff? That should insure you a hearing all over the house. I am told you'll have all Warsaw at your feet this time.'

'Talk seems to have been busy with me and my affairs,' Frédéric returned her a smile that felt like a grin of a skull. 'There will be only one person in the house to whom I shall play tonight: only one whose judgment can uplift or lower me in my own faith.' And because he could not trust himself for fear of what he'd say, or do, he clicked his heels and bowed again, and left her.

He passed the remainder of the day in bed, for now more than he wanted Constantia did Frédéric want rest. He must conserve his energy. Thanks to that meeting in the church and the scene that followed it, his emotional reserve was half-depleted. He felt like an hourglass in which the sand is running out, and must be reversed to be replenished. Now, only he craved sleep; oblivion. The sickly panic that always preceded any public performance had come upon him. His head ached; his stomach turned; he shivered and was hot, sweated and was cold, and refused to eat the meal prepared by his mama and brought to his room by the little maid, Kataryna. Her round-eyed peasant face, so calm and placid, almost imbecile in its void innocence, filled him with envy. 'If only,' he told her, 'if only by some fairy's touch you could be transformed for this one night into me — Frédéric Chopin, and I could be you, Kataryna. What is it like to be you, I wonder? To have no thought beyond soap-suds and dishes and slops. You will never die a hundred deaths before your last, and at each death suffer every torment of the damned. No, you will die only once and go straight to the arms of Our Lady and be a cherub singing in the holy choir for all eternity. It is to be hoped you won't sing flat up there as when I've heard you caterwauling at your wash-tub! However, flat or true, my child, *you* will sing in heaven while I play my piano down in Hell.'

Jésu! Paling, her mouth agape, she crossed herself.

He laughed. 'And now I've scared you properly. Pay no heed to me, my little rabbit, I was talking to myself — or to the black imp on my shoulder whose game it is to torture me before a concert. If you could only know! Here, take this filth away. How do you suppose I can eat? Take it — and don't drop it! Run. Run! No, wait!' He seized her arm as she prepared to bolt. 'Poor child! How you shake. Why can I not love such a simple one as you, who would never break my heart or even crack it, but would be for ever dumb — my God, yes — dumb! What a boon *that* would be — to love a woman who is dumb and faithful as a dog. No scratching claws —' He took her hand. 'Ugh! Worse! Disgusting! You have none at all. You bite your nails. Go!'

He released her and she scuttled to the kitchen with a tale. The young master was possessed. She had seen him speaking with the devil — very strange and wild. She had seen horns growing out of his head while he talked. There were bad things happening in this house. She'd not stay another night here — no, not she! The young master called the devil to him with his music. There, in that very room, she'd seen… And so forth till she infected the whole staff, and Pani Justina looked to lose her servants.

Then Jan arrived with a soothing draught, and Frédéric had some hours' sleep, and the house some peace. He awoke refreshed, but still refused to eat, although he drank three cups of strong black coffee.

'All my future, my whole life,' he told Jan, who stayed with him while he dressed, 'depends on the result of this — my second concert. Till now I have been known only as an amateur. Tonight decides… If only to God Titus were here!'

'And why,', demanded Jan, 'is he not here? I should have thought the least he could have done for his *bel ami* is to be present in the flesh to wish him luck.'

'It is his mother's birthday. He entertains for her at Poturzyn. She would be bitterly offended if he were not with her tonight. But,' sighed Frédéric, 'I miss him.'

'I have no doubt,' said Jan, unamiably, 'that he could have come if he had wished.'

Frédéric turned from his dressing glass. 'Do you mean to imply,' he flashed, 'that Titus didn't *want* to come?'

Jan shrugged a shoulder. 'I know nothing of Titus or his wants, or his desires.'

'You don't like him!'

'I don't love him.'

'Because I do?'

'Because,' growled Jan, 'he wastes himself. I grant him charm — and quality. He's a good showman but he skims along life's surface. He never dives beneath.'

'As you do, my dear, to stir up mud. But don't for heaven's sake let us quarrel over Titus, to upset me at the last minute. How do I look in my new mulberry suit and lavender breeches? It is the newest combination. Titus tells me nothing else is being worn in London.'

'Charming,' murmured Jan, 'I am sure you are completely *à la mode*. But keep your distance. I don't like your scent.'

'I prefer the smell of *Peau d'Espagne*,' retorted Frédéric, 'to that horrible aniseed or vinegar, or whatever it is, of which you invariably stink when you come from your odious hospital. I don't know how you can bear to pass your life among a pack of diseased, verminous people.'

'They may be diseased but they are not all verminous,' said Jan.

Frédéric smiled, and turned to his glass again to brush his hair. 'What I love most in you,' he said, 'although it riles me beyond endurance, is that you are so reliable. So very like a rock. And I — I am the quicksand that whirls around it. Those who put their faith in me might sink, whereas with you, my dear, one knows instinctively, here is one who will never let *me* sink. But I do wish, sometimes, you would be a little *less* reliable, so that one could say to oneself, "Hey, now! What can have happened to old Jan? He is actually ten minutes late for his appointment." Or, "I wonder now, what Jan can be about, so mysteriously — slinking off in a hurry with excuses." But you are never in a hurry, and you never make excuses. Nor are you mysterious. You are the most guileless and honest soul alive — though believe me such honesty becomes at times a trifle tedious. How hellish of me to say that! Now you're hurt. You see — somebody else scratches me, then I scratch you and so it goes on — *ad infinitum*. We are all — and always — pricking and scratching at each other to find the tender spots.'

'And some,' said Jan, 'are born with a skin too few. They bleed.'

Frédéric nodded. 'Yes, me! I'm one of them.' He spun round. 'If I could tell you! Shall I tell you? That girl, that angel, devil — bitch — you know who I mean? How she has made me suffer from her scratches and her pin-pricks you would not — Hallo there? Yes?'

Louise was hammering at the door to tell him that the carriage had arrived to take him to the concert hall.

'Come in,' shouted Frédéric. 'Don't stand there banging to unnerve me. Come in!'

'I can't. You've locked the door.'

'Unlock it, Jasia, while I get my cloak. If I don't barricade myself in this house I'm besieged. You see how it is? My cloak! Where's my cloak? Where in Hades is my —?'

'Here,' Jan took from the chair-back the velvet cape where Frédéric had flung it.

'Thanks, thanks. My hat? Do I want a hat? No, it will spoil my hair. Ah, my pretty! There you are! You have a new dress, too. Look at her, Jan. Isn't she a little beauty? Look.'

Jan looked, with her heart in his eyes. Louise, in pearl grey and demure as a nun, lowered hers. Her lashes were stupendous. She had hair of coppery gold, and a nose as freckled as a cowslip.

'There are no prettier girls in Warsaw — in all Poland,' declared Frédéric, 'than my two sisters. I used to think you had a penchant for Isabella, Jan, only that you let Barcinski get there first, but there is still Louise! If I were not her brother, I vow I'd marry her, so — why don't you?'

'Don't listen to him, Jan!' Louise implored, turning pink as coral. 'The excitement of this concert has affected him. He's crazed.'

'Am I?' Frédéric put his head to one side and gazed from the blushful young lady to the pale young gentleman.

'Eh? So-ho! Have I stumbled by chance upon a secret? What is that English proverb? There is many a true word they speak in joke. *Eh b'en!* Bless you, *mes enfants*!'

'Was there ever such a fool!' cried Louise in a mighty flutter. 'Let me look at your new suit. Turn round.'

And while her brother strutted up and down for her inspection, Louise stole a glance at him who stood so grave and quietly beside her; and she gave a little sigh, and shook her head so imperceptibly, that he saw nothing of it. There was much Jan Matuszyński did not see. If, for instance, he had seen the veiled light in Louise Chopin's eyes when they met his, or their shy, tender question, his life, and maybe hers, might have had a different ending… But Jan, beyond his medicine, saw little more than that which might be written for all the world to read; and though his blood might speak, his lips stayed sealed, and he over-modest in his reason — or his home. That was his tragedy; perhaps also it was hers.

'You look wonderful, Fryck darling!' Louise bit back a second sigh and turned her shoulder on this tiresome, obdurate, sulky Jan. 'I shall be so proud of my little brother when he takes his bow!'

'Yes,' Frédéric gave a complacent hitch to his cravat, 'I have learned better how to take it now. Titus showed me. He said I jerked too much, like a puppet on a string. Look now, both of you —' he inclined, very stiff, head to knees — 'left, right, then eyes up to the boxes. Messieurs, mesdames … is this a pleasant smile?' And he grinned to slit his face.

Louise giggled. 'Don't, Fryck, for mercy's sake! You look like a play-actor. And you aren't rouged — are you?'

'No, my colour is quite natural. It is excitement, not ruby salve, that paints the lily. But there's one thing you haven't noticed. See this?' He turned his right cheek. 'I have been trying to grow one little whisker on the side I present to the audience. It is not much of a success because I only started growing it three days ago, so I'm afraid my gilded bristles won't be seen beyond the front row…'

He paused. God in heaven! The front row… And she…

'The time! The time! What is the time?' screamed Frédéric. 'I must be starting. I must go! Louise, my sweet, my lovely!' He flung his arms round her. 'Wish me luck. Pray for me… Bless you! Bless you!' He embraced Jan. 'My soul! You too must pray for me. And don't forget to keep your ears open, and store up every word you hear for or against. Don't spare me. O God! I *know* I look like a play-actor…!'

And he rushed headlong from the room.

FOUR

From Frédéric Chopin to Titus Wojciechowski.
Warsaw, March 17th, 1830.

*Never have I missed you so much! One look from you after the concert
would have meant more to me than the praise of all the critics.*

*You know what the programme of the 1st concert was. The second
began with a symphony by Nowakowski (par complaisance) followed by a
repetition of the 1st Allegro of my Concerto. Then the Theatre concert
master Bulawski, played de Bériot's Variations, and I my Adagio and
Rondo. The second part began with my Rondo Cracovienne, then Pani
Meier sang — better than ever — something from Soliva's opera 'Hélène
and Malvina', and to conclude I improvised on the Volkslied which
greatly pleased the Front Row!...*

*To be quite candid I must tell you I did not improvise to please myself.
Perhaps if I had, nobody would have understood it... I am rather
surprised that the Adagio was so universally appreciated. I hear from all
sides the most flattering remarks, but you must have read the newspapers
so you will know that this time I have scored a success.*

*I have received an anonymous poem and a large bouquet. Both sent to
my house from I don't know who! And somebody or other called Orlowski
has asked if he may arrange a series of mazurkas and waltzes from the
principal themes of my Concerto! Everyone is begging me to give a third
concert which I have no desire to do. You can't imagine how I suffer for
days before a performance. I hope to finish the first Allegro of my 2nd
Concerto before the vacation, so I shall have to wait, at any rate, till after
Holy Week, if I decide to play again...*

I don't want to stop writing but I must — though I have not told you anything of real interest — yet! I am keeping that back for the dessert when next we meet!

Meanwhile here is nothing more fruity to offer you than a hearty embrace from, Your

Fr. Ch.

It would seem that he was learning self-restraint. He could have told Titus a good deal more than these bald facts of his success, which in view of all that followed was for him the lesser triumph. Applause, bouquets, the critics, these mattered nothing now, for the unbelievable had happened.

She, Constantia, of her own will — unasked and uninvited — had sought him in the artists' room, where, when all was over, he had stood in pandemonium, surrounded by a clamorous group of friends and parents, sisters, Jan, and all the *haute volée.*

For days afterwards he fed on the survival of that moment, relived each word she spoke. Every hour spent at his piano, every phrase that flowed from his pen, recaptured Beauty's spell in those inspired fantasies, which, a few years later, when the bardic voice matured, englamoured sterner passion. Just when his individual ego materialised, or how much this earliest love of his vibrated through the silver moon-world of a nocturne, or the delicate irony of the A Flat Ballade in which a young lover's confusion is indicated so deliciously by hesitation — who can tell?

She, with flowers in her hair, had come to him, and her eyes had held tears.

'Chopin! You...' her words a broken whisper, her red underlip drawn in to stay its trembling, 'I take all back ... all my wicked teasing. You are on the mountains and I … am on the plains.'

He could have died for her then, at her feet. But because he was her fool, he had no answer; he could give her nothing but his oafish bow, his smileless grin, while others pushed and jostled to grab his hand, to mouth and jabber with no more to say than apes.

Disembodied faces, some strange and some familiar, swam before him. Prince Radziwill, kindly, white-haired and always vague, was murmuring: '*Incroyable!* An incredible improvement. Monsieur Chopin,' he addressed the beaming Nicolas, 'it is as I always prophesied. I have watched. I have observed. I have seen how he has practised to overcome the disadvantage of hands too small for extended arpeggio chords. It is amazing how that little hand expands and covers a third of the keyboard, like the mouth of a serpent opening to swallow a rabbit… But how wise you have been neither to force nor to suppress him. Let him fly. He is an Ariel of the piano. You will allow him to spend a week, a month, a year, or as long as he desires with me and the Princess at Antonin? He needs rest … he is delicate. So beautiful…' And the Prince faded away, to be replaced by the Wodzinskis.

Casimir, red with excitement, hoarse from the shouts he had raised from his stance in the pit to start the applause, clutched at his arm to tell him in one breath: 'Mama is furious because you didn't reserve her a box, and Papa says you're better than Moscheles!'

They were all there: Anton, Felix, Count Wodzinski with his fierce dyed whiskers, his porcelain teeth and his countess. She, ablaze with diamonds, in crimson, condescended, very gracious 'I shall give a *soirée* in your honour, Frédéric… Madame Chopin, how proud you must be of this *succès fou*…'

Justina, indeed, was overpowered; not so much perhaps by her son's success as by the Countess Wodzińska's toilette; her jewels; the bird of paradise perched upon her flashing turban, her gold-wrought Indian shawl, her towering presence, that almost entirely extinguished the countess's young daughter, standing demure, and robed in blue organdie at her side.

Frédéric stole a glance. Maria! The bud of two summers past had grown to a sprig of a girl with roses in her cheeks and mischief in her eyes — for remembrance.

He blushed. A saucy piece! Would he never be rid of that nonsense? Neither she nor Casimir, it seemed, were in a hurry to forget it. 'Maria! Come, my darling. We must not monopolise the evening star!'

Countess Wodzińska might be gracious with her patronage and hospitality, which did not, however, extend beyond a certain range. Maria, *bien entendu*, must perforce be out of bounds in her mother's calculations. The little Chopin with his airs and graces, his seductive music and his chestnut curls, might prove something of a nuisance — in the future. The countess had been tolerantly blind and deaf to a holiday *blague* between a boy and girl, but this modish young Adonis who tonight had brought the house down with his playing was a boy no longer, and Maria more than half a woman at fifteen. The absurdity of children might well become a threat. The countess had her own ambitions for her daughter, and the pianist son of a man who kept a boarding school was certainly not one of them, and so: 'A thousand thanks, dear Frédéric,' gushed the countess. 'You have stolen all our hearts. Goodnight. Goodbye.'

Thank God!… The crowded room was emptying. Frédéric mopped his forehead and looked wildly around, but She had gone. She had a trick of vanishing. Once more he must have dreamed her. He heard his father muttering, 'I have had no supper. I am hungry as a wolf. Let us, for heaven's sake, get rid of these *canaille* and then go home — and eat!'

But Frédéric could not eat, nor when he retired could he sleep.

He lay restless, dozing, waking, burning, until dawn when he was up and working feverishly at his new concerto. Then, as soon as he heard the housemaids sweeping on the stairs he shouted for his breakfast. No time to be lost. He must be out and on the steps of the Conservatoire to catch her going in. He would risk all — his life, or her displeasure, to declare himself. He had suffered in silence long enough. Now he would speak. Last night she had been angelic in her tenderness and grace. This morning, maybe, she would have changed again, to show her claws. However, one would have to take a chance. If only the *mot juste* could always be a note in music!

He felt ill, and for all the care he took to dress, his mirror showed him an unflattering reflection. Haggard, pale, heavy-eyed and parched of lip, a pretty sight to go a-wooing. And that ridiculous side-whisker! He must shave it — and he did, and cut himself so deep that he had to stick a plaster on the place, and looked more than ever foolish. He gulped his coffee and went out.

The day was fine and sparkling, the sun high, and the streets full of early folk: workmen in their belted smocks, little milliners in poke-bonnets tripping, very pretty, with their band-boxes, to bring to ladies' bedsides the latest Paris *modes*.

Paris! Frédéric paused before a jeweller's where a bearded giant was taking down the shutters. The shop bore an international name. London, Bond Street. Paris, Rue de la Paix… Magic cities. And he wondered, would he, Chopin, ever play before that world of which Warsaw was a mere provincial suburb?

With his nose against the glass he gazed. If he could only afford to buy offerings worthy to lay at her feet! O for a fortune! Still, one never knew what might come about when he had earned the just reward of fame — even though it were doubtful if this second concert, great success artistically though it might be, would pay its own expenses any more than had the first, since to fill the house half the audience had been presented with free seats. However, that was the least of his concerns. This display of gems before his eyes ... now, here was something, truly! Diamonds — rings and bracelets of rainbow fire; rubies like fresh spilled blood; emeralds glowing green for jealousy; sapphires, night-blue, mysterious; pearls for tears. Necklaces, ropes of them to wind round her throat and strangle her when she tormented...

'Out of my way, young gentleman. I have to sponge this window, if you please!'

'Is the shop open yet for business?' Frédéric loftily enquired, less from a desire to know than to save his face. He objected to being hustled to one side by a hairy smelly fellow in a smock.

'If Your Excellency is prepared to wait...' The window-cleaner's tone was now obsequious. Here was a customer, a nobleman, no doubt, and certainly eccentric, as were all such higher beings who could spend on a trumpery glass stone — wealth enough to keep his wife, his seven children, his old mother and himself, for the remainder of their days in a new-thatched cottage with a garden full of onions and a goat. *Hé*, well! The Lord was just. There would be cottages and goats for all men, rich and poor, in heaven. Meanwhile the young gentleman was feeling in his pockets. Behind his beard the window-cleaner smiled. This was to be a lucky day for him. He had bowed three times to a skewbald horse on his way to town from his hovel on the outskirts of the city. A skewbald horse was always a good omen. To make certain he had stopped to kneel before a shrine. This had been noted, and here was his reward. If the Good God were merciful, a zloty.

It was, however, not a coin the nobleman produced, but a crumpled piece of paper and a pencil. On this, which he spread flat against the window glass, and to the window-cleaner's wonder, he began to write — in the signs of the devil, for sure. The window-cleaner crossed himself and spat. So much for skewbald horses, to say nothing of his prayers! Tomorrow he would offer up an *Ave*.

But those twinkling jewels on their pillows of white velvet had given Frédéric the motif for a Scherzo, and with its first phrase dancing in his head and his fingers itching to be playing it, he hastened on to take up his position at the students' entrance to the Conservatoire.

He had not long to wait. She came, but not alone. That shark-faced maid of hers was with her. Hell!

He, however, was prepared for that. As Constantia approached in her new spring bonnet with a cluster of cherries under its brim and cherry silk ribbons to tie it, Frédéric slunk behind a pillar of the colonnade that circled the rear of the building, and there stood hidden. She, stepping daintily as though on eggs, passed with a flutter of skirts. The students' door swung open to admit her; and, at her heels, with his chin in his coat collar and his hat over his eyes, went Frédéric, hurrying in.

'Why, if it isn't Monsieur Chopin! You here so early? After last night's triumph I should have thought your student's days were over now — for good and all!'

Was she at her tricks again? The door, though shut against her maid who had no right of entry there, was opening incessantly to admit newcomers hastening to their classes. The long stone corridor echoed with footsteps and voices to drown his own.

'My student days are never over. One must be learning always.'

She may or may not have heard him; nor could he know if her eyes, shaded by her bonnet's brim, were kind or cruel. 'And do you take your lesson here today, Monsieur Chopin? Such zeal! Fancy! You, who are now acclaimed a virtuoso, coming so modestly to school. Have you seen what the critics say of you? They have lost no time in putting you in print.'

'I have not seen any newspapers yet, Mademoiselle.'

'So you do not know that the Gazeta Polska says that the Poles will one day be as proud of you as the Germans are of Mozart?'

'Which,' stammered Frédéric, scarlet, 'is palpable nonsense.'

'Do you mean that I speak nonsense, or tell lies to flatter, Monsieur Chopin?'

The formal repetition of his name added more to his confusion. 'No, no! Heaven forbid. Pray do not misunderstand me. But such exaggeration —'

'Not at all. The same critic goes on to say that if you had fallen into the hands of a pedant or a Rossinist — is not that an absurd expression? — you would not have been what you are.'

'That is very true. I have Elsner to thank for what I may become.'

'Another paper, the *Courier* I think it is, advises you to hear Rossini but not to imitate him.'

'I?' That had drawn blood. 'I, imitate Rossini? Good God! What next?'

'I have not learned all your critiques off by heart, Monsieur.'

'Indeed, no! Certainly. It is more than gracious that you should interest yourself enough to —'

'Would you have the goodness,' deftly she broke in upon his mumblings, and drew from her bodice a gold trinket, 'to tell me what o'clock it is? My watch has stopped.'

He blushed again to have to admit that he possessed no watch. 'But I think it must be almost half past nine.'

'Horrors! I must not stay chattering here — I shall be late for my rehearsal. Excuse me, Monsieur Chopin, I must fly!'

And he with her. She would not so easily escape him.

'I too,' he fabricated, 'am due for a rehearsal with the orchestra.'

'The orchestra?' She paused, her eyebrows up in genuine concern. 'Is the orchestra to accompany *you* this morning? I understood that we — the choral group — were to have the orchestra today.'

And now he was in a quandary, and his lady in a pet.

'It is too tiresome,' she shrilled. 'There are always these annoyances. They don't mind how often they put the singers on one side for the pianists. Of course, I do not allude to *you*, Monsieur Chopin — who are now a full professional and have the right to demand entire monopoly of the orchestra if you wish to, but still — for my own satisfaction, I will enquire at the bureau if the authorities have sanctioned the cancellation of *my* rehearsal.'

She flounced away and left him to recover his wits.

'Panna Constantia!' He went rushing after her. 'It shall be as you desire — I can arrange — I can postpone my own rehearsal which is nothing — nothing, I assure you. I do not need the orchestra today. Tomorrow, next week, any time will do, but pray do not go to the bureau!' It would be extremely awkward for him if she did.

'Good gracious, Monsieur Chopin! Do you think I would deprive you? No doubt you wish to practise for another concert.'

'Indeed I don't. I have had enough of concerts to wish never to play at another. I beg you will proceed with your arrangements, Mademoiselle, as though I — were not here.' He greatly regretted at the moment that he was. 'But,' he proceeded at a venture, 'if you will grant me this one boon, that I may be permitted to sit in the hall at your practice —'

'What? To hear me sing? Goodness, no! I'd die of fright.'

'Please, Panna Constantia… Let me hear your voice.'

'I am in no voice today. My throat is husky. I have had a cold. And in any case, it is not for me to give or withhold permission. The auditorium is open to all students — or ex-students — here.' And she smiled to draw the heart out of his body. 'But if you care to honour me, I trust you will not judge too harshly — or condemn.'

'Condemn! You! If you could but know how I adore — I worship —'

It was out: and in another moment he would have been on his knees to her there in the passage before the whole school and its scholars, but for the loud clangour of a bell that called him to his senses, and Constantia to her rehearsal.

He took a back seat out of sight, prepared perhaps for some amateurish *coloratura*, but certainly not for the range and power of a voice matured beyond its years, and of a quality so exceptional that he sat amazed and more than ever captivated. Was there no end to her enchantment?

She was rehearsing the part of Agnese in Paër's opera of that name, which revealed not only the pure richness of her tone, but the excellence of her acting. When she had finished her scene and had come from the stage to take her seat in the stalls and watch her fellow students, it needed all his courage to approach and take his seat beside her.

'Panna Constantia!... What can I say? Beautiful! Sublime! Words are entirely inadequate ... I can only express myself in clichés. Nothing less than a Shakespeare or a Schiller could do justice to ... perfection. The way you took that high F and G! And, quite apart from your magnificent acting, your shading is past all belief, glorious! I am dumbfounded.'

This panegyric, delivered in a rush of whispers through the noise of the finale to the first act, with the whole chorus and orchestra at full blast, fell somewhat short of its effect.

'What?' She bestowed on him a careless frown. 'I can't hear a word you say,' and approached an ear so close to his mouth that her ringlets tickled his nose, further to increase his agitation. 'But tell me,' and her frown became a smile, equally as careless, 'what you think of my performance. Did you like me?'

'Like? *Like?*' The last remnants of his self-control deserted him. He seized her hand and crushed his lips into her palm and half-suffocated by emotion and half-smothered, gasped, 'Constantia! Beloved! I am beside myself. Have pity!'

'Monsieur Chopin!' Her hand was snatched indignantly away. 'Do not, if you please, make yourself ridiculous before the whole academy. I ask a simple question —'

'It is *not* a simple question!' And although he shouted now against the chorus which in full-throated abandon was roaring louder than ever, he might as well have been dumb and she deaf. 'So! I am ridiculous!' He gave a hollow laugh. Was that then how this passion of his life appeared to her? Ridiculous! 'But nothing so ridiculous,' his voice squeaked on a note of hysteria, 'as your fantastic chorus yelling itself hoarse with all its mouths wide open to swallow the house! As for the whole academy —' He took a hasty glance around. Almost all the seats were empty. The few students who comprised the audience were intent upon their scores. 'None cares — or is concerned with me — or you. And if they *wish* to hear — then let them! Let them see me offer you my heart, my soul — to be rejected. Let them know — let the whole world know! Pitiful heaven!' He clapped his hands to his ears. 'Is it possible that the human voice can reproduce so realistically the howling of amorous cats? The sopranos sharp, the tenors flat — and all the basses off the beat. Who is your chorus master?'

'I have asked you,' her hair was tickling his nose again, 'a simple question. Can't you answer without making these grimaces? Are you unwell?'

'Pardon! Pardon!' And he released his ears. 'But I assure you I cannot tolerate these sounds. This chorus is disgraceful — an offence, an insult to your voice. Only a heavenly choir could be a fit accompaniment to —'

'Please!' She tapped his arm to call him to attention. 'Watch this entrance. It is mine, but Wolkow is taking it. She, too, is studying the part.'

A fay-like creature, with a lorgnette in one hand and her score in the other, now came down to the front of the, stage and stood, her eyes on the conductor's baton. 'Such a pity,' sighed Gladowska, 'that she is so near-sighted. But *such* a good actress. Charming, is she not? Though perhaps not quite imposing enough for the part, do you think?'

He was past thinking.

'And she suffers shockingly from nerves. Her voice goes completely flat at a performance — from sheer fright, poor girl. If they decide — pray God! — that I make my début as Agnese, she is to be my understudy. You know,' once more her head inclined to his to drive him frantic, 'but this is strictly *entre nous*, I am sure her range is not quite full enough for opera. Perfect for the concert platform or *Opéra Comique*, of course — but Grand Opera, do you think? I may be wrong. That high D now, for instance, faultless!'

And, lips pursed as though ready to kiss, Constantia nodded with every sign of rapt approval: then, with a slight, the very slightest intake of a breath, she shook her head. 'But her *diminuendi*, I find, are incomplete. Chopin…' Almost caressing, so he dared to fancy, was this murmur of his name. 'Tell me the truth. Be honest. I value your judgment more than — or quite as much — as any other's. There are some, a few, who prefer her voice to mine — thin though it is, and, poor darling, sometimes, a soupçon flat. But having heard us both, what is your opinion, entirely unbiassed? The truth, please. No flattery. Is her voice better than mine?'

'Better than —? Good heavens! It is sacrilege even to suggest—' cried Frédéric, who, what with this delicious conspiracy of whispers fanning his cheek, and the fragrance of her nearness, was completely incoherent. 'A comparison? What comparison? Who can compare the screech of a parrot —'

'A parrot?' She half-rose in her seat to flash her eyes at him. 'Do you imply that my voice is like —'

'No! No, no! A thrush! A nightingale… O God, help me!' He grabbed at her skirt and caught a cherry-coloured ribbon: it came away in his hand with a rending of silk. 'And now,' he groaned, 'what have I done?'

'Nothing, nothing at all, beyond ruining my gown. Give me the ribbon... What you have *said* is more to the point, Monsieur Chopin.'

What *had* he said? And what could he say but to repeat that he adored her? Nor did he give her the ribbon, but clutched it to a rag while he pleaded for a hearing.

'Only hear me ... let me tell you...' Since the first moment he had seen her he had been utterly and absolutely hers. If he worshipped her before he heard her voice, how much more precious was she now to him — as artiste! 'And as such, and on that plane we can meet as equals. As a person you are infinitely above me. As a person I am nothing but your fool. And as your fool I —'

A sob tore at his throat: it was no good. He lacked the power to articulate in words all that his music could tell her. While volcanic tremors swept him, he could only stutter like a schoolboy. No woman was ever in such fashion wooed — or won. And to hide the tears that for the life of him he could not have controlled, he bowed his forehead to the plush back of the seat in front of him, and sat with shoulders shaking, loathing himself for his weakness, till in his misery he could almost have loathed her.

'Poor Chopinetto!' Yes! Her name for him: why not Punchinello, and have done with it? What was he to her but a figure of fun? He felt a touch, light as a moth's wing on his hair, heard a rustle and a whisper, unbelievable: 'You shall tell me all this again, and then ... again. And you may keep my ribbon.'

But when, incredulous, he started up to follow her, she had glided away, and was talking calmly to a fellow student and a friend of his, one Julius Fontana, whom at that moment he could willingly have slain.

Then others claimed her and her master called from the stage: 'Panna Gladowska! Once again the aria.' And though Frédéric for the remainder of the morning sat dazed and palpitating in the stalls, he had no chance of further speech with her. He was, however, more encouraged to pursue. She had asked — invited him to speak; had offered him her ribbon, as a keepsake. What did that portend? That she was not entirely indifferent? It could only mean that: but even while he hoped beyond all hope that she had melted, his heart misgave him and he was haunted once again by doubts and fears. He knew her well enough to take the sign of grace she had bestowed on him for as much as it was worth — a breath on glass, and, like a breath, as swiftly fading. No, he dared not hope. She had been excited by his appreciation of her singing. She valued his professional opinion. That was something for which at least one should be grateful. His wholehearted enthusiasm had pleased and softened her. And tomorrow? Why, tomorrow she would be herself again.

FIVE

Tomorrow and tomorrow... A succession of tomorrows while she played her game with him, was glacial and warm, and kind and cruel in turn, and Frédéric half demented.

That his passion was entirely cerebral with nothing more solid to feed on than a glance, a word, a whisper — at most a ribbon from her dress — is evident from the letters he wrote Titus, and his indecision at this time, when from day to day he changed his mind as to whether he would or he would not remain in Warsaw: or give another concert, or wait another year before he made a next appearance; or devote his life to composition and never play again.

His father was in favour of him making the Grand Tour, starting at Vienna, and so, by way of Paris, to London. His success in Warsaw had been enough to obtain him a hearing on any platform in any capital in Europe: a hearing, yes, but not, perhaps, a triumph. He was still unknown and unestablished. He must go slowly, feel his way, for as he repeatedly told Nicolas, 'Warsaw is not the world ... and if it were, no man is a prophet in his own country. Who can tell if they will cut me into pieces if I play here again? I have my enemies. There are many who find my impromptus mere sensationalism. There are some who say I am too subtle, and all declare my execution is too weak. I had better turn to selling cheese than writing music. No one of importance has yet heard — or ever *will* hear — of me.'

Nicolas shot a glance at the boy's mutinous face, the over-bright eyes, the transparent skin that blushed and paled like a girl's. Could the reserve of nervous energy stored within that sensitive small frame atone for its lack of physical force? One needed the strength of a cart-horse to withstand the fierce demands of the Polish climate, which had already taken its dread toll of one beloved youngest child. The father pulled a long lip. He must get the lad away, abroad and out of danger: even London fogs would be less harsh to combat than the ravages of another winter in Warsaw.

'There is no turning back on the road to success, my son. You must push forward — always forward, and only by your own efforts can you reach your goal. The great successes of this world are never due to chance, but are the result of supreme effort and determination as all failure is due to lack of faith in oneself and one's ego.'

And Frédéric's ego at that time was non-existent. Constantia had deprived him of faith, of resolution, and almost of his hope. While he spent himself in restless yearning, she, fully aware of her conquest, and not a little proud of it, went her careless way to the envy of all the young ladies in Warsaw.

He was sought after now, the little Chopin, the pet of drawing rooms and titled dames who induced him, *con amore*, to play, and flattered him and fêted him, for his *beaux yeux* as much as for his music. But while all this was balm to Frédéric who could never have enough of adulation, and was equally at home in scented salons as on the concert platform, he continued to sigh and burn and suffer at the mercy of Constantia.

So spring blossomed to full summer, and for all his father's good advice, his future plans were vague as ever. He would go to Paris, to Vienna, London, or Berlin. No, he'd stay in Warsaw. *Why* should he leave Warsaw? If for twenty years he had endured this miserable climate, surely he could stand it for another year — or two? Why this sudden urge on everybody's part to send him into exile? Or should he go to Milan? The seat of opera. Italy! Now there was sense — and sun! He'd follow the sun. Yes, he *would* go abroad.

That, then, was decided. He'd have his passport visaed... but not quite yet: not until, perhaps, he'd played again. Yes, certainly he would have to give another concert here in Warsaw before he left for foreign parts. Elsner had advised him, and Prince Radziwill. All his friends and patrons advised another concert... And so on, until his departure must be still further delayed owing to the disturbed state of Europe after the July revolution in Paris. The excitement in France had not yet subsided, and was nearing boiling pitch in Italy. Also a new difficulty had arisen owing to the limited issue of passports. Although the storm of unrest rolling eastward from Paris did not hurl itself on Warsaw till the end of the year, ominous signs were in the air and gathered impetus all through that summer. The Diet had met after an interval of five years, and the national discontent over Russian administration was expressed in a mushroom growth of secret societies and heated debates.

None of this, however, seems unduly to have affected Frédéric beyond the postponement of his continental tour; and that this procrastination depended more upon his lady's favour than political intrigue, may be gathered from his letters to Titus, which a trifle too emphatically deny any such cause for indecision.

I do not know when I shall start my journey now. I shall probably be here all the summer. In any case the Italian Opera season in Vienna does not begin until September, so I need not hurry. All the better. The Rondo for the new Concerto is not ready yet. I have been in no mood to complete it...

The Adagio in E Major, conceived in a romantic half-melancholy spirit,
gives the impression of a quiet much-loved landscape on some still, spring
moon-lit night. I have written a violin accompaniment con sordini. *Will*
that have a good effect, do you think? Time will show.

And though the reply from Titus has not been recorded,
Frédéric's answer gives some insight as to its content.

You are a beast! Why, pray, should you think I have any special
reason for staying other than those already stated? If you have a suspicion
that something — or someone dear *— detains me, you, like many others*
here in Warsaw, are mistaken… Believe me, I can rise above my Ego,
and if I were in love, I hope I could manage to keep my unhappy
condition to myself…

Which is precisely what he seemed incapable of doing; but he
may have been self-conscious or self-flattered if he thought the
whole town buzzed with his infatuation for Gladowska. She,
not he, was in everybody's mouth. Her teacher and impresario,
Soliva, had seen to that. He, determined she should appear —
not as a star in gradual ascension but in full blaze — had her
well exploited weeks before her début as 'Agnese'.

One can imagine in what state of mind Frédéric attended her
first night at the Opera House; how he ransacked every florist
in Warsaw for bouquets, how he sat, speechless and
enraptured, in a first tier box with his friends Julius and Jan on
either side of him — Jan dumb and black as a boot, and Julius
hypercritical, indulgent and derisive all in turn as became a
music-student: how, while the orchestra was tuning Frédéric
must write a note addressed to 'The Incomparable Gladowska',
craving her permission to pay his respects in her dressing room
after the performance: and that he sent the scowling Jan to the

stage-door with the message, and waited in a fever through each entr'acte for a reply which never came. And how that an hysterical account of the event was retailed to Titus, who, although he preserved the letter for posterity, may or may not have read it at the time; in which recording we are told again and yet again of the beauty of Gladowska and her voice: her acting *(Splendid — one could wish for nothing better)*; her high register, her phrasing *(a delight)*; her shading, *(glorious, superb!)* The string of adjectives is inexhaustible. *She was, naturally, a little nervous. Her voice shook the merest trifle on her first entrance, but she soon recovered and sang — divinely.* He was more than ever charmed with the aria in the second act to a harp accompaniment, so cleverly arranged he was certain none but he could tell that it was played by a pianist in the wings.

His divinity's success was, however, not entirely in the fond imagination of her slave. The audience, though less rhapsodic, was enough impressed to recall her seven times, and finally to have her come before the curtain, where to the shouting house she curtseyed amid stacks of flowers and with her arms full of bouquets. Frédéric looked for his. He had sent three. All, he was gratified to see, were there, and more each minute were being pelted from the boxes, or handed up to her by powdered flunkeys. He would perhaps have been more gratified if the roses she held in her arms had been his, but that was hoping for too much. Again and yet again she curtseyed, right, left, eyes up to the gallery, her lashes demurely lowered to the stalls. Then, as a ravishing finale she laid her flowers at her feet to free her hands and blow kisses from her fingertips … to him? O God, if he could think so! Had she seen him? Possibly not, but he took good care that she should hear him, leaning so far out of the box that he was in imminent danger of crashing down into the pit while he yelled his *Bravo*s till his throat was raw, and Jan more than ever scowling.

At last the curtain stayed down and the audience got up. 'Come on, now, for God's sake,' muttered Jan. 'Let's go.'

'Go? *You* may go — and I shall go behind. Julius! You will come with me? Let this death's head take himself away, I intend to see her — to speak to her — to offer my congratulations. *What* a performance! Exquisite. Glorious. She is now assured. Sontag herself is the merest squeak beside her. Go *on*, then, Jan, nobody's keeping you! The mere sight of your face is enough to make anyone sick. Surly brute. So much thanks I get for giving you a ticket. Come, Ju-ju!'

But 'Ju-ju' was no more to be persuaded than Jan. 'Not I. And if you take my advice you won't push yourself in either, where you're not wanted. Soliva has a bunch of critics with him and she'll be surrounded. You will never get near her. I'm going to Fukier's for supper.'

'You can both go and hang yourselves for all I care,' Frédéric retorted. 'But I tell you I'm going behind.' And he went, queueing up in the passage outside her dressing room and ready to kill those favoured who were ushered in first.

For hours, it seemed, he stood there flattened against the wall, while people fought and jostled past him and each other to gain entrance. All Warsaw he noted, bitterly, was at her heels. All the first night *habitués*, all the elect, some nonentities and half the chorus had come to pay her homage. He caught a glimpse of Count Wodzinski — not the countess. It would not do for a lady of society to visit an opera singer in her dressing room — oh dear no! But that old *roué* with his dyed whiskers and his leer and — merciful heaven! — a cushion of flowers in his arms — what right had he, the lecherous old rip, to give her flowers worth a fortune?... And there was Radziwill with his saintly smile, and not so much of a saint as all that, either, elbowing his way along with a mumble of apologies, determined to get there before anybody else, while those not born of princes must be denied admittance. What did *he* want in her dressing room? To offer her an invitation to stay at Antonin? Doubtless.

A cold dew broke out on Frédéric's forehead; he writhed, he gnawed his nails. She was lost to him for ever now. He could never hope, never again aspire since she had gained the patronage of princes. Much they knew or understood of art... Huh! Yes. Art. A pretty name for an ugly motive. She must be protected. She, so pure, so chaste, must not be exposed to the licentious desires of all and sundry and in particular of senile old men. As for that grinning hyena, Wodzinski...!

And while he lashed himself into a frenzy over the imagined lusts of the inoffensive count — who for all he looked the very villain of the piece was innocent to the verge of imbecility, and far too frightened. of his wife to offer more than flowers to any woman in the world — Frédéric received a further shock. Soliva appeared at the door of Constantia's dressing room to make an announcement.

'Sirs! Panna Gladowska thanks you all a thousand times for your generous appreciation, but regrets she cannot receive any more visitors tonight. Her room is overcrowded and she is quite exhausted. She begs you to excuse her, and if any of you care to return tomorrow evening, she will endeavour —'

Frédéric heard no more. Bent double he made a dash for it, wriggled, dodged, and pushed himself out of the queue to arrive panting and dishevelled, his damp collar under one ear and his hair on end, at the threshold of that doorway. 'Pan Soliva! I beg you to allow —'

'Ah! Frédéric! You? Yes, certainly. I feel sure Panna Constantia will make exception in your case — a fellow artist —' And with bows and ceremonious stage smiles masking a hurried aside, 'Come then, quick, if you're coming,' Soliva pulled him in and shut the door.

But although now within a few yards' distance of his goddess, and squashed almost to annihilation in the crowd that packed the small apartment, Frédéric remained unnoticed. She stood surrounded by a clamorous group, composed as far as he could see entirely of men and Madame Sontag, the world-famous prima donna who had been gracing Warsaw opera all that season with her presence. Immense in sapphire velvet and a turban of gold lame festooned with grapes and wheat-ears, she towered, a complacent Ceres — so Frédéric wildly conceived her — offering Proserpine to be raped by not one, but a dozen Plutos.

Of Constantia he could see nothing but her eyebrows and her hair, so hemmed in was she by admirers. All were toasting her in beakers of champagne. Someone pushed a glass into his hand and straining on tiptoe he had a moment's sight of her face, heard her voice ring out: 'Friends! All — all — I thank you!' Her glass was raised, her lips were moving but he could not hear another word she said above the din. He drank: he threw his glass to the ground and stamped his heel upon it and the corns of Count Wodzinski, whose foot happened to be in the way. The pained count backed and Frédéric yelled, 'Gladowska! Queen!' None took the smallest heed of him. Everybody talked, or rather roared at once, and in all languages. He even heard English drawled on the lips of a fair young man with the face of a borzoi, the figure of a god, and dressed to perfection, in just the *right* shade of mulberry suiting, which Frédéric now realised his own was not. These English!

They had all the looks and all the tailors. Who could this one be? A nobleman making the Grand Tour? An attaché at the Embassy? A rival, without doubt, and a head and shoulders taller than himself.

'Mademoiselle! I have heard opera in every capital in Europe, but never a voice to be compared to yours.'

Frédéric caught that one last sentence and, grimacing, mouthed it silently, repeating, *'Toe bee cawm pawhed toe yawhss...'* Bah! What a hideous, impossible language to rasp your uvula and stick in your throat. Why couldn't he speak French like a civilised person? Why? Because no Englishman *is* civilised or *can* speak French. He can speak nothing but his own barbaric tongue. For all that, this English dog-face with his quizzing-glass, his broad shoulders and his lazy lisp, seemed to charm her...

Muttering, perspiring, straining every muscle and his neck completely stiff, Frédéric tiptoed again to see her smiling sweetly up into those damnable blue eyes, as she had never smiled down — at him. Oh, for some height! Why was he not six feet tall — and English? Barbarians though the English might be, and uncultured and slow-witted, a race of shopkeepers with a pampered aristocracy that lived for nothing but horse-racing and the hunting of little foxes and the shooting of innocent birds, a people that ate porridge and biff-steak for breakfast and was drunk from morning till night, a people on whom the sun never shone in a land of perpetual fog, they could yet win every last battle in every war they fought and breed Apollos — and — yes, produce a Shakespeare. That was something, truly! Was it any wonder, thought Frédéric, with his teeth at his thumbnail which by this time he had gnawed almost to the quick that their, first invader called them Angels and not Angles? Yes! And if he could get his fingers round *this* blue-eyed Angel's throat he'd gladly throttle him…

And now there was another at her side: equally imposing but not so elegant, and nothing like, he was relieved to see, so handsome. Him Frédéric recognised as one of Warsaw's wealthiest citizens: Jozef Grabowski, a sleek, black-haired, paunchy fellow.

Riches! Ah, now if he had riches to pour at her feet, he could win her, of that he was sure. Any woman could be won by money. There was not a pin's difference between the *cocotte* of the streets and the *jeune fille* of the boudoir who was sold by her mama to the highest bidder. As for a stage or opera star, all the world knew that having gained distinction she must be financed to keep her place. It was only money that had gained this fellow, this oily merchant, entrance here. Grabowski. What a name! Probably assumed. Yes, more than likely with that money — and that nose.

And he was speaking now.

'Gentlemen! Panna Gladowska desires me to ask you to be so good as to leave her to disrobe. Will those of you who have received her card for the reception which I have the honour to give tonight at my house in celebration of…'

Frédéric went limp and all but slithered to the floor. A reception! This beast was giving a reception. For her? And in his house? Her card! She had sent cards. To whom? To Prince Radziwill? The Englishman, Grabowski, all the critics? To Soliva and to half Warsaw…?

But not to him.

'Please! Let me go!' The words broke from him in a strangled croak. He turned, violently to shove aside the jubilant Soliva who stood a pace behind him, wrenched open the door and stumbled out into the passage, sweating.

That final snub decided him. His pride no less than his self-esteem was shattered. Henceforth he would be done with her and unrequited love; kill the canker that gnawed at his roots, tear the thought and sight of Gladowska from his mind for ever, and devote himself solely to his art.

For a week at least he did, and with enough determination to complete the Concerto in E Minor. This done, he was as restive to leave Warsaw as before he had been desirous to stay. He would take himself and his compositions to Vienna. There he would be certain of a hearing to astonish the world — and her! Yes, when all Warsaw rang with the echo of his fame, she would regret that she had spurned the little Chopin.

With that incentive as ambition's spur he persuaded his father to finance a farewell concert. After endless consultations with Elsner, Ernemann, Soliva and all the rest of the musical bigwigs, it was arranged that the concert should be held at the Opera House on the 11th of October. By that time it was assumed that the political disturbances abroad would have died down, and in any case, since he had planned to visit Vienna before proceeding to Paris there was not much danger that he would contact any difficulties with his passport.

His father saw to that.

Hitherto, Nicolas had chosen to ignore the rumours of Frédéric's infatuation for Constantia. He had dismissed it as an inevitable malady of youth, no more serious and far less unbecoming than a rash of pimples. Nevertheless it were best, as a precautionary measure, to get the boy out of the danger zone. The girl was a flirtatious hussy, his son an irresolute ass.

Thankfully, Nicolas encouraged Frédéric's decision to be gone, and gave him no chance to retract. The preparations went apace; his passport, not without some string-pulling on the part of Nicolas, was visaed for Vienna and London, via

Paris. Justina bought him a brand-new trunk, and Louise under Isabella's supervision packed it.

Isabella, in her newly acquired wisdom as a matron, could be relied upon to know all masculine requirements, even to the particular brand of shaving-soap most in favour with the gentlemen. Three new suits were ordered by Chopin Junior at Titus's tailor, and debited to Chopin Senior's account. And yet, with all these activities to monopolise his time and his attention, and notwithstanding his rehearsals, his vows, and Constantia's cuts, Frédéric was by no means disembarrassed of enchantment.

But, he wrote in another of his interminable letters, *in spite of lamentations and complaints I have the firm will and secret intention definitely to depart on Saturday week with my music in my trunk and a certain ribbon on my heart: thus into the post-chaise. And although throughout the town from Copernicus to the fountain and from the Bank to King Sigismund's column, tears will flow in streams, I shall be cold and unfeeling as stone…*

He was not, however, to be let off so lightly. Fate, or that wily publicist Soliva, intervened. He, who for months had noised abroad the name of his pupil Gladowska, was not content to let the first flash of her success simmer in the pan. Although she was not to be presented in opera again that season, she must continue to shine in the public eye and where better than at Chopin's concert?

Frédéric was not consulted, nor did he know until the last minute that Soliva, with Elsner's collaboration and consent, had arranged the programme starring 'The Gladowska' with himself.

His reaction to this shock was a mixture of dismay and delight. At least he would be near her, and on a level of equality to share the evening's honours with one who, after all, was a fellow student and even more of a novice than he who had played in public, counting his earliest appearances, eight times to her once. True he had only received payment for two concerts, both of which had left his father out of pocket; but she, Constantia, had not been paid at all. This he had learned on the authority of Wolkow, her bosom friend — a gentle, pretty creature — even if her eyes were weak, who had told him that both she and Gladowska were being educated as singers at the State's expense, and who, by command of Mostowski, the Minister of Public Instruction, were to continue their studies under Soliva at the Conservatoire for another year.

He may have been relieved to hear it. A year! He would have returned long before that time crowned with glory, to find Gladowska still a child of the State, though she might have half a dozen Apolloesque attachés from the British Embassy, and all of Warsaw at her feet. Still more relieved was he to hear that Wolkov was to appear in the second half of the programme co-starred with Gladowska; and he might have been more than human if he had not briefly hoped that on this occasion the little Wolkow would outshine her, providing that the little Wolkow did not also outshine him.

And now he must suffer once more again all the preliminary anguish of the day preceding his appearance; and again, too, it was Jan who stood by to support him, and not Titus. That young gentleman, perhaps wisely, managed always to steer clear of contact with the temperamental Chopin at these times, and relied on the letters that unfailingly followed each performance for a first-hand account of the affair.

This, his third, was to be the most successful he had held that season: but none there who heard him guessed — nor, for all his dark 'presentiments', did Frédéric — that never in his life again was he destined to play before a Polish audience in Warsaw.

The concert was to be held at the Opera House. Frédéric, in a fever lest he should arrive too late, came very much too early, and, accompanied by Jan, had to sit for half an hour in the artists' room before even the members of the orchestra appeared.

The first item on the programme was a symphony by Görner; then he was to play his allegro from the Concerto in E Minor, to be followed by an aria, with chorus, by Soliva and sung by Wolkow — for which he thanked God. He would not have to face Gladowska and her taunts — or, if she were in gracious mood, her sweetness, which might be even more upsetting.

It was, however, not Wolkow but Constantia herself who, when the orchestra had filed to its seats, joined Frédéric in the artists' room. She wore a puritan dress of white satin with white flowers in her hair, and a smile which so completely ravished him that Jan, seeing the colour drain from his face, said, 'Steady, put your head on your knees,' for he thought him like to faint.

Ignoring this advice, Frédéric half rose in his seat to go to her, and was pulled back by his friend who, linking an arm in his, muttered, 'Now, now! Don't excite yourself. Come out and have a vodka.'

'Have a vodka? Do you want me to collapse? You know what vodka does to me. Leave me be, will you?' And with a jerk that set him free of Jan, Frédéric sprang to his feet. 'Panna Gladowska!'

She was all smiles still. 'I am more than honoured to share the programme with you, Monsieur Chopin.'

Trembling he bowed, to touch with his lips the small gloved hand she offered. 'The honour is mine, mademoiselle.'

Her indifference, her cruelty, her malicious teasing were all forgotten now. This was the real, the exquisite Gladowska whose eyes were azure pools of gentleness to drown you: whose lips were dewy, flagrant, kind. How terrible, how shaming, to have no words to give her but banalities. 'The honour is mine...' Why could he not shout to highest heaven that he glorified and magnified her for ever, as he glorified the Virgin whom at this moment she so entirely resembled?

'I have come early so that I may hear you, Monsieur Chopin. I would not for worlds miss your allegro.'

'Thank you, thank you ... I shall play only to you.'

'Ah! If I could only believe it! I fear sweet flattery comes as ready to your tongue as sweet music to your fingers.'

He swallowed, blushed, bowed again and went from her for fear of what he might not say or do before that roomful of onlookers. Soliva, who had arrived in charge of Wolkow, was almost dancing with nervous excitement, and violently beckoning Constantia. 'Mademoiselle! I forbid you to talk. You must not tire yourself. Come with me to your box. Stay still. Be tranquil. Panna Wolkow! I entreat you not to speak. Did you gargle your throat before you left home as I instructed? Here is now the symphony commencing. Mesdemoiselles — *if* you *please!* Come, come!' Small, rosy, rotund, and not unlike a motherly, distracted hen, Soliva drove his charges, fluttering, before him. 'Ah! Frédéric, my dear boy! All success to you. Have no fear. You will play magnificently. I, myself, have corrected your score that the orchestra can read it. Quite, *quite* beautiful. In particular the Rondo... Now, young ladies, pray do not either of you speak another word above a whisper.

These most precious larynxes must remain sealed until the moment that you sing.'

She was torn from his sight, turning as she left the room to waft him to the skies with a gesture of a finger to her lips, for all the world as though she breathed a kiss upon the air. Good God! If he could think so!

Now he would play as never in his life before. Now he was strong and proud: no weak-kneed snivelling rat, a hybrid growth, half woman, with a craven heart and palpitations — but a giant. Now all his blood and essence would rise again in song, in rapture and thanksgiving due to her: now was he, Chopin, music itself made manifest, and be her re-created…

That night, when all was over, when till dawn, wakeful in a dark oppressive vacuum, too stunned, too shocked to suffer, as one who has been drugged may watch the surgeon's knife perform its work, unpained, he lay and watched himself.

Strange how through that acheless calm, perception in its tense passivity revealed him: how grown ten years older in an hour, he could see the tempestuous fervour of his boyhood's dreaming stripped like a garment that has been snatched by the wind to leave him cold and sterner, and a man — while somewhere deep within, a something mocked; something of him that he had never known, a shadow twisted out of shape, a stranger, and yet one with whom he felt a quiet comradeship: one who henceforth would be his friend: one who more than Jan with his faithful dog's love, or Titus with his charm and his caprices, would be his mentor. Now he and this other self had met and were united. So, as Titus once had told him, man and woman should have been — each contained within the other, as man was in the beginning, till God thought fit to make of him male and female: two entities, for all man's earthly sin — and for his sorrow.

In the darkness, with his chin in the sheets, his eyes wide and staring out at nothing, his lips smiled. This then was life: reality. Not a pantomime, born of fevered sense and self-suggestion, but a solid truth... Survival can only be attained through and in one's ego. A hundred idiot voices may scream and shout, each claiming, 'This is I,' but only from one clear, unpolluted centre can the controlling 'I' be heard: only from that one point of contact with the Absolute, can the human spirit rise to its fulfilment. Not in false images, false gods or spurious emotions can security be reached, but by a cleansing of visionary obstructions, fears ... and lies.

How unutterably he had been deceived! But not by her. Can one blame the rose for the worm in its bud? Or the almond blossom for the frost that bites it? No, he and he only was his own source of disillusionment. He had been too eager, greedy, young.

Carefully, with undismayed precision, he reviewed the birth and passing of first love from love's inception: its storms and ecstasies, equally delusive, equally exaggerated; the whole pitiful tragi-comedy with himself the leading figure, small, a trifle crude and over-emphasised, groaning in mimic anguish, or uplifted in puppet transfiguration by some imagined favour, by a word.

But henceforth no more words need be spoken to rouse bewildered tumults in the blood and steal from youth all youth's defenceless faith, and stifle it: no more of seedling loves and abortive mimicries of passion, no more insensate longings: no slaking of one's thirst upon dry ashes, no dark hunger in secret hours, no torment of the body to touch and to possess … nothing of that. Just emptiness, and somewhere deep, the sound of laughter, thin and cracked…

He dedicated, pledged to her, had played, that all who heard him marvelled; that even the most critical were dumb. He, not she — and not the little Wolkow whose bell-like clarity of tone was preferred by some to Gladowska's fuller range — he alone had been the evening's star, and its success.

There was a ring of *veni, vidi, vici* in this conquest, which, however, left him strangely unaffected while he bowed to the frenzied audience, and when recalled for encore, improvised; but when with his self-depreciatory shrug and slow boy's smile he sat and played again — the waltz composed for her, then, and then only did he know his own triumph.

For she had come to watch and listen on the stage, her lips parted as that fateful first time he had seen her, and it was to her only that he spoke as she stood in the wings, shielded by the folds of the curtain from the audience below who pressed close to the platform, up-gazing and transfixed.

And when at last they let him go…

He found her in the artists' room; with her was Soliva, Wolkow and… He sensed rather than saw one to whom she turned as he advanced, one whom in his dazed confusion he recognised, but could not quite remember. Then, as he came to her to speak and tell her — what? To stammer croaking in his clumsy hesitation, or to take her there and claim her his before them all by right of love? As he waited while the surge within him settled and his lips were framed to speech, her hand, warm and clinging, came out to take his. 'Chopin! What is it that you, more than any player I have ever known, possess? What lovely trick to tear one's heart to bits?'

But her words were less to him than the sweet surprise of touch, and her eyes on his, tender, shining, through held tears of pure emotion. 'And here is Pan Grabowski who wishes to compliment you. Allow me to present...'

Mechanically he bowed. No slimy financier could now disturb him. Mechanically too, dry-tongued, dry-mouthed, and with a grin stretched tight upon closed lips, he received that pompous flattery, until his ears were plugged and he could answer nothing but his parrot phrase: 'I am glad my music pleased you...'

'And is it true that you are leaving Warsaw, Monsieur Chopin?'

So! Grabowski had been nosing round for information. Why?

He repeated his bow of a marionette. 'There is some talk of it, sir, but —'

'You must not leave before December. We cannot let you go, can we, Jozef? We cannot spare him. He is far too precious. You must stay with us here in Warsaw...' Her hand touched his again, like a caress. 'You must be in Warsaw for my marriage, Chopin... Yes, you must play at my wedding ... for me.'

He smiled again, not hearing, or if he heard, his ears were numb before reverberation came: a spark of red was lit behind his eyes, and then the crash as of all heaven falling.

And she was speaking still.

She looked like a drowned woman under water, blurred, pressed out of shape, and staring, her smile as rigid and as false as his.

'You did not know that I am to be married, did you? Nor did I ... till yesterday. To Pan Grabowski. It is to be announced tomorrow. You should be honoured, Chopinetto... You are the first to hear.'

In the darkness as he lay there in his bed Frédéric smiled as though in answer to that dead smile of hers; and watching himself calmly, he applauded. He was not disgraced. There had been no hysterics, no pantomimic gestures from the grotesque toy clown who stood before her with the sawdust trickling from its wound. Indeed, he thought he had grown taller by an inch or two to meet her eyes unflinching, to bow over her hand, to raise it to his cold lips while he gained voice to murmur, 'Honoured, indeed, Panna Gladowska... Sir.' Bow left, bow right as on the platform, grin. 'It is my one regret in leaving Warsaw for my continental tour, that I shall not be here to join in the celebration that will make you, Pan Grabowski, the most envied of all men. Mademoiselle, to you ... all joy.

With eyes unseeing, his quivering chin held high, he had turned and left the room, and, avoiding the family group that waited ready to seize and waylaid him, made for a back-door exit. There, Jan who saw all had followed, to put him in a droshky and escort him home.

'Thanks, old fellow. No. I ... prefer to be alone. If you would kindly tell my parents that I have gone and am too tired to talk... There will be all tomorrow for post-mortems. Tell them not to come to my room. I shall lock my door. I must ... I must have ... sleep. Goodnight, my Jasia. God bless you.'

SIX

The last day dawned; the longed-for moment of departure had arrived, the post-chaise was at the door.

Some tears were shed, but not by Frédéric. Dry-eyed, and passive, he stood enveloped in a flutter of sisters, clinging arms, and kisses.

'If only you could take me with you, Fryck!'

'If only I could, my darling. But just as well I can't. All Vienna would be strewn with broken hearts... Isabella, don't forget I am to be godpapa, and if it is a boy call him Frédéric Francois for me... *Ma petite mère.*' He turned to his mother; he held her close. 'Dearest, I'm not going to Siberia, you know. I'll soon be back.'

She took his face between her hands and looked at him and tried to smile. 'Six months,' she said, 'is a long time to lose you. Write to me.'

'Every day, I'll keep a diary. Goodbye, *mon père.* I can never thank you enough for... everything. I'll try,' his voice faltered for a moment, 'to be worthy... Yes, Mama, I'll take my cough mixture, I promise. Cross my heart... Yes, I'll consult all the doctors in Vienna at the first sign of chill. Don't worry, sweet. I'll be home so soon you won't have time to miss me.'

'May God keep you safe,' she whispered, 'and bring you back to me.'

Always after he remembered her as she stood with his father and sisters, small and brave, her lips moving in a voiceless prayer, waving her handkerchief, blowing him one last kiss, until a blindness came and hid her from his sight.

The post-chaise set him down at Wola, the, first village on the outskirts of the city. Here it had been arranged he was to meet the diligence and partake of a farewell luncheon given by Titus in his honour, to which all his friends and Elsner were invited.

All was in readiness, the guests assembled in the inn parlour, and Titus, watch in hand, impatiently awaiting his arrival. 'You're half an hour late. There'll be no time to eat.'

But if the whole day had been his to command, Frédéric could not have eaten. He drank, a sufficiency of champagne and the good red wine of France that Titus had ordered. He answered toasts, and listened, with a lump like a rock in his throat, to a cantata composed by Elsner and sung by a choir of students. Then more wine was handed round, and a boar's head, and finally a silver goblet presented by Titus with due solemnity and an elaborate speech.

'Frédéric Chopin, this vase, filled with the soil of our beloved Poland to which half your blood belongs, this token of our love for you we offer as a parting gift to speed you on your way. We, your fellow countrymen, expect great things of you, that your name shall live for ever in the history of our land. Take with you on your voyage abroad our prayers for your success, all the love of our hearts, and this silver urn, that wherever you may be in foreign countries, among strangers, you will carry with you always a slice of your native earth to keep and cherish — as we cherish you!' And overcome with emotion and a mixing of wines Titus sat down, amid cheers.

Frédéric got up, but not to speak; no words could pass the ache in his throat. He stood, with mumbling lips, unheard, while those dear faces, swam before him in a smarting mist: the grey-haired Elsner, a-nod with smiles and a shake in his chin: Jan, with his eyebrows like black eaves to meet above his nose, scowling at his empty wineglass twirled between bony fingers:

Titus, with wine stains on his shirt front, flushed and bright-eyed, blinking through his tears to laughter. And the young voices of his comrades, rising, falling to a thread of a sound in the blast of the post-guard's horn.

So Chopin went from Poland, with his face to an unknown future, and his youth in the grave of a dream.

PART TWO: PARIS, 1835-1837

SEVEN

Paris in the 1830s… City of enchantment and revolt: youth's Utopia, where in an era of hope, of action and excitement, the cage door of convention was flung wide to eject the barren formalism of an earlier age and admit new movements, a new philosophy, new culture. The storm of discontent and rebellion that had risen with the wrath of a tornado, to shatter in the compass of three July days the old dynastic order, and place Louis Philippe on the throne, had penetrated to the very core of life and living.

Paris offers anything you may wish, wrote Chopin. *You can amuse yourself, mope, laugh, weep, in short do whatever you like. Everybody goes his own way.*

A way that had hitherto been barred by inanimate theorists and systems, and the tyrannous limitations of the pseudo-classicism of the first Empire: a way that led through the Champs-Élysées and the attics of Montmartre to the cloistered circle of Romantics. No matter where or how or in what garb or 'new' disguise the spirit floated, sooner or later it must gravitate towards, and be dissolved within that faery ring of poets, writers, artists, philosophers and friends.

The torch of militant idealism, relit by Victor Hugo from the dying candles on the altars of Chateaubriand and Madame de Staël, burned fiercely, proclaiming no other laws but Nature's, no other god but Art.

Yet, surely never was doctrine less akin to Nature than that which plastered Art's temple with a façade of distorting mirrors, wherein a carnival parade of soulful-eyed young men and women bowed and postured in extravagant hyperbole.

Hugo, de Vigny, Deschamps, Sainte-Beauve, these were their masters: Saint-Simon their spiritual guide. His picaresque gospel, resurrected and revised, underwent remarkable developments. Even Saint-Simon himself might have been scandalised at the contemplation of such articles of faith as 'Free Love', or 'Progressive Union' as a substitute for marriage, and Communism — so the socialistic creed was beginning to be called — as the first principle of that Equality and Liberty on which were based all Christian rights of true republicans.

And what an arrogant young army of disciples rallied to the cause of Truth, Regeneration, and Romance, some to fall by the wayside, others to rank among the chosen of immortals.

Alfred de Musset, publishing verse in his teens, a drunken young Dionysus at the feet of the Saint-Simonians' high priestess, Aurore Dudevant alias George Sand: Delacroix, that dynamic genius, using his brush like a broom to cover enormous canvases in loud clashes of colour orchestration, he who led the knights templars of Romance in art, as did the great Hugo in literature. The daring and gifted Berlioz with his *Symphonie Fantastique* was music's trumpeter, partnered by a youthful Liszt with his mystical Raphaelite beauty, his delirious extravaganzas and his charming, slightly tarnished little golden Comtesse d'Agoult.

Such then was the circle of élite in Paris in the thirties, of whom none was any older than the century itself. Most, indeed, were younger, all dedicated to the Universal Life — *la vie Bohème*, whose shocking 'new' morality had even filtered from the Quartier Latin to the salons of the *ancien régime*, there to be discussed by the ladies of the *ton* with bated breath and whispers. And while this dainty boudoir chatter was tossed like a gossamer puff-ball from lip to lip, rumour gathered up the gleanings to make a story of names bandied, that lost nothing of embroidery by repetition.

First of all, and more than any other most intriguing, was the name of Madame Dudevant, that mysterious, bizarre and unbelievable *bon garçon*: the trousered, strange, cigar-smoking 'George Sand'. Altogether 'shocking' was this creature, who dressed like a man and had written a best-seller entitled *Lélia*, which caused such a clamour of tongues for its heresies, its blasphemies, its scandalous corruptions, that superlatives among the ladies on the right bank of the Seine were exhausted before they read the book.

She it was who had snatched the pale, blond, exquisite dipsomaniac de Musset from his doting mother's arms, and dragged him all over Italy to Venice where he lay at death's door in *delirium tremens*.

'Est-ce toi dont la voix m'appelle,
O ma pauvre Muse! est-ce toi?
O ma fleur! O mon immortelle!
Seul être pudique et fidèle...'

Thus may have raved the hapless Alfred, while his 'Muse' was seducing the handsome young doctor in attendance on his case. What an *histoire* to set all Paris rocking and to terminate a union of souls! And scarcely had the last of that subsided amidst titters than *l'haut monde* became hysterical over Madame Sand's divorce suit against her husband, Casimir Dudevant, who on the testimony of half a dozen servants was proven in the courts a promiscuous adulterer of low tastes and brutish habits, unfit to be a husband or a father.

If the pure and chaste believed, or may have hoped that the notorious George Sand would not induce a jury to agree upon a case in which the defendant was certainly more sinned against than sinning, they were likely to have met with disappointment. She won her case but her triumph was short-lived. Casimir appealed, with a rope of compromising evidence to hang her.

So, with a band of trusted friends as her support, and the most brilliant advocate in Paris to defend her, Madame George Sand-Dudevant, who at the first hearing had not appeared in court, came to be judged.

Never had a suit excited so much interest among all classes of society, and in particular among the ladies who thronged, and, let it be whispered, fought, to obtain front seats to watch an entertainment that promised as many thrills as any comedy presented on the stage.

Those who had already been afforded glimpses of Madame Sand at the opera, or in the distinguished salons of those more advanced *grandes dames*, Madame la Baronne de Rothschild, and Mesdames les Comtesses de Potocka and Esterhazy, were prepared to see the most celebrated woman novelist in France habited for the occasion in her famous Amazonian attire of *pantalons* and velvet jacket, with her hair on her shoulders and a Byronic flowing tie. But not at all. Contrary to expectation, Madame appealed, drooping upon her counsel's arm, and wearing the most simple of young-girlish gowns, a flowered shawl and a chip bonnet. Her veil was modestly lowered, as were her dark-fringed eyelids hiding her unfathomable eyes, which, however, when uplifted to gaze upon the jury were suffused, so it was seen behind the shield of gauze, with a grave, heart-rending melancholy to melt the stoniest.

Was this gentle olive-skinned beauty, whose responses uttered in dulcet husky tones from lips that curled in proud disdain at the base insults and allegations hurled against her virtue — was it possible that one so undeniably distinguished could be guilty of the infidelities and unsavoury associations ascribed to her? An avowed republican and the friend of republicans, whose way of life was known to be equivocal and who, on her husband's oath, had been the mistress of some several men, among them...

Hush! *Noblesse oblige.* Let not the name of the Vicomte de Musset be dragged through the slime of the courts. Let him, the innocent impressionable poet, so unscathed for the sake of his greatly to be pitied long-suffering mama, if not for his youth and his genius. If one must choose a scapegoat, then choose at least a man of lesser quality and no significance. The penniless, misguided Dr Pagello of Venice, a mere apothecary and a foreigner to boot, who owing to his absence could not defend himself.

Since, however, sufficient evidence against the unfortunate Pagello could not be produced, the first cause of the first rupture between the husband and the wife must be revived.

With a sigh of silken petticoats, and some agreeable tremors, the ladies settled in their seats to listen and enjoy.

The case for the appeal as presented with oratorical aplomb by Maître Thiot-Varennes, revealed the startling Sand as more than ever shameless. As far back as 1825, it seemed, the creature had been engaged in a 'friendship' — purely platonic, *bien entendu!* — with a certain Aurélien de Sèze, *avocat-général* at Bordeaux, whom Madame had met in the course of an excursion to the Pyrenees, and who, so counsel emphatically stated, had been responsible for Madame's downfall from propriety, and her ultimate pollution.

How, it was argued, could such a liaison be termed 'platonic'? All knew her private life would not bear scrutiny — a woman who neglected her innocent husband and children, brazenly to flaunt her illicit passion before the world, and on the plea of 'spiritual' relationship! What mockery, what sacrilege! 'Your books, Madame —' thundered Thiot-Varennes, while behind her veil Madame gazed, unmoved — 'your books confess you. They reek of the poison that devours your mind. Gall and bitterness pursue your triumphs. In worldly gross desires do you seek contentment of the soul and find it not. Well then, here is the road to it. Return to your husband, and resume your position as a God-fearing wife and mother, take this last chance offered to you for repentance, and walk henceforth in righteousness, in virtue —'

And so on till Madame Sand's supporters on the left could scarcely hold their splutters of derision for this pompous ass, and the ladies on the right were all in tears. Poor Monsieur Dudevant who had nurtured in his breast this snake, this viper, this woman taken in adultery. It was to be hoped she would be punished with due regard for her impenitence. A whipping at the cart's tail was no more than she deserved.

'Messieurs! Your attention if you please.'

Maître Michel de Bourges was on his feet... What now?

With discreet inhalations the tender-hearted and the too-tight-laced relieved their aching sides. A very different front to the affair. Within five minutes de Bourges had jury, judge and ladies by the ears, to make all feel the least bit guilty of intolerance: a bourgeois sentiment, unworthy of the cultured... Intolerance, yes, and something more, most mortifying when thus indicated, that a too hasty, even crude interpretation had been perhaps attributed to a friendship between intellectuals.

Madame George Sand and Monsieur Aurélien de Sèze could not be judged by ordinary standards or as ordinary persons. These two were extraordinary, and as such and on that plane inhabited by higher beings, where spirit controls the mind, and soul the body, was it not inevitable that the materialists whose grosser way of life could impute but *one* motive, one infamous desire to the contact of man and woman, would condemn that which was beyond their understanding? To know all is to forgive all. The duty of him, her advocate, was not to plead the mercy of the court for one whose innocence was unimpeachable, but to reveal the truth, the whole truth, concerning this most lamentable misconception.

'Messieurs, let us return to the beginning of the marriage, when the conduct of the husband — conduct so foul, so revolting, so atrocious that no human lips can describe it — compelled this unhappy lady to leave her home. He, and he alone, is guilty of and responsible for this separation between man and wife, and its *débâcle* which has brought this gentle creature to the pillory.'

The gentle creature was here seen to lift her veil and apply to her eyes a diminutive square of lawn: a gesture undeniably affecting. And with emotion thickening his voice, her advocate proceeded: 'What was the intelligence of this coarse brute compared to hers? Where his chivalry or duty as a husband in leaving a young and lovely woman...'

The ladies were inclined to disagree: not even the most tolerant could call her lovely. Her chin was too full, her shoulders were too broad, her skin, or as much as could be seen of it, too coarse. And certainly not young.

'...to her own devices for near upon ten years? And how did she employ those years and to what noble achievements? Ask yourselves and find the answer written on the walls of fame. A woman of genius who courageously made attempt to earn her own maintenance, and who has so admirably justified her self-esteem in her self-chosen profession. Is it a guilty woman who reveals her beauty of soul in the writings that have been brought as evidence against her? Books that will live in the proud memory of France, when you, Messieurs, and all who slander her have been forgotten...'

If this stirring oratory produced a murmur of dissent, de Bourges was equal to it. Producing his trump card, as it were, from the sleeve of his gown, he raised his hand to call for silence. 'Sirs, I ask you, what manner of man, what animal, what type of hypocrite is this, who, having accepted — nay more, *invited* Madame's honourable friend and literary associate, Monsieur de Sèze, as a guest to his house, appeals with lies, with cajolery and promises to his wife's tender nature, and induces her against her better judgment to return to him? And then, having shown every sign of penitence and acknowledged himself at fault, he strikes — to plunge a dagger in her heart!'

De Bourges sat down.

To such good purpose had he used his histrionics that the judges failed to agree. The case was finally, and in spite of the invective slung from side to side, amicably settled out of court; with this proviso. That the parties remain separate, since it was certain they would never live in peace again together, and the wife was given custody of the two children.

This, then, is the truth of that *cause célèbre* which set the whole of Paris buzzing, and which brought forth from the cinders of one scandal, the phoenix of another, to link the name of George Sand with that of her advocate, Michel de Bourges.

Was the woman indefatigable?

Evidently.

And while those ladies who, for the moment, had rallied to her side shut their doors upon her with eyes up-raised to heaven, the gentlemen, among themselves, laid wagers on a possible successor to de Bourges.

The stakes ran high and higher: their speculations proved unlucky. He whom Destiny had chosen was yet to come upon the scene.

On a late afternoon in the summer of 1837, George Sand was at her desk in her apartment in the Rue Neuve Laffitte, engrossed in her weekly article for the *Revue Indépendante*. Her quill, busily scratching across the page, had written:

I cannot separate the idea of Republic from that of Regeneration. For the sake of the world's future it seems to me necessary to destroy in order to construct... I dream of Homeric combats, that solitary upon some mountain top I watch, to plunge, drunk with holy vengeance in their midst. I dream also of some new day after storm, of a sunrise clear and splendid, of flower-decked altars and wise legislators, olive-crowned in the rehabilitation of human dignity. I dream of man freed from the tyranny of man, and woman freed from the tyranny of sex ... Let me mourn, let me pray for a Jerusalem that has lost its gods and not yet found Messiah. My vocation is to hate evil, to love good, to fall on my knees —

Her pen fell from her hand. 'The devil!' muttered George, scowling at the splutter of ink which had almost obliterated the last sentence.

'Open! Open!' The door handle rattled; fists beat upon the panels, and a girlish voice intoned with plaintive sweetness:

*'Ma chandelle est morte
Je n'ai plus de feu*

Ouvre-moi ta porte
Pour l'amour de dieu.'

'Name of a pipe!' In two impatient strides George crossed to
the door, unlocked and flung it wide. 'Come, then! Come, if
you must.'

In tripped the little Countess d'Agoult, adorable in flesh-pink
muslin, flounced and banded with lace of a cobweb fineness;
on her yellow curls a bonnet of rose-quilted satin, more lace,
and floating ribbons; on her lips two kisses that left a ruby
smear on either cheek of her scowling friend.

'Are you busy? Can you spare for Franz and me one
moment?'

'A hundred,' George retorted, 'since all my moments have
been scattered now.'

'Before such swine as we are! Let us then endeavour to
rethread the pearls,' chirped the countess, unabashed. 'My
dearest! You look tired.'

'As a dog. It is almost my bedtime.'

'Ah, now! We had forgotten that you go to bed with the sun
and rise with the dawn. Send us from you then. Franz! We go.'

'Liszt,' murmured George, extending a hand to a shadowy
figure in the doorway, 'you make me feel like the man in the
Indian legend of Twashtri. When I see your face I know I can
live neither with you — nor without you. But today, my dears,
I am in myself, sufficient. You are both *de trop.*'

'Shame on us!' cried the countess. 'God knows we would not
quench the sacred flame. But we have been thinking, Liszt and
I, that perhaps you work too hard, you drive your energy too
far. We ask you, therefore, to take a holiday; relax — if only for
this one night. We come to offer you amusement.'

'Amusement!' George laughed without a smile. 'And I with two articles to write, two novels unfinished, the rent unpaid, two households to provide for and two brats to keep. Amusement! Sit then, my children, if you can find a seat. You may throw those proofs on the floor, but don't muddle the pages. They go to press tonight. I have nothing to offer you but some bad wine and a good smoke. Liszt?' She handed him a box from her desk. He shook his head. 'Well then, I will.' She selected and lit her cigar, lowered herself to the floor, and sat, clasping her trousered knees, her gaze impassively fixed upon the faded pink-and-white little beauty who had perched herself on the arm of Liszt's chair.

The room reflected the personality of its owner. High up under the roof of the Hôtel de France, it was indeed scarcely more than a garret, with windows heavily curtained in blue velvet, the walls hung with engravings after Raphael, and vivid, unframed colour splashes by Delacroix. Books lay everywhere — and pipes. Rugs covered the parquet, and a rosewood piano stood between the shuttered casements under a portrait of Madame by Calametta. On the desk was a litter of papers, quills, and conveniently placed at the writer's elbow, a bowl of water in which floated the sodden dead ends of cigars. Dust was prevalent, and ink stains — on the walls, on the rugs, on the pale pointed index finger of George Sand.

Liszt, who watched her through the thin fog of tobacco smoke, noted, not for the first time, the striking contrast between these two women, within whose lives his own was entangled beyond all hope, he vaguely feared, of extrication. The one his mistress, the other his friend and confidante, his fellow voyager along the same experimental path: she who spoke his own mystic language in the same exalted symbolism of expression. He stood divided, shared equally between earthly passion and the consecrated union of souls. If only one could be merged in the other! If only his delicious, childlike love possessed more of that sacred flame of which she talked so glibly and so often, and if only his *femme-héros* had a little something more, perhaps, of gracious womanly appeal — but even so, were she as delectable as Venus, he was already pledged and given — utterly.

His hands, the strong nervous hands of the pianist, tightened round his lady's slender waist. Such thoughts were unworthy of the love she had so generously bestowed on him, her music master: yes, even before all Paris had pursued him, even before he had been acclaimed first favourite, until another came to steal... No! Not to steal but to usurp, by virtue of his greater superiority as artist, that place upon the pedestal of fame and fashion which Liszt had made his own. One would be more than human if one did not, occasionally, feel the prick — the faintest prick of rancour, which must, however, perish before art's loyal acclamation of so illustrious a colleague.

Yet she, his love, had remained faithful, unallured by the magic of this frail young Pole who had captured the heart of Paris; she, his pupil, lover, wife in all but name, who had renounced her old husband, her young children, and the society to which by right of birth and breeding she belonged, to follow him; she, whose feet were like hands and whose hands were like lilies, and whose eyes were no less sparkling than her wit that had already expressed itself in one admirable first novel under the *nom de plume* of 'Daniel Stern'... How monstrous, then, to criticise or to ask more than sheer perfection of his Marie, his sweet saint. As for his woman-hero, this female Don Juan, what of her? 'Despairing as Manfred, rebellious as Cain, and inconsolable as either.' So he himself had described her. Why? Because she had never found a man sufficiently feminine to love her as she desired to be loved: to pay her the homage of confiding blind submission. She covered her breast with a cuirass of masculinity, and yet behind that vigorous disguise, behind the dark-fringed eyelids, woman, dominant, discreet as the grave, stood revealed, insatiate and lonely, lover of herself rather than the lover of any other.

Maddening creature, with the dignity of Pharaoh and the manners of a *gosse*! The heavy-lidded, long Egyptian eyes, ringed round with amber, repelled by their inscrutable detachment and magnetised by strange promise unfulfilled. The disdainful high-bridged nose, the short upper lip shaded by incipient down, the full round chin, the olive-dark complexion reflecting bronze lights from a frame of unexpectedly feminine curls that fell parted on sturdy shoulders — yes, there were some who found her beauty undeniable: others who denied it. Enough for Liszt she was his friend, his favourite *bon garçon*, and as Balzac had once remarked to him, her male equal would be hard to find.

'Franz! How you stare!' His lady's hand fluttered like a butterfly across his face. 'One would think you'd seen Medusa.'

Liszt smiled. 'Perhaps I have.'

'But will you listen to what I have been saying? Twice I have asked you. Will Chopin be at the Marquis de Custine's tonight?'

'He said he would be there, but you know,' Liszt shrugged, 'what Chopin is. If the mood takes him he will go; if not he will stay at home and write innumerable letters, or a nocturne—'

'Ah! That new Nocturne in D Flat Major! How exquisite it is. He has dedicated it to Madame d'Appony, but he gives her nothing more than — music lessons. He is always so correct, the little Chopin.'

'I am told,' said George, 'that he has a rooted aversion to all women.'

'Only to one, my darling,' purred the countess. 'You!'

George removed her cigar from her mouth to knock ash on the carpet before replying. 'Yes, I have been told that too, so often, I am almost ready now to disbelieve it.'

The countess gave a little crow of laughter. 'But it is true, I swear. When he saw you first at — where was it? I can't remember — he made the classic remark that he found you utterly repellent — but only in self-defence, I feel convinced. And he is possibly the only man who has ever dared admit his fear of you. He has received some hard knocks from our sex, or I should say from *my* sex since you, dear George, are neither woman, maid, nor boy, and certainly not man, and therefore must remain unclassified and unapproachable. But to return to our *moutons* — or to our timid lamb who is hunted day and night by a pack of ferocious female adorers — he can scarcely be blamed for keeping his distance from you, whom — should you turn your glance upon him — no man above eighteen or under eighty can resist. He is only just recovering from an almost fatal blow. That heartless, unscrupulous little flirt, Maria Wodzińska — I hear she has given him his *congé*. Did you know they were supposed to be engaged?'

George shook her head. She could not keep pace with this mercurial dexterity of speech, and therefore she resented it. But more than Marie's badinage and innuendoes did she resent the interruption of her work.

'I know nothing of Chopin more than that the *jeunesse dorée* ape his scent, his gloves, his one side-whisker, and that his name appears in all the social columns of the journals. Even here —' she turned to retrieve from the floor a crumpled sheet of newspaper — 'though certainly the headlines today give more space to the death of the English King and the succession of his schoolgirl niece than to the name of Chopin, we find him billed to appear — ah yes! you are right — at the Marquis de Custine's *soirée*.' George tossed the paper to one side. 'How can a man — an artist — which I grant you, undeniably, he is — so waste himself? He cares more for the cut of his coat than the creation of his music.'

'No!' Liszt raised his head; his mane of hair shook with emphatic denial. 'No, my dear George, there you do him an injustice. I know how he works and how he suffers at his work, to achieve that bold originality, that perfection of detail which has made him what he is — unrivalled, head and shoulders higher than anyone of us whom he has surpassed. I am the first to admit it. Schumann too. He is too great for us to envy. We can only bow before one who is infinitely superior. And if you could see how he labours to capture that intricate elaboration of design —'

'For my part,' said George, bluntly, 'I find him *too* intricate. His music is embroidery on chiffon, and his playing, though he executes the most incredible contortions, makes me feel as though his fingers are about to faint upon the keys. I admit that I have only heard him twice, and on one occasion I was slightly deaf from a cold in the head, which might account for the strain of my ears to catch the notes. And of course — I am no critic.'

'There are some critics,' smiled Liszt, 'who share your views, though I am not one of them. I acknowledge him a master, and excuse him his small vanities for the sake of his monumental worth.'

'H'm!' George closed her mouth.

The countess opened hers. 'I agree with George entirely; his playing is too lady-like and gentle, and his compositions! — What, I ask you, has he yet produced that is likely to live or can be compared to the strength and passion of our Franz's rhapsodies? But pray let us not enter into arguments on music, which I am truly quite unqualified to discuss — but let us come to the point of our visit, so that George may return to her bureau, as I know she is longing to do. Listen, love, Franz and I are going to de Custine's *soirée* this evening. Chopin is to be there. Come with us and you will meet him. It is only right you should.'

'And why is it right I should?' George rose to drop his cigar end in the bowl of water on her desk, where it expired with a hiss.

'Because —' Marie jumped from Liszt's knee, her hoop swinging in a froth of lace — 'because it would be so amusing to see the effect two such confirmed misanthropes would have on one another.'

'That is the first time,' drawled George in her husky voice, 'that I have been called a misanthrope. As for your Chopin, I have seen enough of him to know that I am likely to find him a consummate bore.'

'Now that indeed I promise you will not. He is old beyond his years.'

'Which are too young for mine.'

'Nonsense! You are ageless.'

'Thirty-six,' remarked George calmly. 'Well?'

'He has an ironic sense of humour.'

'And I believe that I have none.'

'I should hate to contradict you! But Chopin's humour has been embittered by repeated disappointments in his loves.'

'Come, come, my angel, don't exaggerate,' Liszt prompted. 'Only two.'

'So he may have told you. Paris gives him a round dozen.' George, her hands in her trouser pockets, a fresh cigar between her lips, and a frown between her eyebrows, said, 'I am completely tepid about Chopin and his amorous excursions, but since it is obvious you are bursting to tell me, and won't go until you do — who are these two? No, Marie, let Liszt say. I can vouch for the truth from him.'

'Not from me, my dear George. I refuse to repeat the confidences of a friend.'

'Pooh! When Chopin can keep no secret of his own?' cried Marie. 'I should have no scruples. Very well then, as I have never been his *confidante*, I am at liberty to speak. He is the most inconstant, fickle, and inflammable of men. There was first of all an opera singer when he was very, *very* young — be quiet, Liszt! The whole world knows it. He has told everyone — and even *me* — her name. No, not in confidence, I assure you. Merely *en passant*. And her name I have forgotten and could not pronounce it if I remembered, for you know what jaw-breaking names the Poles have. That, my dears, was a tremendous thing of a grand passion. He floundered to the verge of extinction, full of despair and almost suicidal. He mourned her for at least three months or even more. Then after some lesser ventures in Vienna, and here in Paris — he was caught again by that artful little minx, Wodzińska, whom he followed to Marienbad where his father was taking a cure — ostensibly to meet Papa, but —! The countess turned to adjust her bonnet strings before a mirror on the wall, and to repair her complexion with surreptitious dabs of rouge. 'Was there ever such an unbecoming colour as this pink?' She spun round, her eyes agleam between their darkened lashes. 'What a glum pair you are, to be sure! You give me *no* encouragement to gossip! And you know how I love to gossip. May I go on?'

'Please,' said George, with her mirthless smile, 'and then — go out.'

'Now what — after that — can I say? Come, Liszt! We will leave Chopin's latest love-story, like Schubert's symphony — unfinished. In any case I think it would have come to no conclusion. There is nothing permanent in Chopin but his cough. And he *does* cough — very gracefully. So you will come with us, tonight, George, *mon adorée*? Ah, do! We will call for you at ten o'clock. Is it a promise?'

'I make no promises. It is six o'clock already and my bedtime.'

'My God! Was there ever anyone so unaccountable? Please yourself, then. We will arrive at the hour and if you are asleep — we'll wake you up! *À bientôt, chérie.*'

From the door George watched the sparkling countess trip down the stairs on Liszt's arm; nor till the last shrill sound cipher had died away, did the writer return to her desk and her interrupted sentence.

… *to fall on my knees before beauty.* Her quill paused for a moment, then, her dark brows bent upon her work, she resumed:

I believe no longer in the nullity of the grave nor in safety bought at the price of a forced renunciation. All must be made happy that the good fortune of the few be not a crime nor a curse. As the labourer sows his wheat he must know that he is helping forward the work of life, instead of rejoicing that Death is at his side. We must no longer consider Death as the chastisement of prosperity or the consolation of distress, for God has decreed it neither as the punishment nor the compensation of life…

Her head lifted; her eyes strayed to the window. She stretched an arm to draw aside the velvet curtain. Paris lay below her, caught in a net of light. Above grey roofs and spires the sky was tender, clear and flushed as the face of a bride...

And this I know: that to be fruitful, Life, wrote George Sand, *must be enjoyed.*

EIGHT

'Thank you, thank you, Madame la Princesse. It is enough. We are both exhausted. We will continue tomorrow, if you please, at three o'clock.'

The hours of restraint put upon his patience during a succession of lessons to mediocrities, had drained him dry. It was unfortunate that she should have been the last pupil in a crowded day. He had nothing left to give her.

She rose from the piano, her timid hare's eyes fixed on his, adoring, questioning, fearful of his verdict. He forced a smile, and, taking both her small soft hands, he kissed them.

'Princess, we understand each other, yes? You know it is always a pleasure and never a penance to teach you. Some are wooden and unresponsive as this —' he rapped his knuckles on the ebony case of the piano — 'but you are vibrant ... as the notes that lie inside this shell of wood. Still, and this is no reproach but merely my advice from long experience, music should be effortless. It should flow like water from a fountain, pure and clear from these little fingers, that are as much a part of me as they are of you. Have I not trained them to speak, exquisitely? But not when they are fatigued, for then the fountain becomes blocked.'

'Yes, Monsieur, with a frog ... that croaks. I am sorry ... sorry. Forgive me, I do not know why I am so bad today. I have practised nothing but scales all the week ... I have indeed. I have obeyed you implicitly. You said not even to *look* at the Berlioz score. And I did not, though I was tempted. And now…' Tears brimmed. She took a lace-edged handkerchief and mopped them; her eyelids pinkened.

He watched her, unloved, remote, incapable of sympathy: too tired.

He had known her all her life. She was Marcelline, Prince Radziwill's youngest daughter, a childish wisp of a thing with a white-skinned, slightly blurred little face, pale blunt-cornered lips, and ash-blonde untidy hair. Not yet twenty, she had been conveniently married at sixteen, to the courteous, rich, entirely indifferent Prince Alexander Czartoryski. Her rare gift for the piano would have brought her to the concert platform if she had been of lesser rank. In music, or her music master, she may have found some consolation for the sacrifice of talent to society. But Chopin, though unsparing of himself as teacher, was niggardly of any tender nuance that could be more romantically construed; and if the Princess Marcelline, in her lonely young girl's heart and the solitude of her boudoir, suffered from his immunity, she was by no means singular in that.

'Tomorrow, then, Monsieur Chopin, at three o'clock. You have been very patient.' She was buttoning her gloves, her eyes downcast, her underlip drawn in to hide its trembling. 'I will try to be better, I promise.' She glanced aside, afraid to look at him lest she betray herself. 'I will try to adopt this new method of fingering…'

'My dear Madame, do not be over-zealous. I admit it is a difficult method to acquire, but once you have become accustomed to it, you will be astonished at the agility and the control — above all the *control* — that it produces. So much do I believe in it, I am ready to swear that none, not even Thalberg himself, could play certain of my *études* unless he adopted this method, which, *faute de mieux*, I was forced to invent because —' his eyebrows lifted, his voice dropped to draw her with him in an intimate, whimsical conspiracy — 'well, because I had to invent something to atone for this —' he extended his hand to show her — 'this limited stretch and these absurd dwarfish fingers with which nature has so grudgingly endowed me. Shall I tell you a secret? As a boy, I used to sleep with a piece of wood, rather like a clothes peg, stuck between my fingers, to stretch them apart. It was so dreadfully uncomfortable that it used to keep me awake, and I would get up in the middle of the night and play till all hours — I always had a piano in my bedroom. But after the first few months I became so accustomed to it that I ceased to notice it at all, though I remember how ashamed I was to have to resort to such device. I told no one but my parents.' *No one,* he added mentally, *other than Jasia, and Titus and, well, perhaps…*

'And so, my dear Madame, I confide to you my secret, for what it is worth, should you care to try the effect of the same means to an end. Your hand,' he took hers, gloved now, in his again, 'is similar to mine in shape, but smaller still: a child's hand. When you first came to me you had ten little sticks inside your fingers. Now, praise be, they have vanished — turned to jelly! From your elbow to your wrist, from your wrist to your fingernails, you are pliable as India rubber. But firm, and strong! You have fairy pads at each fingertip to make the notes sing. You have worked — I know how you have worked to discipline your hands, your arms — like a ballet dancer must discipline her body. I am proud of my pupil but I ask more of her, still. I ask that she learns now how to use her strength. No matter how irksome it may be, study my method of fingering. Practise if you like, away from the piano, on a table, on your knees, when you sit idle for a moment. Practise! Practise! That you may express… There is no joy in the world like the expression of oneself, one's ego, in whatever medium you choose. Yours and mine is music. But, Madame, you are pale. You must not work too hard. That I cannot allow. You are one of the most willing, most painstaking of my pupils. Take a holiday from practice, then. Forget it for a day, two days, a week. Play for pleasure, and in whatever way you will. Never mind your ogre of a teacher. Play Bach, play Mozart, play the masters for your joy. Tomorrow there shall be no horrible tedious exercises at our lesson. You shall play me my new waltz. No one has played it yet but myself. You shall be the first.'

'Thank you, *Maître*, thank you. I can never thank you... You are too kind.'

He released her hand. '*À votre service, Madame la Princesse.*'

Dismissed. She beckoned her maid. Convention demanded a chaperone. If only he would whisper, 'Send away your woman. Why must she intrude upon our privacy? Now we can speak. Now I can tell you...'

But he would never whisper, never tell.

His man came to show her out. She went with a sigh in her heart, and a last backward look at him, who answered with his slow, bittersweet smile, his stiff little bow of a marionette.

'...one of the most willing, most painstaking of my pupils...' One of a hundred: no more, no less. His waltz! And she the first to play it. Was that true? She knew it was not true, unless he had forgotten. But Madame d'Appony had told her with her own lips that she had played it to him the very day that he composed it, and that he had dedicated it to her... *O Mother Mary, in your divine pity, let him dedicate a waltz to me...*

Was such suffering to be endured? Yes, and more. One must suffer crucifixion to be near him, to hear his voice, to earn his praise, to see the warm appreciation in his eyes when her playing pleased him. Others of his pupils, some who were already minor *virtuosi*, complained of his violent temper, his intolerance of clumsy interpretation. Sometimes, when exasperated beyond control, he would snatch ornaments from the mantelshelf and fling them down, and break pencils between his hands, and clutch his hair and shout, 'Is that a dog barking?' How terrible! Thank God that she had never caused him any agony of that sort unless, of course, he considered her unworthy of such torment. Perhaps it was a compliment to incur the wrath of Chopin. Yet he had said she persevered, was willing... Oh, and once, never to be forgotten, he had leaned over her while she was playing Mozart, to say, 'An angel passed in heaven...'

She cherished that memory, lived on it, held it close. 'Willing' — yes, indeed! Willing to die if for one moment he could be made aware of her. *An angel passed in heaven...* But she knew that it was Mozart to whom he spoke, not her. To him, she was a child. He had known her as a child; thought her, perhaps, too young. She looked younger than her years. Her husband often told her so... Her husband! So much a stranger that she never called him by his name in her thoughts of him. What a mockery of marriage!

Long ago — or was it only three years back, her wedding night? — she had been terrified, unutterably shocked, had frightened him in her hysteria, her stupid infantile ignorance. Inexcusable. He had never forgiven her: had never touched her since. Polite, attentive, irreproachable in his courtesy, and nothing more. She was alone, always alone; alone by day, alone by night in his great ugly house; he, a figure in the background, rarely seen except when he appeared with her at functions. Always she was conscious of her youth, her smallness, her lack of charm, of social flair, of repartee, distinction. She could not talk; she had no words. Only her music spoke for her and in the name of Chopin, Chopin … Chopin.

His man, a wooden-faced automaton, bowed her to her carriage, and returned to his master.

'M'sieu?'

'Ah! Yes, Daniel. I shall dine at home and go to bed immediately. I feel chilly. Put a warming pan in my bed. I think I am going to have a cold.'

'Yes, M'sieu.'

'Has the tailor sent my suit?'

'No, M'sieu.'

'Why the devil not? Go and fetch it. I may change my mind and wish to go out tonight. In any case, he has broken his word to me. It was promised for today. Go to him with a message. If the shop is closed, smash down the door. Tell him I will withdraw my custom. It is criminal to disappoint me. Tell him he is the son of a bitch. Tell him — God in heaven! I had forgotten! I *must* go out tonight. I am pledged to appear at the Marquis de Custine's *soirée*. Why didn't you remind me? I shall have to play, and I must rest.'

'Yes, M'sieu. What does M'sieu desire for his dinner?'

'Anything. An omelette. Soup. But hurry, please. You should not have let me forget.'

'I reminded you this morning, M'sieu, when I brought your *petit déjeuner*.'

'Yes, when I was asleep. Never mind. Go now. Be quick. Tell that animal, the tailor, that he will not be paid for the suit. He can take it back or give it to you. No, you are too tall to wear my clothes. Cut it down, then, and give it to your little boy. How is his poor leg? Does the doctor hold out any hope? Will they have to amputate?… My poor Daniel! How hellish of me to worry you with my nonsense when your child is lying in the hospital with his leg crushed to a pulp. Poor little angel! That drayman deserves to be guillotined for not taking more care of a child playing in the road. But he had no *right* to be playing in the road… Here, take this.' He dug in his pocket and drew out a handful of gold and notes. 'Buy him all the toys he wants, and bonbons. How much is there? Count it and take five louis… Be *quiet*, man! Those are my orders. Good God! Don't I spend more than that on *boutonnières*? Hurry now, and put out my things… Sancta Cecilia! To think, thanks to that pig, that I have to appear in last year's suit… You needn't wait up for me. Go and see your boy. I hope your sister is kind to him. You ought to marry again, Daniel, a nice comfortable woman, who could be my cook and live here, and then Jean could come and live here too, and we would all be *en famille* together. No, on second thoughts *don't* marry. She might not want to be my cook and then I should lose you. And she would be sure to ill-treat your poor Jean. The intentions of all stepmothers are murderous… Of all women, except my own beloved mother, for that matter. Leave me then, *mon vieux*. I ought to rest if I intend to go to this insufferable *soirée*. If I don't ring for you in an hour's time, come and call me.'

He flung himself on a couch. His servant placed a cushion behind his head, drew the curtains, lit discreet candles in their silver sconces, his movements, swift and capable, his face impassive; but his eyes, as they rested for a moment on his master where he lay, held something of the moist devotion of a dog.

The door, with its heavy *portière* of purple velvet, closed; the room retreated in a vast obscurity. A pool of light centred on the piano, slid along the polished floor, struck sparks from the winey depths of mahogany and turned the white brocaded furniture to ghosts. A recent portrait of himself stared from the shadowed wall, a pale oblong of a face peering from a dim Rembrandtesque background: neatly chiselled features, raw sienna with clever high-lights of chrome and amber for the hair, a twist to the lips ... mocking? Sardonic?' The artist had spared his nose but over-emphasised the frail articulation of bone structure: too fine, too delicate... *Was* he delicate?

He winced away from that twinge of alarm. His chest... Nonsense! He was not robust, certainly, had always been bronchial, but Jan, and all the doctors had assured him there was nothing organically destructive. Jan, though, poor dear, was himself a sick man. He had lost two stone in weight — a living skeleton. He worked too hard in his laboratory and at that infernal pest-house of a hospital. Shabby as ever, unacknowledged, a sacrifice to science: his life, his brain, his youth, his manhood — all were given and absorbed in perpetual research. Poor Jan! Paris had no place for him, an out-at-elbows doctor with a string of letters but not a penny to his name. No! No place at all for him here in this Paris of human comedies, of free expressions and emotions wrought to highest pitch; a puppet world of insincerities, kaleidoscopic, shifting, the world Chopin had made his own.

His eyes roved, resting on known familiar objects, his... all his. Success substantiated. Even now, after all this time, the novelty had not entirely worn off; the faint surprise that he, the little Chopin, diffident, oafish, shy, he whose sole possession of worth was an emperor's ring, which his father guarded for him in a safe, he who once had owned nothing, not even a watch, was now owner of all this: so much, and yet so little. Trinkets, jewelled snuff-boxes, rare porcelain gleaming from behind the glass panels of a marquetry cabinet, homage of grateful pupils, ardent admirers, personal friends; anonymous gifts or the gratification of a passing whim; cloisonne vases, a jade dragon that had cost — what he would only have thought a fortune. And solitary, aloof, among these lesser things, stood his one treasure, the silver urn that held for him all earthly token of his beloved Poland: static, unalterable.

For the rest, what mattered? Did he compose better music at a Louis Quatorze bureau in a room in the Chaussée d'Antin, than at the little worn old writing desk his mother gave him to furnish his attic under the eaves … at home?

Home! How long, O God — if ever — before he could go home? Letters were not enough and news, when it came, was disquieting. He read between the lines: his mother ailing, *not quite herself.* The winter was so cold, the summer so hot, the servants so tiresome, and Warsaw so changed since the revolution: or it might be old age creeping on… Always defying, as it were, the menace of her illness.

He had not seen her since he had left her standing at the door, waving him away. That memory lingered, unchanged, unforgotten. Was it yesterday? That clear October morning, his little sisters, bright-haired, gold and copper mingled, two Tanagra figurines, entwined; his father, tall, lean-jawed, calm-browed, his shoulders slightly forward; his mother small and bravely cheerful, her face transfigured with her love… Was it really seven years ago?

His mind went searching back.

Vienna…

It had taken him four weeks to get there, breaking the journey on the way at Breslau, Dresden, Prague… Swift impressions, crowding, shifting, nothing saved to cherish; nothing of himself, no contacts, beacon-clear, to light the haze of distance. Even his ultimate destination had been vague. Vienna, Paris, London… yes, London was his Mecca. His passport had been visaed for Paris, with intention of a visit there *en route*: a visit that had lasted seven years! 'I am passing through Paris.' It had become a standing joke. *J'y suis, j'y reste.* He was rooted here now, the seed of his father, a branch of a tree felled from its trunk, to grow and flourish in its natural soil.

That last soul-searing night at the Opera House when he had lost and found himself, had marked the passing of his youth and his awakening. He was left islanded upon a barren ledge between what had been and what was yet to follow. Beyond that he saw nothing: no landmarks, no bearings, no star to guide him; his keyboard and his mind of music his only weapons of defence against a hostile world, against humanity and the dark cloud of his loneliness. Torn prematurely from the protective shell of boyhood, sore and aching with his hurt, he had amplified his disillusionment, dwelt on it, nursed it, brooded. And though he bled, and healed, the scar remained, never entirely to be erased from his smile, sweetly bitter, his facile sardonic humour; youth mocking at its youth with eyes grown bold to meet a woman's glance, and glance away...

His wit sharpened; he had a store of fun to spare at the expense of those who slid and floundered in the debris of emotional concussion, from which he had escaped, young enough still to overemphasise, a trifle, his scorn for such as these; and more than ever now the friend of Titus, who applauded his return to sense.

And what of that second visit to Vienna...? Even after all these years he shrank from the reminder of that long buried but never quite forgotten wound to his pride and conscience. Raw, quivering, from the one deep hurt that he already had received, exposed and sensitised to feel more keenly behind his ineffectual armour of cynicism and defiance, he had been prepared to anoint himself with the soothing unguents of praise, of delighted acclamation at his reappearance: a prophet come from a far country to bring glad tidings… He shook with inward laughter at that quick descent from sublime arrogance, to ridiculous abasement: a puppet shaken to its *papier-mâché* bowels, when the slow purge of realisation had taken its effect, to drain him of all faith in himself, his work, the critics, music, God…

What exactly had he asked for? Homage, engarlanded by insincerities? Applause from the herd? The lowing of cows and calves to drown the howl of a pack of critics?

With what high hopes and letters from the Court of Saxony to the Vice-Queen of Milan and Princess Somebody-or-other in Rome he had started out to conquer all Vienna!

Indescribably tedious were those royal sisters to whom in Dresden he had been presented, and who had so graciously bestowed their patronage on him whose fame had reached even to their deaf ears. But why Milan, Rome, Naples? He had no desire to see Naples and die. Italian opera was never to his taste. However, letters from Their Serene and Ugly Highnesses — merciful God! And what ugliness! Turkey-jowled and bearded, yes positively! Grey hairs sprouting from pendulous chins, their teeth fallen out, their mouths fallen in, talking guttural French: quite revolting. Still, such favour from such source must be all-powerful. He may have bragged a little, or too much, of his acquaintanceship with minor royalties. He may have arrived in Vienna with a swollen head, to say nothing of a swollen nose caused by a mosquito bite that caused him great discomfort and more fear, lest he lose his 'proboscis'. A judgment from God for having so often complained of its size. Better a big nose than no nose at all. Suppose it should be poisoned and the surgeon decide to cut it off to save the poison spreading? He suffered a torment of horrors.

Titus, who had come to meet him in Vienna, had no patience with his fantods and left him to write his misery to Jan. *I am sad and feel so lonely and forsaken here...*

Vanity kept him indoors. He would not pay visits till his nose had returned to its normal proportions. He went to church instead and was haunted in his prayers by painful memories and fragrant ghosts.

I leaned against a pillar in this House of God, so, in his letter to Jan. *The grandeur of the arched roof cannot be described: one must see St Stephen's with one's own eyes to believe it. Around me reigned a profound silence. The echoing footsteps of the sacristan who came to light the candles sounded loud in that lonely place. Behind me was a grave, before me a grave, only above me I saw none... When the lights were burning, and the cathedral began to fill with people, I wrapped myself up more closely in my cloak and hastened to my lodgings to indulge in melancholy fantasies on my piano, and then to dream ... of her.*

Dreams, always dreams... But Vienna was awaiting him. He had only to say, 'Open Sesame', and all doors would be flung wide. He, Chopin, would be omnipotent... His health improved. He put on weight. His nose had ceased to swell. He could now be seen and would announce himself. There would be invitations. Concerts, publishers (Haslinger?) on their knees to him. He had some good scores to his credit. A sonata, two concertos, a new set of Variations.

Vienna was in gracious winter mood: the air like sparkling Moselle, the sky clear, the ladies lovely, and he enchanted. All was as it had been: everyone delighted to renew acquaintance with him. Thalberg and Moscheles were giving concerts. The halls were packed to hear them. He went too, and listened, unimpressed; perhaps a trifle green-eyed. *Thalberg plays famously but he is not my man. He is younger than I.* (Something of a blow, that.) *He seems to please the ladies, plays pot-pourris, and the fortes and pianos with the pedal, but not with the hand, takes tenths as easily as I take octaves, and wears diamond studs in his shirt.* As for Moscheles — *He does not astonish me. He too writes concertos.*

Let the ladies pant and flutter round that precious pair. Chopin could bide his time. There was work to be done and finished. He had a polonaise, some more mazurkas, waltzes, *But they are not intended for dancing.* Though Vienna did nothing else. *They call waltzes* work*s here…* His were different. His waltzes *were* works. Not to be danced, to be played.

And then…

How and when did he first come to realise that Vienna's memory was short, and the name of Chopin insignificant? Chopin? A Pole? The name sounds French. Who is he? Nobody. Nobody at all. What has he done? Nothing. Some national dances: mazurkas, they call them. A waltz or two. Not to be compared to Strauss. He says himself you can't dance to them… Almost only waltzes were published now. (And Haslinger had politely refused his!) Should he hide himself for shame or affect indifference? Hold his tongue? Be silent. Bury the disgrace. Forget it. But who could?

He was unremembered. The concerts he had given only two years since, had left no more impression than the dawn mist that rose from the Vistula at home. All Vienna danced to the waltzes of Johann Strauss, father of another Strauss destined to be more famous. Beethoven, Mozart, Bach were now *démodé*. Let us be gay! But Chopin was not gay. If French blood flowed in his veins, he had Slav marrow in his bones — and gall in his heart when Haslinger, having refused his waltzes, refused also his concerto.

He had been half-blinded by that blow between the eyes, and wholly stunned. Haslinger refuse to publish *him*, while he grovelled hands and knees before that popinjay, that strutting showman dancing master, Strauss? Not possible.

Titus laughed at him. 'Why make yourself ill over it? There are a thousand music publishers in this great world, and Haslinger is only one of them.'

Slowly, painfully, but still incredulous, he was forced at last to realise that Vienna had no use for the 'brilliant young pianist' whom, when he had played two years before, all the critics lauded to high heaven; nor was he urged to play again. But play he must, to save his face. And play he did, at one negligible concert in the only booking offered him — off season, when all society and musical Vienna had left for their summer haunts. The critics, yawning in their seats, had scribbled a few bored notes and left before the programme ended. Most of the papers ignored his performance entirely. The *Allgemeine Musikalische Zeitung*, that once with sickly gush had fawned upon him, dwelt at ecstatic length upon his fellow countryman Serwaczyński (who for a brief interval shone, a flashing meteor, to sink unrecognised and die unknown), and dismissed in three lines:

...Chopin, who is also from the Polish capital. In the execution of his concerto in E Minor, we see no reason to revoke our former judgment of one who deserves our genuine esteem.

Also from the Polish capital! An also-ran beside one whose name had never once been heard in his home town! What irony! He laughed while his flesh shrank from the cut; laughed and tore the paper into rage, plastered his hurt with a swaggering indifference, and turned a brazen front to the swine who kicked him down… He'd rise again. They couldn't kill him or the music he held within, to be released in his own time. Given time he'd show these carping critics that they had scorned a master. Only wait!

But self-boasting could not restore self-confidence. A fanfare blown from his own trumpet could not penetrate beyond his own four walls. He was losing faith, was sick at heart, and apprehensive of his future. If in Vienna he was no more than a nonentity, would London and Paris, perhaps, disclaim him, too? The English! That most unmusical of all nations. Paris? But how could he conquer Paris in a fortnight? He was only passing through. London was his goal, though God alone knew why. Perhaps because he feared a sterner audience than those beef-eating John Bulls, who would take him as they found him, and didn't know Handel's *Messiah* from 'God Save the King'. Surely to bank on London for success was to admit himself a failure. Would life hold nothing for him now but the applause of English bulls? Must all his hopes lie shrivelled in the dust, a fall of autumn leaves in springtime … a dead orchard?

Plunged in melancholy, he wept himself out at his piano, but wrote nothing. His creative sense was numbed. He needed a further shock, some mental volcanic eruption as a stimulus to vigorous activity. He had gone stale on himself.

The shock, when it came, was a thunderclap: Warsaw had risen in revolt against the Russians.

The patience of Poland, that for fifteen years had endured the capricious and despotic rule of the Czar's brother, the Grand Duke Constantin, was at last depleted. Inflamed by the example of the July revolution in Paris, the youth of Poland massed their forces in the capital, and with banners flying and a herd of peasants at their heels armed with pitchforks, pikes, rakes and muskets, marched forward in united purpose to avenge their wrongs.

At the first news from home of the insurrection, Titus rushed from Vienna to join the rebel army. There was no holding him. His lazy nonchalance, his pose of cynicism, all his affectations were discarded. A stranger, eagle-eyed, sword unsheathed to strike at any who would stay him, stood revealed. 'My place is with my people. I must go.'

'I too ... I must be with you.'

Even now he could not recall that moment without a flush of shame. Titus had said, hard-lipped, his voice knife-edged, '*You* can't! What — *you*?'

Contempt? Sarcasm? What lay behind that curt denial — love?

'Yes, I. Why not?' Quivering, stung, he was on his feet, hands fisted at his sides. 'It is *my* country, too. My people. My place is there beside you.'

'No. Your place...' A flicker of those stone-bright eyes, a pause. 'Your place is here. You have your niche in your own sanctuary. You are one of the chosen — to remain.'

As a lay figure? A weakling, not built to bear the sword of a crusader: a pampered toy, a musical box. Let others shed their blood to spare him his for the little it was worth — to be spat up in a fit of coughing in his handkerchief.

'You think I'm not strong enough, physically? Is that it?' No reproach upon him as a man. Blame nature.

'Neither physically, nor...' Again that glance had probed to make him shrink still smaller, 'nor mentally,' said Titus. 'You could not fight as men must fight. You'd break. You would spew out your bowels to see the sights that must be seen.'

'I can see them now in my mind's eye. Have I no imagination?'

A smile hovered for a moment behind that stranger's mask. 'You have too much. You have also work to do that must be done. You can serve Poland better by saving than by giving your life for her. As one of a million soldiers you would not be missed. As Chopin you can never be replaced.'

His laugh rang out staccato, harsh, to snap the thread of tension. 'You flatter me!'

'No, my Fryck, God only could do that.' Then Titus kissed him warm and fiercely, and was gone...

Life narrowed to a time of waiting for fresh news and letters from home, between long intervals of despair, suspense, and loneliness unbearable... An exile in a foreign land hiding behind the plea of his ill health while his country bled and suffered. God! How to endure it? Why had he not gone with Titus? What had held him back? Not cowardice. He had never been a coward; he had no fear of death, though he did fear annihilation of himself, his ego, externalised in music. But if he could not give his life for Poland, he could give his soul in titanic utterance...

Thunder reverberated through those wakeful nights to shake the house, when, alone with his torment of anxiety, vision multiplied to reproduce itself in strident battle-hymns, the clatter of arms, the tramp of feet, the shouts of victory and challenge, a giant's protest against his puny frame. He remembered how when news came of Warsaw's capitulation he had been racked to the verge of madness, hearing no word from his parents, sisters, friends. The fevered jottings in his diary record it:

O God! Do you exist? Do you exist and not avenge us? Have the Muscovites not committed crimes enough for you? Or are you too, a Muscovite? Are you a Czar?...

143

He saw his parents murdered, his mother ... sisters... Horror heaped itself on horror. His scribbled ravings testified to a mind if not entirely unhinged, a trifle dislocated. His pen screamed of ghosts and corpses.

In this very bed where I am lying now perhaps more than one corpse has lain... I too, am a corpse. A corpse knows nothing of its father, mother, sisters, Titus, Jan... All these perhaps are corpses. As cold as I am now. Death is the best and Birth the worst state of being...

A shameful exhibition of hysteria, but he had kept it for no other reason than to show the world that never in the written word would Chopin find his medium. It might be of interest to his descendants. If he married.

The 'Revolt' Polonaise in E Flat Minor was his first musical reaction to the agony he suffered when he heard of Warsaw's downfall. Hugely heroic, breathing defiance in smothered explosions, and gloomy war cries ending in an important death rattle. Melodramatic. Not his best. Almost his worst. Unworthy. He had believed it unpublishable and it had remained so for six years. But nothing now would ever stay unpublished, unless he wished it... That abortion had been followed by the spirited lusty 'Militaire', not to be published yet. Not bad. Not good. It would need further revision before he offered it. Paris would take anything he cared to give. Paris had taken his Grand Polonaise in E Flat, preceded by the graceful *Andante Spianato*, and dedicated to Madame la Baronne d'Este. Poor stuff and much too long.

His head moved restlessly upon the silken cushion. His eyelids opened, gazing on the room. The delicate half-tones of grey, chalk white and lavender were blended in the sheen of purple curtains, in the grape-bloom dusk of shadows, fragrant with the breath of violets massed in bowls on tables, the piano, all about him. Luxury, comfort, ease…

Yes, it had all been much too easy. Not for him the stone of Sisyphus, the weary climb to reach the heights. His work might have been greater if he had fought against life's violent rebuffs in the struggle for existence, to be dragged down instead of borne aloft on the pinions of success.

There had been one blank period but not long enough sustained to leave a scar. He had arrived in Paris with letters of introduction to Kalkbrenner, that gouty old curmudgeon and greatest of all teachers, who had brought him into contact with a constellation of musical celebrities under whose dazzling light he stood eclipsed: the glimmer of a tallow candle blinking in obscurity beneath the radiance of all the stars in heaven… Mendelssohn, Rossini, Berlioz, Liszt, and the cellist Franchomme, who was to share with Jan and Titus a friendship that endured till death… and afterwards, in cherished tokens saved to give the world.

Mendelssohn… The wonderful young man who had taken all Europe by storm, and before whom, at first sight of him at a concert in Berlin, a raw youngster in his teens had sat, awe-struck, and too humble to obtrude upon his notice; he, Mendelssohn, received him in his own exclusive circle… received him. Yes, but each man for himself, and God for all.

Mendelssohn had found a name for him: 'Chopinetto'. A startling coincidence, though he had schooled himself to hear it without flinching. He had learned to hold his tongue. While 'Romantics' flourished all around him, his own romance must lie for ever dead; no dragging out of dusty memories to be served up as a *bonne-bouche* in the daily menu of confidence and gossip in the cafés of Montmartre. No, not even to enhance his self-importance among his brother-artists who boasted of their *amours* and *amourettes* could he speak of that which he had buried with his youth. He was still young enough to wish himself much older.

It was Kalkbrenner who helped him to arrange his first concert. Kalkbrenner, who had offered to teach him gratis for three years and had been bitterly offended when he refused. It had needed some courage to stand up to the pernickety old fool, whom Heine so aptly described as a *bon-bon that has been rolled in the mud*, but he had done it, fortified by Elsner to whom he had written for advice before he committed himself.

Elsner's reply that *piano-playing is, after all, only a subsidiary branch of music — Mozart and Beethoven were both accomplished players, but as composers they overshadow any achievements at the keyboard*, decided him. He would take no more lessons. He would follow his own method of instruction, and trust to luck.

But luck was not disposed just then to favour him. Kalkbrenner showed a god-like magnanimity by offering, not only to promote his first concert, but by composing a perfectly atrocious sextette for it, in which he, Hiller, Chopin, and several more were to take part at six pianos. The proposal was met with no enthusiasm. Chopin? Who was Chopin? And who would buy tickets to hear him? None in Paris, certainly… Strange to think that there had ever been a time when in order to get a hearing in Paris, he had to pay for the hire of a hall, and to be paid nothing, not a *sou*, for his performance: an artist cannot live on art alone.

For the first time in his life he had faced poverty. His money dwindled to a bare sufficiency to last a month. He could not write home for more. The revolution had drained his father's limited resources. He must stand or fall by his own efforts. While his friends were ready enough to render him lip service and advice, his future darkened. He had been persuaded to give another gratuitous performance in Pleyel's rooms, and in aid of the Polish refugees; but on this occasion, although his name had been starred on the bill, it was not he, but an oboe player who enraptured the audience, while the critics dismissed him with the usual complaint of *the small volume of tone which M. Chopin draws from the piano*, and his concerto with the hope that *the music of this artist will appeal more to public taste when it becomes better known.*

So, he must appeal to public taste or starve! Offer his musical conscience in exchange for a meal. Too proud to borrow from his new acquaintances in Paris, or for that matter, from his old friends in Warsaw, he wrote to Titus frothing of his financial worries, although his letters at this time were all a repetitive dirge:

How I long to have you here beside me ... I have no one with whom I can sigh. My heart beats, as it were, in syncopation. When shall we see each other again? Perhaps never. I am tormented with gloomy presentiments, unrest, bad dreams, sleeplessness, and indifference to everything — no desire to live — and no courage to die. In short, I can't describe my feelings.

Which, when all was said, amounted to nothing more than an empty stomach. But this Titus did not know, nor was he told until such time as one could make a joke of it. As for his health, he caught cold upon cold and developed a bothering cough. He saw a doctor who laid an ear to his chest, pulled a long face, ordered him south for the winter, and charged him two louis, which left him with five.

He sweated at night, ran a fever by day, and was hungry. Five louis stood between starvation and defeat. It would be too humiliating to be compelled to return to Warsaw to live upon his parents who had all to do to keep themselves. Since the revolution his father's school had been closed, and his savings swallowed by his wife's illness that only death could cure.

And so he came down to his last ten francs, and to the end of his tether. Nothing left to him but to acknowledge his failure, eat his pride, and go round with the hat. Liszt and Mendelssohn between them might lend him enough for the journey home: when he got there he would sell his ring — the Czar's ring — to repay it. He could always give music lessons. Prince Radziwill had once suggested he should teach his talented young daughter, Marcelline. He might scrape together enough pupils among his wealthy patrons in Warsaw to earn a living, and when he had sufficient in his pocket for the voyage, he'd sail to America to find his fortune.

Meanwhile he was hard put to it to find a meal.

It was a wintry afternoon with snow in the sky, a biting wind in the air, and few pedestrians abroad when he left his humble lodgings in the Boulevard Poissonnière, and turned towards more fashionable quarters. If he could not afford to eat, he could feast his eyes upon the sights that Paris offered and so forget his troubles in the lively motion of the streets, the carriages dashing past, the spirited horses, the dazzling shop windows, the gay, bold colours of women's dresses, jewels... These always had a fascination for him. He paused to gaze at a display of trinkets, bracelets, rings, snuff-boxes, here for his choosing, and in imagination to enter and to buy.

Was it providence or accident that guided him, just then, to the Rue de la Paix?

To most of us there comes in life a day, perhaps a moment, of significance, that may be set aside in memory as a centrifugal force from which all other points converge. All history is founded upon trifles: a queen's necklace, a game of bowls, the blind eye of England's sailor, or the sword of Sobieski, Poland's hero. Such trifles floated into legend, become static, to endure when the greatest of events, calamities or triumphs are forgotten. So it may be that had he not on one cold sunless day halted before that trinket shop, taken with a snuff-box set in pearls and exquisitely enamelled in a design of shepherds and shepherdesses dancing at a *fête champêtre*, so microscopic that one had to strain to see them; had he not paused to peer just at that moment when Prince Radziwill descended from his carriage to enter there, Chopin's story might have stayed untold, and the echo of his music lost, unheard…

But why speculate? The fact remains that fate had turned the scales when Chopin turned his steps towards that shop.

Prince Radziwill!

Even now he could not recall that moment without a jerk of his heart and the ache of tears unshed. A friend from home, here in this alien Paris; a friend who was more than a patron, almost a father, and in his loving-kindliness, a god.

'Why, Fryck! my dear, dear boy…' From under the curved hat-brim, above the chin-high sable collar of his coat, those mild, slightly prominent grey eyes had searched, incredulous and anxious. 'Is it true? Dear child!'

The sound of his own tongue, the affectionate warmth of that greeting, had all but unmanned him. He croaked an answer. 'Prince! When … how…? I had no idea you were in Paris. When did you arrive?'

Some days ago, it seemed, and he had always the intention of seeking out his little Fryck whose good parents had furnished him with the address. 'But you know how it is —' the familiar spread of the hands, the vague smile — 'so many calls to make, and commissions for my wife — my daughters.' Time flew, and he was here for only a few weeks before returning…

Actually, he was seeking a house in Paris for his family. It was his intention to make his residence here — a rueful shrug. 'Warsaw is quite impossible. No longer the capital of our beloved land, but a colony of Russia, swarming with Cossacks, Muscovites, and every kind of vermin. No self-respecting Pole given the chance or sufficient means to escape, could endure to live there under such conditions...'

And what now of Frédéric? What were his plans? What arrangements for the season? His good friend, Monsieur Chopin, had told of some minor disappointments in Vienna. But what could one expect of such a people — a race of children, these Austrians, as effervescent as their own sparkling wine. Charming, charming — but for music? No taste, no sensibility. They were completely superficial... Yes, he had heard of this craze for Johann Strauss and his waltzes, that had set all Vienna jigging. They said also that Strauss was jealous of his seven-year-old son, who was already writing better waltzes than his father! 'But how is this, my child? You look ill. You are thinner... you must not be so thin.' That pale glance had hovered, but did not penetrate beyond the outward visibility of dress; the lavender suit, the irreproachable neck-cloth, the waisted greatcoat and tall hat — one of the new 'chimney-pots' bought in Vienna, straight from London: nothing there to tell of the rat that gnawed a hole in his inside. He would sooner die of hunger than go shabby.

'You look,' the Prince said, 'much too frail. How is that?'

Try starvation, he just saved himself from saying. 'I have not,' he said, 'been well.'

'Ah!' The Prince wagged a roguish finger encased in yellow suede. 'Too many late nights, too much gaiety, festivity and entertaining — eh?'

Entertaining nightmares, corpses, and the devil's own cough… 'Perhaps.'

They laughed together; sharing the *double entendre* of those late nights. The Prince was pleased to flatter his little Fryck, now grown into a man to taste the gaiety of Paris, as men should.

'Well now,' the Prince cast an absent eye upon the jeweller's glass front, 'what did I come to buy in here? This unexpected sight of you, dear Frédéric, has driven all thought from my head…'

Never at the best of times, too full… Perish the disloyalty. An angel.

'*N'importe*! It will keep. A little gift for my dear friend, la Baronne de Rothschild. It is her birthday. *Ma foi!* Of course. Today. Tonight … I must send her at once a little *affaire*. Come with me to choose it.'

'I have been admiring this…' No. Madame la Baronne would not, of course, take snuff.

They entered. The Prince spent half an hour making up his mind before he bought a bracelet for the price of six months' lodgings and one year's solid food.

'Now, my dear, we will drive to my hotel and you shall tell me all your doings…' And with any luck be offered dinner? He was, however, offered nothing but an invitation from the Prince to accompany him to the Baroness de Rothschild's that night.

The turning point.

Looking back upon it now it seemed fate must have had a hand in it to set the stage, and cast him as chief player in that scene chosen with a master's eye for decorative effect.

Too nervous to be conscious of the hole inside his stomach, he complied with the request of his hostess to play.

'Prince Radziwill has spoken with great enthusiasm of you, Monsieur. If all he says is true, we have a treat in store…'

Clearly Madame la Baronne did not believe in Prince Radziwill's superlatives. Blandly polite, she uttered banalities with the dignity of a Sheba. Her voluminous breadth of yellow velvet increased rather than detracted from her stature. She towered immense, superb, ablaze. Her great black eyes outrivalled the dazzle of her diamonds. Behind all that elaboration of smiles, queenliness and poise, her warmth, her generosity, her simple womanhood was all-embracing.

He remembered he had played as encore a nocturne, and how she came to him where he stood trembling, awkward, and so empty that his inside squeaked its protest, heard, happily, by none above the shouts of unrestrained applause… Yes, these people, the elect of Paris, had stamped and called for him as though they were the rabble of the streets. The ladies wept and laughed and split their gloves in the prettiest show of hysterics; all the gentlemen were cheering, and the baroness, her regality forgotten, while tears blackened with mascara rolled unheeded down her cheeks, had kissed his hands. 'You wonderful, wonderful boy! I am dumbfounded. Are you an angel from heaven? Who are you? *What* are you?'

'I am hungry, Madame.'

It was out, and his mouth stayed open with the shock of his own words. Let the earth swallow him now! Let him die.

She threw back her head and laughed to show all her white teeth, her red palate. 'My poor child! How incredibly thoughtless of me! But your exquisite playing has made me forget my duties. Have you not yet supped?'

He was saved, and she charmed at his modesty that turned her homage aside with a debonair gesture; deliciously gauche.

'I too, am hungry. Come with me and we will eat and drink together. Come, all of you and drink a toast to…Tell me your name again. That, too, I have forgotten…'

Seven years ago. And from that night he had gone marked with the brand of success: the protégé of Rothschilds, to be exploited as Madame la Baronne's own discovery, a new star in the musical firmament, outshining all before him. Liszt, Kalkbrenner, Hiller, even Mendelssohn paled in the light of Chopin's glory. Pupils flocked to his door in the Chaussée d'Antin. He could afford to be selective and turned many away, taking a first choice of talent. Concert managers outbid each other for his name upon their programmes. He had all Paris in his pocket and a balance in the bank. Lionised by society, acclaimed by the public, envied by his fellow artists, his progress was a triumphal march along the road to fame. Life went to the beating of drums, with flags flying, gay and splendid. Seven months of poverty against seven years of fortune's favour. Luck? Call it luck if you like. He deserved it. He had something to give … something that would live long after him; more and yet more to create. Time was short, and life full.

He turned uneasily upon his couch; his eyes closed… Yes, life was full, but not full enough: always somewhere a sense of frustration, an emptiness: always a striving for that which lay far beyond reach. His soul yearned for the unattainable that only perfection could satisfy: the perfection of art, god-like, remote, unrealised save in a moment's ecstasy, to snatch at vision dizzily revealed, and hear it fade in song too faint for capture, the descent from heights imagined and untouched; the ache, the loss, the loneliness of strangled birth and melodies unsung. In love alone would he find peace: in adoration and surrender, his fulfilment. He had sought and almost found it, to be flung back again upon himself, disowned and disillusioned.

But he was older now. Such hurts could not cut deep with inward bleeding. He had been perhaps too certain of his victory, had been repaid in his own coin.

It had begun as an amusement for them both, the lightest of flirtations... He would always think of her as a child, for all she was a woman, a mischievous elfish thing, dark and lovely as he saw her that first night here in Paris when he, to his undoing, had met Maria Wodzińska again.

No doubt she led him on to let him down. She was notorious for her caprices, with a host of victims to her name and her discredit. Scandal hovered, predatory, to pounce. There was the titbit of her escapade to Dijon with her coiffeur. Shocking! And entirely untrue. Other tales, highly spiced, were constantly recurring. Her mama was in a fret to see her placed.

She had come to him for lessons, and he had refused to teach her. That began it: none before had dared deny her what she wanted... If it were only music lessons that she wanted!

'You are afraid of me!' She stood there in this very room, with the devil's smile in her face and a rose in her hair. She had come to him alone and unattended one evening last July to tell him that ... and more.

'You are afraid.'

'Who would not be afraid of beauty, Mademoiselle?'

'Ah! If I could think you meant... But I know better. It is not me you fear. No! Nor my beauty. Do you really find me beautiful? Am I changed from the stupid little schoolgirl you kissed when ... you remember?'

'Who could possibly forget?'

He smiled, and she stamped and blushed pink as the rose in her hair. 'I could hate you for the way you look: the way you purse that girlish mouth of yours. Are you a cynic? A misogynist? I am told that you hate women. Do you hate me?'

He could but look at her, and shake his head, while his pulses raced to her nonsense.

'Or do you refuse to teach me because I have no talent ... am not worthy to be taught by Chopin? But I knew you once as ... Fryck!'

Her voice was shaking with tears — or laughter? He strove madly for control. Oh, she was beautiful, with her deep-fringed eyes that held two golden dancing imps, her ripe young mouth, her hair, black and fragrant as the summer night.

'You should not have come here.'

He had attempted, primly, to reprove her, make her see reason, be rid of her for her own sake and his, since he was almost gone, and past himself. He had his hand on the bell-rope to call his servant. Yes! A mighty effort that, for if ever man was tempted... But she was at him with a drenching sweetness in her eyes, her words, her fluttering breath... Good God! One should have been cast iron to resist her... And he had not resisted. But who could?

'So now you will follow me to Marienbad, my Fryck. Promise me you will. You will? You will?'

To the ends of the earth, if she asked it with her lips on his, and all her lovely body for his taking... He had enough sense left to save her from that last crowning folly: just sense enough to keep his head, though she lost hers.

'No promises. Go now.'

'I can't! I can't ... I love you. I've loved you all my life. I shall love you for ever.'

'No... For God's sake!'

He laughed, wry-mouthed, remembering how so nearly he had been seduced; how at his final ebb he had dispossessed himself of her and her persuasion; and how he had the strength of mind to summon aid, he never knew.

'You beast! Cruel monster! Cruel! You — you rang the bell!' Hysterics, pouts, more tears, a swift last kiss before the door was opened.

'*Oui, M'sieu?*'

'Mademoiselle left her bracelet when she came for her lesson this morning.'

Daniel, discreet, cat-footed, took his cue. 'The room shall be searched, M'sieu.'

'Tomorrow. Mademoiselle must not be detained. Are you positive, Mademoiselle Maria, that you wore your bracelet this morning? I do not myself recollect it.'

'No... Yes... No. Perhaps not... Oh!' She breathed fire at him as she turned in her billowing muslins away. 'Pray don't give yourself and your man the trouble to search, Monsieur Chopin. It is of no consequence ... I *hate* it! And if it is lost, so much the better. Call a *voiture* for me, if you please. Goodnight.'

'My servant will escort you home, Mademoiselle.'

Yes, he had saved her from that folly, only to commit a worse. What had induced him to follow her to Marienbad? Or what induced his father to choose that of all spas for his cure?

Accident again? But accident in this case might have been averted. She, fired by his first rejection, tried again. Was she shameless? Yes, irresistibly, adorably. What was it had been said of England's Byron? *Mad, bad and dangerous...*

Dangerous indeed. He had been paralysed, made drunk with the sheer joy of her; pledged, betrothed, handfasted, a few hours after his arrival, with her father's blessing, her brothers' cheers, and the gracious sanction of her mama who once had spurned him. But Chopin was now a match for any girl... And he a Benedick? Ah, well! He could go back to Warsaw, write music and live like a prince on the generous portion of Wodzinski's only daughter. Meantime he *must* go back to Paris for his concert. She would follow after, in a month.

A month.

Much may happen in a month. In a week. Worlds may crash and dynasties may fall in a few hours, in a day... It took three, to be exact, before she jilted him in the cruellest of sweet letters, that arrived an hour before he was due to play at Pleyel's rooms with all Paris there to hear him.

He played, and never better. The world would never know that Chopin had been thrown over by the artful, heartless, heart-breaking Wodzińska.

But the world did know. She took good care it should, when she announced the news of her engagement to Count Skarbek.

So much for that. Did he regret it? Not perhaps irrevocably. His pride, not his heart, had been scratched. He preferred to think so, and forget.

But had he quite forgotten? Or was this ache of loneliness, this stifling melancholy that drifted down upon him like a fog, merely the symptom of his illness? For, in all truth, he was ill. Damned ill. And coughing blood sometimes, a pure bright stain upon his handkerchief. Alarming.

He worked too hard. He needed a long holiday, a rest in some dear peaceful place ... at home. He was so very tired.

He must sleep.

'M'sieu?'

What now? Another day?

He woke blinking to the mild beam of candles and Daniel's face above his own, composed.

'It is eight o'clock, M'sieu. Will M'sieu dine?'

'Ah, yes! My dinner … and my suit! Has it arrived?'

It had: laid out in readiness upon his bed. Never such a suit! Skin-fitting, raven blue; a floral waistcoat, primrose gloves, blue satin cravat.

'But this tailor is a master! A superman! Without him what am I? He is forgiven! Come dress me, Daniel, heat your tongs, and curl my hair…'

Chopin stood, the finished article, before his mirror. 'We will make a sensational entrance,' he said, 'at the Marquis de Custine's tonight.'

NINE

He had timed it to advantage, to the minute when the vast rooms were not yet so overcrowded with celebrities that any one of them might pass unnoticed, and the host was not yet wearied of receiving.

There he stood, the little marquis, at the head of his grand staircase, small and monkeyish, his cone-shaped silver head a-bob, his wizened face split into innumerable smiling grimaces, his thin, ringed nervous hands gesticulating an accompaniment to the ceaseless stream of talk that flowed in a cracked falsetto from his painted lips, as though he were a clockwork doll that would — that *must* — run down at any moment, placed in an attitude backed by crimson velvet curtains... What a house! A palace.

Even now, although well enough accustomed to the mansions of the chosen who sat at the feet of Louis Philippe, even now when princesses and Rothschilds bowed to the name of Chopin, he was still a little over-awed by the lackeyed pomp and extravagant circumstance of which the Marquis de Custine's establishment was a most shining example.

Situated in the Faubourg St Honoré, approached by a courtyard under a porte-cochere on which the arms of the de Custines were flagrantly emblazoned, it had survived two revolutions and would possibly survive a third.

The grounds, enclosed within high walls, were not extensive but elaborately ornate, and gemmed with twinkling fairy lights that vied with the Milky Way in the sky's black river. Behind vast plate-glass windows, reflected in countless mirrors, the colourful guests paraded, the gowns of the ladies scarcely less varied though more brilliant in hue than those of their more sober-suited partners. The painted ceiling, supported by Corinthian columns, depicted sophisticated cupids, nymphs pursued by satyrs, bacchantes at their revels and naked gods and goddesses at love.

A pale guard of statues lined the staircase walls: all the chimneypieces were of carven marble, all pilasters, panels, cornices, of gilt; these and the crimson flush of carpets, hangings, brocade upholstery and gilded furniture, were repeated in prismatic rays from crystal lustres.

The curtains had been drawn aside, revealing in the upper windows a full view of the entertainment to a huddled group of spectators in the street below, who had come from their sewers to stand in their rags and gaze with wonder at this vision of a world as far removed from theirs as hell from heaven.

Chopin, assurance fortified by his elegant new suit and the appraising glances it attracted from all sexes, returned his host's effusive welcome with a soupçon of condescension, as from one who knew himself to be the guest of honour.

'How good — how good of you to come, my dear — my dear!' gushed the little marquis. He said everything twice to give point to his words and when he had said all had said nothing. 'I despaired of you, I did indeed — indeed! I thought never, never will Chopin come tonight — in the height of the season. I know how you are in demand — in such demand! And now that you are here —' The marquis pawed his sleeve — 'now that you are here, my friend, I have not the courage, positively not the courage to ask you to play for us. That would be too much — too much. If you would. If only, if only you would! But no! I am the most despicable of mortals to suggest

— ah! My dear — my dear Madame la Baronne! How I am enchanted —'

Chopin, his lips pursed in a smile, his eyes everywhere, passed on, and took his stance conveniently near a marble column behind which, should undesirables approach, he could seek shelter. From that vantage he surveyed, a trifle superciliously, the scene, acknowledging bows and greetings, and carefully avoiding those whom he wished not to see.

The Marquis de Custine's company was acknowledged to be mixed. At his *soirées* the low inhabitants of Bohemia mingled with the high nobility of France. The Marquis de Custine favoured the arts; he favoured the Romantics; he followed Saint-Simon, adored Chateaubriand and loved no woman but his mother, who had been fifteen years dead. He received all the painters, the writers, the poets. Society flocked to his house certain to meet there all the old lions, some new ones, and some embryonic.

Tonight Chopin noticed, however, none present who was not the elect — of both worlds.

Balzac, his cascade of double chins sagging on a wide expanse of soiled shirt front, hands crossed on his paunch, lolled on a yellow plush sofa with a worshipping dowager either side of him, while his ironic glance recorded the kaleidoscopic pattern of yet another *Comédie Humaine*... A mastermind buried in a wall of flesh, corpulent, oily, florid, he affected an eccentric nonchalance to fashion and wore a moth-eaten, grease-befouled suit and diamonds on dirty fingers. He talked little, but nothing escaped his keen eyes, the only striking feature in that flabby-lipped Friar Tuck face. He had run through two fortunes, was always in debt and spent the immense sums his books brought him in aping his betters — the aristocrats — in luxurious living, carriages, mistresses, horses, priceless *objets d'art* and horticulture; had prefixed a *de* to his name, and yet came to a *soirée* unwashed… *Astonishing creature,* mused Chopin. A rare enchanter touched with magic, imprisoned in a tower of obesity; a vulgarian destined to rank among immortals, perhaps to live for ever as the greatest penman of his age.

His lips framed a voiceless response to Balzac's nod of greeting, then the heavy bulk heaved itself from its seat, bowed right and left to the ladies, and strutted on absurdly small feet towards him.

'Ah, my old! How goes it? Exquisite as ever, I see. Why do we come to these performances? Do I come to gaze upon you — or do you come to gaze upon me?' His voice, deep in his throat and thickened with catarrh, rasped unpleasantly upon the ear. Without waiting for a comment or reply to his remark, which indeed called for none, his face, expressionless save for those black, piercing eyes fixed on Chopin with a look that seemed to bare him to his bones, Balzac continued, 'I feel in highest fettle. I have discovered *la rose bleue* for which London and Brussels have offered a reward of five hundred thousand francs.'

'Tu dis, dis-tu?' murmured Chopin.

'On which undertaking,' Balzac, with elephantine doggedness, pursued, 'I am prepared, in my turn to offer interest of five thousand francs for the immediate loan of twenty thousand.'

'Twenty thousand! I owe my tailor double that.'

A sound like a sigh filtered up from those ponderous depths concealed beneath a waistcoat whose pattern was erased by countless dried droppings of food. 'I had not really any hope. Perhaps your friend, Monsieur le Baron —' he mouthed the word fruitily, 'de Rothschild — Do not he and his family finance the world?'

'The subject of finance,' said Chopin tiredly, 'is beyond my —' His breath caught on a cough. Pressing his handkerchief to his lips, he stifled the spasm while, eyes narrowed, his face a bulbous mask, Balzac, imperturbable as ever, watched him.

'You are thin, my little one. Too thin. You should take a holiday in Switzerland. The mountain air —'

'I detest mountain air,' Chopin, frowning, interrupted. 'And one is better too thin,' he pointed a glance, 'than too fat.'

For the first time Balzac laughed to show his yellow fangs and shake his chins. 'Come, then!' He placed a hand on Chopin's shoulder and propelled him forward. 'Come! I have a mighty thirst upon me. I could drink a hogshead of good wine. I am told de Custine's cellar is quite fabulous. But,' he lowered his voice to a whisper, 'let us at all costs avoid Dumas. He is hard on our heels. My physique, I grant you, has its disadvantages. I cannot hide behind a pillar as you can... Ah! Too late!'

Tall, massive, his gestures flamboyant, his waistcoat too floral, his magnificent teeth exposed in a grin to the molars, Dumas, uncrowned King of Romance, extended a hand to each.

'Chopin! Balzac! Well met! Three champions of art — three musketeers! My God!' He released a hand to clap his forehead. 'What a title! What a title for —' A dramatic cough choked utterance. Hastily drawing from his breast pocket a silken handkerchief, he held it to his lips.

'Et tu, Brute?' smiled Chopin, bittersweet.

'I suffer,' Dumas rolled his eyes, 'from a slight summer infection. I sweat at night and cough by day. I hope — I trust — I am assured by my physician — nothing phthisical.'

Chopin's smile broadened. Producing from under his coat-tails a gold snuff-box, he delicately inhaled.

Dumas shuddered. 'How you *can*! An abominable habit. It would kill me.'

'Nothing,' muttered Balzac, 'will ever kill you.'

'Nothing indeed,' retorted Dumas, glaring, while a coppery flush surged upward to his eyebrows. 'Neither success nor — rivalry.'

'Alexander the Great,' Balzac said, suave, 'has no rival. But success makes corpses of us all...'

From a distant corner of the room where her husband politely had placed her beyond accessible range of himself, Marcelline Czartoryska watched him whom she had come to see. If he did not address one word to her or send one look in her direction, she was content to sit, and gaze, and listen to the whisper of his music in her ears. Perhaps the marquis would induce him to play.

Hands folded in her lap, her eyes darted scared from faces that she knew, fearing the rebuff of non-recognition. She was painfully aware of her own insignificance, of her hair that would never stay curled, and her new dress which somehow or other had turned out a failure: or so her husband's chilly glance conveyed as she came down the stairs from her robing. Yes, these latest styles were ridiculous for one so small as she. The immense sleeves, the wide bell-shaped skirts, spread over a hoop (a fashion much favoured at court) almost entirely extinguished her. The harsh apple-green satin, sloping from shoulders too thin for exposure, accentuated the greenish pallor of her skin. His blank stare, his empty, artificial words had confirmed her mirror's condemnation. 'Charming, my dear! Charming! A *primavera*. True daughter of spring.' On a night of hot summer? Her closed childish lips curved to a smile, unmirthful.

She saw him whose wife the law and Church but never God had made her, moving among the ladies, debonair, graceful, remote: uttering platitudes, carefully restrained. No caressing murmur, not one stealthy glance to probe the whiteness of a bosom; no word, no breath of scandal must tarnish his great name. Not here in his own world did he seek satisfaction, but one suspected: and imagination fled before the vile fantasies arisen from heaven alone knew what evil things, unguessed… No, not here, though before the night was gone he would approach her. 'You look very tired, my dear. Would you care to go home?' Prompting her answer with his cold glassy stare.

'Yes, I am a little tired. But please do not trouble to accompany me, I can go home alone. You would, I think, like to stay?'

'No, no. I too am tired. I will accompany you…' So that they might be seen leaving the room together. And having deposited her at the door of his house, he would take himself to his secret ways, his dingy loves. All Paris pitied him, thought him a saint, too forbearing to show such devoted fidelity to his plain little mouse of a wife… Yet perhaps tonight she would not be taken away quite so early. The rooms overflowed with celebrities. Her husband patronised the arts. He liked to talk to famous persons. He professed himself delighted to meet Chopin, but he would never entertain him or any artist in his house. Some day she would assert herself; hold her own salons, be a hostess in her own right. Could she dare? Certainly many famous persons cultivated a revolting exterior. Balzac, for instance…

Her eyes strayed again to the group by the pillar. Chopin, she thought, looked like a butterfly caught between two hideous stag beetles. Strange that anyone so unprepossessing, so uncouth as Balzac could write such masterpieces. A magician. She had heard that his patience, his industry were phenomenal and that he revised his proof sheets at least a dozen times. *One must not be deceived by appearances…* And that Monsieur Dumas who had three plays running at once, the most popular of dramatists. Prolific. *People say he is very sensitive about his black blood. The most kind and good-natured of creatures but such a dreadful taste in clothes. He coughs a good deal…*

'Chopin has made coughs the fashion.'

She heard her own whisper and pulled herself up. *Really! I live so much alone I am beginning to talk to myself.*

And now Madame de Girardin had attached herself to Chopin and was leading him away. Very beautiful. She had been the actress, Delphine Gay, before her marriage. Not unlike a Muse or the pictures of Marie Antoinette, built on a large scale. *She is said to be the wittiest woman in Paris. She is coming this way. She is looking at me. She is smiling.* Ciel! *Must I…?*

Marcelline moistened her lips and half rose in her seat. Madame de Girardin, on Chopin's arm, her magnificent bosom out-thrust and white as a swan's, charged down upon her.

'Madame la Princesse! What a pleasure! But why do you hide yourself so modestly? Allow me to present Monsieur Chopin.'

'I have already the honour.' He bowed over her gloved hand. Did she dare to fancy his lips lingered?

'Yes, Madame de Girardin. Did you not know? I … I am a pupil of Monsieur Chopin.'

'One of my most gifted pupils, Madame.'

For one second, Madame de Girardin's superb tact deserted her, but only the most astute observer would have discerned in that marble countenance the faintest tremor as she covered the gaffe, and inwardly recorded a black mark. Of course! How could she possibly have forgotten or overlooked so essential a point to be noted? She, who kept a dossier of all the leading lights in Paris, that memory should not betray her; she whose salons were even more famous than de Custine's for the intellectual society and the great names, from the King downwards, who honoured her rooms by their presence.

Her recovery, however, from that brief lapse was a miracle of grace. '*Ça va sans dire!* But I understood, Madame, it was a secret to be guarded until such time as your estimable husband will permit you to appear upon the concert platform, that the whole world may hear the Princess Czartoryska. Is it not a sin to keep so exquisite a gift in retirement?'

'My husband would never allow me to appear in public, Madame de Girardin.'

'Nor,' interposed Chopin smoothly, 'would I advise it. The Princess plays for the love and joy of music. The applause of the herd is not what she seeks. Is that not so, Madame?'

'Yes, Monsieur...' It was the merest whisper; those soft brown eyes, so like a startled hare's, sought his in trapped appeal. Poor child! A spirit in bondage.

'But,' he said, steadying her eyes with his, 'there is no reason why Madame la Princesse should withhold her music from ... her friends.'

'And,' cried Madame de Girardin gaily, 'we are all friends here tonight. A coterie of souls.'

'Of damned souls, Madame?' queried Chopin gently.

Her laugh rang out a shade too shrill. 'Monsieur Chopin! If I did not know that you hold the key to heaven in your fingers I would think you had been voyaging in hell.'

'Perhaps I have. Our hell is as we make it here on earth.'

'Then for God's love give us paradise — and play to us!'

He stiffened. 'If I may appoint a deputy, Madame?' And turning, bowed again. 'Princess?'

She restrained a hand from leaping to her heart. 'No,' she breathed. 'Please, Monsieur ... no.'

The faint mask of mockery that shielded his face slid from it in a smile that drained her of resistance. 'If I ask it, Madame, for my own pride's sake? The excusable pride of a teacher.' And he added in a whisper, *Les études.*'

She was lost; surrendered. 'If you ask it, then...'

'I do.'

Yes, she would play, and in her playing speak to him in his own words, as none but she could speak, his own creation. Had he not told her at her very first lesson when she had come to him from Czerny with whom till then she had been studying, 'I thought that only Chopin could play Chopin ... till I heard you, Princess.'

She was unfastening her gloves, prepared to follow him, strengthened by his presence, upheld by his faith in her. She would not fail.

'Chopin!'

Like a blown blossom in her rosy froth of tulle and silver gauze, the Countess d'Agoult descended, as though she had been wafted there upon a breeze. Behind her came Liszt ... and another.

A chill, icy as the first grey breath of dawn, touched the Princess Marcelline, to send a shudder to her spine and estrange her in a moment's pause from him who was her master.

Unnoticed and forgotten she sank back on the settee and with involuntary precision replaced her gloves, resumed her posture, hands folded in her lap, while between herself and him it was as if a shadow hovered.

'Madame Sand! This is indeed a happy meeting! I thought you were at Nohant.'

The high-pitched voice of Madame de Girardin splintered the second's charged expectancy. The Princess raised her eyes.

At last it confronted her, that face, never seen till now except in drawings or daguerreotype...

George Sand!

Was this the trousered Amazon, half-man, half-woman, whose republican principles and social hatreds, eccentricities, liaisons and loves had become a byword of the gutter? Was this the seducer of effeminate young men, disciple of Sappho, and Liszt's *femme-héros*? Impossible! Truth had no foundation in such whispers. Rumour's tongue alone had spread its poison to infect her name and smear her with its slime that even her creative art and craftsmanship was held in evidence against her. Cruel. Unjust!

Some colour flushed in Marcelline's white cheeks. Was there no end to the spite and malice of this world? Success had made this woman envy's butt, to bring her dishonour and shame. Yet those smouldering eyes, those proud firm lips, that aggressive chin, denied, defied, all slander. Not beautiful, she conveyed the impression of beauty in a subtle self-assurance and reposeful dignity that had something of the grandeur of an Elgin marble.

She wore a gown of ivory satin lightly veiled in black lace, the low-cut heart-shaped bodice Revealing robust shoulders. Her bronze dark hair was wreathed with violets and she carried a little tight bouquet of violets arranged round one crimson rose. Could any man resist her?

Ah, yes... one.

Marcelline released a breath.

He had bowed, he had turned, he had left her standing there between Liszt and the Countess d'Agoult. He had stayed no longer than the formality of introduction demanded. He had gone from the room. Was he leaving the house?

Marcelline rose to her feet, gathered her skirts, her fan, her fading flowers that she had laid aside, aware of a clammy dew upon her forehead and a faintness at her heart. She was tired, suddenly... One lived too much in one's emotions, with no release, no outlet. If she could have played as he had asked her ... *les études*.

The faces of Mesdames de Girardin, d'Agoult, the carven face of that strange woman swam before her in a mist, converged in a dizzy waltz with the room, with the windows in a curtsey, with the dying voices of the company and the echo of his music heard from some far distance as in another life...

'*Pauvre enfant!*'

A woman's arm supported her; a vinaigrette was applied to her nose. She gazed up into a pair of eyes, soft, velvety, tender as a mother's; she smelled violets. 'It is the heat.' A whisper brushed her ear. 'These rooms are stifling.'

She was surrounded.

The countess, fluttering and twittering like a canary that has seen a cat; Madame de Girardin, calm, monumental, waving back the helpless irresolute Liszt and importunate enquirers. How terrible, how shocking to attract so much attention to herself. What had happened to cause that moment's giddiness? Had her maid laced her corsets too tight?

'It is nothing ... nothing. I am quite recovered. Yes, the heat... Thank you, Madame...?' She glanced from the face above her own to Madame de Girardin, who, ignoring that timid enquiry, hastened to lift her from the sofa to the shelter of her wing. It would not do, emphatically it would not do to present the Princess Czartoryska to George Sand. She had served her purpose, had offered her vinaigrette, a trifle too officiously, one thought. Further encroachment on the guarded borders of that world which the Princess Czartoryska represented, must be forbidden. It was the duty of Madame de Girardin to hold the gates. Her own position in that territory was sufficiently precarious; it dared not be endangered by the risk of a false step.

'Come with me, Princess. I will find your husband. He will take you home. What a loss to us all! We were to have heard you play. A pleasure, I hope, that will not be long postponed.' Madame de Girardin was never slow to seize a social opportunity. 'No longer, shall we say, than this day week? When I will give a musical matinée, Madame, if you will be gracious enough to honour us... Ah! *Voilà! Monsieur le Prince!*'

His solicitous concern deceived his wife no more than it deceived Delphine de Girardin. She was handed over to her husband, snatched from contamination, led away.

George Sand stood looking after her, raised an eyebrow and queried abruptly, 'Pregnant?'

'If so,' Madame de Girardin shrugged a shoulder, '*he* is not responsible, I can assure you.'

The countess put in her word. 'Oil and water, my dear George! They never mix. Can you blame him? Tied to that miserable little white rabbit.'

'She plays Chopin like an angel,' murmured Liszt.

'So Chopin says. I am interested to know,' the countess with engaging artlessness pursued, 'if it is a mere coincidence that all Chopin's most talented pupils are members of the aristocracy, or if it shows how much the bourgeoisie,' she glanced appealingly at George, 'misrepresent us when they declare we are degenerate, effete, out-bred? At his last pupils' concert the only untitled performer was the child Filtsch.'

'Ah! That marvellous boy!' Liszt's face lit up. '*He* knows how to play Chopin. When that little one begins to give concerts I shall retire.'

'You said the same thing when you first heard Chopin, but you have not retired yet.' Again the sprightly countess flashed her eyes at George who stayed withdrawn and unresponsive.

'Well, and what do you think of him?'

'I have not heard him play, I cannot tell.' George answered evenly; and she raised to her lips her posy of violets, as though to hide a smile.

'*Stupide!* I am not speaking of that infant prodigy but of our Frédéric, who,' the countess bubbled into laughter, 'has turned his heel and fled. And after *all* my pains to bring you together! Why did you let him escape?'

'Perhaps,' Madame de Girardin suggested gently, 'to prolong the ardour of the chase.'

George stared, not at Madame de Girardin, nor at the little countess, but at some unseen point in space between the two. 'Can you wonder,' she asked of no one in particular, 'that I shun the society of women?'

'My dear George!' The countess made a dramatic gesture of recoil. 'What a thing to say to *us* — your friends.'

'My friends today may be my enemies tomorrow,' George rejoined with provocative quiet, and turning to Liszt she took his arm. 'I detest these crowded salons. Shall we go into the garden? I find the air here too oppressive.'

He had no choice but to go where she steered him, towards the windows that opened on the terrace. There she paused with a backward glance across her shoulder at the two whom she had left. 'You may return to your ladies, my good Franz.

They need your support and attention. I don't.' And with that hidden smile on her lips, she stepped through the open window into the night.

The terrace overlooked moon-silvered lawns, where in the subdued glow of fairy lights suspended like a necklace from the trees, decorous couples wandered, their muted voices mingling with the cool plash of unseen fountains.

A night of stars, breathless, fervent and so still that the far inexorable hum of Paris seemed to take upon itself an individual significance, remote, but vividly alive with the myriad hopes, loves, passions, and despairs of human multitudes. *How near and yet how immeasurably distant,* mused George Sand, *are the blind alleys, the foetid lairs and dingy dwellings that spring like fungus from those filth-sodden cemeteries where men are born and bred in putrefaction. How long — how long before the cleansing of life's sewers will be completed, that all mankind may dwell alike as gods and not as vermin?*

She leaned her arms upon the parapet, her eyes uplifted to the sparkling sky as if she sought her answer there. Rapt, immobile she stood, lost in the moment and apparently unheedful of a figure that until her arrival on the terrace had been similarly occupied sky-gazing; nor, at the sound of a stifled cough, did she betray by any movement an awareness of his presence till she spoke, her voice poised on a whisper, as casual as though she had recaptured the threads of conversation interrupted.

'Do you see this fiery white-hot star directly above the cypress at the end of the lower lawn? How fiercely it burns — as if it would devour this miserable speck of dust we call the earth. I think I never saw a star so near. Is it Mars or Venus?'

He bowed stiffly, halting there beside her, his face a pale blur in the moonlight. 'I do not know astronomy, Madame, but surely your star must,' he paused, 'be Venus. Never Mars.'

Without turning her head she looked at him, a long slow glance from under those heavy lids. Seen in profile the sweeping eyebrows, the curved nose, the short disdainful upper lip, were entirely Egyptian, unreal, fantastic, as though carved in bas-relief upon the night.

She laughed softly. 'I had forgotten you are as renowned for your sarcasm as for your music, Monsieur Chopin. But I warn you, sarcasm is wasted upon me. I have a poor sense of humour; a slow wit.'

'Madame,' he answered lightly, 'I apologise, though I was not aware of sarcasm in my remark. An observation, merely.'

'For me too obvious an observation. I have little use for the embroideries of social chatter.' She raised her violets and smelled them, glancing round at him again. The dying flowers gave out an aching scent, the very breath and passion-mood of darkness. 'I am a clumsy talker, Monsieur Chopin. I find it easier to write words than to speak them.' Her tone rather than her speech showed a faint hesitation, half-defiant, half-appealing. 'There are many who write,' she added, 'and say nothing.'

A crooked smile came upon his lips while his eyes reluctantly appraised her. Acknowledging her witchery, he held himself defensive to her charm. If she were at her tricks with him — so be it! He could deal with her, play the role demanded, a duel if needs must. She was transparent. This ingenuous approach was not what he expected. He must go warily lest he or his judgment be deceived.

'So!' For the first time now she turned a full penetrative look upon him. He felt rather than saw the movement of her lips, screened by her fainting violets. 'In spite of your deliberate avoidance, we two meet at last. That was inevitable. But I am puzzled to know the cause of your antipathy to me. I should have thought that Chopin —' was there a suggestion of mockery in that trifling emphasis upon his name? — 'would have been immune to the stench of gossip that like blow-flies on a dung heap surrounds the name of a woman who dares assert her individuality before the world.' Her speech, more forceful than her tone, delivered this oration on a breath; almost without pause, giving an impression that it had been rehearsed or written. That most likely...

A queer emotion seized him. It was as if he had stood just here and in this moment through some dim remoter past, seeing her face engraved upon a moonbeam, hearing her voice with its husky, bitter intonation, her words that said so little and so much, rediscovered from some lost palimpsest.

'Are you afraid of me — or of yourself?'

And a coldness came upon him as he listened, aware of some subtle change in her of which she seemed unconscious: an impalpable sixth sense strained above the regions it normally inhabits. Extraordinary being! Was she in truth an enigma, a sibyl of magic spells and secretive enchantments — or the Eternal Feminine whose intelligence born of instinct rather than of mind, prompted her to bury her too insistent womanhood in the guise of a buccaneer? Woman, yes! That undeniably... In a moment's swift perception he saw in her the mirage of a personality as false to her inner consciousness as the disguise that she affected; he saw her Self in essence, fertile, bovine in its simplicity, rich with the grace and awkwardness combined of some lusty peasant bred from the earth, pagan, bare-breasted, a mother to all men.

He made an indeterminate half-gesture of retreat. He would have gone, have left her there, have shaken off those irresistible slow coils that she flung out with all her power to ensnare him — if he could. But he could not. Suspended in a blind, sudden panic, bereft of social platitudes and the parrot repetition of phrases tuned to an emergency, he stood, bound...

Reborn. Regenerated.

He was a child again; a boy untried, expectant; a man with knowledge savoured, whose blood surged shouting through his veins in the maddened urgency of sense matured, and ready for its crowning.

Her body swayed towards him; her hand warm, narrow, sought for his and turned from a melting softness to live steel. He saw the torment of her breathing in the valley of her breasts and the whiteness of her teeth between her lips; he heard her speak in wordless sound; he knew her touch upon him, and in the storm of his surrender, stood, possessed.

Then from some timeless void, from some crushed fragrance, he felt her mouth dissolve into a sigh. 'Unlock your eyes,' she whispered. 'Look at me.'

Her face, found in that pallid light, was strangely smiling.

The Marquis de Custine's *soirée*, the most important social function of the season, had been universally acknowledged a triumph. Chopin, who so rarely could be persuaded to play before an audience *privée*, had stayed the last departing guests by a gratuitous performance.

Next day all Paris clacked of it: how George Sand, in full view of the assembly, had staged a dramatic announcement. With Chopin in attendance she was seen to approach her host, to tell him, 'Behold, Monsieur le Marquis! I succeed where you have failed. Chopin consents to play tonight … for me!'

For her: and all must know it. He stood branded with her seal. Another victim?

No escape, retreat, redress. He was foredoomed.

INTERLUDE: IN ARCADY

A hundred years ago, the passage from Barcelona to the Balearic Isles was no light undertaking. A sturdy little steamboat, much vaunted possession of the Majorcans, rolled back and forth once a week between the wide stretch of Mediterranean that severs the Spanish mainland from its offspring, and was, then, the islanders' sole means of communication with the outer world; and even this limited egress might not have been acquired but for the exportation of live pigs, that brought a sure and profitable trade to the islands, which at that time were almost undiscovered.

Thus, the few hardy travellers who would brave the perils of a passage by steamer on a sea that, for all its azure beauty, could be uncomfortably rough, must give second place to their more important fellow passengers, the cargo.

On a morning in November, 1838, the little steamer, divested on this its homeward voyage of its squealing charges, belched and puffed its way to harbour, and deposited on the quayside at Palma a party of French tourists.

The Majorcans, who, unlike their temperamental and more excitable progenitors in Spain, viewed life and people with a stoical phlegm not entirely devoid of churlishness, paid more heed to the unloading of their precious sties than to the comfort and convenience of their visitors.

These consisted of a bustling lady in a cloak, which did not at all disguise the fact that she wore no skirt beneath it, but what appeared to be uncommonly like a pair of pantaloons. Her wind-blown hair, guiltless of a bonnet, fell in curls upon her shoulders. She carried a heavy portmanteau with remarkable ease and was attended by a pallid slight young man, who tottered rather than walked behind her down the gangway. Hard on his heels came a maid-servant with a child attached to each hand, followed by two scowling porters loaded with luggage.

The day shimmered in the heat of a brassy noon: the sun blazed from a molten sky: the sea was all shades of blue ranging from purple to faint hyacinth, from cobalt to indigo, foam-flecked and dancing. The stench of untenanted pigsties soared strong above the scent of oranges and lemons, and a fantasy of flowers that poured from every wall of every villa on the hillsides.

'We have found our Eden!' cried the lady; and depositing at her feet her cumbersome portmanteau, she unfurled a parasol.

'Eden indeed!' returned the pallid gentleman, the sickliness of whose smile detracted somewhat from the heartiness of his reply. 'It is sheer heaven!'

To be fixed on *terra firma*, certainly, removed from a heaving deck and unspeakable smells. What misery! What a boat! Insanitary, disgusting, manned by the filthiest of crews and passengered by brigands and swineherds.

Deprived of his faithful Daniel he had survived the crossing only by God's mercy, lying stretched, abased, while the shocking vessel plunged and played at somersaults, and his lady in her gentlemanly fashion strode the deck.

So completely unaffected by the antics of the boat was this incalculable creature, that she stood nonchalantly smoking — to the agony of Chopin — a cigar, leaning on the bulwarks watching for the dawn, her mind busy with impressions for her notebook.

The night was warm and dark, illumined only by an extraordinary phosphorescence in the wake of the ship; everybody was asleep on board except the steersman, who, in order to keep himself awake, sang all night in a voice so soft and subdued that one might have thought he feared to wake the men of the watch or that he himself was half-asleep. We did not weary of listening to him, for his singing was of the strangest kind ... a reverie rather than a song.

And a nightmare rather than a reverie for one to whom each wave was a convulsion. And there was still the return journey to be faced. If the passage out had been, on all accounts, comparatively calm, what horrors would attend one in a storm? So, no matter how ecstatic might be an idyll in this 'Eden', one could not quite forget that it must end.

'Divine!' exclaimed Madame, her nostrils savouring the perfumed air. 'You will regain your health and strength within a week in this exquisite spot!'

She was enraptured: with the town — so *picturesque* with its *magnificent*' *cathedral, its royal palace; its peasant huts and the half-naked large-eyed children who played outside them in the dirt* — never *was* seen *so much dirt!* And with the landscape, *whose vegetation is richer than Africa* (though she had never been there), *and has quite as much breadth, calm and simplicity ... A green Switzerland under the sky of Calabria ... A promised land.*

But one cannot live on promises alone. She had been promised habitable apartments by others who had gone before; or failing such, had hoped for an hotel that would provide some suitable accommodation. Not at all. Though they made the circuit of the city in an execrable conveyance drawn by a decrepit pair of mules through swarms of flies, they came upon no sign of hostelry. Even the spirit of a Sand was slightly dashed, while Maurice and Solange, her son and daughter, whose patience and deportment until then had been angelic, who had slept the night through undisturbed by qualms, and had eaten an enormous breakfast of fried ham — to poor Chopin's undoing — now set up a roar for food to shake your ears. Then her maid must develop a toothache and sit with her hand to her face and her back to the mules, and her eyes up to heaven — a martyr. And he whom, next to God and her devilish brats, she loved most in the world, looked and behaved like a ghost, wilting and fading away at her side that one doubted he'd last through the day.

Above all — and what could be more vexing? — when they came to the house recommended, they found it closed up and to let. Never mind! They would find somewhere to rest for the night. And though her heart misgave her, hope never faltered. She urged her charges on with bravest cheer; and at sunset, when her party one and all were out of hand; her angels whimpering and whining — when they were not tooth and nail at each other's throats; her slut of a servant in tears, and her spectral swain sunk in an ominous silence, George's courage was rewarded by the offer of two rooms ... almost entirely unfurnished, to be sure, but what of that? Be thankful for a habitation that contained one folding bed, a three-legged straw-bottomed chair, no sanitary arrangements, and the most villainous of hosts, who served them at supper with a knife in his belt and a peppery mess of raw goat's flesh, pimentoes and garlic.

Even the indomitable George agreed that 'simplicity' could have its drawbacks. The Simple Life by all means, and Nature at her grandest, but not with scorpions for bed-mates and cockroaches in the soup.

True, the view atoned in a feast to the eyes for what the body lacked in nourishment, but still ... with her darlings turned to demons, racing vermin on the table; with her maid in the vapours and her lover in the sulks, the most picturesque of scenery must pall.

As for the Majorcans — surely never was a more unprepossessing, inhospitable and uncouth race of beings bred from beauty. Resentful of intrusion upon their rocky fortress, the islanders regarded every stranger with suspicion. They demanded exorbitant prices for the most primitive of lodgings and nauseating food. One refused to be imposed upon by a band of desperadoes, who would take your money and then stab you in the back.

So the ever-dauntless George explored the town, tramping in her trousers along noisome ways and refuse-laden gutters unheedful of the jeers that she attracted; pausing here and there to gaze in wonder at a Moorish ruin where in the crannies of its yellow walls, the roses dropped their petals, red as blood; or to smile at some lovely, scowling girl in her gay-striped petticoats, her bodice shamelessly agape to show her breasts, a ragged lace mantilla on her black grease-sodden hair, bizarre mimicry of Spanish *modes* and fashion brought to Arcady. And Arcadian it was indeed, at the turn of a mountain road to come upon a brown, cross-gartered goatherd perched upon a boulder with a reed-pipe to his lips, playing his shrill tuneless little tune, evil-glancing and equivocal as a young Pan.

Or, in the height of the noonday sun, she would drive with the suffering Chopin to view the countryside and drag him, who was past protesting, in a scramble up rough hill-sides where road there was none; or down the pebbled slopes of a dried water-bed, to arrive sweating, dizzy, on a precipitous ledge to find a panorama, more exquisite than any, well worth a scratch or two. The sea, turquoise and sapphire, the cypress-wooded valley, the shadowed gorge, the grey-tawny shoulders of the mountains rising to jagged peaks where the golden eagles sheltered: one could watch the majestic downward pursuit of some small invisible prey; could hear the piercing shriek of a creature caught between relentless talons, the savage triumphant cry of the hunter appeased; and everywhere the lavish wealth of Nature's coffers: the bewildering riot of flowers, the luscious fruits, the palm, the myrtle and the twisted cacti; the burning blue, the blinding sun...

'The sun! Always the sun!' She would throw out her arms, to embrace it: to see was not enough. She wanted to possess, to tear from its womb this exuberant stored passion of the earth. Vision was inadequate, one must touch, must grasp, devour...

In her frenzy of sightseeing she all but devoured him. He was weakened by a succession of fierce colds, and had not slept since he landed on the island. His cough, his horror of the bug-scarred blankets spread upon a mattress on the floor, kept him sitting up in a chair at night in shuddering wakefulness. But nothing kept her awake. She would lie like a child deep breathing, and was up again at sunrise with her eyes full of light, and her face full of health, ready for adventure and the day: another jaunt in that jolting *birlocho*; another search for lodgings more delectable.

These were found at last: a villa on the outskirts of the town terminating in a valley enclosed within the mountains and with a glimpse of the yellow walls of Palma and a sparkle of the sea.

Passably clean, having recently been whitewashed, the house was to let furnished; and, though the furniture was scanty and deplorable, the villa had its necessary convenience, and was well ventilated: too well ventilated, one might have thought, when a miniature cyclone came sweeping up the valley to tear the trees from their roots, to bluster at the doors, and rattle at the windows and blow dust from Palma's gutters through every crack and crevice of Son-Vent — 'House of the Winds', aptly named.

Such slight discouragements, however, were nobly met. It did not behove a man on honeymoon with his beloved, to find fault with that which providence and his lady's unfaltering determination had provided. They had left Paris in the cold mists of November; they found their island basking in full summer heat. 'As sun-worshippers,' said George, 'we should be thankful.'

One strove to be, at least.

To his friend Julius Fontana he catalogues his blessings.

My Dear,

I am in Palma, among palms, cedars, cacti, aloes, olive, orange, lemon, fig and pomegranate trees, as seen in les Jardins des Plantes *only under glass. A sky like turquoise, sea like lazuli, mountains like emeralds, and the air like heaven. All day the sun and everyone in summer clothes. All night guitars and song — (everybody sings till all hours). Vine-festooned balconies, Moorish walls, and every view looking towards Africa...*
Enfin! *The perfect life...*

Until the rains came and deluged the House of the Winds. Then the walls, so fresh and white, were whited sepulchres that swelled to the damp like a sponge. The house possessed neither stove nor chimney, for the Majorcans, though accustomed to rain, were unprepared for cold, and this winter was to prove the coldest yet experienced in living memory.

The humid mists rising from the sun-baked earth, draped a mantle of ice around the villa and oozed a sluggish slime from walls and ceilings. As a further discouragement, no servants were to be had, and George found herself responsible for half the chores and all the cooking. To a friend, Madame Marliani, in Paris, she wrote despairingly:

If you could know what I have to do! I am not only the chef but serving-maid as well. Our one domestic is a brute: bigoted, lazy, gluttonous, a veritable son of a pig. (I think they are all that here!) Luckily the maid I brought with me from Paris is very devoted and does the heavy work, but she is not at all strong and I have to help her. Besides which, everything is very dear, and proper nourishment almost impossible to obtain. Believe me our stomachs revolt against a surfeit of rancid oil and pig's grease, and unless I myself prepare his food, Chopin is sick after every meal. In short, our expedition looks to be the most frightful fiasco.

She was, however, not to be defeated. It had needed much persuasion to induce Chopin to join her on this adventure, that, as she was at pains to impress on her familiars, she had been forced to undertake on account of the health of her boy Maurice, who suffered from rheumatism, for the cure of which the House of the Winds could scarcely be considered the best of all locations. Chopin, too, had been a trifle obstinate. He was not anxious to leave Paris with so much work on hand, nor did the prospect of a holiday *en famille* — with two children and a nurse — present unmitigated bliss; but a succession of chills and an attack of influenza had finally decided him.

What, therefore, could have been more unhappy than the choice of Son-Vent as a home for convalescents?

The lack of adequate heating arrangements, the swampish walls, the omnipresent moisture, proved too much for the enfeebled Chopin. He developed a violent irritation of the larynx, due to the smoke from an improvised brazier, bought for a fantastic price from a tinker in the town; and scarcely was he recovered from that indisposition, than he developed a congestion of the lungs.

George, seriously alarmed, sent for not one, but three doctors, who met in consultation on his case. They gave the gravest verdict and ordered a quantity of drugs, most of which were unprocurable in Palma.

Meanwhile the invalid, in a state of agitation occasioned by the non-arrival of his piano, delivery of which had been supervised by Pleyel, was writing frantically to Julius Fontana: *I must have my piano! Ask Pleyel by what route it has been sent. You shall have my preludes soon...*

And then:

I cannot send you the MSS. They are not ready. During the last two weeks I have been as sick as a dog, notwithstanding 18 degrees Centigrade, and roses, orange, palm and fig-trees all in blossom. Three doctors, the most renowned in Palma, were called in. One smelt what I spat, another poked whence I spat, and the third listened when I spat! The first said I would die, the second that I am dying, and the third that I am dead already. But I am still alive!

Tell Jan I cannot forgive him for not warning me of my condition which he will persist in calling acute bronchitis. However, I fought against their bleedings, blisterings, and such-like operations, and am slowly getting better. My illness has had an abortive effect on the Preludes, which you will receive — God alone knows when.

Incidentally, we are moving in a few days' time to take up our abode in the ruins of an old Carthusian monastery: the most beautiful spot in the world. Sea, mountains, cloisters, mosques, thousand-year-old olive trees, a church of the Knights of the Cross, and a most poetic cemetery ... what more can man desire?

Kiss Jan for me, and if you write to my parents, don't let them know I've been ill. *I don't want them to worry…*

It was George who had the worry.

How much of a 'fiasco' this idyll proved to be, only she could tell, and has told in her letters and the history of her life. Not only the doctors urged the patient's prompt removal from the morass that a month of rains had made of her 'picturesque' villa; rumours were afloat, and the Majorcans superstitious. Their ignorance of illness magnified their fear of it: and although medical science on those benighted islands was in its infancy, the inhabitants had gleaned enough knowledge, passed from mouth to mouth, to declare the 'Frenchman' a consumptive — and consumption was infectious as the plague.

A curse had come upon them with the entry of these strangers to their island. And such strangers! A woman who dressed like a man! That alone would be enough to bring the wrath of God on all whom she contacted: and a man with the face of a woman, who coughed blood! Their presence was a menace and their flesh contaminated. The natives crossed themselves and muttered, *'Retro me Sathana!'* when Madame in her trousers stalked the streets.

Then the landlord, Senor Gomez, wavering between his greed for gold and general opinion, decided it were best to play for safety. He could not afford to quarrel with the pig breeders from whom he bought his wealth-producing livestock to sell to the mainland. And he could always make the strangers pay for the trouble brought upon him and his house.

So one morning he drove through the pouring rain in a *birlocho,* to be received by Madame smoking a cigar. That, however, did not shock him. Many women in Majorca, his own good wife included, smoked cigars; nor, though the lady, who for once was wearing skirts, offered a cigar to him, was Gomez melted. He must be wary. This woman was undoubtedly a witch. Behind his back he crossed his fingers, and wished profoundly he had paused at the church on the way to the villa to entreat the intercession of the saints.

George could speak no Spanish, but he had a little French. He understood that she had bid him enter. What? To court infection? By Bacchus, no! He had glimpsed through the open doorway that thin-faced shivering rat (her lover, son, or changeling — who could tell?) sitting huddled in a chair, his hands like perished monkey paws spread out to catch the warmth of the charcoal-burning brazier, the smoke of which had disgracefully discoloured his white ceilings... *May their bones rot in hell,* prayed Senor Gomez to his saints while his mind registered his damages' account. For every drop of blood that living corpse spat out, for every stain upon his walls and ceilings, he, Gomez, would draw in... Gloating, he rolled the estimate upon his tongue, and bared his teeth in smiles.

George, disgustedly, surveyed him. A cut-throat devil incarnate if ever there was one, sprouting five days' growth of beard, with eyes like a snake's sunk in yellow fat, and lips as red as though they had been painted.

He had dressed himself for the occasion in his *festa* suit; black velvet bolero over a soiled white shirt, a scarlet sash-band with the hilt of a knife half-hidden, his whiskers gummed in two flourishes upon his cheeks, a rose over one ear, gold rings in both, and a wide-brimmed black sombrero over all.

'No, Madame, I thank you,' he told her pointedly, 'I will remain outside the door.' And in the shelter of the porch that saved him somewhat from the driving rain; and having refused the olive branch and her cigar, he extracted from a pigskin case his own, an evil-smelling object, never grown in Cuba, to waft its nauseating fumes through the open doorway and down the 'Frenchman's' throat. The fit of coughing that ensued hastened Gomez to dispense with overtures and explain without delay the object of his mission.

He regretted deeply but he begged Madame to understand that, although unwilling to incommode his patrons, the law of the island prohibited the harbouring of an infectious illness beneath a private roof. The poor gentleman — Alas! how he suffered for him! 'It is I, Gomez, who speak, Madame, from all my heart and in the deepest pity. I am chagrined to my soul — but what would you? It is the law.'

'A recent legislation, I presume?' George in honeyed tones enquired.

But no, Madame, she was assured. An ancient law. One of the most ancient of all laws, passed during the great plague of many centuries ago, by the then ruling monarch. May he, Gomez, his wife and his beloved children be struck dead and left to mortify, unburied, if what he told Madame was less than truth — on all that he held sacred he would swear it. And was it not, in fact, a sensible sanitary law which rendered liable to imprisonment any person who sanctions the retention in a house — a private house — of any case of disease that is infectious?

'You, Madame, will understand. You, Madame, are a lady, very gracious, very clever, very good. Of a goodness that one sees shining in your eyes —' And Gomez leered into her face with such a smile on his own, that she was hard put to it to keep her nails off him. 'You, Madame, are the mother of a family.'

'Of two young children,' George curtly interrupted.

'Ah, so? Now I have six, and another —' Gomez crossed himself as a sop to the Evil One who surely was about the

189

place and in this woman's eyes — 'another on the way — may the good God bring it safe to pass! Six little ones, Madame, whose lives are threatened should they return to this house before it has been purged of all infection.'

In view of which and the repainting and replastering that must, perforce, be done to make his palace habitable and cleansed, the oily Gomez made it clearly understood that evacuation should take place without delay.

So much for that; too much for George, and not enough for Gomez, who further named his price. A monstrous price: an outrage! More than treble a month's rent, and their unexpired term of tenancy into the bargain.

But sooner than prolong the unsavoury interview with this glutinous mould of flesh, whose cigar and garlic-tainted breath was proving more than even George could safely stomach, she decided to agree — or have her throat cut, or be sick.

Very well then — they must go. But where, under heaven in this God-forsaken island — *and* in God's Name — where?

She had not yet discovered the monastery at Valdemosa, and moreover:

Our invalid was in no fit condition to be moved, especially by such means of transport as are available in Majorca; and in such weather! And, since the rumour of our 'phthisis' had spread like wild-fire, we could no longer hope to find a shelter anywhere, not even for one night, and at no matter how high a price. If it had not been for the kindness and hospitality of the French Consul, who gathered us all under his roof, we were faced with the prospect of camping in a cave.

Then by nothing short of a miracle we found our asylum for the winter.

In the Carthusian monastery at Valdemosa dwelt a Spanish refugee who had hidden himself there, for what political reason I do not know, nor did I care. Visiting the monastery I was much impressed with the gentility of his manners, the beauty of his wife, and the comfortable, if rustic furniture of their cell. The poetic savour of this monastery enchants me. It happened that the mysterious couple wished precipitately to leave the country, and that they were as delighted to dispose of their furniture and cell as we were to acquire them. So for the moderate sum of a thousand francs we had a complete establishment, but such a one as in France we could have procured for 300 francs: so costly and so difficult to get, are the bare necessities of life in Majorca.

And though to George the bare necessities of life were secondary to love, it seemed the cruellest twist of fate that once again her lover had become an ailing child. Another Alfred to be nursed and soothed and waited on a hundred times a day, with doctors in attendance; and a scurvy set of rogues indeed they were. No soft-eyed, soft-lipped Pagello to give her sympathy and counsel in a gondola... Ah! If only this were Venice! But most definitely it was not.

A monk's cell in a ruined monastery did, however, offer a more romantic setting than the mildewed, soaked and desolate Son-Vent. So soon as her invalid was well enough to leave the kindly consul's house and take the journey up the mountain, they departed.

The two children and the maid had been sent on in advance; George followed with her love in a *birlocho*. Coughing, shivering, swathed in shawls and padded with poultices till he resembled nothing so much as a bolster, the hapless Chopin was in no mood to echo Madame's raptures.

She, braced to meet emergency and determined at all costs to make the best of her 'fiasco', saw everything *couleur de rose* even through the rain. While their staggering *birlocho* bounced and slid and jolted up the streaming roads, she exclaimed upon the beauties of the scene.

'What could be more sublime than these rocky heights, these deep ravines, these miniature Niagaras?' — that thundered in yellow torrents down the mountainsides, slicing up the soil and tearing palm trees from their roots, to render the slushy tracks almost impassable.

'How exquisite,' sighed George, 'to live up here upon an eyrie with the eagles. The rocks above, the sea below, and the ghosts of vanished monks for company.'

Chopin palely agreed. He was past speech and past complaining. Since the way had proved too stony and too steep for the rickety wheels of their conveyance, the final stage of the ascent had to be made astride the mule.

That sagacious animal, oblivious of its driver's oaths and prods or the feeble protests of its rider, took its own time and its own, precipitous, direction to the summit, walking unconcernedly on the edge of an abyss till Chopin deemed each second was his last. Rain-drenched, splashed to the chin with clay and mud, the invincible George clambered up on the heels of the mule, to arrive panting but undaunted ahead of her cavalier, to see the first cloud-break, the first sign of a watery sun. A good omen!

She had triumphed. She had brought her little Chopin through the deluge. The floods were receding. Romance need not be drowned. The sun had come to pour a blessing on their love and their new home. In that tremulous silvery light the weeping world shone, smiling, through its tears. The sky had ceased to frown, was mildly blue. The sea, five thousand feet below, was changing from a sulky violet to a gay cobalt; the mournful cry of sea birds was lost in a chirruping overture as the feathered choir in the orange groves tuned up for evensong.

Valdemosa!

The very name was poetry; their monkish dwelling a haven of peace, crowning the lofty mountain ridge and girdled by terraces of vine and olive, and cypress-studded avenues that wound in serpent coils down to the misty plains.

Their 'cell' divided into three was approached from the cloisters by a dark stone passage and a door of oak. On the south side each room opened on to its own small square of garden, insuring privacy from its neighbour by ten-foot-high stone walls. A terrace, roughly hewn from the rock by the monks, ran under the lee of the wall and overlooked a vineyard, which ever since the monastery had fallen in disuse had spread in riotous confusion among the orange orchards and the ancient olive trees; under the gold and amber vine leaves one could see the purple ripened clusters of the grape. Despite the rain all kinds of flowers, not yet torn away by the winds, blossomed in the gardens.

The mists were lifting from the valley: the fragrant earth breathed out a message of hope, and George a sigh of thankfulness. All was well with the world, and — she prayed — with Chopin.

At least his room was dry. No damp could penetrate the solid thickness of those walls; or so she reassured herself and him. For move again, she would not. Having dragged him to a mountain peak, there they must rest, aloft in their lonely grandeur. And if she could not control the elements she could at least procure him a modicum of ease.

With the furniture bought from the Spanish refugees, and some supplemental purchases made at considerable cost and a neck-breaking descent down the slippery pass to Palma, she provided their trestle-beds with mattresses, which, if not soft, were clean; also some quilted coverlets and several yards of gaily patterned chintz for window curtains. She begged goose feathers from the consul's wife wherewith to stuff a cushion for her Chopin, spread the cold stone floors with matting and sheepskin rugs — approximately white, and partitioned off an alcove with the aid of a tartan shawl.

An eccentric stove, fashioned in Palma by the resourceful tinker, whom they found to be a trifle more obliging — or less surly — than his townsfolk, provided a moderate heat by way of an iron cylinder with a pipe attached and an outlet through the window. On top of this singular contrivance, and to disguise its conspicuity, George placed a Moorish vase, and filled it with trailing vine leaves: all declared the effect was very pleasing.

In the ruins of the chapel she unearthed a Gothic chair, and persuaded the sacristan to lend it her; also an oaken chest to hold their books and manuscripts. Nothing now was lacking to complete their home from home, except Chopin's piano, without which he swore he could not live.

When at last, after weeks of delay and the payment of six hundred francs as duty, the instrument arrived, and was hauled up the mountain by half a dozen belligerent porters, George felt that she dared ask no more of life.

As for Chopin, he writes to Julius:

Here I am, stuck between rocks and sea in a ruined monastery at Valdemosa, a few miles distant from Palma — with my hair uncurled, without white gloves, and paler than ever. Picture me in a coffin-shaped cell, the doors of which are larger than the gates of Paris, dust on the vaultings, and a small window opening on to orange, palm and cypress trees. My bed faces the window under a Moorish filigree rosette, and at my bed-side stands an ancient square box of a thing intended to serve as a writing-table, but which, I need hardly tell you, does not answer its purpose: on it a leaden candlestick, holding the greatest of all luxuries here — *a tallow candle!* — *some works of Bach, my own scrawls, and other scrawls (not mine) and nothing else* — *but silence. Such silence you could scream, only nobody would hear you!...*

I cannot send the Preludes, for as I keep telling you they are not ready yet, but I am getting on with them slowly.

Schlesinger is a cur to take my Waltzes from me, which I only gave him because he said he wanted to put them in an album to send to his old father in Berlin — *and then to go and sell them to Probst! There's a louse for you! But he can't bite me here!*

How is my servant, and what is he doing? Give my concierge twenty francs for a New Year's present from me, will you? And pay the chimney sweep's account — *it won't be much. I will send you the money. Have I any other debts to clear?*

By the way, your last letter, just received, was wrongly addressed. You say you forwarded one from my family, if so I never had it, and I do so long for it!

Tonight there is a most wonderful moon — *I never saw it more lovely. Under these skies everything breathes poetry. All nature is divine, and all the people thieves. They will give you an orange for nothing and rob you of a trouser-button!*

My piano has been waiting in the harbour for 8 days! These swine want a mountain of gold to deliver it.

For God's sake write, and please put enough stamps on your letter, and address correctly, *Palma: Valdemosa...*

As the winter advanced they became more inured to their discomfort. The stoical George could, indeed, adapt herself to any circumstances however hard: not so Chopin, the epicure.

The humid atmosphere, the crowding mists, the ceaseless onslaught of rain and damp which even the sturdy walls built by dead and gone Carthusians could not keep at bay, took its toll of lungs predisposed to weakness, and already impaired, by recent inflammation.

While with symptomatic optimism he made light of his complaint, he suffered desperately from lack of those trifling elegancies which were as vital to his body as was music to his soul.

His squeamish appetite revolted at the greasy food, the sodden bread, brought up the mountainside on the back of a donkey, and waterlogged before it reached their hermitage... And the insects! He went in mortal fear of the slimy, lurking, crawling things that oozed and pattered and buzzed on the walls of his cell: these more horrifying, even, than the ghosts, whose voices wailed in dreary chant to the howl of the wind as it went shrieking like a tortured witch along the gorge, to drown the roar of the waterfalls and freeze you to the marrow, and petrify the laughter of the children and drive them from their games into corners, afraid of what might be... Some monkish, black-robed revenant perhaps, who would glide from the cloistered dark with clank of chains and rattle of bones, to stare and beckon with a dead white finger, and on its death's-head face, a grin to send them screaming to their mother's arms for shelter.

If George's courage wavered in these abnormal atmospherics, how must Chopin, so much more sensitive, have been oppressed?

Isolated from the outside world by the storms that kept all ships in harbour, they could not have left their mountaintop no matter how they may have longed to do so. Life narrowed to a battle for existence. Even the poorest quality food was hard to come by, since the raging mountain torrents made the three-mile descent into Palma virtually impossible. George's letters were at this time a continuous lament. *What would I not give to be able to offer our invalid some nourishing beef bouillon or a glass of Bordeaux wine!*

Nor was Chopin's disgusted revulsion to the Majorcans' ways and means entirely unfounded. *Will you believe me,* writes George, *if I tell you that when one day a lean chicken was brought to table, we saw jumping on its steaming back several enormous* Maîtres Floh (fleas)*, to the intense delight of my children, who laughed till they fell from their chairs!*

Those two, with the recuperative adaptability of the very young, were soon hardened to conditions. The despairing shriek of the wind that echoed through the dark deserted cloisters, ceased to terrify. They played hide-and-seek among the ruins, and went ghost-hunting with a candle flickering like a will-o'-the-wisp in and out the shadows.

George, thankful for the respite their activities allowed her, indefatigably went about her own: the preparing of Chopin's meals, the cleansing of their cells — which her *bonne* who had not looked to rough it when she undertook the journey as a nursemaid — refused to do: and over and above all the tedious routine of daily housework, she found time to teach grammar to her daughter and classics to her son. She was taking him laboriously through Thucydides. Then, when at last she had packed them safely off to bed, she would sit down and work all night on a new book.

In the creation of *Spiridion*, conceived and written during those months of exile, Sand, at her desk, could forget herself and all externals. The shroud of fog that wreathed the crumbling arcades, the cry of the famished eagle, the bangings and the crackings, the rustling whisper of dead leaves, the shadow-haunted corridors and all their dreary solitude, held no ghosts for her, the writer, whose pen translated the mysterious harmonies of nature in a faithful record of impressions for posterity.

But for Chopin, the musician, such harmonies became distorted, and he — though we have only George's word for it — 'demoralised.' While he suffered illness with amazing fortitude, he could not overcome his superstitious fears. *For him the monastery,* says George, *was full of phantoms.*

Which have left an echo down the ages in the despairing melancholy of the Second (C Minor) Polonaise, the yearning, sad Mazurka in E Minor, in which one can discern a heart-aching nostalgia for his own lost land: and then, the Preludes…

There has been much controversy and contradiction as to the actual date when these spontaneous sketches were composed, of which Schumann writes:

I confess I expected something quite different, carried out in the grander style of his studies. But these are the beginnings of studies in which ruins and eagle-wings are strangely interwoven… He is the boldest, proudest poet of his time.

While almost all authoritative sources declare that the majority of the Preludes were written before he left Paris, there is no doubt the series must have been enlarged and greatly influenced by his visit to Majorca.

The storm-clouds, the reverberant thunder of sea upon rocks, the 'eagle-wings' of Schumann, the shades of dead monks, the ghostly chantings, the febrile rebellion of a sick man and the rage at his enforced imprisonment; the swift flashes of humour streaking through sonorous caverns of gloom as bracing as the sting of spray on pale cheek, or the glitter of sun upon rain — all are here: the surface and the deeps of his emotion, carved in cameo in his most lovely of mood-pictures.

Let the critics continue to haggle: one must at least believe that the Prelude in D Flat was composed in some such hour, on some such night, and from some waking dream as George describes it, when, *he saw himself drowned in a lake, while the heavy, ice-cold water dripped upon his breast...*

Even as the ceaseless drip-drip of rain on the stone roof of his dismal cell.

That was the day when, braving the glowering sky, George had taken Maurice to Palma on a shopping expedition.

The rain which had stopped for a brief interval came down again with renewed vigour to inundate the mountainside, so that the return journey was accomplished in something over six instead of under two hours.

Since the driver of the *birlocho* had abandoned his fares at the first downpour, George and the loudly protesting Maurice were forced to make the ascent on foot. They arrived at midnight in a parlous state. Maurice, indeed, was so far gone, having lost a shoe in the mud, that his mother had to carry him pick-a-back most of the way. By the time they reached the summit George had lost her boots, Finding it impossible to gain a foothold in the squelching slush, she had removed and flung them down the abyss where they went hopping gaily to destruction, one behind the other, to send a covey of startled curlews screaming up into the mist.

George completed the last lap of the journey up the steep incline on hands and knees dragging Maurice after her, who, between fright and discomfort, was yelling to burst his lungs.

Convinced, as time passed without a sign of them, that they were gone for ever, Chopin was half demented when at last they did appear. The feverish anxiety of hours had congealed to a frozen despair at the visions of catastrophe his imagination conjured. Then, the certainty that he would never see his lady's face again, that she lay battered out of recognition in some rocky gorge, and that vultures were already feasting upon Maurice, dissolved him in floods of tears. At his piano he sat and played their death dirge; nor did their arrival in the middle of it at once relieve his mind, for *On seeing us,* wrote George, *he rose, uttered a great cry and with a wild look and in the strangest voice, he told us 'Ah! I knew that you were dead'.*

And born of that night's exaggeration of alarms, translated into sound of raindrops, heavy, monotonous, eternal, lives his Prelude — the 'music of tears that fell from heaven' on his heart.

Tout passe … Even the dreariest winter.

Chopin awoke one morning from his restless sleep to find the sun in splendour and the birds at song, and in his square of garden a spray of almond blossom: magical, joyous.

The long nightmare was ended. Spring danced again, and never surely with such lavish sweets to offer, as though she could not enough atone for those merciless dark months when she lay hidden.

The leaden clouds had lifted; the torrents slowed their headlong flight and gushed sportively in sparkling cascades where they had roared; half-drowned buds shook off their weight of rain and burst their sheaths to perfume all the air. Flowers enamelled every hillside in a starry pattern of anemones, narcissi and jonquils. Violets nestled on the graves of the monks whose ghosts had vanished and whose worthy bones lay rotting, undisturbed. Grass, long and fine as hair, covered the bald rocks with springing green where once more the young goats grazed, and the goatherd played on his reed-pipe his tuneless song.

And music flowed from Chopin in a hymn of thankfulness — sunny, blossom-laden, that most beautiful of nocturnes in G Major.

But notwithstanding the delightful prospect of a Majorcan spring, the miseries of a Majorcan winter were yet too raw in memory to be forgotten. As soon as the boat resumed its weekly passage to the mainland, they decided it was time for them to go.

They went: and with no hesitation, although it seemed doubtful if in his weakened state, Chopin could endure the journey. However, nothing else to do but take the risk; and despite the island's transformation from a witch's cauldron to a bowery arbour swept by gentle zephyrs instead of blasting storms, and where no insect more noxious than the great honey-bees buzzed about his open window, Chopin told himself that he'd had his fill of honeymoon, and told his mistress that he must get back to work.

For his dread of the sea was nothing compared to the agonies he had suffered on land.

So, towards sunset on a golden February afternoon the little party wended, not unjoyfully, its way down the mountain path to Palma, where the steamboat, snorting at the quayside, awaited them and its more favoured passengers — the pigs.

This time at least a hundred were brought aboard. The noise and the stench of them could be heard — and smelt — all the way along the sea-front: and this, in conjunction with a nearer sight of the treacherous ocean, brought to Chopin a swift return of qualms.

Gone was the placid blue of the Mediterranean, that, viewed from the mountaintop had looked as quiet as a lake. Now, as far as apprehensive eye could reach, one saw the tossing manes of wild white horses a-gallop.

'I won't go,' said Chopin flatly. 'It's too rough and I can't face it. We must stay another week.'

George restrained herself. 'Now, now! Pray don't be difficult, my angel. What you see is just the merest breeze —'

But mere enough to tear the words from her lips, and her angel's hat from his head, to send it curvetting gaily in the gutter. Then Maurice (*surely,* vowed his mother, *the devil's own spawn and not mine!*) must leap from their chariot and go racing after it, while its owner, his hair on end, and shivering with cold, since the wind, out of sheer contrariness had changed from the south to the east — was taken with a sudden fit of coughing to spit blood.

A pretty how-d'ye-do!

Only an inhuman monster would make her little one undertake the crossing on such a day and in such sorry state. But where to go if they decided at this last minute to remain on this accursed island for another week?

'There, there, my treasure!' George hastily supplied the pale Chopin with a clean, white handkerchief, 'Hold your breath…'

What could be more unfortunate than that her precious 'Chip-Chop' should have one of his attacks just here on the sea-front, and in this hell-fire *birlocho* with its driver turning to mutter and make the sign of the cross on his filthy chest, and attract a threatening crowd.

Then, while the unhappy patient almost choked himself in the effort to do as he was bid and hold his breath — until another bright red stain appeared — the driver, who was done with muttering and prayer, began to shout. He scrambled from his seat, he thrust his frightful face within an inch of Madame's: he gesticulated, foamed, and, incited by the growling comments of the onlookers, demanded three times his fare by way of damages for the infection of his carriage.

It was almost too much for George's resourceful energy to cope with; but she made a superhuman effort to command the situation. Her maid, passing from laughing to crying hysterics, was threatened with instant dismissal if she did not hold her noise. She recalled the errant Maurice — still chasing Chopin's hat — with a peremptory, 'Let it go! What matter? He can wear mine.' She hushed her whimpering daughter, ignored her 'Chip-Chop's' protests, who between coughs and splutters gasped that he would not lose his hat; and promised their brigand of a driver anything he asked — 'only for God's sake, man, drive on!'

Embark, swore George, they must and would. Sooner be drowned at sea than stay on this damned island to be murdered.

Chopin's fears for a rough time were not unfounded. Scarcely had the ship left harbour than it began to plunge that even George was compelled to fling her half-smoked cigar overboard. Chopin was already in that state when he could have thankfully flung himself after it.

Weak, exhausted, propped against the rail of the deck, he watched the sun's cremation unfurl in banners of crimson and gold above the mountains of Majorca: like a slow andante to a funeral procession the trailing pennons passed across the orange sky, while hoods and veils of lilac dusk were gathered round the day, and night closed upon evening…

And the island melted to a shadow between a swinging moon and the rim of the sea.

TEN

He had hoped to be home within a fortnight, but three months had elapsed before Chopin saw Paris again.

At Barcelona he was taken with a haemorrhage that delayed all travel for a week, and when he recovered from the shock and fright of that, George hurried him to Marseilles to consult with Dr Cauvière, a lung specialist.

Although Cauvière insisted that the patient be kept under his personal observation in his own house for a while, we may take it his report was reassuring, for Chopin's letters at this time are less concerned with his state of health than with his business.

To Julius Fontana — who acted as his agent and whose job it was to translate into more propitiatory language the composer's correspondence with his publishers — he writes:

Tell Jan that I am not strong yet but getting better: that I refused to allow the medicos to bleed me, that I still cough (a very little) in the morning, wear woollen vests and am not — or at least not yet — consumptive! I don't drink wine. I don't drink coffee, I drink milk — and I look like a girl!...

What heaven, what bliss to be out of that maelstrom into the sun on the friendly French shore of the Mediterranean! Daily his health improved. *I begin to play, eat, walk and speak like other men,* he wrote a week after his arrival; and before the end of March was sufficiently recovered to attack his publishers, red-hot.

The reply from Julius:

Thanks — thanks — a thousand thanks, my Life! The way you run all over the place for me. I tell you! I did not expect these German tricks from Pleyel. If he makes any more fuss about the Ballade and the Polonaise, just give him this letter — here enclosed — and take the Ballade to Probst. If you can get 500 francs from him — close — if not offer it to Schlesinger. If I have to deal with a Jew I would rather it were a real one. Probst may cheat me. Schlesinger has cheated me, but he always makes it worth my while. He'd not want to let me go. Better be polite to him. He may call himself a Jew but he hates anyone else to!

So, if Probst jibs — then go to Schl. and tell him he can have the Ballade for France, England and Germany for 800 fr., and the Polonaise for Germany, France and England for 1,500. (I don't suppose he will give me that, but I won't take less than 1,200.) If he wants the Preludes tell him they are promised to Pleyel who begged me to let him have them before I went away — which is perfectly true. He did! You see, my dear, I wouldn't mind breaking with Schl. for Pleyel but I'm damned if I will for Probst. After all if Schl. makes Probst pay double for my MSS. I don't get anything out of it. Probst always undercuts me and besides he has no establishment in Paris. I will say this for Schl. that he has always paid me on the nail, and Probst has often made me wait. Anyhow they are all scoundrels... Good God! when I think of Pleyel! How he has always adored me — and now! Perhaps he hopes I will never return to Paris alive. Well, you can tell him from me, I shall — and I'll pay him a surprise visit!!

We can scarcely envy Julius his task of unthreading the main theme of his instructions from half a dozen such, entangled dialectics; but there is evidence enough to assume that a satisfactory agreement was eventually secured with Schlesinger:

To whom I would rather sell my manuscripts for nothing as I used to do, than bow and scrape to fools...

Don't speak to a soul about the Scherzo. I don't know when I shall finish it for I am not really well enough yet to start work...

How did Wieck play my Étude? I think she might have chosen something better than just this particular Étude which can be of no interest to anybody who does not know that it was written for the black keys.

Hide my MSS. so that they don't appear in print before I have a chance to go over them. If the Preludes do appear, it will be another trick of Pleyel's. But I have given up caring... God! You can finish the litany for me. You know it as well as I do.
Your Ch.

Chopin's tenancy of his house in the Chaussée d'Antin having expired, devolved also upon Julius the search for new apartments. Chopin's letters to his friend on the subject of house-furnishing and decoration appear to be a great deal more coherent than the diatribes he hurls against his publishers. He insists on dove grey wall-paper for bedrooms and sitting rooms, with a border of dark green. There must be no smoke, no smells, all windows must face south, and overlook a garden... *In the Faubourg St Germain or St Honoré are many gardens. Find something quickly, something splendid. Not a hovel.*

The patient Julius, with more regard for Chopin's pocket than his, a trifle, grandiloquent tastes, compromised between the something splendid and a 'hovel', and managed to secure a suite in the Rue Tronchet. George installed herself nearby in the Rue Pigalle.

This arrangement of two separate *ménages* did not entirely meet with Sand's approval. Although she presents herself as a sister of mercy in her attachment to Chopin, and is for ever emphasising his dependence upon her, it may be that she dwells too often and too much upon the virtues of this 'chaste' association. It is also possible that she deceived no one but herself. Her viewpoint of the relationship is startlingly naïve: *We were driven by fate into the bonds of a long connection which we both entered unawares.* Thus, blandly, she justifies her deliberate approach and his ultimate subjection, completed by their 'idyll' in Majorca.

The intimacy of their shared discomfort, his unhappy illness, her transformation from a *femme fatale* to a sick nurse enshrouded both in mutual obligation: on his side gratitude for her unfailing care of him: on hers, a moral charge.

She could not rid herself of conscience-pricks, and the thought that had she not insisted they remain upon the island, ignoring his unspoken prayer that they leave before the winter had set in: or if she had suggested a holiday in Provence, or Italy, or some less benighted spot — though to be sure she could not blame herself for unprecedented weather in a climate that had never known such rain; or if she had not dragged him to a monastery upon a mountain peak in her search for new adventure and 'copy' for her books — if she had done a thousand other things she did not do — he might not have contracted that weakness of the lungs to develop into God alone knew what.

But it is doubtful that he could have escaped her domination, even had she given him the chance. He had become her child, docile, submissive; in her he found a substitute for that motherlove, which more than love of woman his soul craved.

And George confesses she had no illusions on that score: *My love for this great artist was a kind of maternal adoration, very warm, very real; but I was still young enough to have to fight against my natural desires.*

This may have been dust thrown in her own eyes; for there is no possible doubt at all she was his mistress; or one might more reasonably say, his master, and he content it should be so. One can believe her *exigeante* in her demands, and him complacent. But while he gave her his devotion and respect, he gave her little of his confidence. Only to those most intimate friends of his boyhood — Titus, Jan and Julius Fontana, and a young Pole, Count Gryzmala, with whom he had become acquainted when he first arrived in Paris — to these selected few he stands revealed in his letters as his followers preserved them; hot from his pen, unrestrained, unguarded. The letters of a schoolboy, a helter-skelter mixture of French and Polish, and misspelt even in his own language, they have no literary value as have the letters of Mendelssohn or Schumann. But more than any studied record can one trace the very essence of this spriteish being in every swift, capricious change of mood; his *gamin* wild high spirits; his melancholy and his laughter, his almost childish delight in simple things: some new engrossing toy: *In the Palais Royal, on the theatre side is a big shop with two show windows filled with ornaments and odds and ends. Ask there if they have one of those tiny ivory hands for scratching your back — you must have seen them — a little white hand with bent fingers.*

And then his love of perfumes and of clothes. *Buy me some good soap at Houbigan Chardin's in the Faub. St Honoré, and a bottle of* Bouquet de Chantilly... *And tell my tailor to make me a pair of grey trousers at once! You can choose the shade of grey. Also a plain black velvet waistcoat with a tiny inconspicuous floral pattern... Write to me three times a day,* every *day, and — go on loving me!*

So we have it, here for our keeping, a lifelong unconscious diary of daily trivial surprises, in which the artist is forgotten in the whimsy of a moment, attaching to his signature *a thousand, thousand kisses* or a diabolically clever caricature.

But even his most favoured intimates are not permitted entrance to that remote recess where Chopin dwells unique, withdrawn from the superfluous fluidity of life; a shrine so sacred and enclosed that those who knew him best would scarcely have suspected its existence had they not listened to the echo of his soul, shaping dreams into abiding sound. *Ready to give everything,* says Liszt, who more than any other had the sight to see, the ears to hear — beyond, *yet he never gave himself...*

On his return to Paris Chopin took up residence in the apartments Julius had found for him in the Rue Tronchet, and began to prepare his manuscripts for press, to receive pupils, and compose again. His activities resumed after a period of comparative stagnation, were all-engrossing. Gutmann, one of his most brilliant pupils, was about to make his first public appearance in Paris. Moscheles, too, had come to Paris, and both he and Chopin were invited by command of Louis Philippe, to play to him and his court at St Cloud.

One may believe that neither Moscheles nor Chopin were delighted to share this honour with the other. Both thought it would have been a more tactful royal gesture to have bestowed on each a separate distinction rather than that they should appear together, the same evening: but no sign of such mean sentiment passed between the favoured two as they drove out to St Cloud in Chopin's carriage, in mutual admiration and the pouring rain, to hurry under the dripping umbrellas held over them by flunkeys, up the marble steps into the palace. The damp had put Chopin's hair out of curl, and Moscheles out of temper. Nor did the fact that his exquisite rival — in an enviable *corbeau*-coloured coat — was requested to precede him at the piano, sweeten his humour; though none to see him would have guessed Moscheles bitter. Certainly the *soirée* was informal. One reclined in an arm-chair, with, the Queen and her ladies similarly at their ease and at their needlework; the King in solitary state upon a sofa, drumming his sausage fingers on his knee — and completely out of time — to the series of nocturnes performed with a great upturning of the eyes and swaying of the hips and a great deal too *piano*, to the accompaniment of 'Divine! Delicious!' from the Queen and sighs of rapture from her ladies.

His face fixed in smiles and with rapt attention, Moscheles sat it out until his own turn came. Then the same subdued applause and sighs, and whispers, the same head-wagging from fat Louis Philippe who scarcely knew a crotchet from a quaver, but who thought it better to please everyone, artists, artisans and *bourgeoisie* alike; for who knew how long before the murmurs of the rabble turned to roars? And this little Chopin was the *bel ami* of that outrageous writer-woman Sand, a communist! But one must make friends from enemies. That woman's pen will cease to spit its fire after this... A politic manoeuvre, a *bonne-bouche* for the *juste-milieu*. As for Moscheles, — why, the Jews held all the money, and the Rothschilds were his bankers here in Paris. So muddle-headed Louis Philippe may have reasoned, while his throne shook with subterranean eruptions, not yet to burst in lava from the whirlpool of volcanic discontents that seethed below.

Both artists were obliged to give encores, and both played their compositions: Moscheles his sonata in E flat; Chopin his twelve studies, and for *finale* they played together a duet, with, as Moscheles confesses in his diary, increased abandon and a kind of musical delirium: *Indeed Chopin's transports were so* exceptionally fortissimo *that they infected the whole audience who burst into fresh eulogies until their vocabulary was exhausted. Then, as they still refused to let us go, I improvised.*

To set Chopin gnawing at his thumbnail, black-hearted. What a trick, to steal *his* sole prerogative! No time left for *him* to improvise. The hour was midnight and the King a-nod — as Chopin was not at all displeased to see. It was obvious he'd had enough of Moscheles.

The drive back may have been as equally amicable as had been the journey out, since both performers had received a present from the King; Moscheles, a dressing case with silver-mounted fittings, Chopin a cup and saucer: solid gold. But this especial favour did not restrain him from a parting scratch in his farewell.

'Does the King give you this charming travelling case as a reminder that you will soon be leaving us, my dear?'

'Does the King,' returned the smiling Moscheles, 'give you a gold saucer to lap milk?'

Even genius can have its foibles. Chopin arrived, boiling, at his apartment in the Rue Tronchet to find Sand, ensconced in his salon awaiting him. She had fallen in a doze; his entry woke her.

While Daniel served him with a cold collation, for he had been offered no refreshment at the Palace, he gave George a full account of the evening's entertainment, with some malicious cuts at Moscheles. But George had only half an ear for this. Her thoughts were elsewhere — on a plan that she had nurtured till the time was ripe to launch it; and now the time had come. She interrupted his excited flow of chatter.

'You will never sleep, my angel, if you drink so much black coffee at this hour.'

'I will, I will! Pour the coffee in my gold cup, Daniel. Look, my cup from the King! This is the second royal trophy I've received. There remains only the Queen of England to approach me.'

'Pooh! Kings and queens — and guillotines!' growled George.

'That's treason! All the world knows you're an anarchist. You'd knit at the foot of the guillotine while the King's head bounced into the basket, if you had your way, like Madame la Harangère, your grandmother.'

That sly thrust at her bourgeois descent brought the blood to her face, for although she had inherited a château at Nohant from her father, who claimed to trace his ancestry from Frédérick II, King of Saxony through the celebrated courtesan Aurore von Konigsmark, her mother was a *midinette* from nowhere.

'Take care to keep your head upon your shoulders. It looks like to burst with too much honour,' George retaliated, flushed. 'And send your man to bed. Go, Daniel — you're falling asleep on your feet.'

Daniel, unmoved by this command, awaited his master's confirmation of it. Chopin nodded. 'Yes, go, my old.' And as the door closed, he added pointedly: 'I too will go to bed within five minutes.'

'Certainly.' George smiled with closed lips. 'I will not detain you longer than you wish.'

'Which, were I not as tired as a dog,' he returned, behind a yawn, 'would be at your own pleasure.'

With a swift gliding movement she dropped on her knees beside his chair and slid her arms around him. Gently he disengaged, gazing down into her upturned face, her bronze-dark liquid eyes. Such eyes she had! Moist and mild as a cow's. What unfathomable depths, what mystery lay beneath their torpid calm? What unguessed secrets did she hold under that closed Mona Lisa smile? He would never know...

She was wearing her man's suit, a short velvet jacket over red trousers, and — absurd, coquettish touch — the prettiest, most feminine of gold slippers trimmed with fringe. Her shirt, carelessly unbuttoned, revealed the warm dusky skin, the full firm throat.

'You are like a beautiful boy. You ravish me,' he whispered. 'I love you most when you are not a woman, for as woman you are terrible. A Sphinx. A goddess — Sekhet — implacable and adamant as stone. What is it you want of me now? What new device have you contrived for my damnation?'

She reared her head: the movement was like a snake's about to strike. 'Is that how you take me then, as one already damned, to drag you down?'

'You misinterpret me.' He passed a weary hand across his forehead and showed her his fingers, wet. 'See! I am sweating. These cursed sweats! They come at me at night — always at night. Sometimes I wake with my shirt soaked through that I have to get up and change it… I am so tired, my darling. I can't talk now. Let me rest.'

'Yes, here.' She drew him to her and instinctively he turned, as a babe to the breast, seeking, while with her lips against his hair she murmured on, 'Do you know what I have been thinking while I sat waiting for two hours in this room? Listen, my little one, and I will tell you.' She could invest her voice, her tone the most ordinary utterance with magic, that one was forced to listen as to an oracle, although she told of nothing that the porter's wife could not have told as well. Only on the rarest of occasions did her speech betray the writer's art, and then one was inclined to think that it had been said already — by her pen. 'I have been thinking,' she continued, her words tickling his ear, 'that my treasure is not happily placed in his casket. These rooms are dark, unhealthy, and they smell.'

He drew himself away. 'No, never that! I could not live in a bad smell. I burn pastilles every hour —'

'Pastilles burning in a salon are like the cheap perfume used by a *cocotte* to cover the stink of her armpits.'

He winced, not for the first time, at her crudity. 'And also,' George proceeded, unaware of or ignoring his recoil, 'also I find these rooms are damp. I have made a careful survey in your absence. There is moisture on the walls, and a brown trickle, like perspiration, on the ceiling above your bed. As for the closet — my God! I retched my heart out when I —'

'Yes.' He rose abruptly from his chair, while she still knelt. 'I know that patch upon the ceiling. It is an old stain but quite dry. In the hurry of removal there was no time to have it whitewashed, but the landlord has promised me it shall be done.'

'It may be an old stain, but the damp that comes from it is new,' persisted George. 'And wringing wet. I felt it. Do you want to take your death, then, in these rooms? My faith! I wouldn't sleep here if you paid me — and my chest —' she banged a fist upon it — 'is strong as a drum.'

'Death will come to me — and to you,' Chopin said, 'no matter where or how we sleep. For sleep is death's half-sister. Each time we fall asleep,' he mused, 'is perhaps a preparation for the time to come when we shall never wake.'

'How true! As Hugo says, *Nous sommes tous condamnés à mort avec un sursis indéfini.*' George got up and stood before him squarely, her hands in her trouser pockets, her eyes under bent, thoughtful brows, on his.

'Well?' He regarded her quizzically. 'How long do you give me? I don't care for an indefinite reprieve. Let's hear the worst.'

'Don't be morbid,' she said, briskly. 'There's a suite prepared and waiting in my house. The rooms are sunny, well-proportioned, and large enough to hold three concert-grand pianos if you want them, and more than all your furniture — her swift glance swept the room, came back to him. 'I have a cook — a *cordon bleu*! Superb! A *valet de chambre* far better-mannered and better trained than your surly deaf-mute Daniel. If he were my servant I'd drown him.'

'I love Daniel as my life,' he said.

She laughed. 'You and your loves! Then you shall have your Daniel.'

'I thank you, lord,' said Chopin, dry.

'My dear!' She took his hands and held them to her face. 'Why do you so wilfully frustrate me? All I want is your happiness and comfort.'

'How boneless your hands are,' he said, 'and yet — how strong! There are no bones in your whole body. You should have been a circus trickster — a contortionist.'

'You should know,' she answered, nodding. His sarcasm was always lost on her. She could not, or she would not, see it. 'My body is all yours, my heart, my blood — yes, I'd bleed for you, beloved. You — like Juliet — could *take me and cut me out in little stars* and throw the pieces up to heaven, or tread me underfoot, I'd still be yours. You can hurt — can bite me — I would give you kisses for every torment that you make me suffer. Why don't you hurt — and hurt me more? Crush the life out of me…'

Her eyes harrowed, her breath quickened to the surging tide that now encompassed her. She might so easily have been ridiculous, dramatic or obscene; but she was none of these. She was imperious, exalted. Sounds shuddered on her lips, inarticulate and savage, to strike slow answering chords that rose more fiercely urgent and to stranger music, till her body was a sword of flame upon him and her whispers died…

'For there is no possible doubt whatever these rooms are damp,' she said.

Out of some drowsy vacuum her voice returned to him. He stirred in her arms and raised himself upon an elbow to watch her face, serene, reposeful. Her eyes opened, staring up unseeing, lost in the blessed aftermath of convalescence.

Incalculable creature! Not a sign, not a flutter to tell of that convulsion that had unloosed its frenzy upon him, and consumed her. She lay, a tempest-tossed, obliterated Aphrodite, slaked and calm, her thoughts busy on the trail of her words to recapture the main thread of her argument as she had left it — before she left herself.

'For,' said George, 'your bedroom is undoubtedly a death trap. That stain upon the ceiling is proof enough. A mausoleum. You must — yes, I insist — you must, my angel, come to me and let me care for you in my own house. I'll not intrude. We can have separate apartments, but at least I shall be there to watch — and guard your health. Good heavens! Haven't I caused you harm enough already by taking you to that infernal island? Let me make *some* reparation for that unforgettable *débâcle*. You shall have your own garden, too,' she said, working it all out behind knit brows, 'I'll build you a pavilion so that we can sleep in the fresh air… Yes, certainly. Together! Why should we hide our love as though it were a physical deformity?' demanded George, flinging wide her arms in appeal to invisible gods. 'Do you think all Paris, from the King to my concierge, does not know that I'm your lover? Yes! George Sand and Chopin are coupled now for ever. The immortals! They will name us that hereafter.'

'What a pity,' murmured Chopin, 'that one has to die to live.'
And he rose from the couch to snuff a guttering candle.

'To hell,' continued George, 'with the conventions! We're
above them. I find this mockery of two establishments an
odious compromise —' she stood to refasten her clothing and
smooth her disordered hair — 'against all my principles of
liberty, thought and action. I claim the right,' she said, 'to
conduct my life in my own way. I claim…' Then seeing him
turn pale where he leaned against the mantelshelf, she stopped.
He crumpled the next instant in an armchair. Her transports
had been too much for him: he had all but fainted.

She flew to fetch him water, but Daniel was there before her
with a phial. (Had the fellow, she wondered, been waiting all
this time upon the mat?) And Daniel's arm supported him until
the spasm passed.

'You see, Daniel,' said George decisively, 'how these rooms
are fatal for Monsieur? The damp is everywhere. It even affects
my bones — they are beginning to ache now. I should have
rheumatic fever if I stayed here another night. Positively he
must leave tomorrow.'

His face a mask, Daniel went to pull apart the shutters: the
rain had ceased; a pale light was in the sky.

'It is already morning,' muttered Chopin.

'Then,' George smiled, throwing her cloak about her
shoulders, 'you can make arrangements to leave your rooms —
today.'

ELEVEN

So for the next eight years his life with her became a marriage in all but name.

The Rue Pigalle of those days was a quiet street of medium-sized houses with gardens at the back. The rooms allocated to Chopin he found not altogether to his liking. They were neither as large nor as sunny as George had led him to believe. His piano crowded the salon which had been decorated to her taste and not his. She ran to garish colours, he to subdued half-tones. Nor had he enough space for his most cherished pieces of furniture most of which were relegated to the attic, and although George did not intrude upon his privacy, having a separate entrance up a narrow staircase to her own apartments, he was always conscious of her presence. It hovered, possessive, in the background, unseen but none the less predominant, to watch — or so he uneasily imagined — from behind her curtains the comings and goings of his pupils, the visits of his friends. Daniel, whom she had reluctantly conceded him as his personal attendant, could always be relied upon to stand as buffer between his territory and hers; but Daniel could not intercept her shadow or the telepathic messages that called him to her by day, at night, or when she willed.

They dined together every evening in her salon; after dinner she would visit his, or if she were entertaining, which she seemed to do five nights out of seven in the week, he was expected to play host to her 'Hostess' as in all his letters home he named her. He named himself her *malade ordinaire*.

Thus their winter life in Paris. In the summer he accompanied her to Nohant for a long vacation. The musical papers regularly announced his return to town, sometimes at the beginning of October or November.

Whether Chopin did or did not love country life, or whether he enjoyed the 'Society of Friends' gathered round his 'Hostess' at the Château Nohant, where she kept liberal open house, of one thing we may be sure: he always longed for his return to Paris.

To call George's rather ugly dormer-windowed, two-storeyed villa a château is a trifle euphemistic, since its only claim to such pretensions lay in the ruins of a fourteenth-century feudal castle on which site the house in 1767 had been built. Screened by a shrubbery and chestnut trees, it stood in a walled garden on the roadside between Châteauroux and La Châtre. Not far from the house, beyond larch-bordered meadows, the river Indre wound through the broad flat-lying fields of Bas-Berry.

For George, the house, the placid river, the village with its huddle of cottages and its grey church tower, were girt about with memories of childhood. Here she had lived with her grandmother, that impeccable old autocrat Madame Dupin; here too, at the bend of the road on the way to La Châtre by the tall poplar tree, George's madcap father, Maurice Dupin, had been thrown from his horse and killed; and on the gravelled terrace that skirted the dining room the little Aurore Dupin had been taught her lessons, under supervision of Grand-mère. In those meadows edging the Indre she had ridden her white pony bare-backed and astride, to be punished for that outrage by such a birching that for days she could not sit. To this house she had come as a bride with her handsome stolid young husband, who had not yet shown his temper or his tendency to drink. Here she had borne her babies, dreamed her dreams of a new world to be by her created, and had fallen in love for the first time — with that Aurélien de Sèze, whose name had been dragged up in her divorce suit.

And from this house, too, she had escaped, leaving her children to the questionable care of, till then, a complacent husband, while her pen spluttered the 'New Doctrine' in an attic in Montmartre.

That was Nohant in its quiet days; but days at Nohant were not always quiet. From the panelled walls of the dining room, the portraits of arrogant Dupins stared down upon strange scenes and stranger company. The house was always full — too full even for George's free and easy hospitality. She would arrive with Chopin for a 'quiet' weekend, to find a dozen 'friends', some of whom she had never seen before, assembled there and perfectly at home. 'What can I do?' she asked despairingly. 'How can I feed a regiment? But if I make a fuss they'll say I'm stingy.' She was anything but that, generous to folly; over-lavish. She would stint herself sooner than shut her doors to anyone who chose to enter. All were welcomed with wide arms to her table that groaned under the goodly produce of the farm. Short staffed — for she could never keep a servant — she would if need be do the cooking for two dozen, commandeering help from those friendly 'souls' who were not at their devotions before the shrine of Art.

Liszt, his sprightly countess, Balzac, Delacroix, and a young opera singer, Pauline Garcia, a heavy, black-eyed Spanish girl whose powerful soprano went throbbing through the night to set the nightingales in the poplars trilling an accompaniment — all came, all went; but Chopin stayed — and out-stayed his predecessors.

So year after year the pageant was repeated, familiar faces vanished, reappeared. Heine came, with serpent's poison in his poet's tongue, to make spiteful puns at everyone's expense, to whisper his malicious gossip into Chopin's ear, and make love to Sand to sweeten her while he made trouble. All Paris tittered when he hurried back to spread his tales, highly spiced of the *passetemps* at Nohant; of how George had built herself a small theatre, of how in short doublet and long hose she pranced about the stage, and played dumb charades — with insinuating gestures — while Chopin, lost in reverie, would improvise behind the scenes, all unconscious that the fun waxed faster and more furious till the charades ceased to be dumb, and developed into Rabelaisian pantomime enacted with much gusto and the circulation of more wine, until the morning.

Small wonder, then, that Chopin pined for Paris. Such wealth of entertainment in George's Liberty Hall must have, a trifle, jarred. George, naively, could not understand why, when he was in Paris he always longed to be at Nohant, and when he was at Nohant he always hated it...

There seemed to be no suiting him. George attributed his dislike of the boisterous revels that were the order of the day — and night — at Nohant, to his ill health. If he had been more robust he would surely have delighted in that happy-go-lucky holiday life where genius met genius to play at guttersnipes, dispensing with the pomp attached to fame. But her little *malade ordinaire* did not always fit in with this holiday humour. Although there were times when he would keep the table in an uproar with his mimicries, and act the clown, play monkey-tricks, and be as jocular and waggish as the worst of them, one was never certain when he would turn prude to cast a damper on the gay proceedings. He was squeamish; he could not adapt himself to cap and bells. A coarse jest would set him sulking the whole evening, to sit apart and moody — *prim,* said

George, *as an old maid who refuses to wash below the waist for shame of her own navel.*

There was the time, for instance, when an April Fool trick was played on a distinguished visitor who called to pay homage to Madame. George thought fit to be funny and to hide behind a curtain while she sent her maid — dressed up as herself — to receive the stranger, and split her sides to watch him bowing and offering all sorts of honeyed compliments to the giggling tongue-tied gawk. He departed none the wiser and with more eulogies upon his lips for this *literary genius, who was as simple and unaffected as a child.* And there was worse than this, to rouse the gentle Chopin to a scorching fur: that occasion when a certain Monsieur Pelletan, a quiet, modest, very shy young man, tutor to Maurice, was the victim of a monstrous perpetration. All in the best of fun, no doubt — but such excess of wit was not Chopin's.

The unfortunate tutor, having come a little late to table after a long session with his pupil, whom he was coaching for a near examination, was presented with a delicacy on a dish which he made attempt to eat and which he discovered to be something so utterly revolting that the poor youth fled the house never to return. The story was told by Madame d'Agoult, who witnessed it. She may doubtless have been equally disgusted for she, born *grande dame*, had as little taste for pleasantries of this sort as had Chopin. The affair had to be hushed up and Chopin pacified: but took all George's cajolery to do it. He had almost had enough of Nohant, if not yet enough of her.

After that affair his influence at the château was, unobtrusively, beginning to be felt. He would countenance no obscenities, no hideous 'practical jokes' in his presence: gradually he weeded out the undesirables, and decided who of his own chosen friends should be his fellow guests: these few were invariably limited to Liszt and his little lady, between whom and Sand might be observed a growing coldness; Franchomme, Fontana, Gutmann, Chopin's favourite pupil, Delacroix, the painter — and once, for one whole month to cherish, Louise his sister, come from Poland to be with him, and married now, but not to Jan — this the first time in fourteen years that they had met: a joy to be remembered.

So season succeeded season, and the past became the present, fraught with memories of those loved ones at home, whom he would never see again. His father had died, while his mother, in her lingering malady, still lived, mercifully soon to follow him without whom life was already ended.

And in his first anguish of sorrow, Chopin turned to George for the comfort that only she could give; never did she fail when he needed her.

Her rooms in the Rue Pigalle had become hateful to him. 'I can't work here,' he said, 'the colours clash.' But it was not only colours that clashed. More and more her 'Chip-Chop', her third child as she would sometimes call him, was learning self-assertion: imposing his will and his desires upon hers; she knew better than to cross him. She gave in. They moved: lock, stock, and barrel, Maurice, Solange, and all, to a charming house of Chopin's choosing in the more select Cité d'Orléans, near to the Rue St Lazare.

Here, then, we find him, joint ruler of her kingdom, and prince in his own domain.

The Cité d'Orléans was — and still may be — a small square overlooking a grass plot with a fountain in the middle and a private gateway to guard it leading from the Rue Taitbout. There, in company with Madame Marliani, wife of the Spanish Consul, and one of. George's most favoured intimates, a *ménage à trois* was established. George, to whom the exigencies of housekeeping — unless on holiday — were irksome and a tiresome deterrent to her work, contrived that she and Chopin should take their meals with her dear Marliani.

To this arrangement he raised no objection. His rooms at least were his own. For that much concession he had stipulated when they entered into mutual agreement of the leasehold. And to his apartments and the solitude he loved more than the society of women, more than the clamorous voices of young people in their teens — for Maurice and Solange were growing fast — there to his own dominion he retired, withdrawn, locked in, at peace, untouched by the stream of life that passed him by; the daily, almost hourly visitors who ceaselessly arrived, with or without invitation, at the house of the celebrated couple, to gossip, take 'pot luck' and lounge till George unceremoniously turned them out.

Both now were in full blaze: their *affaire*, from the salons of the Rothschilds to the dens of the *apaches*, was known to all. George made no attempt to screen it. She flaunted her love and her lover sky-high. When he made a reappearance on the concert platform after several years' retirement, she attended in the front row and in full fig — a *toilette* completely *à la mode* — with smiles on her lips, his jewels round her throat, reflecting the flashing triumph in her eyes. She held his flowers, a bouquet of violets, his favourites, it was noted: a harp of violets and a laurel wreath, her gifts to him, were handed up at the end of the performance. She claimed her right to call him hers before the world. None could gainsay it. Were they not twin stars, a Castor and Pollux in the Milky Way of immortality?

Yes, and more: it was generally accepted that she and she alone had saved Chopin from death. He owed his life to her self-sacrifice. She was his nurse, his *garde-malade*, his wife, his mother. Soul and body she possessed him; even his music growing greater as her passion grew in him, was inspired by her adoration.

So the whispers of society fanned smoke to flaming gossip around these two, the most criticised, most talked-of pair in Paris, till none knew truth from slander, and some called Chopin a pimp and Sand a saint, his saviour. Others named her his evil genius, a vampire who fed her insatiable thirst on his frailty, to drain him of his life's blood with her demands.

If rumours such as these reached the ears of the Princess Marcelline she did not heed them. Her king could do no wrong; and who, she may have reasoned, could blame that sinister dark woman for the love she gave and had inspired? One might suffer in the knowledge that this irresistible Delilah had been granted all that makes life bearable, but one could not hate her for her witchery, though one might fear it.

Something of this, perhaps, was in the thoughts of the Princess Czartoryska when, on a May morning in the year 1847, she came to Chopin for her lesson. She had been away in the South of France for the winter, and had returned to Paris for the spring.

Descending from her carriage at the gates of the Cité d'Orléans and attended by her maid, she walked along the private way to Chopin's house. In the centre of the grass plot round which the square was built, a fountain sprayed a fairy shower, catching the rainbow light. All the lilacs were in bloom and a laburnum, weighted down with purest gold. A marvellous sweet day it was, filled with nameless flower-scents and pricked by an impish wind that played with the leaves of the plane trees and sent the dust whirling in tiny cyclones along the cobbled path and under Marcelline's springing hoop that she must press her hands to her sides to hold it, and laughed for no other reason that that she was glad though she could not have told why.

As she stood on the step of her master's house, the door opened, not to admit her, but to allow another to pass out. Marcelline stood aside, and in a moment it was as if the sky had clouded. That woman! In her velvet jacket and her trousers, with her hair on her shoulders and smiles on her lips.

'Madame la Princesse Czartoryska, I believe?' And before Marcelline could find the breath to answer, that voice, deep-throated, husky, spoke again. 'We have met — once, I think, before. Some years ago.'

'Yes, I...'

'You will not know me?'

There was no challenge in the query: no hostility in that searching glance, although it seemed to Marcelline that she had been stripped naked and stood there in her skin.

'I remember meeting you, Madame. I ... had no opportunity on that occasion to ... to thank you for your kind attention.'

'Pooh! That!' And 'that' was dismissed with the snap of an ink-smudged finger. 'You have come for a lesson, Madame?'

'Yes, Madame.'

'I hear that you are exceptionally gifted. Why do you not use your God-sent gift — to give away? Why do you not share it? Why are you so seldom heard in public, and then only for some social charity performance?'

'I am not a professional pianist, Madame.'

'Professional! What exactly is the meaning of professional? One is, or one is not, an artist. You, Madame, are an artist — but an artist in prison. Do you speak English?'

'Yes, Madame.'

'Then perhaps you have read that sublime English poet William Blake who says, *A robin redbreast in a cage puts all heaven in a rage*... You, Madame, are imprisoned in the stone walls of your class from which you can no more free yourself than could Blake's caged bird or a galley slave from his chains. Have you no longing — no desire to escape to your own kingdom? All art is concentrated in the search for an ideal truth, and it is, after all, the simplest ideas, the most trivial circumstances that inspire the creation of the artist. I,' that impassive voice continued on a warmer note, 'am not unobservant. I have seen you when you have not seen me. At Chopin's concerts I have watched you more than I watched him. You are lonely ... you are lost, Princess.'

Had that been said, or whispered? Or was it the mocking breeze that spoke in the plane trees? Was it the scent of lilacs or what overpowering sweetness that left her dumb, bewitched, agape like any schoolgirl? With an effort Marcelline gathered her ebbing dignity about her like a cloak, her mouth framed to words, unuttered, her body poised to bow, and pass. This woman had presumed too far. One did not — in one's right senses — accost a stranger with such a personal approach: or was it an *im*personal approach? Was this extraordinary creature merely giving utterance to her own mental observations? Was she aware, actually, of the presence of ... of one so insignificant as Marcelline Czartoryska?

Then, before she could collect herself or her reeling thoughts, she found her hand possessed in a strong narrow clasp. 'Forgive me, Madame la Princesse, for my uncouth behaviour. I have no *savoir-faire*, no manners. What comes to my lung leaps out on my tongue. As you see and hear me — so I am.'

And like a panther, or some swift gliding animal, she went, so silently one would think her feet were padded, down the path, into the gate next door; and where she had been, stood Daniel.

If he had heard or seen, or listened, his face betrayed no sign. A man of wood, who returned her murmured greeting with a movement of his lips as though they were pulled by wires.

And, still with that same feeling of unreality upon her and that woman's touch still burning through her glove, Marcelline, bidding her maid attend her in the hall, was admitted to the waiting room to find it already occupied by two gentlemen in talk that hushed as she came in. Both rose, both bowed to her entrance, reseated themselves, and, heads together resumed their conversation, which Marcelline with a thrill of pleasure noted was in Polish.

So seldom did she hear her language spoken in this, to her, always alien city — for not even with her master did she speak anything but French, and to her husband she scarcely spoke at all — that she sat listening not so much to their speech as to the grateful sound of it.

To the Princess Marcelline, perception, perhaps from solitude, had been limited to that degree when life beyond her music was less lived than studied, as through a microscope one may examine the curious phenomena of a busy universe contained within a drop of stagnant water; so to her did the inhabitants of that outer world in which she lived but had no being, offer an acute and sometimes painful interest.

Unobserved, since after that formal acknowledgment of a lady's presence neither had glanced in her direction, she watched them. Each presented a striking contrast to the other: the one so tall, so thin that his clothes hung upon his bony frame as on a scarecrow; a crop of black untidy hair streaked with silver receding from a high dome-shaped forehead, and eyes like restless coals sunk deep in their sockets under peaked bushy brows. His linen was by no means fresh, and his long nervous fingers were stained to the knuckles as though he had been dabbling them in dye.

From behind the lowered veil of her bonnet Marcelline regarded his companion, he as point device in elegance as the other was shabby; his buff pantaloons so tightly strapped beneath his boot, and so creaseless it was wonderful that he could move without a split; his coat of bottle green so waisted one could not doubt but he wore stays; his hair shining with pomade and carefully arranged to hide a baldness; his rosy face, round and whiskered, after the style favoured by the English 'dandies', as also were his clothes, tailored to that perfection which only Englishmen could carry and not appear ridiculous. But there was nothing English in his manner, in his gestures, in his bearing, or his face to which her gaze was drawn again — and then again, in lightning recognition…

She all but spoke his name aloud, but he, now, was speaking louder, entirely forgetful of her unobtrusive presence, while his shabby friend sat moodily, his chin in his stock, a finger worrying his underlip, his face as dark as thunder.

'For,' vehemently declared the whiskered gentleman, 'it behoves us to restrain this outrage — this monstrous libel on his name. It must not be permitted to appear in print. It must be instantly withdrawn from publication.'

'It is already published,' returned the other with a sound in his throat like a snarl.

'It must,' the whiskered gentleman repeated, 'be withdrawn.' He rose. On the table lay a book; he picked it up, he opened it, and slammed it down again with an explosive comment — in Polish — that brought a blush to the cheeks of the Princess,

229

who, however, was sufficiently intrigued to read the title of the volume, and glad, for once of her long sight which necessitated the wearing of spectacles when she read music: a vain sorrow, that, to her — even though she knew Chopin would never notice if she came to her lesson in a mask.

And with a little twist to her lips that had learned to smile that way — at herself, Marcelline registered the name of the book and its author: *Lucrezia Floriani par George Sand.*

Published? Already? Then only just; perhaps this very day, for the Princess had a standing order with her bookseller to send her all the latest works by Madame Sand the moment they appeared.

'We may yet be in time to suppress it.' The fashionable gentleman seemed very put about, lashing himself into a fine fury as he turned to deliver this pronouncement. 'I tell you, Jan, I will not tolerate the publication of this abominable caricature, this damning insult to one whom I revere above all men — to one whom all Poland reveres! I take this as a personal affront not only to him but to —' the gentleman thumped his chest — 'myself, as a true patriot. Are we Poles to sit meekly by and watch his great name cast before these French swine to be mocked at and abused? Are we to watch this filthy display of connubial bed-sheets aired upon a public clothes line? What a cesspool of vulgarity must be the mind of this hag, this harridan who —'

'Pan Woyciechowski!'

Marcelline was on her feet, and following that clear, peremptory interruption had crashed a heavy silence. With all expression save that of astonishment swept from his countenance, Titus surveyed her who spoke his name.

He saw a trembling little woman in a last year's model of a gown that should never have been just that *wrong* shade of mauve: and a shawl too largely patterned for so small a figure: and a veiled bonnet tied with ribbons scarcely whiter than her face, and wisps of hair, hay-coloured, straggling under it. Her eyes, like brown velvet, were fastened upon his with a look of startled defiance.

'I realise,' she said, and moistened her lips to say it, 'that you are unaware I speak your language. It is my language too... You did not know me, Pan Woyciechowski. But you used to know me ... once. A long time ago. At Antonin.'

He knew her then, and was beside her; and almost on his knees. 'Princess! Princess Czartoryska! Am I to be forgiven? You were a child when I saw you last. How could I have forgotten the little Princess Marcelline!'

A crooked smile came upon her lips. 'We must all grow older, Pan Woyciechowski. But I never forget — a friend.'

And then she held her hand out, and Titus, fiercely red, bent over it and kissed it. Her gaze slipped past him to that other who stood watching. Titus turned. 'He also is a friend of mine and Chopin's... Dr Matuszyński.'

'And a compatriot, too,' she said softly. 'Have you recently arrived from Poland, Doctor?'

'No, Princess. I live in Paris now.'

'But I,' said Titus, interposing, 'have just arrived. Last night. And since we are all friends,' he paused, 'of his — of Chopin's, may I speak freely, Madame?'

'If,' she looked with timid searching from one to the other, 'if that of which you speak is right to hear.'

'We can speak no wrong of him we love, Princess,' said Titus, pompously. 'I have come to Paris on a mission. Have we time to talk?' He glanced at the clock.

'I am a little early for my lesson, sir, and Monsieur Chopin forgets time when he is teaching.'

'Then, Princess, if you will allow me to explain.' Titus took the book from the table and handed it to her. 'This is an advance copy of George Sand's latest novel which has been sent to me by another loyal friend — Julius Fontana — for my opinion. I received it two days ago, and did not read it all, but enough to bring me as fast as train and diligence could carry me to Paris in the endeavour to prevent the circulation of this scurrilous attack on one who —' Titus hesitated, cleared his throat and hurried on — 'whose name and fame have already been too much the subject of slanderous criticism from the *canaille* of Paris studios.'

'I think, Pan Woyciechowski,' said Marcelline, low-voiced, 'that no work of fiction and no pen, however able, can damage the name of one who is as far above slanderous criticism as the sun is above the earth.'

Jan nodded in sullen agreement, but Titus would have none of that.

'Your sentiment, Madame,' he said with a hasty gallantry that barely concealed his impatience, 'is admirable, and admirably expressed, but the world, alas! does not think in terms of sentiment. The world is always prone to find a poisoned lie much sweeter than a truth — that has no spice in it. And I maintain,' persisted Titus, his eloquence increasing to an excitable crescendo, 'I maintain that we, his fellow countrymen, cannot permit the name of this great son of Poland to be publicly associated with an illicit connection and discussed open-mouthed as a result of that —' he pointed to the book which Marcelline had replaced on the table — 'of that indictment penned by a malicious fiend who, not content with her conquest, must needs malign him.'

'But how?' queried Marcelline, who in total ignorance of the contents of the book, was at a loss to understand Pan

Woyciechowski's indignation. 'And why should this lady seek to malign him?'

'Revenge,' said Titus, darkly.

'*Revenge?*' whispered Marcelline, dry-mouthed.

'Yes, Princess, revenge. Is it not obvious?' Titus appealed to the silent Jan, but receiving no more support to his statement than a ferocious glare, he turned again to Marcelline. 'Is it not so, Madame? Believe me I have watched with the deepest disapproval and regret the progress of this unhappy relationship from its beginning, years ago, when I implored our friend to dissever himself from an entanglement that could only bring him into disrepute. But would he listen? Would he heed me who have loved him as a brother? No. Obstinate. Our friend, Princess, is obstinate. Always was and ever will be. Headstrong. As I see it, then,' continued Titus, waxing warmer as his listeners waxed cold, 'our friend seeks to free himself from a situation that was never of his choosing. It was forced upon him by an influence stronger than his will. This book presents a deliberate — a cruel misconstruction of the character of Chopin, but oh! so artfully disguised as the weakling poet, the peevish "Prince Karol", that there is no mistaking its diabolical intent. Read it, Princess! You will see for yourself,' and Titus rolled his eyes so wildly while all the blood in his body seemed concentrated in his face, that Marcelline might well have thought he looked to have a fit, 'you will see — and you will wonder at the depths of depravity to which this unholy being has sunk, in order to inflict pain upon one who has been her avowed —'

'Pan Woyciechowski!' Again Marcelline's voice rang out to silence him. Her face was now as pale as his was red. 'I feel bound to discontinue this discussion. The private life of

Monsieur Chopin must remain private — even among his friends.'

Titus turned, if possible, a deeper scarlet. 'Your reproof, Princess, is merited. Nevertheless, I feel bound,' and he looked at her straightly, 'to persevere in my crusade to annihilate this book. And as our doctor here will take no part in my activities on his friend's behalf, I shall pursue my campaign unaided. I thought — had hoped, Princess, to enlist *your* aid in this crisis.'

'Mine, Pan Woyciechowski?' She crushed her hands together. 'How could I...?'

'Your name, Madame,' urged Titus, too intent upon his mission to be aware of her distress, 'is all-powerful in Paris. If you could have made known your disapproval —' His words faded as hers were gently interposed.

'My husband's name, Pan Woyciechowski, admittedly is influential, but I who share his name have no influence at all. And if I spoke —' that faint crooked smile came upon her lips — 'there is none would hear me. I have not read the book, sir, nor in view of its effect upon yourself, do I think that I would care to read it. Still more, if its intention is —' she hesitated — 'is disloyal, do I feel that I — that we — the friends and compatriots of Chopin, should ignore it.'

Jan from his distance nodded. Encouraged by that truculent concordance, she continued, 'We who love — who honour him,' and behind her veil now her eyes were starry, 'can honour him most by ignoring any sign or word, or whisper that could be even remotely misconstrued by the — unworthy.'

Then, before she had quite recovered from the effort of this, almost the longest speech that she had ever made; before she could still the tremble in her heart as the word 'love' had left it, the door opened and Chopin was in the room.

He saw not her, not Jan who stood like God condemning; he had eyes only for Titus.

She watched those two embrace, seeing in the boyish exuberance of Chopin's greeting yet another facet of that personality in which her own was wrapped.

'Madame la Princesse!' He was full of feverish apologies. Here was a friend from Poland just arrived. Quite unexpectedly. Madame would understand? Ah! But of course! The Princess Czartoryska and his good friend Titus had known each other since the old days at Antonin — so Madame would excuse — would be so gracious as to excuse him for a few — a *very* few moments and wait in the music room where she would find on the piano a new waltz, an amusing trifle of a thing written —

'I will tell you how it was written, Princess. The other day we — Madame Sand and I —' she marvelled at the ease with which he spoke that name, without a tremor — 'were watching Madame's little dog chasing its tail round and round on the hearthrug. It was so droll to see it! "Improvise me a waltz for my little dog," said Madame Sand. And so I did — and I've called it *'La Valse du Petit Chien!'* You will find it a wonderful exercise for the fingers, Princess. Perfect for you! Go and play it now, if you please. And then when you have read it through — you shall play it again for me. Daniel!'

But Daniel was already there to conduct her to the music room; and like a child, obedient, she went.

A new novel by George Sand had always been regarded as a literary event, but the appearance of *Lucrezia Floriani* was a beacon. Although Titus had arrived too late to do more than add fuel to the blaze, he and all the friends of Chopin were loud in their condemnation of the book as a deliberate libel on his name, and an affront that should be challenged.

If the voice of Titus rang the loudest, the voice of Heine was more often heard. *Sand has treated our Chopin disgracefully in a divinely written novel...*

There was no suppressing it. Everybody flocked to read the book, gloatingly to identify in the character of Prince Karol, a young gentleman of *exceeding charm and frail physique*, the prototype of Chopin, and in the saintly unselfish Lucrezia who nursed him through a lingering illness and ultimately died of her untiring bedside attentions, a self-portrait of George Sand.

The most intimate details of a relationship that for years had been the favoured slice of talk among the 'Chosen' were now uncovered: an astounding revelation, ruthlessly adroit in its subtle rendering of two temperaments diametrically opposed. The first causes of dissent, the gradual expansion of mutual hostility, the delicate insinuations of a master-mind thrusting its analytical probe like a surgeon's knife among the fibrous tendrils of a love that had sickened of its own malignancy — all was here, for all to run and read.

Why had she done it? What perverted sense of humour had caused her to produce this preposterous caricature of her devoted lover? Could it be that he was tiring and that she had chosen this unkind means to a revenge?... Titus possibly had loosened that motive to be scattered as straws on the gossiping winds. The ladies seized upon such whispers joyfully. The men were more inclined to disagree. It was Sand who sought to break off an association which had become a nuisance. After all — a man who was but half a man with half a lung, what use could he be to a woman Hercules? She had worn him out, had drained him dry, and was now ripe for his successor.

In Paris salons the tongues clacked till they were sore while George's sales mounted. 'But why this hullabaloo about the book?' she asked. *Her* conscience was at rest. If any similarity of type had been created, it had been entirely unconscious. Moreover, she had given him the chance to read the proofs. If he had read and passed them, then there was no more to say.

True, she had given him the proofs, and he had put them on one side to read at leisure, had forgotten all about them, and had never dared to tell her so lest he should cause offence. He offered her, instead, a mouthful of honeyed compliments which she swallowed with gullible credulity and a lusty appetite for more. Even George was not above those human weaknesses common to all mankind and to authors in particular, for whom no praise can be too sweet. And if these rag-pickers chose to put a false interpretation on her work, what did *she* care? Let them babble till they choked. She'd close her ears so she'd hear nothing of it. As for 'Chip-Chop', the poor precious, he lived in a daze. He'd never recognise his own face in a glass.

She was mistaken.

'Mama has put you in a book.' Thus when he arrived at Nohant a few days before the publication of *Lucrezia*, did George's daughter greet him.

Solange at seventeen was a golden-haired imperious young beauty with the profile of an Apollo and a precocity beyond her years. For that one can scarcely blame her.

She had been a problem child, petulant, wilful, violent in her likes and dislikes, and a bone of contention between her parents. At the age of seven she was abducted by her father whose paternal conscience, a trifle tardily awakened, had decided that his wife was no fit guardian for his little daughter. Whereupon, after careful plotting, he stole Solange from the garden at Nohant and her unsuspecting governess, while George was otherwise engaged in Paris. By the time this disaster was discovered, Solange and Casimir Dudevant were well away on the road to Spain.

The distracted George, who, whatever else that she might not have been, was a devoted mother, roused herself to instant action. In a post-chaise full of gendarmes, with an armed escort and a warrant for the arrest of Casimir, she pursued the fugitives three days and nights, finally to overtake them on the frontier. Since Casimir Dudevant had forfeited all claim to his own child, there was nothing for it but to hand Solange over to her mother who returned with her in triumph to Nohant.

The adventure was not without its triumph for Solange, who notwithstanding her extremely tender years, had a good sense of her self-importance. This had been considerably enhanced by the battle royal between her parents for the possession of her unworthy little person. With the advent of Chopin in her mother's life Solange became still more aware of herself as an entity. Between Chopin and this *enfant terrible* existed a very real affection based on a tacit alliance, a mutual sympathy with and understanding of each other. Both chafed against the influence that dominated their environment, both resented the strangely assorted company who visited the caravanserai at Nohant. Solange had come to a premature maturity with a full awareness of the relationship that existed between Chopin and her mama. Since her earliest infancy she had been an innocent spectator of unbridled excesses and haphazard intrigues, and had developed an unchildlike distrust of and contempt for those whom she contacted. She read enormously, wrote a little, had no great opinion of her mother's novels, and held decided views on life as she herself would live it.

From her strait-laced great-grandmother Dupin, Solange had inherited a strong streak of conventionality. All in her that was bred from the squirearchy against which the young Aurore

Dupin had revolted, recurred defiant and protesting in the daughter of George Sand. When Solange left the schoolroom, the clash of arms increased. Solange had her ambitions, her own private dreams, and an inborn contempt for those lower orders whom her mother so stoutly championed. Solange was royalist to her backbone; she despised Louis Philippe, the self-styled 'Citizen-King' who hung on to his throne by hobnobbing with the bourgeoisie, rubbed shoulders with the rabble and was a traitor to his crown. Had she lived at the time of the Great Revolution she would have proudly died upon the guillotine. She wove romances of herself as heroine, driving in the tumbril holding to her nose a handkerchief soaked in *Peau d'Espagne* to keep away the smell of the common people. She longed to inhabit that *beau monde* which she had only been permitted to glimpse through the wrong end of a telescope, distorted by her mother's views and doctrines; a world of distinction and breeding where women were ladies and men gallant; a world where the love affairs of one's mama were kept a secret — not shouted to the roof-tops of Montmartre: a world where obscene jests were never witnessed, never uttered, never known, and where girls were well enough endowed with ample *dots* to marry high-born husbands. But for the daughter of a *mésalliance* whose father was a drunkard and whose mother was a whore — Solange could be outspoken to herself — what hope had she of a footing in that guarded world which she so longed to enter?

This then her grievance. George had a name for it: 'You're too full of your own snobbery. You and Chip-Chop are a pair. You two should have been mated.' George had always openly discussed the facts of life — her own and other people's — with her children. 'He'd have been happier with you than with me. You both say your prayers to a title. We all know Chopin was nursed on the knees of princesses, and that you would sooner entertain a marquis to your table than the Son of God.'

In Chopin Solange found a staunch ally. She knew that she could do with him as she pleased. From the first he had adored and petted, spoiled her, gave her pin money and showed in a hundred ways that he favoured George's unruly little daughter more than George's cherished son.

And here was another problem. As a young boy Maurice had been devoted to Chopin, attended him when he was ill, bought him delicacies, listened enraptured to his music, and sat in worship at his feet. But that was before he understood the intimacy that had existed between his mother and his hero. When Maurice grew old enough to realise the truth he turned insanely jealous of the fragile invalid who had usurped him in his mother's affection, and was the acknowledged master in *his* house.

Thus the *ménage* gradually became divided into two camps, with Maurice and Solange perpetually at war, George as go-between at pains to keep the peace, while Chopin, all unconscious that he was the main cause of dissent in a hitherto united family, continued to regard George's son as his young brother and George's house and daughter as his own.

'Mama has put you in a book,' Solange triumphantly announced. 'Did you know?'

She was well aware that 'Chip-Chop' did not know. If he had read those proofs he would surely not have let them go to press without revision.

So, from God alone knew what obscure desire to bring about a crisis in the family, Solange enlightened him. She put a copy of the novel by his bedside. He read it long into the night: he read until from wounded pride and mortification he could read no more, and lay feverishly reviewing his past life with his

Lucrezia, tracing back each episode from that first disastrous 'fiasco' in Majorca, when but for her, he told himself, he would have died. Now that his eyes had been forced open he could see, and seeing wondered that her love for him could have survived the strain of his, as she portrayed him; weak, ineffectual, irresolute, exacting… A merciless exposure. Was it true? Was that indeed as he appeared to her? He had sometimes noticed, or thought that he had noticed a constraint in her manner towards him during a recurrence of one of his 'attacks'. He had fancied that on these occasions her visits to his bedside were made as an unspoken protest, a kind of moral obligation and not from any keen anxiety on his behalf.

Her frequent reappearances with bowls of broth and bottles of wine did not altogether nullify the effect of her glum face and martyred silence: the impatient jerk of a blind as she pulled it down in answer to his querulous remark that the sun was in his eyes, or pulled it up that he could see the moon: the changing of his sheets when a night-sweat had soaked them through; all these infinitesimal grains of circumstance were piled one upon the other, until a mountain towered… But, of course!… He writhed in self-abasement, cursing his abysmal blindness. Not to have known, not to have seen how she must have suffered in this role of sick-nurse imposed upon her by his frequent illnesses, attending to his private needs, waiting on him in an intimacy that must have poisoned if not killed the flower of their love.

This, then, was her unconscious protest, this revelation, made — so he excused her — with no deliberate intent to cause him pain, but because she, as artist, must unconsciously release through her own medium the flood-tide of her emotions. He understood. None better. Did he not create from the same source? The mind of the artist is supersensitive, his

241

impressions more violent, his inner world of thought and feeling more dramatic. Every drift of sight or action is retained in its own image, constantly recurring in a perpetual interweaving of colours, textures, sound, to be translated into ardent melody, a poet's song, or some significant association of ideas... But still, the shame of it! The dreadful shame of knowing that all these years together had been for her a penance of self-sacrifice, she who lived to love. Was it too late to start again, or was the novelty of their romance irrevocably befouled by the sickly repetitions of his illness?

So on and on his mind ran madly through a maze of conflicting emotions until he slept, exhausted, to wake so unrefreshed and strengthless that Daniel urged him to remain in bed.

'No, I shall get up as usual,' he said, determinedly. 'I am perfectly well.'

'But M'sieu is in a fever,' protested Daniel.

'I am in *no* fever! And for God's sake, man, don't stare at me as though I were a corpse. All this fuss! There has been too much fuss already about my health. Now get me dressed.'

Daniel shook his head; he had seen a splash of red on the silk handkerchief under his master's pillow. 'Has M'sieu been coughing all night again?'

'Parbleu!' Chopin cried explosively. 'Take your long face away. I have not coughed and I'm not dead — yet. Open that new bottle of *eau de toilette* and pour it all into my bath. I've been sweating and I smell. And if you tell Madame a word of this, I'll kill you! So hold your mouth.'

Daniel held his mouth. He knew better than to open it when Monsieur was in his moods.

Chopin took his breakfast on the terrace with Solange. George never appeared until midday and Maurice was out riding.

'Does your mother expect a houseful this weekend?' Chopin apprehensively enquired.

Solange gave a shrug. 'Who can tell? They come and go. Mama's friends regard our house as an hotel. She has invited a new man — a sculptor called Clésinger. He has written to ask if he may make a bust of her. You'd better look out, my dear,' she added, saucily. 'Mama says he's young. She likes them young. Do you know him?'

'I may,' said Chopin in an icy tone that belied his heightened colour, 'I may have met him.' The little puss! Trust her to find the softest spots to scratch... *Likes them young*. Too true, indeed. But Chopin was young no longer. The seventeen-year-old Solange made him feel seventy.

'Oh! So you've met him.' She wrinkled her nose. 'Is he dirty?'

'My dear child!'

'Well? Aren't they usually dirty, these baboons Mama collects? They never wash, they never shave. And their hands! Covered in paint — and if Clésinger is a sculptor, his will be covered in clay and he'll get drunk and be sick on the floor.'

'Solange!'

'Don't pretend to be shocked. You've seen it happen yourself. Don't you remember, last New Year's Eve, how disgusted you were and how furious you made Mama by refusing to sit down to table with the drunks? I told Mama then that she ought to build a vomitorium in the dining room if she wants to hold Neronian revels there.'

Chopin concealed a grin behind a frown. 'Do you think,' he began pontifically, 'that this is the proper way for a young lady to —'

'I'm not a young lady! I've never been brought up as a young lady. Mama would make me wear trousers if she could,' cried Solange with a storm in her eyes. 'I want to get away from here. I loathe this. house and everybody in it. Life with Mama is unendurable. I don't know how *you've* managed to put up with her all these years.'

But that he would not pass. 'You are right,' he rapped out sharply, 'you are *not* a young lady. You have no self-restraint, no manners —'

'Whose fault is that?' she demanded furiously. 'Is it *my* fault if I've no manners? What sort of example have I had to *teach* me manners? You know as well as I do that this is not a fit *milieu* for me.' Her voice cracked; tears trembled on her eyelids.

Hardening his heart against the wilful charm of her, he attempted a further rebuke 'Your mama is ever watchful of your interests, my dear.'

'*My* interests?' A flag of red flew up in either cheek. 'You mean her own. She is anxious now to get me married. She has a husband for me on the carpet.'

Chopin raised an eyebrow. This was news. He listened to the tale Solange poured into his ready ear, of how she had been shamed to receive 'a half-witted Berrichon squire with a plum in his throat, no tongue in his head and hands like pig's trotters. The best thing about him is his name. Fernand de Préaulx. He is of good family, though I should not be surprised if his crest is a hog *couchant* and his quarterings a calf's liver. He stinks of the stable, and if I marry him I shall only exchange a madhouse for a cowshed. That's what *she* has chosen for me. But I'll drown myself before I marry him,' raged Solange, 'I swear it. I'll throw myself in the Indre. Oh, Chopin!' She raised her tear-wet eyes to his, imploringly, 'can't you help me? You are my friend. My only friend. My father. I wish you *were* my father, then we could run away together. My father did run away with me once. I wish I'd never been brought back. He was kind to me,' she added sadly, 'when he was sober.'

He stared at her helplessly, touched by that spontaneous appeal for guidance. She was so much the little girl behind all her assumption of bravado. But what to do? And who was he to act the part of Mentor to this unruly young Telemachus? His heart twitched. He, her father? Well, so he might have been, if he had married his first love.

She was growing up. Uneasily, his eyes swept her ripe young figure. The childish gown of sprigged muslin, the folded fichu over the firm breasts could not conceal her budding womanhood. Her hair, demurely parted, fell curling on her shoulders, a fiery gold. Her skin was clear and rosy as a milkmaid's. She had nothing of her mother in her face. She was all Dudevant.

'But how selfish I am,' she exclaimed suddenly. 'All this time I talk and talk about myself, while you eat nothing. Here!' she halved and buttered a *brioche*, spread it with liberal honey and passed it to him. 'Eat then, my little one. You are much too thin. You should be fattened. I am sorry I have made you cross with me. *Are* you cross with me? I didn't mean to speak against Mama — but — well!' And she sighed deeply, shook her head and asked with characteristic inconsequence, 'Have you read *Lucrezia* yet?'

He was not to be caught. 'You forget I had already seen the proofs,' he told her warily.

'*Seen* them, yes. But did you read them?' Solange laughed up at him with the sun in her eyes. 'You are the worst possible liar, my angel. You have not read those proofs. I know it — me! I know what I am saying. You stuffed them in the top right-hand drawer of your dressing table. When I went to put in those new lavender bags I made for you I found them there with the pages all uncut just as they had come from the press.'

'That was another set,' he retorted quickly. But she had seen him flush.

'Never mind, my Chip-Chop,' she leaned across to pat his hand, and nodded reassuringly, 'I promise I shan't let her know that you didn't read her book until last night. But you're surely never going to let her publish it?'

'I see nothing in it,' said Chopin firmly, 'that I would wish to withhold from publication.'

For so he had decided. Pride, perhaps, or weakness compelled him to this line of least resistance, but it was too late now to offer up a protest… Let it go.

And notwithstanding the roars of indignation the appearance of *Lucrezia* aroused among his friends, and the crows of satisfaction from his enemies, Chopin stayed apparently unmoved by public criticism, treating the incident as merely — incidental.

Which in a sense it was.

The first link in the chain of catastrophe had been forged between these two, to drag them, fettered still, but with inevitable certitude towards the crossroads at the parting of their ways.

TWELVE

While storm clouds gathered in the skies above the Château Sand, events were moving swiftly on the political horizon. Uneasiness was not confined to the domestic hearth alone, nor the love affairs of two celebrities.

The year 1847 had dawned in gloom: a year of crisis, of upheaval and disputes. The cauldron of grievances that for almost two decades had been smouldering in subterranean craters was now on the verge of eruption. Louis Philippe's bourgeois government headed by Guizot, that great historian who had not yet learned the lesson of history repeated, was powerless to stem the rising tide of revolution. Once more a King of France sat shaking on his throne to await the hour of his doom.

From her desk in her study at Nohant, George Sand trumpeted her challenge to the monarchy. *If France is proclaimed a Republic,* she wrote in an outburst of communistic fervour, *France may have all my possessions. My lands — give them to those who have none. My garden! It shall be a pasture for your cattle. I have a house — it shall be a hospital for your wounded. I have wine, I have tobacco — and my books. Take them — take them all and use them for cannon fodder.*

Joyfully prophetic, she saw an end of those shoddy makeshifts that had diluted the *ancien régime* with a concoction of democracy, to fall where others had already fallen: an end to the tyranny of kings who sought to placate the mob by shaking hands with it. She saw the beginning of a new era for posterity, and she saw herself as Jeanne d'Arc, but she did not see the chasm yawning at her feet; the rupture of her own life and her lover's.

And so preoccupied was she with these labour pains that heralded the birth of a new Liberty, she failed also to perceive the spirit of revolt hammering at her own back door: the younger generation kicking impatient heels while it watched for the moment to declare itself. Poor George! She did not know that Solange, her problem child, was about to turn the tables and put into practice the doctrines of Freedom that her mother so readily preached.

Did Chopin realise the end was near? One can — one must believe so. But he knew the time was not yet ripe for the severance of all those ties that bound them in a union closer than a marriage. Always a fatalist, he saw with surer sight than hers the inevitable course of destiny shaping to its ultimate finale.

And as the months slipped by he was weighted by an indefinable depression less of body than of mind, as though forces out of his control were roused and active, bent on his destruction. He brooded, sunk in melancholy, sick at heart and haunted by 'presentiments'.

'You bring disaster to yourself,' George told him, 'because you look for it.' But the first blow to fall was so unexpected and so great a shock that he collapsed and lay, himself half-dying, when his friend, Jan Matuszyński, lay dead.

Yes, Jan!… His Jasia, a martyr to research, had contracted the disease which he had spent his life in fighting for the benefit of humankind. Jan died — of a chill, it was said — that flew to his perished lungs and killed him in a week. The doctor who attended him told Chopin his own view of the case, of which the plain facts were that for years Jan had been consumptive and none knew it but himself. 'He dies and I still live!' was Chopin's dirge, while he cursed his own blind selfishness and his love that had not loved enough to see till his eyes were opened. 'I might have saved him had I known. I would have sent him south. He should have been cared for, nursed. But he nursed me … my beloved physician.'

His bitter grief and self-reproach depleted his slight reserve of energy and resulted in another haemorrhage. What little strength remained to him had gone, and it seemed more than likely he would follow Jan within a month.

Once more George was at his bedside with wine and nourishing broths and new-laid eggs from the farm at Nohant. All was as before; she ever patient, he more petulant and irritable for the hundred kindnesses with which she overwhelmed him, and which, stabbed by the reminder of 'Prince Karol', he was shamed to accept and too ill to refuse. He prayed that he might die, but surprisingly, he didn't. Though his recovery may have been vicarious it was sure enough to impress his medical advisers to return the usual verdict — 'Nothing phthisical. No cause for alarm. The lungs are bronchial but otherwise sound.' And to the anxious enquiries of Madame Sand, the assurance, 'He can live to be eighty.'

With the return of spring he was himself again and ready to believe it.

He went down to Nohant in April to find open war declared between Solange and her mother. Having flatly refused to entertain as suitor her Berrichon squire, Solange, it seemed, had found a prospective husband for herself; and he none other than the sculptor Clésinger.

Stoutly supported by Maurice — who at that time may have had his reasons for wishing to direct his mother's attentions to his sister's activities rather than his own — George violently opposed Solange's choice, and in a stormy scene forbade the young man to re-enter the house, and hurled after him as he bolted down the steps a torrent of abuse and the plaster cast of the bust he had made of her. She was now holding her daughter in custody, virtually a prisoner and guarded day and night by several spies in her confidence: her maid and Maurice, the gardener, a certain young lady staying in the house, and the *curé* who was more inquisitive than shocked.

Thus the state of affairs in which Chopin on his arrival at the 'château' found himself immediately embroiled.

'For,' said George despairingly,' I look to you to save the situation. You must tackle her. I can't. I always said she was the devil's spawn — if she is not her father's. So do you talk to her. Make her see reason. She will listen to you though she's a deaf-mute to me.'

Chopin was very loth to interfere, but since he had only heard George's version of the case he was not incurious to hear Solange's story. She had a long involved tale to tell which, when she had done, left him little the wiser, beyond the fact that she and Clésinger were deep in love.

'But,' said the bewildered Chopin, 'I understood you had forsworn all artists.'

'He is not an artist — at least not the kind I loathe. He doesn't smell. He is clean and beautiful — and almost as great a dandy as you are. His suits are made by an English tailor. Like you he would sooner starve than wear soiled linen, but — did you see the bust he did of Mama?'

Chopin blinked. Her irrelevancies were a little disconcerting. 'No ... I...'

'You never will. She smashed it over his head when she kicked him out. A masterpiece! And that,' Solange vindictively commented, 'is what made her so savage. It is a superb revelation of what she *is* and not what she *thinks* she is. All in her that is little and all that is big — all her coarseness, her brutality, — *and* her loveliness, is there. He shows her as part animal, part goddess — and she hates him for it!' Solange broke off with a laugh that was half a sob and stared out of the window at the arrowy rain falling through the April sunshine, at the flat grey-green meadows and the river winding through them like a silvery translucent snake. 'Look! There's a rainbow!' she said pointing, and she gazed up to heaven with the rainbow in her eyes and tears on her lashes. 'Even Maurice,' she went on, hardily, 'even Maurice whom I used to adore has turned against me now. But that's to suit himself. He has his own *affaire*. You know Titine?'

Chopin knew 'Titine,' affectionately so called by George and Maurice. Her full name was Augustine Brault, a demure retiring young person with the face of a Botticelli Virgin. A distant cousin of George's on the somewhat disreputable distaff side, she had been a frequent visitor to the house during the past year, acting as a sort of secretary to George.

'She's a bitch,' said Solange, inexcusably. 'Yes, she is! And I shall say it. She and Maurice are lovers and Mama encourages them. Oh, yes, they are! They sleep together... Is that so surprising in *this* house? Believe me — it's true! I've seen him coming out of her room — and — I've listened at the door and heard —'

'Solange!'

'But why should you look so disgusted? It's natural, isn't it, for a man to lie with a woman? — at least so I've been taught. I only wanted to make sure that my suspicions were justified. And yet Maurice, the sanctimonious little beast, dares to preach to *me*, dares to turn *my* lover out of doors — or egg Mama on to do so. It's all the same. Oh my God! This household! If only you knew all that I've seen and heard in it. And yet I — *I* who desire only that I am allowed to marry the man I love who will take me away from this *brothel* —'

There was no stopping her. The demons of emotion were released in a hurricane of hysteria. 'Listen to me!' yelled Solange, stamping down his scandalised protest, 'I know what I'm saying. I've been wanting to say it for years. This house is a brothel!' And on a shrieking crescendo, her face distorted with passion, she repeated it — 'Brothel! Brothel! Brothel! Has Mama taught me to mince my words? Does she mince hers? And is it a sin to love? In this house love is as free as tobacco. "*Free* love"! I've been brought up on that dictum —'

Chopin nervously backed to the door. Sancta Cecilia! What a virago. True daughter of France — with that temper.

'But is *my* love —' the pitiless young voice pursued him — 'is *my* love allowed its freedom? Ah, no! *I* must be married to a husband my mother chooses for me, no matter though he be the village idiot. Yes! Figure to yourself how she, the great democrat, the true republican, rams down my throat night and morning this clod of an aristocrat — his family, his château, his lands and his name till I'm sick to death of the sound of it. A de Préaulx has asked for my hand — what an honour! Mama has promised me a *dot* and his parents are for ever nagging her to raise the price. Mama tells me what a saint she is — how she has scraped together every *sou* she earns the better to endow me. I'm to be bought and sold — and to stand by while they bid. *Bon Dieu*! Am I a slave in an open market? Is this Turkey? Are we barbarians, then? Mama is, truly! She has even written to my father whom for years she has refused to see, asking *his* intervention, but I've written too. I could have loved my father. He is kind. I am more his daughter than hers. I have written to him begging him to forbid marriage to a half-wit.

Do I want to breed idiot children? Oh, Chopin, my pigeon! You must help me! You must, *must* help me!' Her mouth crumpled; tears coursed unchecked down the lovely crimson cheeks and splashed on to her bodice. She flung herself into his arms and sobbed uncontrollably.

Torn between his sense of duty and his pity for the passionate young creature, he strove to soothe with encouraging pats. 'There, there, *ma poupée!* Pray don't distress yourself. Be calm. We will see what can be done.'

Her hands clutched him convulsively. 'But soon! Do it soon! Am I to be kept under lock and key like a criminal? They watch my every movement. Clésinger is in the village — waiting to meet me and I can't get *out!* You must contrive to let me out. I can sneak out a night and meet him in the garden. I'll *kill* myself if this goes on much longer —'

'No, no! Of course!' uttered Chopin ineffectually. 'All shall be as you wish. Only leave it to me — and pray do compose yourself.' She was a heavy young thing and it took all his strength to support her.

'Do you mean that?' she asked him fiercely, raising her head from his shirt front. 'Do you mean you *will* help me? Will you tell Mama how wicked she is? Will you? You must. And you must tell her, too, what I have told you about Maurice and Titine. We will give her the benefit of the doubt and presume she doesn't know. Turn her attention from me to them. And if Maurice dares to dictate to me I'll expose him and his whore… Oh, yes! I know! Shocking. But who has taught me these words? Promise! Promise you will help me?'

He would have promised anything she asked to be rid of her.

So much for the peaceful holiday at Nohant that after his recent illness he so greatly needed. It seemed he had uncovered a wasps' nest into which he would be forced to plunge his hand, and receive, no doubt, the queen wasp's sting if he dared declare himself an ally of her daughter.

Solange's account of an *affaire* between Maurice and Augustine did not at all surprise him. It was an open secret, although he had never approved of George's protégée as an addition to the household. Still less did he approve Maurice's pursuit of Mademoiselle 'Titine', whom, however, he deemed well able to look after herself and her own interests. As sly a little minx as ever tickled trout to land an eligible *partie*. And if that which Solange had seen and heard were true, then Maurice would have to marry her. But what a coil! Admittedly Solange had just cause for grievance if her mother allowed her son to follow the natural course of his fancy under her very roof and with a young lady whom she had taken under her protection, and yet could present so stern a front to Solange's choice of the inoffensive Clésinger. There seemed no sense in George's attitude, and Chopin did not hesitate to tell her so.

It might have been better had he held his peace.

'You talk like a fool,' George said, 'Maurice is a man. He must live his own life his own way. I am not responsible for his peccadilloes.'

'But that child, Titine,' objected Chopin. 'You are responsible for her. She is your protégée.'

George looked down her nose. 'She may be my protégée but she is not a child. And believe me, my friend, I have saved her from a worse fate than to be the mistress of my son. When I took her under my protection she was about to be exploited by her mother as decoy in a house of ill repute. Did you know that?'

He did not know that: nor did he find her apologia convincing. She had an aptitude for self-justification, allowing her exuberant imagination to envelop fact in an embroidery of words and sentiment.

'And surely,' she insisted, 'it is better that Maurice should receive his pleasures here at home than to buy them off the boulevards?'

'Good God!' ejaculated Chopin softly. Long custom should have inured him to her astonishing code of morality, but this blatant acquiescence in her son's relationship with her young kinswoman, was more than he could pass.

His narrowed eyes, the wry compression of his lips, his stiffened body spoke more than his half-whispered protest. George glanced at him, gave a shrug and walked over to her desk to take a cigar from the box that stood there. He followed her movements closely. It was as though he were seeing her now for the first time. She had stoutened. Her jaunty velvet jacket and her trousers accentuated rather than concealed the fallen breasts, the fleshy hips. With a sudden pang of contrition he realised that she was middle-aged. The contours of her face were blurred, her skin a little coarsened, and the whites of her still lovely eyes had yellowed.

'You smoke too much,' he said.

'I have always smoked too much. But that is not what you wished to tell me.'

'You read me like a book.'

'The print is large, my dear. You disapprove of this marriage I have arranged for Solange.'

'No,' he corrected, 'I disapprove of your inconsistency. In seeking to make this cold-blooded conventional alliance for your daughter against her own judgment — and still worse — against her instinct, you emulate the methods of the bourgeoisie you so frankly despise. You do not scruple to desert your principles when it suits you to do so, and yet you encourage your son in his pursuit of a questionable —'

'Name of a dog! This is too much!'

At this explosive interruption both started and turned to the window. There, head and shoulders framed in its open space, stood Maurice who, unobserved, had crossed the lawn. Swinging his legs over the sill he came to his mother's side. 'You will kindly leave me out of this discussion,' he said, in a swollen voice and with a vein like a cord in his forehead.

He was a heavily built, squat young man, broad of shoulder, short of leg, with the spread nose and square-jawed face of a pugilist. His eyes like his mother's, full and dark under thick jutting brows, regarded Chopin with a steely insolence.

'You seem to forget,' said George's son, 'your own position in this household. You forget, too, that no house can have two masters. *I* am the master here.'

So! It was out. The simmering antagonism of months had come to the boil in open hostility, and Chopin felt a sudden queer sense of elation. The flood gates were opened; he was free to speak his mind.

And standing there before those two — the woman who for eight years had filled his life, and her son whom he loved as his own, and who — his heart twisted to tell him — had returned his love with a boy's adoration, he watched himself. It was as if he were re-living in this room and in this moment of eternity some tragic interlude spun between light and darkness, seeing her face eclipsed and secretive, dissolving in a dream, hearing his words like a whip-lash cutting through the clinging tendrils that held him to her still.

'Your son,' he said, with his bittersweet smile, 'speaks for you. It is his house and I am the intruder. I have taken what was offered. I have drunk from your cup.'

'Was it poison?' queried George, with an answering smile.

'Shall we say rather — anodyne?' he returned, white-lipped.

The smoke from her cigar was wreathed about her face, hiding the expression of her eyes.

'Yes,' he said, with his pitiless air of mockery, 'I have taken my drug as an addict. I have been always too weak to fight. And you have been ... so strong.'

'I have needed strength to fight your weakliness,' she retorted carelessly, but that unveiled implication set his temples throbbing and brought a redness to his sight.

'As you have told the world,' he flung back at her, 'and have not spared me in the telling. A *bonne-bouche* for the gutter — how that Chopin with his name and fame is nothing but a fungoid growth that feeds upon the bounty of "Lucrezia"!' Something gave way in him. Hideously he began to laugh, hearing the sound of his laughter as though outside himself and powerless to stop it. 'Not...' he spluttered, 'it is not a viper you have nurtured in your bosom but a ... pimp!' His breath caught in a cough. Desperately he fought to suppress the threatening attack, the ghastly spasm that would leave him drained, defeated. Not now, not here, not just at this moment when he had dared to meet her on the battle-front, to speak at last and rid himself of his festering resentment that gnawed like a rat at his vitals to destroy his faith, his hope, his charity... Dizzy with the fever of his illness his mind reeled beneath the strain of emotional reaction, and with the talons of his enemy in its stranglehold upon him he sank, racked and shaken with a gush of blood from his lungs to his mouth.

'It is the smoke,' George threw her cigar out of the window and came to him. 'My poor little one ... my child!' Her hand caressed his damp forehead. She placed a cushion at his back, and told Maurice, 'Bring the cognac.'

He gestured a refusal. 'No!' he gasped. 'No!' fighting for his breath. 'I do not... Thank you, thank you, you are very ... kind!' He shrugged himself away from her ministering hand.

'Shall I ring for Daniel? Will you go to your room?' And there was nothing now but pity in her face.

Her son returned with a liqueur glass of neat brandy. 'Drink it,' said Maurice curtly.

With a mighty effort Chopin raised himself from his chair. 'Thank you ... thank you.' He took the glass that Maurice handed to him, but he did not drink. 'I have this to say. The time has come, I think, when I must leave this house. There has been too much conflict ... we do not see eye to eye...'

He gazed at the two faces before him; both were smooth as stone, and their eyes, frozen pools alike in shape and darkness, stared fixedly back; from her even pity had faded. How did one speak to the dead?

'It has never been my wish...' The sickly amber fumes of the untasted brandy rose like incense to his nostrils. He raised the glass to his lips, and felt the raw spirit run through him like a fire. 'It has never been my wish,' he said, shuddering a little, though not from cold, 'to deprive Maurice of his own right in his own house. Conditions have altered since your son and daughter have grown from two children to a man and woman. The ... the situation is untenable.'

It was no good. His moment had passed and could not be repeated.

'You had better go and lie down,' George said. 'You work yourself into a passion over nothing. What is all this about? What are you trying to tell me? That you disapprove of the marriage I desire for Soli?'

'And of my friendship for Titine,' put in Maurice with an ugly look. 'I resent his interference.'

'Hold your tongue!' his mother bade him sharply. 'Enough has been said, and God knows why we three are quarrelling. All was well till that rascally Clésinger arrived on the scene to turn Soli's head with his flattery. And now Soli has gone whining to Chopin with her tales to try and make him fight with her against her mother. You have always spoiled her, my dear. You are always ready to believe her and condemn me — without a hearing. My faith! She's a demon, that one! Don't I know it — for my sins! You had better leave me to manage my girl in my own way. I know better than you what is good for her and what she needs. A proper thrashing might bring her to her senses... So go you now, Chip-Chop, my dear, and rest. You look like a ghost.'

A tepid anti-climax to a drama.

He lay on his couch by the open window in his room that overlooked the garden, and laughed, mocking at life's small ironies, its tragedies, its chagrins, and defeats. Nothing had come of his outburst beyond a further exhibition of his frailty. Was it any wonder if she were sick of him? He was so utterly sick of himself.

Yet he should have been grateful. She studied his whims, his moods, his wishes. This room... She had reserved the best room in the house for him, large enough to hold a concert-grand piano, had papered the walls in softest grey and curtained his bed and windows with starry-blossomed chintz to suit his fancy; and always in and out of season she filled his flower bowls with violets. This was his sanctuary. None could enter here unless he gave permission. And here he could retire when the company below was too freely entertained — or entertaining.

For eight years she had cared for him, playing more than her part of a dutiful wife, and in return had demanded nothing but devotion… Well, he had given her that, and his fidelity. No other woman could so entirely possess him. He had loved her … *had* loved? How swiftly the present turns into the past! The thought chilled him. Did he not love her still? Love! What was this love? Was it a spark in a mad gust of wind, a bright eager flame, a dying down, a passing out — and then forgetfulness? Was it a vapour? Strange how he who spoke love's language in purest melody, could not define it.

Lying huddled, his small mouth compressed, his eyes watching the green afternoon fold tender wings of dusk across the day, Chopin had a vision of his youth, the sweet intoxication of that first delicious fever, that even after almost twenty years he could not recall without a diving and a leaping of his heart. If that devouring obsession were not love, then love was non-existent, the mirage of man's passion for himself… If only one could rediscover it, the magical sweet torment, the restless yearning: if one could know spring's rapture once again before the autumn mists closed in upon his life! His lips smiled a very little. Was he so old? And not yet thirty-eight.

He kneeled on the couch and, resting his elbows on the window ledge, leaned out for air. A greyness slowly settled on the garden; under the whitening sky all colours waned from the pastures where the herdsman's voice urged home his lazy cows. The landscape gathered loneliness and darkened, and the herdsman halted and was silenced to stand, head bent, while the angelus rang out the evensong.

And deep within him Chopin felt the stir and heartbeat of conception; the quickened pulse of his spiritual self striking from muted soul-strings the silvery lament of a nocturne…

It was late when he rose from his piano, exhausted but at peace.

The supper that Daniel had brought him on a tray remained untouched. He poured himself a glass of wine and stood at the window to drink it. A moth flew in his face; he went to snuff the candles, and returned to the window savouring the night.

A night of summer rather than of spring; no breeze, no sound of bird or beast disturbed the stillness; a sickle moon swung by its horns in a lavender sky, and lay drowned, a mirrored ghost of itself in the dark gleaming river. The poplars that lined the narrow banks stood like giant sentinels, blacker than the shadows. Somewhere a clock struck twelve… And while he gazed and listened, his glass raised to drink again, something stayed his hand: a movement, indistinct, uncertain. Was it the prow of a boat that nosed between those black tree stems? Was it the plash of oars, or the scared plunge of some small wild creature he heard, down there by the water's edge?

A leaden minute passed. No, nothing… Emptiness. Imagination.

Suddenly the harsh cry of a nightjar pierced the quiet and over the moon-misted lawn sped a cloaked figure, so silent and so swift it seemed scarcely to touch the ground in passing. Then out of the brooding darkness by the gate in the yew hedge, his straining eyes discerned another shape — a man's. The first had been a woman's.

Two wraith-like figures joined, were one, and vanished.

And to Youth and Youth's madness, Chopin smiling, drank a silent toast.

Early in the morning he was awakened by an uproar in the room beneath his own. Sitting up in bed he cocked an ear to listen and heard his lady's voice raised loud and hot in argument to a booming accompaniment from Maurice.

Curious to know the cause of this commotion Chopin hastily put on his dressing gown and slippers and took himself downstairs.

He found the demure Titine in négligée, Maurice in a nightshirt, and his 'Hostess' in a rage.

On perceiving Chopin she halted her rapid flow of speech to point a finger at him and utter awfully — 'And here — here stands the culprit. The instigator of the crime!'

'Crime!' echoed the startled Chopin. 'What crime? Has there been a robbery?'

'Robbery and murder!' shouted George, advancing with predatory strides while Chopin nervously retreated to the window. 'The robbery of my child,' declared Madame, 'and the murder of my love for her. The slut!'

'Ah,' non-committally said Chopin.

'Ah!' The inoffensive monosyllable as George repeated it became the roar of an infuriated tigress. 'You may well say "Ah"! She has gone! She has escaped me. Her bed has not been slept in. She has taken my portmanteau. My portmanteau. Not her own. Oh no! And she has fled with that mountebank, that ruffian, that animal —'

'Have you,' Chopin gently interposed, 'dragged the river?'

George rounded on him, pale. 'Mother of God! What are you saying? You don't suppose?' Her voice ran down in panic.

'Solange did once express to me,' Chopin remarked reflectively, 'that desperation might drive her to end her troubles in the Indre.'

George gave a sigh of relief. 'Then that dispels all thought of suicide. Those who threaten to take their lives always live the longest. In any case, what should she want with my portmanteau if she desired *that* means to her end? She has taken the obvious way. Her own way — *your* way!' cried George, maternal fear dissolved again in spleen. 'I see! I see it all. You have aided and abetted this elopement. You have always taken her part against me. I insist you tell me where she is! Where *is* she?'

'I should imagine,' Chopin said, unlatching as precautionary measure the window that opened on the terrace, 'I should imagine that by this time she's in Paris.'

'Paris?' screamed George. 'Then you do know —?'

'Nothing,' he said, suavely, 'but what my reason prompts me to suggest.'

'*Your* reason!' It was Maurice now who spoke, thrusting himself between his mother and Chopin, his poise somewhat hampered by the folds of the rug he had dragged from the couch to wrap round him. 'You have no *reason*,' he aggressively stated, 'to be here at all: you have interfered too often in my family's affairs, and now you've interfered for the last time. But before I take the reins of management in my own hands, and in my own house, I will ask you this and you shall answer me — or by God I'll make you — have you or have you not helped my sister's escape with that rat of a Clésinger?'

Silently Chopin looked him over; in his eyes, coloured like old brandy, lurked somewhere deep the red spark of danger, but his lips, though closed, were smiling.

'Will you or won't you answer me?' blustered George's son.

'Answer you how?' asked Chopin, unruffled. 'I have no notion where Solange is at this moment, although I have a shrewd suspicion that she is far beyond your reach — or my redemption.'

'*Tiens!* Such wickedness! Not possible!' With horror in her face and relish in her heart Mlle Titine contributed a series of shocked murmurs, to be interrupted by a shriek from George.

'*Diable!* What are you saying?' But it was not Titine whom she addressed.

Chopin smiled. 'Only this,' he told her blandly. 'Last night I watched a ghostly figure flit across the lawn. I stood petrified.' He glanced from one to the other; his eyes more than his words held them all in a kind of paralysis. 'You know my fear of revenants? This one was cloaked in grey. It looked like nothing human. I am confident it carried no portmanteau. If so I should have noticed it. A ghost that voyages from astral planes, *tout simplement* — and without luggage is frightening enough, but *with* —'

'Idiot!' snarled George. 'Will you come to the point?'

'Certainly.' And with that closed smile on his lips Chopin flung wide the window and stepped out. 'The point is — that which in the light of the moon I mistook for a spectre, I now know to be none other than Solange.'

And leaving George, her son and Titine to digest, in their respective ways, this information, he passed along the terrace to halt beneath his bedroom window, looking up.

'Daniel!' he called. 'Daniel!'

Wooden-faced as ever, Daniel's head appeared above.

'M'sieu désire…?'

'That you pack my bag,' commanded Chopin. 'We are starting for Paris at once.'

THIRTEEN

He had reached but had not crossed the Rubicon.

As a stone cast in turgid waters will leave its trace in ever-widening ripples, so did events in obscure concerted sequence diverge from that night on which Solange rushed headlong from her mother's house into the arms of her lover.

Though George made every effort to recall her, the marriage of Solange to Clésinger was solemnised before any intervention could annul it.

On return from their stolen honeymoon the errant couple went in duty bound to ask forgiveness and the blessing of Mama, to be greeted by a tornado of denunciation and abuse, and forcibly ejected from the château.

At La Châtre in temporary lodgings found above a baker's shop, Solange sat down and wrote this letter to Chopin:

I am ill. I am in misery. I have left Nohant for ever after the most terrible scene with Mamma. Will you lend me your carriage to take me to Paris? Jean-Baptiste left for Paris today, but I am far too upset to take the journey from Blois in a diligence. I await your reply at La Châtre. I positively must see you at once. They have absolutely refused to let me have your carriage, so if you are willing I should use it, please write giving me permission, and I will send to Nohant for it.

It had long been Chopin's custom to place his carriage at Madame Sand's disposal during his visits to Nohant, and although he had removed himself, his man and his belongings from the château, he had allowed his carriage to remain.

On receipt of Solange's letter he sent her an immediate reply.

DEAREST CHILD,
I am much grieved to know that you are ill and hasten to assure you
that my carriage is now and always at your service. I have written your
Mamma to this effect.
Take care of yourself,
Your old friend,
Ch.

Her *only* friend… She had none other to whom *in extremis* she
could turn. Her happy-go-lucky young husband, already up to
his ears in debt, could provide her with nothing more
substantial to live upon than love. From whom then but her
'Chip-Chop' should Solange seek material support?

One evening at the beginning of June she whirled into
Chopin's apartment in the Cité d'Orléans looking radiant and
anything but ill. When he expressed his satisfaction at finding
her so speedily recovered she told him yes, she had been
suffering from a *crise des nerfs* due to the horrible cruel way her
mama had received her and Jean-Baptiste.

He smiled at the air of conscious pride with which she threw
out that name. And, 'What of your Jean-Baptiste?' he asked
her. 'Are you happy?'

'Happy!' She took the lapels of his coat in her hands, laughed
with tears in her eyes, and whispered, 'I'm so happy that I'm
frightened.'

'May you keep your happiness, my dear,' he said; and
touched her forehead with his lips.

'Yes. Every night and morning I ask the Blessed Virgin to
preserve my love and his — but —' Solange sighed and shook
her curls, and broke away from him to perch herself on the

edge of the table. She wore a tight little leaf green jacket and a crinoline of yellow faille: a bonnet of the same shade tied with green ribbons framed her sparkling face and gold hair. With her bell-shaped skirts in silken petals about her she looked like a yellow rose. 'But,' she said and sighed again, 'I have anxieties. Apart from my mother's monstrous treatment of my husband... Did you know —' her cheeks crimsoned at the memory — 'Did you know she boxed his ears?'

Controlling a spasm, Chopin expressed suitable horror.

'Yes, indeed! And the shame — the shame I suffered! My mother is a fiend when she is roused.'

Chopin had reason to believe it.

'And my poor Jean who had come on his knees so humble and polite to offer his apologies for taking me away and to ask her blessing and forgiveness — imagine how he felt.'

Chopin said he could very well imagine.

'Yes! And he had told her that she — great lover as she is — would surely sympathise with lesser loves. And *that* remark, intended to soothe, had quite the opposite effect — to drive her mad. She flew at him. She caught him by the throat. She was as white as paper. Terrible! She looked like an insane Medusa. I know *I* was turned to stone. And holding him with one. hand she gave him a clout with the other. I screamed. That bitch Titine pretended to faint and Maurice said "Bravo, Mama! If you, had not done it — *I* would have!" Then my angel shook himself free from his *belle-mère* and stood up like a king and said, "Madame, you have insulted me. I cannot demand the *amende honorable* from a woman even though —" and he stared at her trousers — "even though she is dressed as a man. But your son," and he bowed very sarcastic to Maurice, "your son who applauds this indignity shall receive the challenge that your sex forbids me to offer you."

'Then said Maurice, black as hell, "If I fight, I fight with gentlemen. Not cads." And then my husband made a dash at him. I thought there would be murder, and I flung myself between the two and dragged Jean to the window and out on to the terrace, and I rushed him away down the garden. Such a to-do! With the whole village out to watch. So we went to the inn where we hired a chaise to take us to La Châtre, and we slept in a smelly little room over the baker's. And the next day my husband left for Paris — he *said* to seek legal advice as how best to deal with what he called assault and battery, but I think by the time he arrived there his rage had cooled, and he went out to buy a block of marble to make a bust of me. So that was the end of that *histoire*.' In the telling of which it seemed that Solange had derived not a little enjoyment. 'So then I wrote to you,' she said, 'and,' her words rippled into laughter, 'here I am!'

Here she was, indeed! And what to do with her he did not know.

She, however, very soon enlightened him. Taking his frail thin hand in her firm one, she pleaded big-eyed: 'Darling Chopin! If you will — *would* — be an angel! My anxieties are killing me. Jean-Baptiste is the sweetest lover in the world, and I adore him — he is so handsome and tender and kind and smells of jasmine — and he bought me this lovely new gown. Do you like it? We bought it in Nice. It cost — oh! Hundreds and *hundreds* of francs. And this garnet necklace — look! And these bracelets.' She pushed back the loose sleeves of her jacket to show him her plump white arms banded in gold. 'But you see — he knows about as much of the mere business of life as I do of housekeeping. Conceive it! Such an idiot I am! I asked the butcher for a *tête de boeuf* instead of a *tête de veau* — and he sent me the whole head of an ox. Tongue, teeth, brains and all. The concierge screamed when she saw it arrive, walking in on the butcher boy's tray! She thought it was the devil. Well, it's the fault of *ma mère* that I did not know any better. She has not brought me up to be a proper wife. And now we have no money. Do you see?'

Accustomed though he was to Solange's inconsequent discourses, Chopin confessed that he did not yet — quite — see.

But Solange had little patience with anyone who didn't. 'Don't you understand,' she demanded with asperity, ' how difficult it is for both of us? We — Jean-Baptiste and I — are utterly helpless as to ways and means. We have nothing. Not a *sou*. Of course, Jean-Baptiste did have plenty when we married. But we've spent it. Or rather *he* spent it — on buying a trousseau for me. Who could expect a wife to go to her husband with nothing more to clothe her than her skin? But that, I assure you, is all I had.'

And ignoring Chopin's pleasantry that no husband could desire for his bride a sweeter dress, she hurried on: 'And only enough in Mama's travelling bag, which I stole — and such a weight it was to carry, I assure you — to last me for one week. So, of course, he had to buy me some new gowns. And all that remained to us after our honeymoon he spent on marbles for his busts and now we're being sued for the rent for our dreadful little attic... Chopin! Angel! If you could — if you would — if you *can* possibly lend us just enough to tide us over for a month or two, till Jean-Baptiste has sold his things and made his fortune! If you could help us just a little... now.'

Help them? Of course he helped them. To the extent of some thousands of francs which the foolish young couple ran through in three months. Which mattered nothing to Solange.

Chopin would always give her all she asked. Nor did she hesitate to ask again.

What a calamity! she wrote when the first ten thousand francs had disappeared:

All the money Jean-Baptiste has borrowed from you and all our belongings have been seized to pay our debts. But I suppose one can get used to everything in time, — even to anxiety. Fancy me with my extravagant tastes — I who used to think that nothing less than a coach and six horses was grand enough to carry me — I who lived in a world of palaces — and poems — I who once would have thrown millions out of the window am now become a miser hoarding up every franc. I assure you I have aged more in this last week than in all my eighteen years.

And not only have I these frightful troubles over money – or the lack of it – but I have a mother who ruthlessly abandons me to my fate or the bounty of the Saints of Paradise. And who knows if anyone of them will give me their protection at this time when I need it most?

Which brought a prompt reply from Chopin:

I received your letter with pleasure and read it with grief. What is all this about? Your husband has borrowed no money from me, and you have already returned me 500 fr. of the sum I gave — (not lent) — to you. You need not have done so…

And when he asked her for an explanation of that last line in her letter, she was proud to let him know she was expecting a child.

One may suppose that George viewed Chopin's favours to Solange with disapproval. Such championship, she reasoned, was deliberately rendered as insult to herself. In every way he sought to antagonise her further by supporting her devilish young daughter in her works. In the most princely fashion he had financed her and her vagabond husband; he had placed his carriage at their disposal, taking it, high-handedly, away from her, who for eight years had used it as her own; and he continued to bestow his patronage and largesse on the unrepentant pair in direct defiance of her wishes, or her condemnation of her daughter's fall from grace.

The coolness between George Sand and Chopin, following his abrupt departure from Nohant, continued to increase till the temperature dropped to zero. While she stayed at Nohant their strained relationship could pass unnoticed by the outer world; but so soon as George returned to Paris, it was obvious to all that the Sand-Chopin *affaire* had reached a climax.

'*Elle et Lui*', so it was rumoured, no longer lived in the same house.

Summer drifted into autumn and the plane trees on the boulevards turned to gold. From his window in the Cité d'Orléans Chopin watched the rusted leaves torn from their branches by the impudent wind that, like an invisible urchin, played with the dust of the gutters and in the gardens of the rich,' with no respect for property or persons.

The ash trees on the terrace of the Tuileries were full of whispers; on the quays beside the river the prankish north wind fluttered the news-sheets, and turned the pages of the musty volumes spread out on the parapets by those traditional retailers who offered for sale the second-hand pearls of great minds. Always in the open air, regardless of the weather, they stood with their blouses loose to the breeze and their faces beaten by the rains and snows and frosts and fogs of Paris, until they had come somewhat to resemble the grotesque immutability of the gargoyles that stared from the grey buttresses of Notre Dame.

The news-sheets fluttered like great white-winged black-speckled moths; the newsvendors opened their morning papers to read the headlines in print still damp from the press, to discuss the leading articles, and with guttural prophecy to mark the way the wind was blowing. The gossip of the faubourgs never reached their ears, and the name of Chopin did not live for them; but the name of Sand shone like a glow-worm in the dank grass of undergrowth to guide the way of lesser folk who had no learning and no words to cry for light in darkness, no power to declare their right to live and to be done with petty tyranny and pseudo-kingship, and all that stood between their liberties and their Republic.

The barricades were rising beside the waters of the Seine that swelled to the rains of autumn as the mutterings increased. The voice of the people was heard in the land, and the quarrelling of turtles was no more than an extravaganza played on Aeolian harps to the echo of past loves and present sorrows.

But in the catteries upon the fashionable faubourgs where ladies assembled to partake of an execrable concoction brewed in par-boiled water from the dust of tea leaves — the latest craze from London known to Parisians as the 'feef o'clock' — the talk that set the ball of gossip rolling was not of those workers, who like ants, were indefatigably building under the swaying throne of Louis Philippe, the formidable termitary of destruction. The blunders and vacillations of the government, the names of Lamartine and Guizot, were of no concern to Mesdames de Girardin and d'Agoult. But the names of Sand and Chopin, 'He and She', so the ladies tittering, passed the latest *'mot'* — these were not yet *vieux jeux*. By no means. The talk buzzed loud as wasps around a jam-pot when Sand and Chopin, it was said, had parted.

The shrill treble of the ever-green little Countess d'Agoult was the first to scatter the spiced titbit: 'Not a drama but a comedy — of errors.'

That perhaps was true enough. There had been no violent dramatics, no upheaval following his passive withdrawal from the château. He had left with excuses, politely. An unexpected summons from his publishers in Paris to settle a query raised in a clause of his contract: also to arrange a date of production for his latest compositions; these, the last to be published in his lifetime. Three mazurkas (Op. 63), three valses (Op. 64) and the Sonata in D Minor. The note he left for George expressing his regret was quite feasible and prolific of apology, but professional exigencies, she would understand, demanded a curtailment of his *vacance*. And he returned to her his carriage, but did not return himself.

We have seen that his carriage was, again politely, requested to be sent to George's daughter to bring her back to Paris: that, the first of some unkinder cuts to come. And, as slow drops of water will wear away a stone, so did an accumulation of unobtrusive trifles leave each their marked impression on the surface of two lives.

Volumes of conjecture have been written as to the actual first cause of the rupture; but, since every event has its own cause, invariable and unconditional, so every event must have its pre-existence, even as Time itself that ties man to its eternal wheel, without beginning, without end.

Meanwhile Madame Sand was storing up a series of complaints against her 'Chip-Chop', the chief of which appeared to be that he, unpardonably, had come between her daughter and herself. She was convinced that he had urged

Solange to her elopement, and nothing he could write in self-extenuation could change her outlook. He, and he only, not Solange, not Clésinger, had connived at this betrayal of her trust in him. He had struck like a snake in the dark, not at her poor misguided child but at her and at her love, seeking by such stealthy means to bring about a shattering *dénouement*.

Then, flinging her trump card upon the table, she wrote declaring that if he persisted in this deliberate defiance of her wishes, and received Solange and her husband in his house, all would be over between them.

To which Chopin made no reply, but he told Franchomme, who has recorded it, that he'd be damned if he would be dictated to by Madame. 'Those two young creatures have only me — shall I desert them? Never!'

So the final blow had fallen. He had cut the knot; he was free.

Despairingly did George proclaim it in a letter to one of her Republican young friends, Charles Poncy:

I have exhausted all of tribulation that the cup of life contains. It is so bitter, so unprecedented that I cannot speak of it, at least I cannot write of it.

Whereupon she proceeds to write, and at wordy length, to this effect:

I had hoped at least for some recompense for the great sacrifices I have made in work, fatigue and long years of devotion and self-abnegation. I ask for nothing but to render happy those whom I adore. Well, I have been repaid with ingratitude, and evil has got the better of a soul which I had thought was the sanctuary and hearth of all that is beautiful and

noble in this life. May God aid me! I believe in Him and hope… But I am broken in body and soul, and I fear my sorrow is incurable…
I have undertaken a great work entitled 'Histoire de ma vie'. *It will not, however, reveal the* whole *of my life, but it will, I think, put me on my feet again, financially.*

From which it would appear that she was not so far gone that she could not foresee a more practical reconstruction in the debris of Romance.

All that winter while Chopin stayed at his apartment in the Cité d'Orléans, Madame Sand remained at Nohant. Both were hard at work. She on another book, he on his sonata. He was also arranging for a concert to be held in the New Year. But although sustained by that amazing will-power which controlled his nervous energy, and by which alone he lived, it was apparent to all who watched him that his physical stamina had been exhausted, and his reserves strained to highest pitch by the crisis from which he had emerged, visibly, alarmingly, weaker.

His small neat figure, always so immaculately tailored, seemed almost hourly to shrink, that his suits must be cast aside unfit to wear. 'I shall have to change my tailor,' he complained to Daniel. 'What has come over him? This coat hangs on me as on a clothes peg. He has sent me a cossack's suit by mistake — or else he has lost his cunning. Well! Let him take it back — or throw it in the river! *Sacrebleu!* Does he think that he'll get paid? What?… *Fermez-le*, you fool! I am *not* thin! Tell me that again, and I'll…' The feeble fists were clenched in impotent fury. He would not have it he was thin — or thinner. He was *not* ill. Who dared to call him ill?

None, likely, dared. There was that in his eyes that stayed their words and held their pity. In his face, carved to a cameo fineness, still singularly youthful, those eyes lit by the flame of fever shone with a strange, luminous quality that those who knew and loved him best were filled with vague forebodings, and he laughed in their long faces, while he clung to life with a desperate tenacity, loud in his denial, 'I am *not* ill...' As though by forceful repetition he could make himself believe it. 'I'll outlive you all,' he told them, 'every one of you. I *have* been ill, but now I'm better. My cough is almost cured.'

For there would be weeks when the frequency of his attacks was lessened; and months before the stain of red appeared, in ever fresh reminder of those microscopic death-hounds that hunted, him by day, by night, hot on the scent of blood.

The Princess Marcelline, with vision clarified by love, watched that avid relentless pursuit and took her fears and her prayers to Madonna ... to save him, to give him long years of peace and of health. And kneeling there in the vast empty church of St Sulpice, she prayed for her own salvation. 'I have lost sight of God in his creature,' she confessed to the Mother of all; and she thought the divine compassionate lips moved as if to breathe a benediction; or it might have been the light from the rose-tinted window above the high altar that lent to dead stone the stirring and semblance of life.

She left the church and stepped into her barouche. It was a mild February afternoon. Paris lay wrapped in misty grey like a woman in furs of chinchilla; and though the streets were busy with traffic, and people engrossed in their own concerns, it seemed to Marcelline peering through the closed windows of her carriage, that the gathering dusk was charged with unnatural quiet, as a heavy calm before a storm. Beneath the muted hurry of the city one could sense a febrile tension, a lurking watchfulness in hidden corners; small clusterings of crowds, stealthy comings and goings from dark doorways, an anxious snatching and scanning of news-sheets from the booths under the naked trees of the boulevards. And what a quantity of loiterers along the kerbstones there appeared to be that day, to stare at her liveried servants, her handsome horses, her shining equipage as it drove through the Rue St Lazare. Their faces, and those of the blue-bloused workmen, even the faces of the gendarmes expressed a peculiar sullen defiance. She was glad when her carriage reached its destination at the gates of the Cité d'Orléans. There she dismissed her maid, and went for the first time alone to Chopin's house.

She found him lying on the couch in his candle-lit music room. He made attempt to rise at her entrance but the effort proved too much for him, and he sank back on his cushions in a dreadful fight for breath.

In an instant she was at his side. 'Master! Pray do not move. You are ill!'

She was shocked to see the change one week had wrought… A week only since her last lesson, and he appeared now to be less like a man than the shade of one there among the shadows of his room. His hands, his wasted face, had the transparent frailty of shells; but his eyes were wide and brilliant.

He shook his head, his lips pursed in a rueful smile. 'No, Madame, I am … better.' His voice strengthened as the spasm passed. 'I am recovering from a very slight attack. So disappointing, for I have been in splendid health till the turn of the New Year.'

'Shall I leave you, master? You are too tired to teach me today.'

'I am never too tired to hear you play, Princess.'

She knelt at the foot of his couch as though at a shrine. Under the velvet brim of her bonnet her small white face looked like a blurred moon-flower: her eyes devoured his. Her slender body in its wrappings of velvet and furs, was quivering with the startling impact of the knowledge that she had the power, if not the right, to serve him: and the thought that in a moment's impulse had risen to overwhelm her with the audacity of her suggestion, now took shape, as she took courage.

'Master,' she whispered, 'Master…'

'At your service, Madame,' he murmured, puzzled at her agitation: then his smile flashed again. 'You look,' he said, 'as though you were preparing for confession. I think I can guess. You have not practised the sonata?'

'No … yes, master … I have worked. But you…' involuntarily she folded her hands over her breasts, as if she would silence the heavy drumming of her heart, 'I pray you not to take amiss what I must say. I know, *cher maître*, that you are ill. I have seen … have watched. You give so much to us, to all your pupils. You think never of yourself.'

'Madame, you overrate my sensibilities. I think too much, too often of myself.' He paused and regarded her attentively; and it seemed as though a film had been skimmed from his sight. Dimly he divined her lonely life's perspective, her young ungiven womanhood, and all her withheld sweetness. 'But now,' he told her, strangely moved, 'I think of you … Princess.'

She answered him with perfect simplicity, for she had loved so long in darkness she could not hope to love in light. 'Let me think for you, master. I have a villa in the south on the shores of the Mediterranean, not far from Nice. There is a garden full of orange trees and orchards of mimosa. You would find it very peaceful. You could rest. The house is fully staffed. It would be my pleasure to offer it to you for as long as you care to stay. I would not intrude on your privacy. I … we …' she hesitated, 'my husband and I will not be going south this year. We shall spend a few weeks at our château on the Loire. But I … *we*, I speak for my husband who I know would join me in this offer … we would be honoured to receive you as our guest. Will you not let me place my house and servants at your disposal, Monsieur Chopin, for as long as you care to stay?'

Her lips remained parted while she waited breathlessly for his reply; she feared she had been too eager, feared, perhaps, he had misunderstood. His answer was so long in coming. But her eyes were downcast and she could not see that his were wet.

At last, 'Madame,' he said low-voiced, 'I am more moved than I can tell you by your offer. I would give much to be able to accept it…'

Carefully he explained why he could not. His speech, his stilted phrasing betrayed no sign of his emotion; and taking his restraint for a rebuff her small face closed as a sea anemone in some shaded pool will fold its opening petals to a touch.

He had arranged, he told her, to leave Paris in March to fulfil a series of engagements in London and Scotland. And also he had been requested to give another concert here in Paris —

London! Scotland!

She heard little more than that. So he was going to Scotland. Would he ever come back? The climate there would surely kill him.

'A command performance,' she heard him say. 'The King and all the court have taken tickets. I was not anxious to appear again just yet, but Pleyel urges me... *Le roi propos, et dieu...*' His gaze slipped past her into distance. 'Who knows,' he said, 'how God will dispose of men and things — and kings — within the next few days?'

Something in his tone, in his too-brilliant eyes that seemed to penetrate beyond the outer walls of consciousness, arrested her.

'Do you mean,' she queried anxiously, but the tremor of fear that shook her was less for the fate of princes than for him, 'do you mean that the political situation is serious enough to affect the lives of individuals? Do you think the mob will really rise against the King?'

His lips tightened. 'I think,' he said, 'that the next twenty-four hours may be decisive. Do you read the daily newspapers, Madame?'

'Not very often,' she admitted naively. 'I do not understand them. The papers shout so much and say so little. But I have read enough to feel there is an underlying menace in the voice of the people today.'

'And yesterday — and all our yesterdays, Madame. What is happening is an accumulation of events that pours like water from a barrel full of holes ... perhaps,' he added thoughtfully, ' to bring about a deluge. Who can tell? However, *chacun à son goût.*' And his eyes with the strangeness gone from them came back to hers in a look so warm, so deep, that her heart fainted to see it and her own eyes filled with swimming loveliness. 'The affairs of government,' said Chopin, softly, 'the whinings of the people, the greed and treachery of ministers, or the foolishness of kings are of less account to me than a bird's song. I would sooner hear the whisper of a nightingale than all the rhetoric of Lamartine or Guizot. The proletariat may take the whole of France if they will leave me my piano ... and you, Princess ... to play it.'

Then, because perhaps he felt rather than saw the shy tumult of her response to words unuttered; because he sensed her unimagined secret shining brave and tender as the sun's red flush on snow: and because in his day's twilight he understood what might have been and now must be … too late; because of all that with his soul, at last, he longed to say, he said, 'So, Madame, to our lesson, please…'

And said no more.

Indifference to the hurricane that menaced the political horizon was not confined to Chopin nor to artists great and small. While Lamartine poetically thundered against the corruption and complacency of those upon the heights; while the propaganda of the Socialists heaped insults upon exaggerated injury; while the worsened condition of the masses was reflected in numerous minor disturbances and inflamed by a vigorous hatred of their betters, the Orléanist party, absorbed in its own exclusive interests, buried its ostrich head in the sands of bigotry, oblivious to the approaching tidal wave.

George Sand at Nohant heard with mingled hopes and fears the ominous reports from Paris. She read of de Tocqueville's warning to his comatose colleagues in the Chamber, of an interchange of ministers and the hectic disputes between Guizot and Thiers, and she decided it was her duty as a patriot to rise and go about her country's business.

'The monarchy is tottering!' she cried, delightedly. 'The monarchy will fall — is falling like a card-house about the ears of the Citizen-King. *Vive la République*! *Vive la Victoire*! To hell — or to England — with Louis Philippe!'

In a hired post-chaise and a frenzy of excitement she drove through the night to Paris and arrived on a clammy February dawn at the house of Mme Marliani.

In his rooms next door, Chopin heard the clatter of her coming and the execrations of the concierge who, having carried on his back a heavy trunk from the entrance gates, was now vociferously demanding double his due for his pains.

Drawing aside his window curtains Chopin peered through the slats of the shutters to discover the cause of the commotion, and saw her whom for six months he had not seen, at Mme Marliani's door. The peremptory tattoo of the knocker was loud enough, he thought, to wake the dead. It certainly woke Mme Marliani who, thrusting her head in curl-papers and a nightcap out of the window, shrieked distractedly, 'The revolution is upon us! I give in. I am of Spanish birth — by marriage! You cannot touch me. I will surrender! My husband is the Spanish consul — he will have you flogged! Don't shoot!'

'Calm yourself, my cabbage!' shouted George. 'No one is going to shoot *you*! The first shot has not been fired — yet!'

'George! Is it you, then! My God! What a fright you have given me! I thought — heaven *knows* what I thought! I have not closed my eyes all night. I dare not stir from the house! My husband is from home and we shall all be murdered! The Place de la Concorde is full of *gendarmerie* and soldiers. What can be afoot?'

'Let me in and I will tell you,' replied George.

'Instantly! I come!' The head of Mme Marliani vanished.

Chopin let fall the curtain and, going to his bureau, took out a letter received from Solange the day before. Briefly scrawled in pencil it announced the birth of her baby — a daughter — and begged him to inform her mother of 'the glorious event'.

George's arrival at this moment could not have been more opportune. He would write a note and hand it in with Solange's letter enclosed... Or should he call and see her? She was here!

And once again her spell was all about him, returned with the sound of her voice, with that swift passing sight of her whom he had once so passionately desired, and by whom he had been so utterly possessed.

Did she possess him still?

Standing there irresolute, dismayed, he felt the subtle tentacles of long association surround and bind him like the pale slow-moving arms of an octopus... Be done with folly! Though a thousand memories ensnared him, though the knowledge of her presence divided only by a wall set the blood coursing madly through his veins, though all his body thirsted for the imperishable fruits of hers; though he be burnt to the bone in a torment of desire, he would not again be magnetised. She had spoiled his life and killed his love and he wished to God that he could hate her.

But he couldn't.

A defensive irony welled up in him and broke in laughter so harsh, so fierce, it brought the ever-watchful Daniel to the door.

'M'sieu called me?'

'No ... yes! Prepare my bath and bring my *petit déjeuner.*'

'M'sieu will not return to bed?'

'What? At this hour? No, I'm going out.'

'But does M'sieu not know? The barricades are up from the Pont Neuf to the Madeleine and the streets are full of soldiers.'

'So much the better. If these Communist rats run out of their sewers I hope they'll be shot at sight. I wouldn't mind taking a pot at them myself. At least I shall be there to see the sport.'

'Sport!' Daniel's mask slid from him; he strode forward and stood between his master and the door. 'I beg that M'sieu will not venture out today. It is not safe.'

'Safe! What do I care for my safety?'

'Others, M'sieu, care for it. Your friends, M'sieu ... your servants.'

Chopin smiled. 'Why, Daniel, do you defy me? Go and get my bath... What?... Yes, yes! I promise. If I go out you shall come with me. Name of a Name! What has come over you that you contradict my orders? Revolt appears to be infectious as the plague.'

And as stealthy in its method of attack.

The barricades had risen like mushrooms in a night. The pregnant quiet of the day before had changed to a buzz of activity as from a hive of bees waking at the end of a winter's long inertia to the trumpet-call of spring: for spring was in the air that day, and in the flight of birds and the restless scurry of clouds across a clear untroubled sky. A pale sun, light-fingered as a woman, touched grey spires and turrets with a dust of gold; the Seine gliding noiselessly under the bridges, flashed in a million sparkling wrinkles; and along the boulevards and in every public garden all the trees were starred with their first buds, as innocent and tender as the nipples of a girl. The singularly mild weather that morning of February 23rd tempted Chopin to discard his winter overcoat and wear his new spring suit of lavender grey, when with Solange's letter in his pocket he left the house to pay a call next door.

He had decided it would be advisable to have no meeting with George, but to give Solange's message to Mme Marliani with a request to pass it on. But although Mme Marliani could still be heard, she was not yet to be seen. She sent a message begging him to wait. She would be with him on the instant. He was shown into the salon where he waited fifteen minutes, which in his state of mind might have been fifteen years, so frantic was he to be gone... Or should he stay and insist on an encounter with his lady, charge her categorically with the ruin of his life, bare his heart and make a scene … or not?

The emotions of a lifetime were suspended in the agony of his irresolution. He sat down; he got up, he paced the room — a hideous, overcrowded room as full of sham *objets de vertu* as a pawnbroker's: the walls papered in a design of improbable roses, the windows shrouded in dusty red velvet that kept out the light and kept in the smell of stale patchouli and garlic.

Disgustedly he surveyed the litter of feminine trifles, the pseudo-Dresden ornaments, the imitation fruit under a glass globe, the latest fashion in monstrosities imported from the English. He stared at the gilt-framed pictures on the wall and at an atrocious lithograph of Marie Antoinette surrounded by her guards at the Conciergerie… He thought he heard the distant beat of drums, the tramp of feet, and the angry buzz of a myriad voices. Was the world going mad, or was he?

Thoughts whirled and whispered in his temples. Yesterday… Today… His little Princess.

Her blurred white face rose up before him, her faint surprised eyebrows, her tremulous, blunt-cornered mouth, and all her subtle fragrance. He experienced again the overwhelming revelation of her secret that had been shaken from her, unaware, and frail-spun as the scattered cherry blossom that floats on a fugitive breeze… Too late. One must not stir the ashes of a dream, must not dwell on all that of life's substance he had missed; the dear comradeship, the shared delight of mind and body, the steady flame of two united burning like a candle on an altar to light his darkening way along the years… All, all too late… Perhaps it were better so. Nothing stayed. No triumph, no ecstasy, nor sorrow, no miracle of love but did not wither in fulfilment. For the way of life is loneliness and hunger, and the human spirit on its upward voyage must follow no star but its own.

His fever of impatience subsided; his mind was light and pliant, and content with the contentment of finality, attuned to the future's unimpassioned coil.

The clock on the mantelshelf struck ten. He had waited long enough; he cared to wait no longer for Mme Marliani. He would call back later in the day. He left the room, prepared to leave the house, and on the way downstairs met George coming up.

He halted.

There she stood below him, cloaked and trousered like a brigand with her hat pulled down over her eyes and her face lifted to greet him. He saw the proud tilt of her chin, and the curved scornful mouth relax to a quick intake of breath; he heard her anxious query: 'You! My friend! But you are changed … so thin… Have you been ill again?'

'*Comme ci, comme ça!* It is nothing. I am better.' As always he was impatient of solicitude. 'And you?' Then, gazing down at her as she looked up at him, the conventional words of greeting died on his lips, and he realised with a sudden tremendous wrench that was half agony and half relief, as though a crushing burden had been lifted from cramped limbs, that her sorcery had lost its cunning; her magic had fled like a witch in the dark.

Shorn of her vaudeville display, her mimic armour, he saw her now in this penultimate moment, not as she would be seen but as she was: no mesmeric sybil who practised black arts on her unwary victims and could transform herself at will from a saucy Ganymede to a sick-nurse or a love-tormented goddess, a great lady or a *bourgeois gentilhomme* — none of these was her true role though she played them all in turn to a mock audience… No, she was a child Quixote seeing dragons in a windmill, an army in the clouds and a Dulcinea in the face of every boy; a child whose preternatural intelligence arrested on the threshold of her womanhood, had left her spiritually and for ever *demi-vierge*.

A great wave of tenderness engulfed him, and although he knew that he had ceased to ache for her, he knew also he had never loved her more; that while he lived he could never love her less.

In silence he took from his breast-pocket Solange's letter; in silence he presented it.

'Well?' George stared. She had recognised that scrawl. 'So she deigns to write! What for? Is it money she wants, and sends you to beg it from me?'

But her insolent aggression could not now anger him; shaking his head he smiled down into her eyes. 'Have you not heard lately from Solange?' he asked. And with another slighter shock he realised that they seemed to be continuing an interrupted conversation. These months of severance were as measureless and as forgotten as the dawning hour is in a short night. All was, at this moment, as before: and, as with fateful certainty he knew would never be again.

He saw her knit her brows in calculation. 'Six … no, five weeks ago, I think. She wrote to me from her father's house where she appears to be very comfortably installed. I wish him joy of her!'

'Then you,' persisted Chopin, 'have heard nothing since? You have not been informed?'

'Of what?' Alarm sharpened her voice. 'Have you bad news that you come here like a raven with your croakings? What are you trying to tell me?'

And, steadily, his eyes on hers he told — that she was now a grandmother, that Solange and her baby were splendidly well, 'And that,' he put the letter in her hand and closed her fingers over it, 'she sends you this.' And raising her hand to his lips that for an instant lingered, 'Goodbye, my very dear,' he said, 'God bless you.'

Then without another word he bowed and passed on down the stairway. The front door opened and closed softly.

He was gone.

And he was followed.

As he turned the corner of the Rue Taitbout he saw that Daniel, with a greatcoat over his arm and as much expression on his face as a stone wall, was behind him.

In mock despair Chopin pushed his beaver to the back of his head, leaned upon his cane, and, eyes to heaven, waited.

'Your overcoat, M'sieu.'

'Thank you, friend. How more than kind! Do you want me to be roasted? It is June today, not February.'

'M'sieu may find the wind is treacherous.'

'And more than the wind, I think,' said Chopin drily. 'The rats from all accounts are turned to tigers... So! You are determined not to let me out of sight. Was ever man so governed by his servant? Very well then, come with me — but first — go and get me a *fiacre*. I am not disposed to walk.'

Eventually he had to. The entrances and exits of almost all the streets were blocked by barricades; but though no horse-drawn vehicle was to be seen, there were mounted police in plenty and troopers armed cap-a-pie. Some cavalry, and a line regiment — as a purely precautionary measure it was understood — had been called out, and, owing to the blundering and mismanagement of the military authorities had stayed out — all night, weary, unoccupied, and entirely provisionless.

Yet, beyond the unwelcome attentions of an audience composed for the most part of *gamins* and unemployed workmen — or rather rioteers disguised as workmen with pistols in their pockets and hand-grenades under their smocks, who joined their *sotto voce* and distinctly hostile growls to the jeers of the street urchins — the city-folk appeared to be peculiarly unimpressed by this untoward display of force. The housewives with their long loaves of new bread tucked under their arms hurried from the bakers' to the butchers' and the wine shops, to haggle, determinedly as ever, over the price of food, bent solely on their efforts to obtain something for nothing — or at least for a *sou* less than it was worth. At the tables under the awnings of the cafés the usual *habitués* were seated, apathetically to stare at the glittering uniforms, the tired, sweating soldiers, or to read their newspapers and form their own conclusions which they may or may not have been prepared to voice above a whisper. And if the eyes and ears of Paris located in the Bourse, or the editorial offices of the daily journals, or in those higher quarters that surrounded the quaking Louis Philippe at St Cloud, may have regarded this unusual restraint as one more ominous sign, Chopin was immensely cheered by it.

'They'll never dare attack when they see the soldiery. The mere sight of the Orléanist troops is enough to quell disorder. How can they attack unarmed? They haven't a musket between them. And what,' he demanded of the unresponsive Daniel, 'do they want?… God alone knows what more they *can* want than they already have. A king who bows and scrapes to them in order to keep his throne — and a ministry that knuckles under every time they squeal. I'm inclined to think the government deserves all it may be going to get. But — good heavens above! To let things come to this pass that the military has to be brought out. It is incredible! The whole country is overrun by these vermin who have never ceased to gnaw their way into the vitals of administration since the day they hurled a king's head into the basket.'

'A king's head may fall again, M'sieu,' said Daniel calmly.

'What?' blazed Chopin. 'Treason! Do you dare to speak it — and to me?'

'M'sieu, I am a servant, unlearned — uneducated. I have no politics and no ideas above my station. I repeat only what I hear.'

'Then keep your gutter-gabble for your comrades,' returned Chopin hotly. 'Go! Join them now — they're waiting. Why do you dance attendance upon me? Fall in and follow your leaders. See! There's a gang of them baiting those unfortunate troopers — poor devils! They look as tired as dogs.'

Like an inquisitive tortoise that has been hit on the head, Daniel withdrew into his shell. Chopin, who if truth be told, knew as little about politics or the causes of the present abortive situation as his valet, gave him a quizzical glance. 'There, there! No one's going to eat you. You're forgiven. But you must keep your observations to yourself. I *loathe* the proletariat. If I had my way I would lash them till their hides were raw and pickle them in brine. I can forgive any sin on earth save the sin of dirt. And these people are dirty because they *like* to be dirty, *not* because they can't afford to wash. Water costs nothing and soap costs far less than the price of the drink with which they souse themselves. You — or rather your leaders, my good Daniel, will tell you that these stinking hordes — these vermin — are our brothers. *My* brothers. They are *not* my brothers. I refuse to believe it. You see, Daniel, these Communist swine who demand a Utopian universe wherein all men are equal, think only in terms of money. They are in fact the usurers who turned the House of God into a Bourse, and thereby earned the righteous wrath of Our Blessed Lord Himself. They say, "I have two francs a day to spend — you have two francs a day to spend. No more, no less. We will all share alike. There shall be no more poverty, no more workless, no more diseased and starving children, no more sweated labour. No! We will buy at an equal price — each his pass through the gateway to heaven." Very good — in theory. But they forget that God in His Wisdom does not dispense an equality of that grey matter in which our brain cells float. He, who by the accident of birth, inheritance, or whatever — has a disproportionate share of intelligence, will surely, sooner or later, turn his two francs into four, or eight, or twelve, and be a capitalist. If I, for instance, were deprived of all my possessions today I would have them back tomorrow — or next week. I have only to give a concert and all Paris flocks to hear me. Your leaders will tell you, "Very well! Put this miserable sickly little Chopin at his piano and make him play for a couple of hours and earn ten thousand francs — for *us*! We will then give him his two francs and take the remainder and share it with those who have not ten centimes." That, my friend, is what is meant by "state control", which as I see it is a comprehensive word for greed, jealousy and the picking of better men's brains to supply the deficit in those that God, for His own exclusive reasons, has overlooked. The doctrine that thrives on the assumption *Ask and it shall be given* is a death trap for the unwary. Shall we drag these pigs from the filth of their sties that they should turn and ask that still *more* shall be given — even to the blood and entrails of the Constitution? However, I perceive that I am talking to myself and so much Greek to you, and I confess I am no politician.'

Daniel did not attempt to contradict him.

'If only women,' reflected Chopin, 'were as dumb as you, my friend, how happy the world would be. Phew! How much farther must we walk? Why did I not order the carriage?'

'It would not have been allowed to pass the barricades, M'sieu. Would M'sieu care,' suggested Daniel, 'to go home?'

M'sieu made it plain that he would not care to go home, although he admitted that it hardly seemed worthwhile to stay out. Whatever excitement had been pending appeared to have subsided. The soldiers who lined the streets, the gendarmes on patrol, might, but for the barricades have been no more than an advance guard awaiting the arrival of a royal procession; and the loiterers, who like Chopin had come to view and to partake in the alarms and excursions of a riot, looked to be disappointed.

For the moment.

But, as Chopin and his mute attendant neared the Boulevard des Capucines, a terrific yell burst upon their ears, and in an instant the streets were seething. From all directions and at some prearranged signal, the mob had rushed from its lurking-places to swarm like cockroaches disturbed in their noisome cellars by a light.

Determined to miss nothing, Chopin darted forward and was caught back by Daniel, stirred from his immobility to peremptory command. 'M'sieu! We must get out of this while we have the chance. There will be fighting.'

'I hope so! I am here to see it.'

'At least, M'sieu,' entreated Daniel, 'take cover in this doorway. You are in danger!'

'What! Am I a girl to hide? Are *you* afraid?'

'For you, M'sieu. Not for myself.'

'Save your own skin. I can take care of mine... Here! Damnation! Let me go.' And like an eel he wriggled out of Daniel's grasp, to regret, an instant later, his foolhardiness. Some-tiling horrible had happened ... was happening. He stood, a pigmy in the vanguard of a charging herd of giants, while, as though agitated by an earthquake, the ground under him heaved in a hideous convulsion, as wave upon vibrant wave the thunderous tide swept on.

He had a confused impression of ravening wolfish faces, of staring eyeballs, of tossing arms that seemed to have snatched their weapons out of vacancy, for all around, above, beside him, the air was thick with muskets, carbines, sabres — even rusty mediaeval lances looted from curio shops or private collections, or from heaven alone knew where — and hoarded stealthily till this first given moment of attack. He heard the yells, the oaths and cries of a mob inflamed to breaking point, the terrified shrieks of women, the stamping and clatter of startled horses... and the staccato rattle of rifle shot, as though Titans were throwing dice in some deadly game.

Resistless as a straw on a millstream he was borne along, submerged in a boiling inferno.

He had lost Daniel, he had lost his hat, he had a stitch in his side that every breath was torture. How more — how more than terrible! Why had he not listened to the advice of his good Daniel? Why had he not taken cover? Why had he come? O God, why had he come to be embroiled in this multitudinous fit of epilepsy! He would vomit, he would faint, he would be killed and crushed underfoot like a beetle... It was a nightmare, unbelievable, insane. All thought, all reason, died in him. As an entity he had ceased, already, to exist. He was no more than a grain of dust in a whirlwind. And although, incredibly, he moved, as if his feet had no contact with the earth at all, he found himself wedged, stuck fast between two ruffians, one in a workman's overall, who, brandishing a carbine, was yelling — what he could not hear; the other, with a thicket of black beard that concealed all of his face except his demoniac eyes, was yelling, too... *'Mourir pour la patrie!'*

Then to his unutterable horror Chopin found that this monster, this malodorous wild boar, had clamped a hand upon his shoulder; he felt the hot breath of the beast upon him, saw the bared yellow fangs, the foam-flecked lips that roared, 'See how it works, my little one! See how we, the ants who labour in the dark, reap our reward! The wheels are set in motion. *Marchons, Marchons —*'

And from a thousand voices the forbidden 'Marseillaise' rang out to be drowned in a volley of grape-shot, the howls of the wounded, the awful scream of a horse in its death agony.

The troops were advancing. Between the upraised arms and surging bodies, Chopin glimpsed the shining slant of bayonets led by a guard of cavalry. Suddenly a deafening reverberation shook the air, and he heard the petrified gasp of massed terror and one maniacal voice raised high above it.

'Vengeance! Murder! To arms — to arms, comrades. Down with the barricades! Down with the tyrants... Down with Guizot... The King! Down with the King! *Vive la République!...*'

Again the cannon belched from the rear of the advance guard. Chopin, enveloped in a pall of sulphurous smoke, was choking. He would die ... if he were not dead already.

Driven to further madness by this attempt to awe them into submission, the revolutionaries poured on and ever on with smoke begrimed faces, and bloody hands discharging pistols, muskets, stones, bottles, dead cats, any and every sort of missile in a frenzy of retaliation. The sickly sound of hand-to-hand combat, of cold steel rasping through hot flesh, was extinguished in the rush and thud of feet and hooves, and the groans of the injured and dying. Fear-stricken men were climbing the lamp-posts, the trees were black with gibbering human apes. One balloon-shaped and obviously inoffensive citizen, whose empurpled visage had turned mauve with terror, had hoisted himself to the forked branch of a tree where precariously he sat, hugging the trunk in a frantic embrace and calling upon all the saints to witness that he had no hand in this outrage. He had cheated no man, had paid his debts, his rent, his taxes. He had saved some money — take it — take it all, but spare his life! Then the branch broke and down he crashed…

Chopin glanced wildly aloft. If he, too, could find a tree! He weighed nothing. He could sit there, perched, in safety.

For some minutes that seemed like an eternity he struggled to find a loophole of escape from the stampede. A bullet whizzed past him and spat itself out in the dust, almost at his feet. He dropped on all fours and felt the pressure of the mob relaxing. He prayed: *Sancta Maria, preserve me!*

Hob-nailed boots kicked him aside like so much offal. The stink of blood, of acrid smoke and foetid flesh was in his nostrils. He sank lower, he lay flat, his head buried in his arms; and the hurricane passed over him, and swept him down…

How long he lay, mercifully unconscious, he did not know: it might have been a minute or it might have been an hour before he returned from his glimpse of hell to find himself in the gutter, and, by a miracle, alive.

Cautiously he lifted his head to see the last of the insurgents disappearing in a thin trail of smoke. He could still hear the baying and howling of the mob and the intermittent bark of musket-shots, but muffled now, although from the opposite direction — the Luxembourg, most likely — came a grumbling detonation as of heavy fire. The revolutionaries must have been scattered in all parts of the city. This was no passing storm; it was a thunderbolt.

He looked up and around. The trees were disgorging their shelterers. He thought he saw the balloon-shaped gentleman enthroned upon an overturned pile of sandbags, and, judging by his gesticulatory remarks, little the worse for his adventure; but, with the instinct of self-preservation uppermost in his mind, Chopin was not greatly concerned with the welfare of his fellow sufferers. Crawling on his hands and knees to a near lamp-post he clung to it and got upon his feet, where he stood swaying like a drunkard.

Astonishment that this horror, which by the grace of God he had survived and which had not, as yet, resulted in one of his 'attacks', ousted all other emotions, while externals gradually protruded on his consciousness.

He saw gnome-like figures scuttling into doorways, heads appearing at and vanishing from windows; he heard the cheep and twitter of sparrows returned from their startled flight, to peck in the red-stained dust.

He surveyed the ruin of his brand-new suit. His trousers were torn, his coat caked with horse dung and spattered with blood. His own?

Hurriedly he felt himself, his ribs, his chest, his knees that had been scraped raw. No! Save for a few bruises and some surface grazing, his skin was whole and he unharmed. But in shuddering reminder of the cataclysm that was raging through the city, he perceived, not thirty paces distant, a twitching bundle of rags, and another stark and twisted and green-faced.

And yet another, with a scarlet gash across its forehead, sprawling… And beside it the stiffened body of a horse.

Chopin closed his eyes.

'M'sieu! Oh, God be thanked!… M'sieu!' Daniel, pale, with grime and sweat on his face and no hat on his head, stood before him; and, amazingly, Daniel was weeping, but as a statue might have wept, without a sound; and though tears coursed in rivulets down his cheeks, he continued in a voice unshaken by these visible signs of stress, 'Master, I have searched and I have found you. When I saw you disappear I never thought to see you alive again. Is M'sieu hurt?'

Chopin shook his head, tried to grin, and swallowed a rock in his throat. 'My old…! My faithful…! Are you hurt?'

'No, M'sieu.'

'Is my face dirty?'

'Yes, M'sieu. Here is your hat. Your coat. Your cane.'

'Is this to be believed?' marvelled Chopin. 'Was ever man so blessed with such a treasure of a Daniel? While the skies fall he saved my hat, my cane…'

'And *le bon dieu*, M'sieu,' said Daniel, 'saves your life.'

Chopin, smiling, blinked away a dampness from his sight. 'You must never leave me, Daniel. Stay with me till … the end. Come! Give me your arm, my friend, and take me home.'

FINALE: MARCHE FUNÈBRE

From Chopin in London to his pupil Adolf Gutmann in Paris:

48 Dover Street, Piccadilly.
May 6th, 1848.
Well, mon ami*! Here I am at last, installed in this whirlpool of a London. It is only a few days since I began to breathe because it is only a few days since the sun began to shine. I have met d'Orsay who is charming and received me very kindly. I have made as yet few other calls, as most of the people to whom I have introductory letters are not in London at the moment, but I receive many visitors and the days pass like lightning.*

Erard has been kind enough to place a piano at my disposal, also Broadwood, and I already have a Pleyel — so now I have three!

I have been requested to play at the Philharmonic here, but I would much rather not. I may, however, have to appear before the Queen at a matinée *held at a private residence to a limited number of the* élite, *but this is only in the air at the moment.*

Write to me often and tell me how you are, what you are doing and all about yourself.

Yours ever, my old 'Gut,'
Chopin.

To his friend Gryzmala:

London,
May 11th, 1848.
My Dear!

I am just returned from the Italian Opera where Jenny Lind sang for the first time this year and the Queen showed herself for the first time in public since the Chartist Riots.

I need hardly say that I was greatly interested in both these ladies but more particularly was I impressed with Wellington, who, like a faithful old dog on guard in his kennel, sat in the box on the tier directly below that of his royal mistress.

Having been presented a few days previously to Mme Lind I was charmed to receive from her what they call here a 'Stall' for her performance, so I had a capital seat and saw and heard splendidly.

This young Swede is truly an originale! *She shines in no ordinary light but in a kind of magical* aurora borealis. *Her singing is infallibly pure and sure, but I admire most of all her* piano *which has an indescribable charm and quality.*

Note! A 'Stall' costs 2½ guineas…

And here is a trashy thing I composed two weeks ago. All desire for work has fled from my soul! I trifle away my time — et voilà!

Yours,
With all my heart,
Ch.

To the same:

Friday, June 2nd, 1848.
…For the last week the weather has been appalling and does not at all agree with me! Nor am I strong enough for the social life that I am forced to lead — night after night till all hours of the morning! I would not mind if it brought in any money, but up till now I have earned only 20 guineas. I have played before the Queen, her German Consort, Wellington and all the haute volée *— No! not at court — at the house of the Duchess of Sutherland — because the court is now apparently in mourning for some old Aunt or other so I don't suppose I shall ever be asked to visit there!*

And I hope I won't have to play at the Philharmonic either, for if I do I shall certainly not get paid. They expect you to play for love here, and to have any success you must play nothing but Mendelssohn!

Tonight I dine — (and at what an hour — eight!!) at Lady Gainsborough's. She has been very amiable. She gave a matinée *and presented me to everybody. If I could only run about as I used to do, if I could go for a few days without spitting blood and making an exhibition of myself, if I were younger … or if I could only start my life again! As it is… However.*

My kind Scottish ladies — Miss Stirling and her sister — are overwhelmingly attentive and drag me hither and thither with visiting cards till I am only half alive. And the distances! After three or four hours jolting in a carriage one might have made the journey from Paris to Boulogne. I am introduced here, there, everywhere. I dined last night with Lady Kinlogh (sic) *and a great company of Lords, Chancellors, and gentlemen with ribbons and orders stuck all over their chests!*

I confess I do not shine in such gatherings because I cannot talk their frightful language, but that doesn't matter because everybody else does — unceasingly. But at least they don't talk when I play, although they seem to look upon me as an amateur!

Believe this or not. The other night at a soirée *old Lady Rothschild asked me how much I charge to play! Well, as the Duchess of Sutherland gave me 20 gns when I played at her house before the Queen, I said '20 guineas!' The good Lady Rothschild was then gracious enough to admit that I play 'beautifully', but she advised me to take less as everyone is practising economy this season!…*

So from his own and all accounts, his visit to London seems to have been more of a social than a musical success. This may be due to the. fact that his three *matinées* were not held in any concert hall but in private houses to a selected audience. The few critics who had managed to secure seats were guarded in their praise, with exception of Mr Henry Chorley of the *Athenaum* who dilates upon *the delicacy of M. Chopin's touch, and the elasticity of his passages, delicious to the ear after the hammer and tongs work on the pianoforte to which we of late years have been accustomed*. Mr Chorley then dwells at some length on the composer's peculiar method of fingering, his treatment of the scale and shake and, of course, his much discussed *tempo rubato*. But for the most part, and for all Mr Chorley's conscientious if somewhat laboured eulogy, Chopin — we must accept it — was not hailed by the English as a master. As a lion, yes — by all the lion-hunters: by Lady Blessington who produced him with a flourish at Gore House, and where he was reluctantly induced to play; by Lord Falmouth, at whose house in Eaton Square he gave a concert which was one of the social events of the season; and by Macready who invited him to a dinner to meet Thackeray, but at the last moment he was too ill to go.

Everyone remarked on his fragile appearance which during the last few months had become so accentuated that his body seemed to be almost transparent. He found it increasingly difficult to walk upstairs and had often to be carried by Daniel, whom he had brought with him to London, and who attended him wherever he went.

He weighed no more than a child of twelve and looked like a boy of eighteen. The ravages of his disease etherealised rather than detracted from his 'beauty of countenance' that enraptured all the ladies. Chopin was so 'poetic', so 'exquisite', so 'romantic'. He was, in fact, the rage… None guessed that he was dying.

He had never quite recovered from the effect of his escapade on the morning of February 23rd. Although at the time he appeared to be little the worse for the fright and rough treatment he had received, the reaction when it came was the more violent for its delay. Within a week he had been stricken with one of his 'attacks', and lay for a month, exhausted, given up for dead by the doctors, and nursed back to life by Daniel who never left him, day or night.

As soon as he was well enough to travel, and regardless of the entreaties of his friends who were convinced he never would survive the journey, he made his preparations for departure. He could not, he declared, stay a day longer in 'this jungle of wild beasts'. The Paris of life and love, and laughter was no more. Mob-rule had changed the face of the city as though a lovely portrait had been smeared over with a dirty rag. An era had been abolished in two days, and the King driven from his throne sobbing while he fled, *'Comme Charles Dix... Absolument comme Charles Dix!'*

The comparative peace, the *laissez-faire* existence of the Orléanist *régime* were finished and done with for ever. A new world might arise from the ruins of the old, but a world in which Chopin had no part. There could be no niche for artists among artisans, or in this new disorder where the bourgeoisie and mediocre joined hands in the despoilment of beauty. 'I cannot exist in ugliness,' he groaned. 'They will put me in the workshops or the national guard if they don't put me in my coffin.'

In London he would find, if not aesthetic appreciation, at least the luxury of the *beau monde* to which he was accustomed; nor was he disappointed. His letters bristle with the names of the British aristocracy:

Next week, I go to Scotland, having been persuaded to accept the invitation of Miss Stirling to stay with her and her brother-in-law, Lord Torpichen, who has a house not far from Edinburgh and who has sent me a personal and pressing invitation. Lady Murray has also invited me to stay at her castle — these Scottish ladies continue to shower kindnesses — but — how they do bore me! From everywhere in England I receive invitations but I cannot go wandering all over the place like some strolling player. Besides, my health would never stand it... My heartiest thanks for your most welcome letter and also for the letter you forwarded from my dear ones at home. Thank God they are all well. But why are you so concerned about me? There is really no necessity for you to worry. I am not ill, but very depressed ... I seem to do nothing but vegetate. I am certain I shall never be able to face a winter here!

He was not sorry to leave London. The depression of which he complains was due as much to mental inactivity as to his physical condition. He had achieved nothing, done nothing, composed nothing worthwhile, on his visit to the metropolis. He had frittered away his time on a round of unprofitable social engagements. He had made a number of new acquaintances, but not one new friend.

Seated in his reserved compartment in the Scottish night express, he felt that for the first time in the last few months he could relax. The noise and rush of the engine was less disturbing than the continuous hurry and bustle of the London streets the interminable carriage drives from house to house, bumping over cobblestones with his back to the horses in the company of his 'good Scottish ladies'. How more — how *more* than tedious had been those endless rounds of visits, the incessant introductions, the strain of trying to understand a language you could never speak.

The English were hospitable, but their manners were atrocious. They had no *savoir-faire*, and the very strangest customs. As for instance, after their 'late' dinner, the ladies retired to the drawing room where they sat at their embroidery frames, and waited for their gentlemen to reappear; but more often than not the gentlemen were too drunk to reappear, and fell asleep at the table — or under it. And *how* they drank! Three bottles of port at a sitting, and this on top of a dozen different kinds of wine served with every course. What heads they must have — these Englishmen: — thick as their castle walls and as insensitive. And then their appetites, their food! Good heavens yes! Their food! Their breakfasts — beginning with porridge and ending with 'biff-steak', with several glasses of some black brew known as 'porter' thrown in, to say nothing of prodigious cups of 'coffee'. At least, they *called* it coffee. What stomachs they must have — and what digestions! But, surprisingly, they did not fatten — as might have been expected — like prize pigs: on the contrary, and notwithstanding all the meals they ate, they remained as lean, as wiry, as their own racehorses. Almost all the men he met were over six feet high, elegant, slim-waisted — and such shoulders! — with the colouring and profiles of Greek gods.

But their women — Dear God, their women! Were they chosen for their ugliness that the men should have no rival? With exception of Lady Blessington who had lived in Paris and had acquired *chic*, there was not one among the ladies of the British aristocracy whom so far he had met, that had style, grace, or beauty. All were middle-aged at twenty-five, with long teeth, large hands and bony necks. Their complexions were good but would have been better were they powdered, and not so often washed; they shone from too much soap and water as though they had been rubbed in bear's grease. They were as tall as their menfolk and as thin and spiked as the iron railings that enclosed every park, every garden, every house. They talked in shrill high voices at the back of their throats and wore gloves all day, and no doubt slept in them. Also, *nota bene* — you must be careful how you pay a compliment. To speak to a lady of her feet, her ankles or her legs, was an unforgivable social *gaffe*. It must be assumed that a lady ceased to exist from the waist downwards, and in order to maintain this illusion their crinolines were of such a vast circumference that they were forced to make their entrance to a room in crab-like fashion, sideways, or they would never get through the door.

One observed too, that on no account must you allude to a lady as a 'woman'. Women were 'ladies' unless they belonged to the *demi-monde* or the lower orders, who were presumably as non-existent as the lower limbs.

As for the *demoiselles*, they, Chopin conceded, were delicious. He adored their little button mouths, their dimples, their smooth ringlets, their secret air of knowing so much more than they were meant to know. Also they never spoke unless they were spoken to — a great advantage. Demure and dainty buds of English roses — but, alas, they withered early. They must be married young or not at all. A virgin of twenty-three was regarded as almost 'on the shelf' (such extraordinary expressions!). A woman of thirty, unmarried, was called an 'old maid', and if she were a wife she was a matron. A strange world indeed that considered women *passé* in their prime.

Another peculiar custom of this country appeared to be that you must on no account embrace a friend when you met or parted. If you did, you might be given a black eye! Men did not kiss each other here in England. Indeed, the warmer their affections the less they must be shown. Nor should you kiss a lady's hand when you were introduced to her unless you wished to be mistaken for her lover. Apparently the only hand that you *could* kiss without remark in Britain was the Queen's.

Chopin recalled the occasion when, at the informal concert held at Stafford House, he had played before Her Majesty… Yes! That undoubtedly had been a triumph. He had stirred a frigid English audience to cheers. The Prince Consort — a barber's block of elegance with curly whiskers round his chin — led the applause and gave the guttural command for an encore. Beside him in the front row, the Queen, a plump, vivacious little lady, clapped her hands, whispered to her consort, and requested in her clear young voice, 'Please play one of your pretty waltzes, Mr Chopin.'

He played '*La Valse du Petit Chien*', which so delighted Her Majesty that she asked him to repeat it, and the Duchess of Sutherland to present him. He bowed, he kissed the small gloved hand so graciously extended, the Queen smiled to show her gums, and said, 'You play with great feeling, Mr Chopin. It has been *most* enjoyable. Do you know Mr Mendelssohn?'

He admitted that he knew Mr Mendelssohn very well indeed.

'You do?'

The Queen's slightly protuberant blue eyes sparkled with pleasure. 'We have met him also. He has played to us in London. *Such* a beautiful composer. I hope we shall have the pleasure of hearing you again, Mr Chopin. Such a *very* pretty waltz…'

No. The English were not musical.

He glanced across at Daniel, who sat rigidly upright nursing on his knees a squat leather case. In it, on a grey velvet lining, reposed Chopin's greatest treasure, the silver urn containing the fragment of Polish soil brought from his native land, and without which he never travelled. Daniel kept the key of the case in his possession. Crown jewels could not have been more strictly guarded.

With a despairing howl the train plunged into a tunnel. From the surrounding gloom of the compartment lit by the feeble rays of one ineffectual oil lamp, Daniel's face emerged, immobile as rock. Only his eyes, fixed in hope-abandoned resignation upon a void above his master's head, expressed their disapproval of this race through roaring grit-laden darkness to that ultimate disaster, which, Daniel was convinced, must be his journey's end. He was prepared. He had made all ready to appear before his Maker; he had confessed, and received absolution; he had written a letter of farewell to his son in Paris, now grown to manhood, and happily married to a good young woman, daughter of a greengrocer, who had brought to his Jean a *dot* of twenty *louis d'or*. He had made his will, by which, thanks to his master's generosity and his own thrift, Jean would benefit to the extent of some five thousand francs. He had left his master's suits in order, each meticulously pressed and packed in their trunks between layers of tissue paper; he had seen those same trunks of which he held the keys, deposited in the luggage van. If he were killed, therefore, and his body undiscovered, and if his master survived — which Daniel deemed unlikely — new keys would have to be provided or the locks forced. That, however, was a contingency which must be left to fate, or his successor. He consigned his soul, into God's keeping. Mortal man could do no more. He was content.

Meanwhile, and in the remote event of deliverance from immediate extinction, Daniel had provided himself with a slender volume entitled *English and how to speak it*, for which he had paid a shilling at a shop in the Charing Cross Road; an extravagance that in view of his imminent decease he now regretted.

The train with the shriek of a tortured soul rushed out of the tunnel into the grey summer's evening. The quiet country with its mist-sodden fields, its spreading trees, fat cows and pastures like green chess boards, flashed by and ceased to flash; slowed, steadied. The engine snorted, groaned, and with a great jarring of wheels on metals, came to a panting halt.

Still firmly clutching his master's leather case with one hand, Daniel with the other crossed himself. Chopin, his nose to the steamy window, peered out. 'There is no station here. Why can we have stopped?'

Daniel's lips moved in silent prayer.

'Ah! Of course! To let the other train go by — the express *from* Edinburgh. Is it not astonishing, Daniel, how science has progressed in these last twenty years? Here we are, travelling over four hundred miles in a night! And this discovery of steam is only in its infancy. When it is perfected the tempo of life — of the whole world will be set to speed. Then, Daniel, men will be gods. Already steamboats can cross the Atlantic in a month; already the distance of days has become hours — and perhaps *one* day we shall travel by steam to the stars! All ways are open to man now, on land and sea but not yet in the air. Who knows —'

The remainder of this monologue was lost in the hurtling approach of the Caledonian express travelling at the world-shaking speed of thirty-five miles an hour. Their narrow compartment rocked as the train thundered by, the windows rattled, Daniel clutched more firmly his master's precious case, closed his eyes and prepared to give up the ghost. His book fell with a slap to the floor. Chopin retrieved it.

'What's this?'

The engine bellowed, and with another hideous grinding of its iron teeth, braced itself to move. Daniel's eyes unfastened. He breathed out.

'M'sieu, I have applied myself with diligence to the study of the English language, but I find it — difficult.'

'*Ma foi!* Difficult! Chinese would be easier. The English spell so many words alike and pronounce them in a hundred different ways. For instance, *raide* is pronounced "tuff" and it is spelled t-o-u-g-h. But *une toux*, which in English is a cough , is spelled exactly the same way and is pronounced "cawff" — not "cuff" . If you say "cuff" it is *une manchette*. But also they have a word d-o-u-g-h which means *pâté*. Now how would you pronounce that, Daniel?'

'"Doff", *n'est-ce pas*, M'sieu?'

'*Non!* Doe — D-o-h! But — and conceive *this* idiocy, if you please. Doe means *une daine*, the female of deer — and 'deer' is a term of affection! Now wait. H'ah-ou-sess. H-o-u-s-e-s. *Mais! C'est formidable! Pas raisonnable!*'

Daniel ventured to suggest that it was more than unreasonable, formidable. It was completely mad.

'You are right, Daniel. The English — we must face it — they are mad. *Eh bien!* This little book appears to be instructive. I shall study it all night, for I shan't sleep. But first, we will eat. What have you in that basket? Open it and let us know the worst.'

From the luggage rack Daniel lowered the supper basket provided — at a more than adequate consideration — by a thoughtful railway company, and, with long-suffering, produced its contents.

Man and master surveyed them in silence. At length, 'Five *shilling* each — for *that!*' ejaculated Chopin. 'I call it robbery. What is it? What sort of animal? My God! Do they eat cats in England?'

'It is labelled "Cawld Rost Shicken", M'sieu.'

'*Un poulet!* They are wise to label it. What are those dead leaves?'

'*C'est une salade, M'sieu.*'

'Not possible! And what is in that bottle?'

After some painful investigation Daniel intimated that the bottle contained 'Drr-rressingg' for the salad.

'"Drr-rressingg" for the salad! What can it mean? A dress is *une robe*. Must they not even serve salad naked in this country? Ah! There is also another bottle. Wine, Daniel! Good — at least we hope it is good — French wine. Bordeaux. Open it. We will eat the *poulet* and drink the wine. On that we shall not starve.'

'There is also *fromage*, M'sieu, *des biscuits, et dessert.*'

'*Fromage*! I know their *fromage*, Daniel. They call it "chiss". I call it white lead. *Merci, non*! And their *dessert*! Dried oranges, sour grapes and hard green apples. Do you want to give me colic? Five *shilling*! We could dine at the Café de Paris for less. Only the rich can afford to eat in England.'

Having disposed of this banquet to their mutual dissatisfaction, Daniel, still sitting bolt upright, fell into a kind of coma, that was more due to nervous excitation than fatigue. Supine upon the opposite seat, his head supported by the railway company's pillow that he had declared had been stuffed with metals left over from the laying of the lines, Chopin composed himself to study Daniel's treatise on the English language. The rushing night tore on; the boxed-up air of their compartment was condensed into a blanket of sooty moisture that smelt of smoke, coal dust, and the dank vaultish odour of tunnels. The jagged edges of noise were dulled, to a murmurous recitative, a subdued hum, a drone, a lullaby, oblivion. He slept…

And woke, to find the sun in his eyes, Daniel on his feet, their baggage on the floor, and in his ears one last long trumpet call, the voice of triumph — or of doom?

Chopin, in great alarm, sat up. 'Where are we? What is it? An accident?'

Daniel told him, calmly, by God's grace it was not — yet — an accident. 'We are about to enter *Édimbourg*, M'sieu.'

If Chopin found the English customs strange, he found the Scottish customs stranger. Refreshed from his journey after a day's rest in Edinburgh, he arrived at Calder House on that same evening to receive the hearty if somewhat startling welcome of Lord Torpichen.

As for Daniel, he had been rendered almost speechless for three days. After which time he had been moved to give voice. That a great milord should so expose himself — in a skirt of many colours, with a dagger in his stocking and bare knees!

'It is,' Chopin explained, 'the native costume. They are still, you see, uncivilised in Scotland. They cling to their ancient traditions. Even their dress is unchanged since the days of their great savage king, Robert the Brute — as they call him. *En effet*, they are barbarians. But they mean well.'

'*Oui M'sieu, mais le milord*,' said Daniel doubtfully, 'he carries everywhere this dagger.'

'All Scotsmen carry daggers,' Chopin answered with false cheer and a 'presentiment' that his admirable Daniel might, if too greatly tried, be persuaded to return by the next mail-coach to London. Even the devotion of a dog can have its limits. 'A dagger in this country means nothing. We are not in France or Italy or Spain. The blood of the British is cold and does not boil easily, though when it does, believe me, it is dangerous. But rest assured. Their daggers will not hurt you. They serve merely — now — as ornaments to their outlandish dress, like these great beards they wear tied round their middles to prevent their skirts from blowing up in a wind.'

'The lord's servants also,' persisted Daniel, unconvinced, 'are dressed in the same fashion as milord. They too carry daggers in their stockings. They also carry guns. They are forever in the park or in the pastures, shooting. M'sieu, what is it they shoot?'

'Cattle, you idiot, for food. Goats, deer, and those magnificent horned beasts with shaggy coats that you see prowling the hillsides. The Scotch bulls are known to be the finest in the world, and these wonderful "beefs" as they call them, run wild in the mountains and are shot in the shooting season. Only the highest nobility can afford to indulge in this game which is so expensive that they call it "dear stalking". "Stalking" is the Scottish word for *la chasse*; "dear" means costly. When they have shot their "beef" they eat it. That is why they are all giants and as "strong" as they say, "as an ox".'

'*Oui, M'sieu.* They have also —' pursued Daniel, with such unwonted loquacity and such a desperate eye that Chopin was ready to believe the varied shocks his servant had sustained on his way north of the Tweed had resulted in some serious derangement — 'they have also a music of their own. A mournful wailing sound played on some savage instrument with pipes and wind-bags such as are used to blow the flames of their great fires. Tonight in the *salle à manger* of the servants, one marched round the table making this most ugly and terrible sound. After that they danced to the music upon crossed swords, with their skirts whirling around them as they kicked their heels and pointed the toe and flung their arms in the air, while all the time they screamed like twenty devils.'

'That,' Chopin uneasily attempted to assure him, ' is, of course, their native music, and their national dance — like our Polonaise. You must not be alarmed at their droll customs. These people are friendly. They dance for your pleasure — and — *sapristi!* Chopin felt his own nerves were beginning to give way. 'Can I help it if they *murder* you! We are here, and here we must remain, for the time being. Can I be so churlish as to make excuses to leave when I am invited for three weeks? You forget I have to earn my living that I may pay your wages… Be quiet! Have I fallen so low that I must accept the charity of my servant? I know that you mean well — but I see that you are not at all yourself. Nor perhaps am I. But I must,' and Chopin clutched his hair, 'I simply *must* fulfil my engagements in Edinburgh and Glasgow. That will bring me in sufficient to take me through the winter. Yes, yes! I know this climate will probably kill me — and you too, and that will be the end of us. What you do not seem to realise is that this milord, who is a chief in Scotland, has paid me a great honour in offering me the hospitality of his castle. Is it for me — or the son of a camel like you — to criticise or to complain of milord's manner of entertainment? Let me tell you it is considered here a compliment to allow these "bags of pipes" — as they are called — to play for us. And so you think I am not stupefied by what I see or hear? But I have better taste than to admit it. I listen. I smile. I applaud. I too have been honoured by these "bags". In Scotland they serve the man with the same courtesy as they serve the master. All through dinner tonight with all the lords of the neighbouring castles in their native dress, we had this music. God knows my stomach suffers for it. I have a formidable indigestion. But I say nothing. I hold my tongue, and I advise you for your own sake to hold yours.'

Thereafter Daniel stayed close-mouthed as an oyster, in a silence sullen and impenetrable as the Scottish mists that wrought their slow and certain havoc on lungs already ravaged by disease.

Was Chopin aware of the slow march of that unseen inexorable army which for ten years, with merciless precision

and without respite, had stormed the very fortress of his life —
to be flung back again and yet again by the indomitable spirit
that upheld him? If in this, his short day's closing, and in
regions far beyond the range of mortal sight, he saw, and.
having seen, accepted, the shadowy approach of those dark
wings that hovered, poised, to strike and overthrow and
conquer, he gave no sign; he may not have believed it.

His letters shrewdly observant, ironic and full of naive
comments, not always free from mockery at the expense of his
British hosts, show him less concerned with morbid fears
about his future than with the problems of his material
existence. He had spent lavishly in the past and had saved
nothing. By his visit to Scotland and the concerts at which he
was booked to appear, he hoped to earn enough to see him
through the winter. As he tells Franchomme:

*If only somebody would give me a pension for life so that I need never
compose again … I am so tired. But here, at any rate, I am at peace. I
have a Broadwood piano in my room and in the drawing-room, Miss
Stirling's Pleyel. This place is called Calder House (pronounced
Kolderhaus). It is an old manor with walls 8 ft. thick, surrounded by a
great park, lawns, trees, mountains and the most beautiful views
imaginable. There are endless galleries and corridors full of ancestral
portraits that glower down at you, dressed in a variety of costumes, some
Scottish, some in armour, some in flowing robes. There is even a ghost that
is supposed to wander about in a red cap, but I've not seen it yet. The
people here are kind but ugly…*

Nor does he hesitate to tell his friend that he is as bored *as an
ass at a masquerade* in spite of the efforts at entertainment
offered by his host, the septuagenarian Lord Torpichen, and
the slavish attentions of Jane Stirling.

She had been a pupil of Chopin's in Paris, was now almost fifty, and cherished a passion for her 'Master' that for years had been no secret. But as almost all his pupils were in love with him, no one paid much heed to the rumour that filtered through from Edinburgh to Paris, via London, that as a consequence of his sojourn at Calder House, Miss Stirling had proposed marriage to Chopin and been rejected.

Whether that were true or not, he may have found her undisguised devotion an embarrassment. She forestalled his every wish. It was she who had ordered from London the Broadwood piano Chopin found, on his arrival, in his bedroom. She sent to Paris for the newspapers. She took him sightseeing, dragged him to the top of Arthur's Seat, to Holyrood and to the castle, taught him English, bought him shortbread, asked only that she be allowed to serve him; and asked no more than that.

In an age that measured woman's worth by woman's visible attractions, Jane Stirling knew she must, for lack of charm, remain a spinster. From early girlhood, she had been resigned to her loveless fate. But, unlike others less luckily endowed, Miss Stirling had been given compensation beyond the price of rubies, or of the marriage bed. Miss Stirling's rugged body housed an artist's soul. Her piano was her solace, Chopin her inspiration. From the study of his method had sprung the fixed desire to meet, to know, and to be taught by him. Miss Stirling went to Paris. She took rooms, applied, for and obtained an interview with the composer. He heard her play, passed judgment and consented to instruct her to the glorification of Miss Stirling, the wonder of her friends and the mild disapproval of Lord Torpichen. He had married the eldest Miss Stirling, and had been a widower some years. His wife's sisters, Mrs Erskine, and the youngest of the family, Miss Jane, acted as joint hostesses when he entertained at Calder House.

Lord Torpichen, a courteous and very kindly host, was at greatest pains to put Jane's 'Frenchman' at his ease. 'Do as ye like, go where ye like — don't trouble to get up for breakfast, Mr Chopin. It'll be sairved in ye room when ye ring. Ye must rest all ye can while ye're here. Ye look as if ye need it.'

As Lord Torpichen's knowledge of French was not much better than Chopin's English that did not extend to the understanding of broad Scottish, conversation between the two must have been somewhat limited. Nevertheless, since whomsoever Chopin contacted it seems he made a friend, it was not long before Lord Torpichen became an avowed ally of his singular guest who put scent on his hair, looked like a girl, and played the piano much better than Jane. 'And that's saying something, I give ye my word!' announced the old laird to his cronies.

Chopin stayed three weeks at Calder House. *And I could stay,* he writes, *three months, three years, or for the rest of my life if I wished to. Lord Torpichen does not want me to leave him, but I must...*

He was booked to play at Manchester on August 28th, from there back again to Edinburgh and Glasgow. Thence, at the invitation of Lady Murray to Strachpur near Inverary; after that, to Perthshire, to stay with the Stirlings of Keir.

The continuous round of visits, the strain of his recitals, for which he confesses he had not the strength to give sufficient preparation, taxed his failing energy to its last resources. The *Manchester Guardian* commented on his fragile appearance:

Chopin looks no more than thirty years of age. He is very spare of frame, and has an almost painful air of fragility and feebleness. This, however, vanishes when he seats himself at the instrument in which he seems for the time to be entirely absorbed… Both his compositions and his playing are the perfection of chamber music. We can say with great sincerity that he delighted us. He has a purity of style, a correctness of manipulation and delicate sensibility of expression which we have never heard excelled.

In Glasgow and Edinburgh the musical critics were equally enthusiastic. The halls were packed, and every seat booked weeks in advance, notwithstanding the — for those days — exorbitant price of half a guinea each for the tickets. Chopin, however, seems to have been unmoved by the encomiums heaped upon him by his British public.

Of his concert in Manchester, he laconically announces, *They received me very well. I had to sit down to the pianoforte three times. I stayed in the country — there is too much smoke in the town — at the house of some land people called Schwabe. He was born a Jew and is a Christian…* And of his recital in Edinburgh: *People say it went off well. A little success, and — a little money.*

That, or the lack of it for the first time since his early days in Paris, was now his chief obsession. He dreaded the effect of the approaching winter on his enfeebled health. If, through illness, he found himself unable to continue giving lessons, his chief source of livelihood would be cut off. He was impatient to return to Paris, where in his own environment he hoped to be able to compose again, although it seemed that the creative urge had left him for ever. *I can't breathe here,* he tells Franchomme, *and I can't work; and although I am surrounded by the kindest of friends, I am alone, always alone. As for the conversation, it is almost always entirely genealogical. Who begat whom; and he begat and he begat and* he *begat — and so on till you come to Jesus. A day longer here and I shall go mad, or die…*

317

The weather had changed. The Scottish season was over. Chopin arrived at Kier in Perthshire on a Sunday, and stood at his bedroom window gazing down upon a vast white sodden cloud.

'This,' he told Daniel, ' is what they call a "Scottische meest" — and it will kill me.'

'*Oui, M'sieu.* Does M'sieu desire that I unpack his things, or will M'sieu depart upon the instant?'

'How can I depart upon the instant? Think, man, think! This is Sunday. In Scotland on a Sunday there are no carriages, no boats, no trains, not even a dog to be seen. Yes! Let us by all means go now — and how? Shall we escape out of the window and ride away on the back of a sheep — and mortally offend our good host here? Go and find out at what hour they dine and bring me a glass of their good drink "hort toddee", for I perish in this fog. What a climate! What a country!'

He could see nothing of it. Grey walls, the still grey lochs and stony mountain crags, the wild trackless grandeur of moor and forest, the seas of wine-stained heather, the stark grazen green — all were blotted out in a white desolation. Even the chatter of tumbling streams, and the dreary voice of sheep was suffocated in that pall of mist.

The damp crept into Chopin's bones and lay on his chest, corpse-cold. His flesh Seemed visibly to shrink from his face, his eyes burned with the brightness of fever. But while stricken to death's door he still can laugh, with his ear bent to catch the whisper of life's comedy above the cosmic echo of life's dirge. His letters written during these last weeks in Scotland are the more poignant for the salt streak of humour flashing through them, as though he weaves a chuckle in his shroud. He writes to Gryzmala:

I am getting worse every day ... I cough all night and am fit for nothing in the morning until after two o'clock, when I get up, dress and gasp till dinner-time. When dinner is over I have to sit for another two hours at table with the gentlemen, watching them drink and hearing them talk. I shall soon have forgotten Polish. I am beginning to speak French like an Englishman and English like a Scot. When they have finished drinking — by which time I have been bored into a trance — we go to the drawing room where I make a supreme effort to revive, for all are anxious to hear me play. Then at last when that is over, my good Daniel carries me upstairs, undresses me, puts me to bed and leaves my candle burning and me to sigh and dream...

Of what?

Of his home in Paris and how to pay the rent? Of his beloved Poland, of the faces of the living, and the dead? Of those deep burning memories lit by the flame of young desire, the smouldering fragments of a young despair, or the wintered ashes of man's self-delusion? Did he dream of these, or of one last flying sweetness, an aching glimpse of love and life, of youth and warmth returned and rediscovered at the barren edge of that pure darkness which is the end and the beginning of all things here on earth?

He lay in his monstrous four-post bed and watched the eerie play of shadows about the gaunt firelit room. The silence seemed charged with unheard voices, loud against the ticking of the clock and the muffled incessant lament of strayed sheep out there in the crawling mist.

On a table at his bedside stood the urn that held for him those cherished tokens of his native land. In the depths of polished silver the fire's red glow gleamed like a watchful eye; or — thought Chopin, turning restlessly upon his pillows — the blood of a wounded heart...

Poland!

Wounded, yes, oppressed and battered, but not broken. The savage drama of life and death wrought upon those battle-fields was not yet won, nor Poland conquered. The fight for freedom would go on, and would resound along the ages, undaunted by the agony of mortal conflict. He, Chopin, had cried with Poland's voice, that challenge in the soul-dance of his music. The spirit of his country had endured its crown of thorns, had suffered martyrdom, and would triumph through blood and tears to an eternal resurrection He thought he heard the march of a great army, and the thunder of its coming was like nothing known to man.

The silver surface of his urn shone crimson as in a red sunrise; and in that strange glowing light he saw again his own beloved Warsaw and the column of Copernicus, and the Church of the Holy Cross where as a child he had prayed: and there, too, he saw himself, white and rigid as though carved in stone, gazing out with eyes that looked beyond the edge of time. Then, while he watched in wonder, he saw, flying high above the world, a mighty host of devils with horned heads, and the spread of their wings in their passing darkened all heaven and hid God's face, and hurled the stars from the sky to crash upon that little city, rending apart the very bowels of its earth. He saw houses fall, and churches. He heard young children dying; he saw the mangled dead, and the statue of himself, dismembered, on a funeral pyre of smoke...

'Daniel! Daniel!'

That cry, piercing the darkness, woke Daniel from his sleep in the next room and brought him to his master's side.

'M'sieu!'

Chopin was sitting up in bed, wild-eyed and pale as death.

'What have you, M'sieu?'

'Nothing... yes.' He tried to laugh. 'A nightmare. We must leave here at once. Tomorrow. For Warsaw.'

'Warsaw, M'sieu?'

'Don't stare! You shall come with me. It was,' he shuddered, 'so much more than nightmare. I have had a great presentiment. My country is in danger.'

'M'sieu is feverish,' said Daniel; he laid his hand on Chopin's forehead. It was wet.

'In danger,' repeated Chopin, loud. 'I must go back. We'll take the first train in the morning. Fetch a timetable. Pack my things. I'm going...' his voice ran down in whispers, 'going home.'

Warsaw... That was his refuge point, and with the grim determination of a drowning man he clung to it through the turmoil, fears, irresolution of his illness. But the urge that drove him on had laid him low. He got as far as London where a pea-soup fog completed the damage done to him in Scotland.

Imprisoned in his rooms at 4 St James's Place and attended by the Queen's physician, Sir James Clark, Chopin forcibly reiterated his intention. 'You must make me well, Sir James. I have to travel. I have to go to Warsaw now — at once!'

Sir James Clark thumbed his lip and shook his head, and answered carefully, 'You're in too great a hurry, Mr Chopin. We'll patch you up and then — perhaps — who knows?'

Not Sir James Clark, certainly, who 'patched him up' with plasters and the promise of a winter in the South of France, 'then Warsaw, by all means, Mr Chopin — in the spring!' And left his patient raging.

In the spring! Six months! Was he to wait six months?

Too long, when days were precious. Once, however, back again in Paris his obsession left him. Nor would he have taken

Sir James Clark's advice to winter in the South of France even if he could have afforded it, which he could not. How to live: that was the burning question. Not how or when or where he was to die. Of death he had no fear, but poverty he dreaded.

Spring came and summer passed, and hope passed too. He was resigned to know he never would return to Warsaw. Increasing weakness, due to a recurrence of 'attacks', compelled him to give up taking pupils. He had taught too long and now could teach no longer. To appear upon the concert platform was an effort far beyond his strength, and since he was unable to sit for any length of time at the piano and could not create away from it, he could not now compose.

Confronted with this absolute cessation of his work, for the first time, and at his last gasp, he attempted to economise. His carriage had gone already: now he himself must go. He would have to move into cheaper apartments. These were found for him by Franchomme in the Rue Chaillot, at a rent of four hundred francs a month, misrepresented as two hundred by his friends who supplied the surplus from their own pockets. Daniel, aware of his master's circumstances, spent the wages that Chopin still insisted should be paid to him on delicacies to tempt the failing appetite.

But there came the time when the last hundred francs for rent had gone and there was nothing left. Franchomme had come to the end of his own resources and had no more to give. Gutmann was equally hard up, and Gryzmala then, and always, penniless. Titus was in Poland and Chopin refused to write to him of his financial straits. 'I have never lived, and I won't die,' he said, 'on charity. Besides, I have enough for present needs. I must move again and take a garret in Montmartre. Better be a prince among beggars than a beggar among princes.'

They dared not let him know the bitter truth: that he was virtually destitute. But what to do? Julius Fontana, who had always acted as his agent in business and money matters, and was now at his wits' end, decided. He would write to Miss Stirling. She was rich. She was kind. She would — she *must* help Chopin. If not she, then who else could?

He had forgotten, for men did forget, the Princess Marcelline. None thought of or remembered her in this crisis, save one … who took himself and his master's case to her on a September morning.

She had been away from Paris for three months and had not seen Chopin since her return, but she had written; she had sent him fruit and flowers, and received a politely worded letter of thanks expressing no wish to see her in answer to her request to be allowed to call. He was not, he said, receiving visitors at present, and no pupils. He had not yet begun to play, could not compose, and he ended with a postscript, *One cannot speak as one would wish to — with a pen.*

Which might mean everything or nothing, and she would never know.

At her desk, his letter in her hand, her thoughts in a cloud about her, she sat and listened, wonder-charged, to her heart's secret and knew herself confessed. No matter what of sorrow's journeying her spirit yet might suffer, she was given; and the knowledge was her surety beyond desire, beyond all life's fulfilment or regret…

'Madame la Princesse.' Her footman was in the doorway, hesitant and doubtful, to announce 'a person to see Madame' who would not give his name. 'He says he comes from Monsieur Chopin.'

'From…?' She restrained herself from that too eager repetition and said coolly, 'I will see him. Bring him in.'

Daniel was brought in and stood before her; and he who never spoke dared to speak then.

She heard him out: she gave him her assurance. 'You have done well to come to me. I did not know…'

'Nor, Madame,' Daniel cleared his throat, 'nor, Madame la Princesse, must my master know that I…'

'He shall never know. That is a promise. He is my master too, you understand, as well as yours. It will be my privilege to serve him now until the end as faithfully as you have served him from the beginning.'

And her smile dimmed Daniel's sight and cracked his voice, and set him stammering, 'I cannot thank Madame la Princesse, but the good God will bless … will bless you, Madame.'

'Is he,' she made her lips firm to say it, 'is he dying?'

'Yes, Madame la Princesse.'

'I will come to him,' she said. 'I will be with him always.'

Daniel recounted afterwards, and all his life he told to those who cared to listen, how she, so small, had, at that answer, seemed to grow in strength and stature with a light about her, and behind her eyes seen only in the pictures of the saints.

The first week of October brought with it an Indian summer. The slow procession of days passed in wistful sun-lost mornings that brightened to pale golden afternoons and evenings touched with skies of muted crimson. Paris had never been more lovely nor in more tender mood than in this autumn of her convalescence from the paroxysm of revolution. Peace and order reigned again, personified in the nephew of Napoleon, who with five and a half million votes was carried to the Elysée and there installed as the President-Prince. The voice of the people had ceased to roar; a silenced and respectful mob stared at this scion of that emperor who for a short span had grabbed the world — to lose it. Would this easy-mannered 'citizen' with his fierce moustachios, his self-assurance and his head full of Caesarian dreams, rule as Emperor again? Anything might happen. It was a day of miracles that could make dynasties or break them in an hour.

Meanwhile Paris was content to hum, not on a note of menace but in satisfied complacence, like some great drowsy bumblebee drunk upon honey wine and the smiling promises of Louis Bonaparte.

Along the boulevards the trees of Liberty stood unstirred by any whisper of ill wind, brave in their autumn dress of ambered green, splashed with a sun-scorched gold. In the avenues of the Bois de Boulogne, Fashion promenaded or drove in its barouches, if in perhaps a little less splendour, with much less fear than in those dreadful days of mob rule, best forgotten. Where barricades had barred the way, social barriers again had been erected, and once more *le monde*, that recognised no world beyond its own, could stroll on velvet lawns where dead leaves crackled beneath a silken sandal, or the swaying froth of crinoline, or the tread of a polished boot. And Beauty, once again attended by her high-hatted cavalier, could bask in mellow sunshine amid foliage and flowers, by miniature cascades, by winding streams and thickets, where formerly footpads and murderers had lurked. And as always, wherever the Countess d'Agoult and her faithful — if a trifle tawdry — following held court, the gossip floated breezily on those fair October mornings.

It was she, the Countess d'Agoult, who had upon her lip the latest bulletins of *ce pauvre Chopin*… Poor indeed! The whisper went that he, reduced to his last *sou*, was entirely supported by Miss Stirling.

All Paris, knew that this Miss Stirling, once his pupil, still hoped to be his wife. It would be laughable if it were not so very tragic. Chopin himself had said to marry him 'would be to marry death'. But here was Madame d'Agoult — and trust her to know the ins and outs of this *grande passion macabre* — ready to vouch that Miss Stirling had come from Scotland to be with him, and had placed at his disposal twenty thousand francs! Some said twenty-five.

Truly these English — or *écossaises*, it was all the same — were unaccountable! If he recovered he would, without doubt, marry her... *Who wouldn't?* may have thought the gentlemen, as they fingered their little black imperials adopted out of compliment to the agreeable new Prince-President, whom it were better to acknowledge than ignore. For who could tell what favours Louis Bonaparte might graciously bestow on the deserving, if the *coup d'état* became a fait *accompli*, and he Emperor of France?...

But to return to their mutton, this 'Plain Jane' of Scotland, was it true, could it be possible that Chopin was living — or was dying — on her money?

Absolutely true, declared the countess, who had it under pledge of secrecy from — no! She could not and never would divulge from whom, but rest assured — she knew! And the tales his friends concocted to account for this upward leap of his finances — that his publishers are bringing out a new edition of his works in Paris and Berlin, and had been induced to pay him in advance: that an anonymous Englishwoman having heard him play in London had sent him a gift in admiration of his music, — anything to save his pride that was so much bigger than his body... But how truly sad!

Sighs fluttered, lips were pursed, curls shook, breasts quivered to the pin-prick dart of envy. Chopin! The little, great, adorable Chopin and that gawk of a 'miss'! That hopelessly unappetising spinster, with the complexion of a crocodile, hair like tow, and a figure like a sack of potatoes! Was *she* to be the last romance in the life of the last 'Romantic'?

None could believe that Chopin, the idol of their drawing rooms, the lion of his day, would not survive to stir their hearts and charm their ears again. He had so often been subjected to these crises, that each time proved to be a false alarm, and after all, to be consumptive had at one time been *la mode*. Even Dumas had affected in his younger days a delicate hacking cough, when all the world was coughing — *à la* Chopin! And Chopin had been dying for ten years. His strength of will was known to be extraordinary. He would, of course, recover. That was certain. But where had they put him? In a *maison de santé*? All were agog to know.

They had moved him to the Place Vendôme — the countess had it pat, even to the rent of a thousand francs a month, paid by Miss Stirling, *sans doute*. Superb apartments with an anteroom adjoining his bedroom where he held audience and where visitors, none lower than a countess, lined up in queues to wait their turn to enter. Royalty could not be better placed or receive greater homage. The carriages outside the house blocked the traffic down the street for half a mile!

And what of Sand, the amused listeners enquired? Was she there?

She! The countess chirped a shocked protest. Not likely! Sand was finished, done for! She had croaked her swansong to the tune of 'Lucrezia Floriani.' If she called she would have to take her place at the *end* of the queue.

The old score of 'Daniel Stern' against 'George Sand' had not yet been paid in full: there was still a balance owing on the debit side of the account. Liszt's interest in Sand, avowed platonic, had never waned, not even, when the war between the friends and foes of Chopin was at its highest pitch after the publication of *Lucrezia*. So — 'Sand?' The countess showed a dimple and all her pearly teeth. 'Even she would never dare intrude where angels ... and *what* an angel!' Eyes to heaven, Marie d'Agoult breathed a name, not Stirling. 'But just as faithful, just as loving, and, alas, — unloved! She is always there beside him. But naturally — why not? — the favoured pupil, the most talented of all his titled galaxy, the star that shines so very near to heaven that its light cannot be seen by lesser mortals here on earth. She never leaves him. She plays to him all day, and sits at his feet all night — while Miss Stirling, in an apron, does the nursing. It makes me cry, it does indeed,' declared the countess, 'to think of the little — the *great* master — lying there between his Martha and his Mary...'

Feckless as the straying wind that danced among the plane trees, revolved the airy bubbles to expire in the dust, unheard by him whose eager spirit straining at the leash, marked time upon the threshold of eternity.

Propped on his pillows in his room facing the window he could watch the sky in all its changes; the misty blue of morning, flushed sunsets and starred canopy of night, lit by a great gold moon with a halo of bronze about it. He was tired, glad to rest, content to lie and see loved faces all about him, and some that he had never thought to see again. His mother, father, Jan, the little sister whose bud had never grown into a blossom ... all were here and undivided by the veil that dims man's sight in this short spell of sleep that we call life.

He had strange dreams while he lay resting there, supported sometimes by Daniel or Franchomme, or Miss Stirling, very starchy in an apron to her chin, and very kind. How hateful of him once to say she bored him! And sometimes it was Gutmann...

'*Cher ami.*'

'Yes, master, I am here.'

'You ... must teach my method. I would have written ... have begun to write a book ... about my method. I would have finished it, maybe ... if I'd had time.'

'I will teach it for you, master... Does it hurt to talk?'

'Not now. No more.'

No pain, no torment of thirst nor fever, only a quiet drifting on a slow untroubled tide of memories, clear as the light that shone, a pure white flame, in the heart of his silver urn... He could smell violets, could see in an enchanted long perspective that violet-grey shadow whose stinging lips had taught him the dark witchery of passion and all of passion's emptiness, down those lost lotus years... But when the sun, the stars, the reeling universe, and time immeasurable dissolved in the struggle for a single breath, one face, one form among all others formless, stayed serene, cloud-pale, with hand outstretched to guide him from his tumult into peace.

He watched himself grow younger, very young, a boy again, standing in the sparkling cold outside the Church of the Holy Cross, where a girl had told him, 'Wait...' He was still waiting with his heart like a drum in his ribs and his hot blood shouting up to heaven... Would she come?

'Poor Chopinetto!' Yes, she was here again as he had always seen her, in her fur-lined tippet and her cherry-coloured hood. 'You look so exactly like a little pinched owl with that enormous beak jutting out over your muffler.'

He tore the choking muffler from his throat. 'I've had a cold on my chest. I am better...'

How she used to laugh at him! She was not laughing now. Her face was full of light, a divine radiance beyond all understanding. He knew her then, and tried to tell how he had dreamed her someone else and was mistaken. 'All my life, Madonna, there has been only you...'

Night ended; dawn was in the sky when she whose soul was watching his saw his lids raised and heard him whisper, 'Play for me.'

'Yes, Master... What shall I play?'

A smile flickered up into his eyes; his lips shaped to a word. 'Sonata.'

Facing him at his piano that had been placed on the landing outside the open door of Chopin's room, the Princess Marcelline began to play the first movement of his Sonata in B Minor.

'No...!' His voice gained strength to stay her, 'no, not mine.' And in his eyes that smile deepened. 'Real music,' Chopin said. 'Mozart.'

In the dusk of that same evening a carriage drove up to the house in the Place Vendôme. A woman, heavily veiled and wrapped in a cloak, got out, walked unmolested up the stairs and came to a landing where a piano stood outside the closed door of a room. There she halted, hesitant. No sound, not a sigh could be heard in the darkening silence, till a voice spoke from the shadows behind her.

'Madame Sand is too late.'

And brushing by her up the staircase Daniel passed, to keep his faithful guard at that closed door.

A NOTE TO THE READER

Frédéric Francois Chopin died on October 17th, 1849, aged thirty-nine, and was buried at Père Lachaise. The fragments of Polish earth contained in his silver urn were scattered on his coffin; his heart, removed and sealed in that same urn which went with him everywhere, was conveyed to Warsaw to be preserved in the Church of the Holy Cross.

Almost a century later, German bombs destroyed the church and everything within it. The statue that had been erected to the memory of Chopin was hurled, broken, from its pedestal, but the head remained intact.

In this story of his life I have endeavoured to present a portrait of Chopin as boy, man, and artist, without encroaching on his great work as a composer. Of that I am not qualified to write; others who are, have already written volumes on his music and will continue to do so while his name and music lives.

I have, however, tried to keep within the bounds of fact in the telling of his story, and although I have created imaginary scenes and dialogue, no character and no letters in this book are fictitious.

It has been no easy task to select from the long, rambling letters he wrote to his friends and family those extracts I have quoted in my narrative; or it might be more correct to say misquoted, since many of the sources available are literal translations which I have abridged, and adapted into more colloquial English while still retaining their original sense.

Unfortunately no letters of any importance between George Sand and Chopin are extant. Some written by George to him were supposed to have been destroyed when the Russians invaded Warsaw in 1869 and ransacked the house of Isabella Barcińska, Chopin's sister, who had them in her keeping, while the most ardent of Chopin's letters to George were burned by George herself.

I am gratefully indebted to Mr Yozef Opieński for kindly allowing me to make use of certain extracts from the collection pf Chopin's letters compiled in the original Polish by his father, the late Dr Henryk Opieński; to Mr Francis Gribble for his courteous permission to quote excerpts from his version of the Solange-Chopin letters in his admirable book, *George Sand and her Lovers*; to my friend Ann Driver whose lovely playing of Chopin's music last New Year's Eve, spurred me to begin the actual writing of this book on New Year's Day; and to all those authors living and dead whose works have aided my research.
Doris Leslie

Sapere Books is an exciting new publisher of brilliant fiction and popular history.

To find out more about our latest releases and our monthly bargain books visit our website:
saperebooks.com